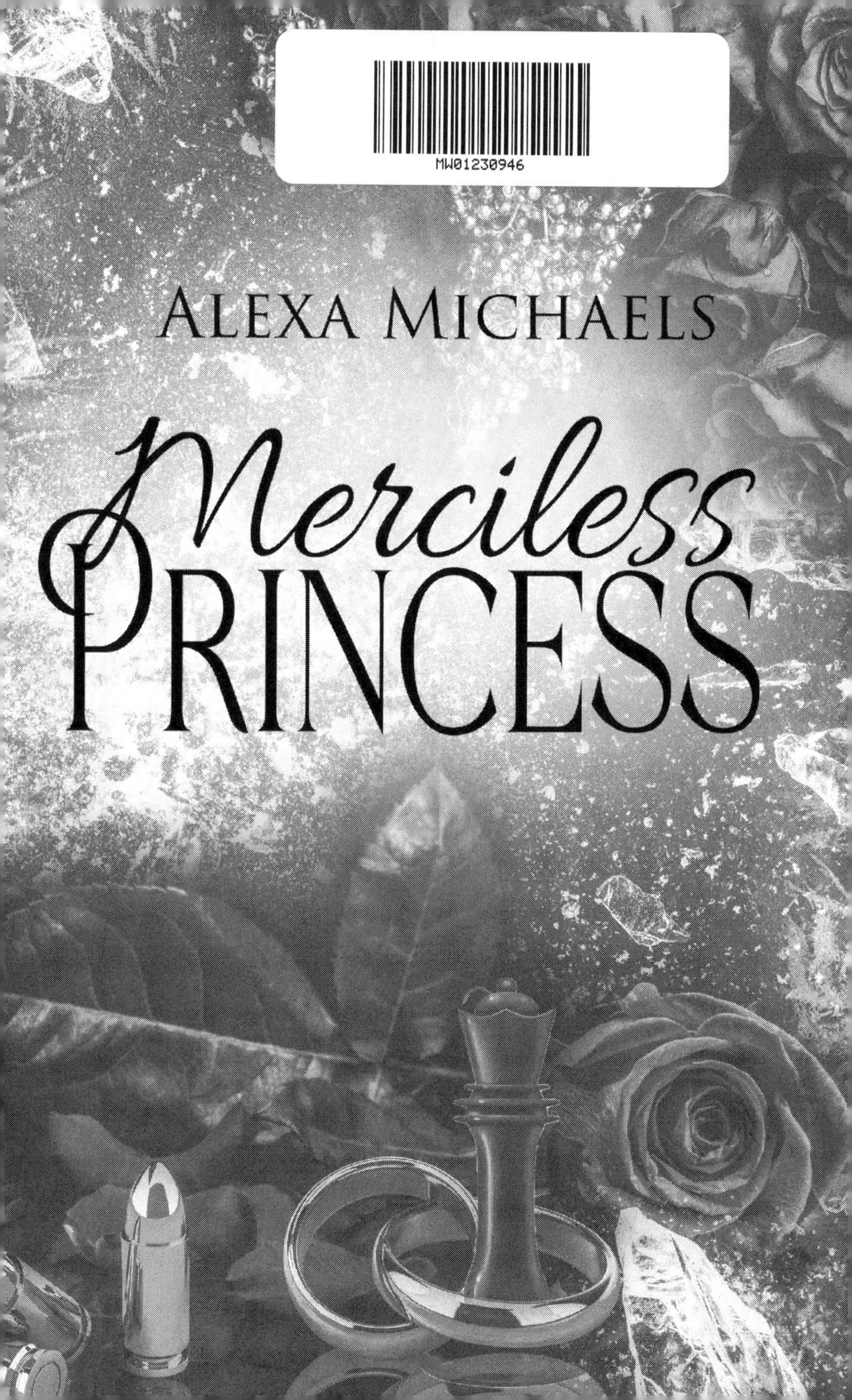
Alexa Michaels
Merciless
Princess

Copy Right

ISBN: 9798327515581

Editor: North Pines Editing LLC

Cover design: Covers By Aura

Interior Art: Atra Luna Graphic Design

About Merciless Princess

It is a truth universally acknowledged that a prince of the underworld in positioning himself to take the twisted crown of crime must be in want of a queen to stand at his side.

LaurelI couldn't let them do it. Let them end the life of the bratva prince. He's a good man; a dangerous one, but a good one.

I had to warn him! I owed the mobster a life debt, even though he's forgotten my face.

I passed him the message and disappeared into the night.

The only problem? When you enter the monster's lair, he might not be ready to let you fly away.

DimitriWhen a decadent vision appears at my doorstep one night, I found myself stunned. How is it that after years of emptiness there is a flicker of light in my dark existence?

I blink, and she's gone.

But my pretty little bird left a feather. It's enough to track her down.

When I find her, I'm going to make her mine.***Merciless Princess*** **is the first book of the Vlasov Bratva series, set in the Midwest Underworld world. It's a stand-alone darker mafia romance, with no cheating, a guaranteed HEA, and no cliffhangers. A morally grey romance, this book may not be suitable for everyone.**

Author's Note

Dear Reader,

Welcome to the Midwest Underworld! If this is your first encounter with the Vlasov family, I'm delighted you're here! If you've already read *Vengeful Dreams,* thank you for returning to this dark and wicked corner of the fictional world.

The story you are about to read is a darker contemporary romance. The male main character is a ruthless businessman and member of a criminal organization, and therefore he's not afraid to do any number of shady things. But the female main character will never take it lying down. In fact, she'll give it right back. While Laurel may be from the "normal" world, it wasn't a safe place for her. She escaped, and now will do anything to protect the villain who saved her. Her monster. Laurel is merciless, clever, and unapologetically fierce. I'm so proud of her!

If you're looking for a safe read with traditional heroics, I caution you. It's not to be found here.

Merciless Princess contains mature content that is not suitable for all audiences. **Reader discretion is advised.** The top dogs in the criminal underworld don't play by any rules but their own—neither do those who venture into the dark with them. If you're new to my contemporary or fantasy books, I write what I like to describe as "darker" romances. My MMCs are hardened villains who would burn the world for their FMCs. There are definitely instances of grey morality, moments of violence and a smattering of cruelty in my books, but this story doesn't have ugliness between the two main characters.

Just remember, Darling Reader, monsters deserve love too. It's the motto for all my books.

Now! If you're like me, and love a bad boy & a smart, breathtaking girl, flip the page and let the action begin. Xoxo, Alexa

Trigger Warning

- *Reference to past abuse, sexual abuse, and rap of FMC*
- *An abusive parent*
- *A verbally abusive in-law*
- *Light stalking, more like haunting her*
- *On page romance*
- *Adult language*
- *Violence, fighting, and criminal warfare*
- *Submission during some sexual encounters*
- *A corporal punishment in the criminal world*
- *Destruction of those who hurt the FMC*
- *Maiming of those who hurt the FMC*

Playlist

- Dimitri's Song "Invincible" by Skillet
- Laurel's Song "Miss Independent" by Ne-Yo

Chapter 1	"Faded" by Alan Walker
Chapter 6	"Gypsies, Tramps, and Thieves" by Cher
Chapter 6	"Do-Re-Mi" from the Sound of Music
	"Diamonds Are a Girl's Best Friend" Christina Aguilera Cover
Chapter 7	"Someone Like You" by Adele
Chapter 21	"My Name Is No" by Meghan Trainor
	"Let Me Love You" by Ariana Grande
Chapter 30	"Princess" by Pia Mia
Chapter 35	"Hot Stuff" by Donna Summer
	"You Say I'm Just a Friend" by Mr. TalkBox
Chapter 48	"How Deep Is Your Love" by Bee Gees
	"Fallin'" by Alicia Keys
Chapter 55	"Stand by Me" by Ben E. King
	"Can't Live Without You" by Mariah Carey

Dedication

Dear Reader,

You were born a princess. Don't settle for a partner who won't make you their queen.

Merciless Princess

The Midwest Underworld: The Vlasov Bratva

Alexa Michaels

Chapter 1 – Laurel

Power and lust filled the air, clouding it like a bad perfume. A collective excitement shivered under the surface as the club beats rose in a false crescendo. The nine o'clock show was starting soon, and the rise and fall in the beats stirred the anticipation. The only women not on stage or working the floor in waitressing uniforms were decked in finery and clung to the arms of moderately wealthy men. Karlgrad Christensen, the owner of the STYX Gentlemen's Club, turned a blind eye to the men bringing their mistresses and escorts to his establishment. Which meant we, the staff, were to do the same.

"The one in the glittery pink number was with her son, right? Just last week!" Julisa hissed under her breath. "Now her *John* is the dad? Incestual much."

She's going to get in trouble! Julisa wasn't discreet to save her life. While I loved gossip as much as the next service industry worker, I knew when to keep my mouth shut and my ears open.

"Be quiet," I sang out in an undertone as my fingers danced across the rack of top-shelf bottles. There was every brand imaginable, even rare or illegal imports. But they weren't full concentrate. I once caught my boss's goon, Kevin Larsen, and Ms. Beck the floor manager pouring cheaper brands into the half-empty bottles one night after close. Since then, I occasionally made discreet marks and realized it was a regular practice for them to dilute the quality of the beverages.

If they just focused on making this place a more classy venue, they could charge more for the drinks. It was simple business math. But...what did a bartender know about running an entertainment hotspot?

I snorted under my breath.

"Dolly P, will you look at this?" Julisa insisted, flicking a bejeweled finger toward the table.

Shaking my head, I stepped around her. "Hold still, you're spilling out."

I helped her tug the corset up her back. Despite the sweat pooling under my boobs and around my belly, my own was laced tight enough to stay in place.

"Look at her! She's practically humping the old man's leg," Julisa chortled, the sound sinking into a deeper baritone.

About to tell my favorite coworker to shut up, the sharp tang of peaches blew into our space behind the bar. The rank perfume was strong enough to overpower the scent of booze, dampness, and yeast. The air turned icy, and acrylic claws sank into Julisa's forearm.

"That had better not be gossip about a client," the floor manager snapped.

With the thunderous drone of pop beats, it wasn't as though the customers at the nearest tables could overhear. Unlike proper watering holes, there wasn't bar top seating. No, we had poles intermittently placed around the bar that were used mid act on the longer shows. Tables were pushed close so more patrons could enjoy without touching. Waitresses serviced the tables, but there was one spot where guests could order drinks straight from the far end of the bar.

"No one is saying anything, Ms. Beck," I said carefully, cutting through Julisa's stammering. "We have a full line of drink tickets, and I would like to clear them before the show starts."

Beck gave me a clipped nod. "You're a smart one, cookie. This one could stand to learn a thing or two from you."

The floor manager stabbed a finger into Julisa's thick bicep before disappearing through the swinging black canteen-style doors.

"Puta," Julisa spat.

I pattered her silky, smooth-shaven cheek as I passed to the garnish station. "You just make a prettier girl than her, and she hates you for it."

Julisa blew out an indignant breath. "It's not like it's hard, Dolly P. If she cared, she could be...tolerable."

Three martinis and two palomas soon stood on the rubber mat, waiting for Precious to come and take them. I grabbed the next drink ticket, only to have it snatched out of my hand as the stench of peaches suddenly overwhelmed the area.

"Table fourteen, go take their orders," Beck said harshly.

I blinked. "I'm bartending tonight." As I did most nights.

"No, Electra screwed their order up and that's an *important* client."

There was no arguing with my manager. “On it,” I said and wiped my hands on the bar towel tucked into my apron.

Beck yanked the black cloth away, snapped her fingers as I untied my apron, and pulled my cleavage down. Julisa let out an appreciative whistle, and I was off, tugging at the short, black, faux leather skirt. It always rode up my thick thighs, but behind the bar and under the apron it didn’t matter.

I’d started at STYX as a waitress, but quickly graduated to behind the bar. My pretty face and full rack were visible, but the curves were concealed. Neither Beck nor Kevin would admit it, but that was the reason. Needing the paycheck, I couldn’t call out their discrimination. With the funds I raked in and squirreled away, I preferred it back here and didn’t fuss.

Hurrying toward table fourteen, which was a circular booth with a good view of the main stage, I plastered a seductive smile on my lips. Working at a strip joint taught me a thing or two about manipulating men. There was a smile for every occasion, and I wielded that asset without remorse.

Two big guys shuffled their gaze to watch as I passed the high-top that was table thirteen. There was a flash of metal under their coats. Bodyguards. Whoever was at fourteen had enough weight to convince Kevin to allow their armed guards in.

I tensed but didn’t let it show as I slid up to the booth. My voice turned seductive. “Gentlemen, I heard there was a mix up with your beverages. On behalf of the management, we’d like to make it right.”

Roving, licentious gazes trailed down my body. The two men sprawled over the vinyl seats drank in my appearance. They couldn’t have been any more opposite if they tried. One wore a button up black dress shirt that complimented his lush brown complexion and made his dark eyes dance. The other wore a baby blue three-piece suit that only needed a straw hat for the Easter Parade.

“Gorgeous,” the man in baby blue rasped appreciatively.

It should have felt good to be appreciated. The other girls loved the attention. But my sugar-sweet act was my mask to protect myself from their penetrating attention. They could look their fill at the girl standing before them, but none would touch the woman underneath.

“We want a round of Blue Label Ghost, and a few other cocktails,” the man in the black button up informed me. “It was a simple order. The shots she brought were *not* Blue Label.”

"And I'm sorry Electra messed it up," I said warmly.

"Why don't we just get a bottle, Khumalo?" baby blue suggested.

I struggled to keep the surprise from my face. I'd heard rumors of Hasani Khumalo, how he was involved with the criminal activities around this city. It was said he could acquire anything for the right price. Having him as a guest tonight was a little like seeing a phantom in the flesh. All the rumors I'd heard swirled around my mind but crediting them to the man before me was a touch surreal.

It wasn't uncommon to see the movers and shakers of the Chicago criminal underworld here. STYX wasn't just a hotspot for men to cheat on their wives, and ladies of the night to entertain their next meal tickets. It was a safe zone of sorts, for those favored friends of Karlgrad and his crime syndicate. However, Mr. Khumalo had never been here. Part of me wanted to ask for his autograph.

"That sounds delightful," Khumalo agreed with a nod. "But I want these craft cocktails."

"The cocktails are on the house, but I'm afraid I'll have to charge for the bottle," I gushed.

The pale faced man waved me away. "That's fine, that's fine."

"I'll have those immediately, gentlemen." I brightened my smile and sashayed away. Curiosity spiked in my veins. What was the famous collector doing here? Moreover, what did the other man want from him? One of my favorite parts about this job was hoarding snippets of information. There was a wicked pleasure in knowing who was whom, and collecting their secrets.

I never did anything with the information, of course.

But I was addicted to eavesdropping.

I made the drinks as fast as humanly possible, but I made sure the garnishments were perfect. There had never been a prettier espresso martini. Thanking karma that past chapters of my life forced me to learn to walk in high heels, I carried the tray full of drinks, an unopened bottle of the expensive Johnny Walker, and shot glasses back to the booth.

"If he's out of the picture, you could swoop in and snap up his businesses," the man in blue insisted, leaning across to Khumalo.

He spoke in German, a language I'd spoken with one of many private tutors since age six.

Pretending to not be listening, I set the drinks down. The conversation ceased and the men watched me pass around the beverages, before making a show of pouring the shots.

"This is beautifully done," Khumalo said, and there wasn't a drop of lust in his sincere tone. He sipped the espresso martini appreciatively. "Tastes as good as it looks!"

"Thank you, sir," I beamed. "Will there be anything else?

"We're good," the man in baby blue snapped.

I wanted to tell him that color of suit was for summer weddings or idiots. And since it was the middle of February, and this wasn't a chapel or country club, it was obvious which one he was. After I moved away, their conversation turned back to the Germanic tongue.

"While I appreciate you thinking of me, it would be a death sentence to stab the Vlasov heir in the back," Khumalo said with a bite.

His tone sent a shiver down my spine. But it was that name that quickened my pulse.

Vlasov heir. *Dimitri.*

I needed to know what they were going to say. This wasn't just about my love of gossip. This could be a chance to repay a kindness. Ducking into a different booth, which happened to be empty, I feigned reaching over the table for a napkin that wasn't there. I pulled one from my pocket and let it flutter to the ground.

"By the time the wee prince's blood is cold, no one in that organization will be strong enough to come after us!" the blue suit protested.

"Quiet, you fool, just because we're not using English, doesn't mean someone can't hear you," Khumalo hissed.

He was right on that score.

"I don't make a habit of collecting bounties. But even if I did, I'm not partaking in Dimitri Vlasov's death," Khumalo added.

Death...they were talking about death. I sank my teeth into my index finger to keep from breathing loudly. Time slowed. My heart refused to work. Scooting deeper into the booth, I made myself as small as possible.

"We'll tell our client that you refused."

"I did." There was a pause that ended with Khumalo's appreciative sigh. "This espresso drink is just the thing."

Baby Blue's tone was acerbic. "Enjoy the whiskey."

"Thank you, I will. And good luck with your contract. Bullets seem to avoid the Vlasov men," Khumalo laughed after him. "Might want to use something bigger."

Baby Blue and his guards left the other way. I lingered another moment, trying and failing to restart my heart. Death wasn't uncommon in the criminal underworld. A good portion of the juicy tidbits I overheard were matters of illegal ventures and private feuds. This time it was different. This time...it was personal. I knew the Russian they were speaking about.

Okay, *knew* was a stretch.

My heart slammed a painful double beat. *I can't let anything happen to him.*

"Then move," I hissed the command to myself. I scampered out of the hiding spot and disappeared behind the bar.

"Dolly P! What's wrong?" Julisa grabbed my arm and wrenched me around. "You look positively sick! Were they inappropriate with you?"

I shook my head violently. "No, just wrenched my ankle."

Julisa tipped her head. Long pink braids tipped in a waterfall to the side. "You're walking fine."

"The show must go on," I said with a forced smile.

She chortled and went to the ticket dispenser.

To reassure myself, I touched the inner pocket, one I'd sewn into all my clothing. The hard lumps were reassuring. It was rare I used them, but they were there, nonetheless. If guests got handsy, or worse, I had my own methods for taking care of them. Gentlemen who fell asleep couldn't leer or touch. Not that they stayed asleep, but when they woke up, they weren't my problem anymore.

I won't be caught defenseless again. Never again.

Robotically, I went through the motions. Clean highball glasses were filled with ice. Fresh juices were squeezed into the shaker. Tonic in one and soda water in the others, I shook each. I poured. I garnished.

Electra, Precious, and Soliste came to grab the drinks for their tables.

My brain finally came back online. The ugly suit wanted to kill the son of the Vlasov boss. A spectral memory flashed to life. Sea blue eyes softening and hard mouth turning up.

The painful double skip of my heart sent an ache through my chest. *I can't let him die.*

I owed him everything.

I clutched the bar. "Shit."

"Dolly P?" Julisa set a kind hand on mine.

"I think I was just handed an opportunity to return a kindness." I lifted my gaze to meet her laughing brown eyes.

Whatever those ruby red lips were about to say was lost.

"Miss, you were the one who made this espresso martini, right?" a rich, deep voice asked from the other side of the bar.

Reality settled around me. I turned and forced a professional smile. "I did. Was it not to your liking, sir?"

Khumalo laughed. "It was delicious. Damn good!"

The rigidity of my spine lessened. But only a fraction. "Thank you."

"Here's my card." Between two long fingers, the collector passed me a red and bright white card. "I would love for you to come over sometime and teach me to make one."

"Stealing my bartender?" Kevin asked, appearing at the other end of the bar.

Khumalo laughed. "When I see something I like, I take it."

And then, he gave me a wink.

My stomach twisted, as I tucked the card into my cleavage and thanked the guest. I should be flattered. I rarely was the one the gentlemen hit on. But I didn't make personal connections. Friends or even lovers were a no-no. It was far safer to be a loner. My coworkers were great—well, most of them. But even they didn't know about my personal life. No, I was all alone.

As the collector left, I let out a shaky breath. There were a couple more hours of work, and then I would be able to do something I'd wanted to do for a long time, but there had never been an opportunity. Now there was. Now I could repay a life debt. That thought sent a delicious tingle singing through my veins.

While Khumalo wasn't signing up to murder the bratva prince, he wasn't rushing to warn him of the threat. A fact I was glad of. My heart skipped double. Sweat made my palms sticky. And what was probably the world's cheesiest smile wouldn't stay hidden under the mask of professionalism.

It was time to make contact with the ruthless Vlasov at long last.

Chapter 2 – Laurel

Nothing good happened after two in the morning. Of course, it didn't matter what time of day it was. Normal people didn't stroll these streets for shits and giggles under the bright frolicking rays of sunlight or beneath the moon. Only something like the conversation I'd overheard could make me desperate enough to venture into this part of town. Popping my freshly colored lips, I shut my compact and returned it to my handbag as the rideshare vehicle slowed. I had the driver drop me off across the street. As if the faux fur coat could protect me, I pulled it tighter as I emerged from the vehicle. Wind whipped down the street. The sharp bite cut through the fabric and excess of natural body padding, and straight into my bones.

But that cruel caress of winter wasn't the thing that made shivers crawl down my spine. How many times had I driven this neighborhood over the years? Always in daylight. Always a few blocks away. Glimpses of the refurbished factory were the only thing I'd seen, because there'd been no reason to venture up to the gates. I had nothing to offer a prince of the underworld to express my gratitude.

Now I stood here, facing the behemoth that was more fortress than industrial structure, with an offering at long last. The high brick wall stared down at me, warning me to run.

A sane person would.

Dimitri is there. Somewhere.

And in danger.

That was the resolve I needed to force the worms writhing in my stomach to calm. With a deep breath, I hustled across the street, careful to watch for patches of unclear pavement. No one stood watch, but it would be foolish to assume I wasn't being tracked. I could feel their eyes on me. That was the job of a security detail, after all. But no matter how watchful, bodyguards weren't allowed to protect from every monster. They were paid well to turn blind eyes.

Swirling, cloying images of the past plumed to choke my brain.

"Don't think about that," I chided myself.

Most days it was easy to forget my old life. After eight years in the Windy City, I was practically a Midwesterner now. But knowing I would see Dimitri brought much of the turbulence to the forefront. Granted, he was associated with the turning point toward the good. It was the past before him that I kept locked away and never visited.

All this time, and I finally am going to see and speak to him again. Every dream scenario, whether it was a chance bumping into him or a planned encounter, I never thought it would be because I brought this morbid flavor of news to his doorstep.

The walls of the repurposed factory loomed overhead. I stepped under their shadow, focusing on the excitement. Would he remember me? I sighed. Probably not. I was many pounds heavier and wore my hair differently. Plus, I was clean, wore proper garments, and no longer slept on the streets.

Standing before the small door beside the double gate, I stabbed the intercom with my cherry red glove.

There was a beat where I shifted my weight. Just because I could walk and work in the skyscraper shoes, didn't mean they were comfortable after a long bartending shift.

"State your business," a thickly accented voice demanded.

"I need to see Mr. Vlasov. Mr. *Dimitri* Vlasov. It's urgent." The cold was numbing my cheeks, calves, and ankles. At least the heels were close-toed.

"Mr. Dimitri isn't expecting anyone," the voice countered.

I pursed my lips. "It's very important. Is he home?"

"Go away."

Working my jaw back and forth, I debated how to proceed. It was entirely possible that whoever was plotting against Dimitri had infiltrated the bratva. An assassination would require intel, which would be better coming from a close source. So I couldn't tell this faceless voice what I knew.

I have to get inside.

Her voice turned hard. "This might sound batshit crazy, but it's the absolute truth."

I moved to a chair and gripped the back. "I'm listening."

She dropped her gaze, shuffling in place. My focus tracked her every move. Excitement mixed with anticipation. It was something big. Something important. The unknown hung heavy in the air, and my pulse doubled in beat. What could it possibly be? While she could be here to hurt me, I didn't sense a threat coming from her. Nerves, she had those in spades. But there was no malice, no danger—none of the usual things that preceded a kill.

"Let's start with something easy," I relented. "What's your name?"

Her lips tipped up. This time amusement played in her smile. "Laurel. Laurel Gundry."

Instead of relief at balancing the scales, something prickled at the back of my neck. *Now why don't I believe you, little snow princess?*

"Okay, Laurel. What brought you to my door?"

That smile vanished entirely. Her eyes glistened and she wet her lips. "Someone wants to kill you."

Chapter 4 – Laurel

Those sea blue eyes closed, and his lips twitched. A short breath that could have been mistaken for laughter came out. "That's a daily occurrence for me, I'm afraid."

Oh, shoot! I took a step forward. "It's true. Hasani Khumalo was at the bar tonight. He was speaking to someone in a ghastly blue suit."

Dimitri's gaze hardened. "The collector."

I nodded eagerly. Reaching into my cleavage, I brought out his card. Moisture was making the paper disintegrate. "He gave me this after the blue suit left."

"If you overheard Khumalo plotting to kill me, how are you here?" suspicion laced his voice.

Waving the card, I held it for him to take. Dimitri slid his hands into the pockets of his sweats and simply watched me. I slapped the tiny, moist paper on the chair seat. "They didn't know I could understand them. They weren't speaking English," I blazed.

Interest sparked in his eyes. "What language?"

Well, shit.... I didn't want it known I could speak almost ten languages. But I put my foot in my mouth with that. "German."

His black brows lifted in surprise. "German," he purred, rolling the word over his tongue. "I know few men who speak that."

"It's not like any Germanic family has an organized presence in the city," I quipped.

Taking a step forward, Dimitri crowded me. Even standing next to him in these shoes, he was tall, forcing me to look up to hold his gaze. "How do you know so much about the organizations in the city? Hmm?"

I gulped and scrambled to hold my resolve.

His gaze dropped to my lips. Something dark flashed in his gaze. "Be truthful, Laurel. I would hate to break something so beautiful to pry out the truth."

Instead of fear, warmth shot through my veins and settled in a needy little ache between my legs. "I pay attention. No one thinks the dumb bartender is listening. You would not believe the loads of gossip loose lips spew once I get them drinking."

"And you just happen to speak German?" The words came out in a damn purr.

I held my breath and lied. "My high school was one of the few that taught foreign languages. I chose that so I could study abroad, which I never did."

His heated gaze roved up and down my body. Gods, I felt like he was stripping me bare! And not just my clothing. No! He was peeling away the hardened layers and was in danger of reaching my calcified soul in one single look.

Before he could speak, there was a shout followed by ravenous barking.

Dimitri sprung to action, going for the door and yelling in some other language. One I didn't know. My lips thinned. Disadvantages weren't something I cared for.

The yammering stilled.

"She came in through the back kitchen when Jasha opened the door," Illya boomed, running down the hall. "That guard, Jasha, was stammering about letting her out to exercise. I thought you forbade the others from caring for her?"

"I did." A muscle in Dimitri's jaw ticked. "I'll have words with him."

"Do you want me to remove the dog?" Ilya offered, appearing in the doorway and shooting a glance at me.

But Dimitri shook his head and whistled.

The prance of paws sounded a moment before the creature trotted through the door. The beast swung that sharp gaze on me and stilled. The russet color of its coat confirmed this hound was actually the spawn of hell.

I took an involuntary step back.

"Don't worry, she won't hurt you," Dimitri told me quietly. To Ilya, he asked, "Did you bring the waters?"

Ilya stabbed a hand at the mutt and with a shake of his head, Dimitri slammed the door.

The whole time the hellhound stared at me. Those onyx eyes promised pain and death to whomsoever pissed her off. Thankfully, the brute seemed to obey Dimitri implicitly.

"Her name is Marena, and she's my dog." Dimitri walked to stand where the hound could see us both at once.

"The Slavic goddess of rebirth," I whispered.

Dimitri cut me a look.

My cheeks flamed. "I read."

"Slavic tales? And you speak German?"

With a shrug, I dropped my gaze so he wouldn't see through me. "I was forced to study the classics, learned to love them, and haven't stopped."

And I've had a fondness for all things Russian for the last few years....

"What else did Khumalo say?" That question snapped my attention.

I could feel the weight behind that command, a physical force drawing my body's focus. It settled deep in my core. A force that I couldn't escape from. Not that I wanted to, but it was nice to have the option. I cleared my throat. "He wouldn't agree to the plot. Said he was a collector of objects, not bodies. But he added that it would be suicide to go against you, because if they failed, it would be certain death."

Dimitri let out another short breath. "Smart man."

"I'm sorry, I wished there was more I could tell you." I took a step clasping my hands. "It's not much."

"It's a start." And then, the most incredible thing happened. His eyes *burned*. The blue became more pronounced.

A shiver rippled down my spine. I couldn't help it. That was a man who was about to raze the city to the ground and dance on the ashes.

Not that he probably danced.

His tone lightened, contrasting with the savage spark in his eyes. "Well, Laurel Gundry, may I offer you something to eat or drink?"

"Oh, no," I laughed, placing my hand on my belly. "I don't drink much, and I have leftover Giordano's in my fridge."

"Ah, there's nothing better than that pizza pie," he murmured.

Something dark and forbidden buzzed in my veins. Would it be so bad? One little taste of pleasure? I could go right back to being a lone wolf right after I took a bite.

He probably wouldn't go for you.

That slap brought me back to reality. I shook myself. He wasn't flirting with me, he was just being nice. Because despite every terrible whisper, Dimitri Vlasov was a nice man. And now that I'd *finally* done something nice for him, it was time to escape.

"I would cut down any man who stood in my way of Giordano's," I laughed, pulling my hat back over my head and reaching for my coat.

Dimitri plucked it from my hands and held it out for me. My breath caught in my throat. Electricity buzzed across my skin under his heated gaze. And we hadn't even touched yet!

"I'll take you home," Dimitri offered as I slid into my fur coat.

He ran his big hands across the shoulders, smoothing the fake fur down. I tried and failed to stare at his hands. So large, but slim and elegant. A mischievous, gleeful little part of me wondered what it would be like to have them brush over my body? To have his touch everywhere? To feel his fingers blaze a path across my skin?

But...I can't. I didn't do one-night stands, and I sure as hell didn't do relationships. I kept to myself; I stayed hidden.

And it was time to get the hell out of here.

That was the flaw with my plan. I'd been in such a hurry to come here, to warn him, that I hadn't calculated my escape. What if he didn't let me go? The butterflies turned to worms in my stomach. *I'll get out,* I promised myself.

"Thanks," I choked out. "But I have an Uber on standby." Shooting out of his personal space, I reached for my purse and succeeded in sending the contents flying wide.

"Blue shit monkey balls!" I fumed, squatting to pick things up.

Dimitri stilled. "Well, that's got to be the world's oddest swear words."

Looking over to comment, I froze. Marena's lip curled back as she pinned me with a warning look.

"Let me get her out of here," Dimitri muttered. He barked a command in that unfamiliar language. The dog moved to his side, and they left.

Flustered, and unable to squat-lean in my heels, I dropped to my knees in a hurry to grab my things and leave.

Chapter 5 – Dimitri

Marena sat in my home gym, and I pulled the door shut. As I returned to the living room after penning my dog, a turbulent stream of thoughts raced through my mind. Even without reason to trust a strange woman's tale, I believed what Laurel said. While the collector wasn't an assassin, Khumalo wasn't above taking a bounty. I was in danger. But since that was part of my existence, I was able to push it aside. The more immediate question was what I did with the messenger.

Did I let her go?

I spun my lighter through the fingers of my right hand. I couldn't very well keep her. While a mistress or a side piece was acceptable, it was frowned upon to bring girlfriends into the inner workings of our business. Unless I wanted to admit that she was a threat, and thus expose the information she brought, I couldn't keep her prisoner here.

Just because I let her free, doesn't mean I'm done with her.

Satisfaction slithered through my chest. There was no way I was done with her. Not after popping into my world on a random night and piquing my interest. I stopped short in front of the living room. There she was, crawling about my floor. I swiped my hand over my mouth.

"Wow," I breathed to myself. *Just...wow.*

The sight of her in that thick black coat on all fours was one of the most spectacular things I'd ever seen.

"Did anything fall under that table," I said a little louder, ignoring the tightness in my pants.

Laurel yelped, rearing up. "Fate! You scared me. I didn't hear you!"

Something similar to a laugh rumbled through my chest. "Sorry." *Not.*

I wanted to do it again.

Laurel turned and rummaged under the table. I bent to collect what seemed to be a button. It was small and black. Bringing it closer, a piece of the mystery fell into place. This was a free drink token from STYX. The strip joint. My gaze cut to the woman stretching under the table to reach for her packet of facial tissues.

No...she wasn't.

Was she?

This snowy beauty was a stripper for the Mikhaylov Bratva? STYX was owned by the captain of another Russian crew, and it laundered money just like my clubs washed for ours.

I fisted the token. I should have been worried that she was a plant, sent here by a rival mob. Instead, a fire in my veins set to boil. Other men saw her naked. Other eyes latched onto that beautiful body? Let her fulfill their fantasies?

No. No, that wasn't acceptable! The force of me clenching my jaw threatened to crack a molar. She said she was a bartender, but she'd already lied to my men to gain access. Who was to say she wasn't a stripper?

I couldn't bring myself to ask her.

No, a far darker thought consumed me. As soon as possible, I would go to that seedier neighborhood and use my free drink token. I would follow her. I would discover *everything* there was to know about her.

"Ready!" she beamed, climbing to her feet.

"So am I."

She walked before me, bundled and prepared for the winter. The way she wrapped the knee length coat around her throat reminded me of the glamorous movie stars of bygone decades. She tipped her face to the sky and drew in a deep breath. "It smells like snow."

It did.

"It's been a crazy winter," Laurel mused, picking her way across the ground.

Jasha stood outside his box. Those vicious eyes tracked us. I glared at him, silently daring him to contradict us. Laurel sauntered right to the side door and pushed it open. That authority in her stride. Damn—it was like she owned the place.

Now there's an interesting thought. A dark laugh flickered through my mind.

"Sir, someone could gun you down on the street," one of the other guards interjected, hurrying forward.

I looked him up and down. Although I outranked him, I was still bound by the same rules he was invoking. Instead of pressing that issue, I raised a more personal one. "If any of you ever touch my dog again, I'll cut your arm off for a chew toy in the kennel."

Jasha's eyes widened. Unfortunately for him, it was a threat that had been carried out. On more than one man. I pinned him with a knowing look. He was the fool who'd messed with my hound. Only the kennel master and I went near Marena. The soldier knew my hound was off limits, but he chose to ignore that. Whatever his reasons, it didn't matter.

"Sir, you can't go out there." Viktor, the oldest and best guard we had, stepped forward.

"Get out of my way, soldier," I barked. "Or else I'll remove you."

Viktor pulled himself up to his full height, which barely came up to my shoulder. "It could be a trap."

Viktor was just doing his job. Protecting our family. Not that he knew it, but Laurel did come from the club of a rival mob. He'd been in the position for half a decade, and before that, he was one of our most valuable soldiers. Like the faithful hounds we kept on the property, he was a fixed piece.

I jerked as the full weight of that thought hit me.

I sounded like my father. Black wrath spiked in my veins. I bit my tongue until the metallic tang filled my mouth. I'd just equated a loyal soldier to an animal. Exactly how my father taught me to behave.

Dear old dad never saw animals as pets, but tools. The same with men—and his only son.

I glanced at where Laurel tapped on her phone on the sidewalk, ignoring us.

I will not be like him. "Viktor, take the men, and fan out down the street. Both sides," I clipped as I stepped through the door.

Relief twitched through Viktor's grizzled features.

Laurel continued to tap on her phone as I ghosted to her side. Inhaling deeply, the smell of ripened summer fruit overwhelmed the booze. If she worked at STYX, it explained the alcohol. "Laurel, I want to—"

She jumped. Missed her footing. And began to topple.

I snatched her arm, finding flesh under the thick layer of fur. "Steady there."

"You can't just sneak up on people," she gasped, but there was a smile in her voice.

The sound drew me forward. I clutched both her arms, holding her in my space. The streetlights glinted off her cinnamon eyes. That color was so unique, so familiar somehow, but I could have sworn I'd never seen this woman before. And that voice? I would have remembered a voice like that, even if her face was changed.

Sweeping one long look over her, I cleared my throat. "I want to thank you, Laurel."

She cocked her head. "For what?"

I twitched in surprise. "For telling me."

"Oh, that," she laughed. "Yeah, it would have been wrong not to. Sorry, it wasn't more information. At least you know now. Because you don't deserve to be...."

Her voice trailed off, and she looked at the others.

I followed her gaze, but then returned it to her face. I couldn't stop looking at her.

She leaned closer, head bent low. "You better keep what I told you to yourself. Or your most trusted men," she said quietly. "You have no idea how deep this thing runs."

Those words were a cold dash of water. Every vicious fiber in my being numbed. "That's wise advice."

Laurel lifted a shoulder in a light dismissal. "It's nothing."

"It's not nothing." I drew my touch down until I clasped the gloved fingers of her right hand. I hated the material separating us. I wanted to touch her skin. "I owe you a life debt, Laurel Gundry. Any day or night, you call and you will get whatever you need. I swear it to you."

Those strange eyes were impossibly wide, and she was breathing hard. I did a double take, struggling to decipher her reaction. She tugged her fingers. I let them go.

Only when she snatched them with her other hand did she let out a long breath.

"Thank you," she smiled, and her voice didn't shake.

I was imagining things. For a second there it seemed like she didn't want me to touch her hand.

"I mean it. You ask, and if it's in my power, I'll give it. Up to half my kingdom, it's yours."

A smirk twitched her lips. "That's biblical."

I narrowed my eyes.

"That painting; John the Baptist's head on the platter?" Laurel cocked her head. She waited in silence, watching me.

The cool night air fanned around us. But the space between our bodies? It wasn't chilly at all.

Finally, laughter played across her lips. "Am I scaring you with my oddities?"

"Enticing. Not scaring."

Her blistering smile sparkled, those pearly teeth flashing behind the crimson paint. "Oooh! I've caught the attention of the lion. A good thing my ride is here so I can escape his den."

She stepped away. I never wanted anything as badly as to yank her close. Unfortunately, I let her go. I couldn't keep her—not openly. She hurried across the sidewalk, movements graceful and elegant, and slipped into the Honda Pilot with the big Ü in the front window.

Walking to the driver's side, I rapped my knuckles on the glass. The man rolled down the window, black eyes wide. "Sir?"

"You drive carefully, and you make sure she reaches her destination," I warned. "I have your license plates and you'll answer to me if you don't."

His lip wobbled. "Yes, sir, yes! I'll even walk her to the door if you want," he stammered in a thick, foreign accent.

"I do want. Thank you," I said shortly with a nod.

The window rolled up, and he began to drive away. The security cameras likely caught the license plate, but I whipped my phone from my pants pocket and snapped a picture. I no doubt scared the driver half to death. But I was serious. She needed to arrive safely at her destination.

Or I would do something drastic. Like scorching the earth. Because I wasn't done with the snowy little beauty. In fact, as I turned on my heel, I knew I would spend the next few hours scrolling through the software programs available to me and find out every drop of information I could.

“How long did you sleep?” Luka shadow-boxed the air to warm his combinations.

I rolled my shoulders and lied. “Five hours.”

A long whistle slid between my cousin’s teeth. “I wondered if it was a good night when you weren’t calling me at five saying you needed a workout.”

What he didn’t know was that instead of coming to the gym when I couldn’t sleep, I’d split my time between creating a nice little dossier on a woman with no history to scrub and contacting a few spies in the underworld. I put out feelers for both information on Laurel and also for the bounty for my own head. The results were futile.

With a snort, I bounced on my toes, practicing my steps. “You want to chat or you want to fight?”

“As if you can best me,” Luka chortled.

“We’re two for two outside the ring. And our record is evenly matched in here,” I reminded him, circling my somewhat insane cousin. “No face shots.”

Luka dropped his hands, threw his head back, and moaned dramatically. His lean frame wriggled. “Man! That’s no fun!”

I relaxed my stance and stepped back, a prepared lecture on my lips.

Luka rushed.

It was like watching the dark-haired girl from The Ring come for me. Body loose and flailing, he dodged every maneuver and dove.

“Goat!” I roared the offensive term. “We’re supposed to be boxing.”

Arms wrapped around my waist, Luka laughed. He was always laughing and smiling. I rained blows on his back, showing no mercy.

He never played by the rules!

“Luka!” I slammed my glove into his left kidney. “You dirty little brat. Why can’t you fight me like a damn man?”

“‘Whenever you are about to find fault with someone, ask yourself the following question: What fault of mine most nearly resembles the one I am about to criticize?'" Luka's laugh was manic. Wild and unfettered. Light and full of his own self-assurance.

"Damn your ancient philosophy!" I seethed. I was going to beat the ever-loving shit out of him.

It was no use, the spry bastard lifted me. Lifted *me!* All 250 lbs. of hardened muscle. And he weighed 190 dripping wet!

My arms went wide, windmilling and trying to clutch anything solid. There was nothing but air.

Luka sat.

Sat hard on his butt.

Which meant I toppled. Despite the bulky boxing gloves, I snaked out to wrap him in a grappling maneuver. We might be on the ground, but I was fast.

Luka grunted, thrashing about as his head stuck fast under my armpit.

"Did you just *bite* me!" I roared.

Deep laughter sounded from somewhere outside the ring, but I didn't pay any attention to the noise. I was furious now. The gym our Bratva used to work out tinged with red. Moving my legs around his middle, I clamped tight.

He struggled, but I had him!

Squeezing with every ounce of strength, I blessed the saints that I did as much work on my lower half as my upper. His chest cavity compressed under the vise of my legs. Luka gasped, unable to keep biting me.

"I will crush you," I threatened, locking my legs tighter and tighter.

"Yield, you idiot." It was Kaz.

"Never!" Luka twitched.

I managed to tear at my tape with my teeth and flung a glove off. Luka didn't have enough hair to grasp—smart goat. But he had two good ears. I grabbed one and wrenched.

Luka yelled.

"You bite me, I do this," I clapped my open palm against his ear.

"Hey, not cool, cuz," Kaz cautioned.

As if I cared. I would beat Luka to a pulp if he wasn't a blood relation. I would—

"Rabid dogs need to learn their place in the pack," a voice not my own bellowed in my mind.

Those words gutted me.

The muscles in my legs had to have relaxed, because the bastard wriggled free. I shook myself from the stupor enough to prevent the blows suddenly pelting down on me from doing any damage. With only one glove, I couldn't give them back.

Scrambling away, I lowered my guard to unwrap my other wrist.

Leaving myself exposed.

Luka jumped to his feet.

"Dimi!" Kaz warned.

The blow cracked on my left.

Stars exploded across my vision.

Every muscle in my body stopped working. I blinked slowly...up. At the steel ceiling far above us.

"Luka, enough!" Kazimir was there, pushing our cousin away. "You win!"

Wild whoops filled the space. The sounds swam in and out of focus, as if we were in a fishbowl.

"Dimitri!" Kaz was looking in my face. "How many fingers?"

"Three," I choked, shutting my eyes for just a second.

"Shit," Kaz spat and lifted me.

How much time passed, it was impossible to say. I was deposited in the lounge area and something foul was brought to my nose.

I swatted the smelling salts away. "Hell no."

"He's *fine*," Luka drawled.

"If he's got a concussion...." Kaz threatened. "We have our hands full as it is without Dimitri laid up."

"I am fine," I said, struggling to sit up.

Nausea bubbled in my throat. *Fuck.*

Kaz had the bucket in front of me a moment later. I heaved into the plastic-lined container. It was nothing but bile. That was how it was with these episodes. I could eat a steak meal and puke nothing but spit and liquid.

At least it didn't burn.

"Shit, man," Luka ripped off his gloves.

"Get everyone out," I shouted.

"No one's here," Kaz assured me. He handed me a bottle of water. "See what you did," he added quietly to Luka.

"You will *never* go easy on me," I commanded, choking out the words between bouts of dry heaving.

My head spun. There was nothing to be done but wait for the agony to pass.

"I thought the puking spells were under control," Luka said quietly.

"They are, idiot, until he gets hit in the damn head," Kaz growled.

I managed to draw in several breaths. The dizziness subsided, and after five minutes I was able to look away from the trash. I didn't dare stand up yet, but I could glare at my cousins.

"No one is to know," I insisted.

It was what we'd agreed on.

"You don't have to keep reminding us," Kazimir grumped. "We'd never let the others know."

I gave them a short nod. "Good, now that that's settled, I have other news."

They waited while I paused to swish and spit. I'd debated long and hard whether I should tell them what Laurel told me. Her advice had been sound about keeping the information quiet, but I needed to believe my cousins were loyal. That they could help me. While they could never understand the weight of the crown, I had to believe they would stand by my side.

Lies...the throne is a lonely seat.

I cleared my throat. "Someone is trying to recruit backers to assassinate me."

Kazimir dropped into a chair. "When you said you wanted to talk...fuck."

Letting out a long breath, nodded again. "Yeah. I know."

"Does Kolya know?" Luka frog squatted, stretching his quads. "He might have contacts in that niche."

"Called him this morning. He'll look around. Oh, and he's got threads on your sex traffickers, Kaz."

"I know, we spoke around midnight."

"Shit's going to hit the fan fast," I drawled.

"We said ten tonight, right? To hit Lazarowicz's shipment?"

I thought quickly. "Ten thirty. I have somewhere to be beforehand. I'll need you as wingman, Luka."

Luka narrowed his eyes. "Where?"

Amusement flickered through me. It was such a foreign feeling that I paused to give it space. "Charron's river."

Neither of my cousins got the connection. But my plastic token pulsed in my gym bag across the room.

Chapter 6 – Laurel

Another shiver rippled down my spine. I frowned. It was far from cold in here. A full house tonight, there were three of us working behind the bar. The fans overhead circulated the stale, thick air, making a cloud of sweat turned into humidity descend on us. Still, I couldn't shake the icy tendrils that seemed to stroke my spine every few minutes.

"Tell me again how you landed a Friday night off?" Julisa grumped, spilling half the shot of Grey Goose on the floor. "Shit!"

I looked quickly around the establishment for Beck. The floor manager was working with the hostess. And Kevin was running around like a chicken without a head, because the club owner was here tonight. So far, neither of the managers had been back here to bother us.

Callie, the third bartender, snatched the two high ball glasses with strawberry mojitos on the rubber mat. "Because she begged Helen to bartend instead of waitress."

"Yeah, and she gets half my tips from tonight," I scoffed. But it was worth it. So worth it to have tomorrow night off.

Beka sailed to a stop, snatched the bar towel, and began to wipe her tray.

"Beka, baby, what do I have to do to get you to cover for me some weekend?" Julisa batted her thick, long, and 100% real lashes at the waitress grabbing the drinks on her tray.

"Show me what's under your skirt? I want to see if it's as long and thick as rumor has it," Beka shamelessly flirted.

Most of the girls working at STYX were constantly begging to get Julisa alone. They were curious because she was a trans female, and they wanted time with her. But Julisa was picky about her partners. They had to have spark, passion, and be willing to explore the wilder side. Compared to my fellow coworkers, I was practically a virgin. But like Julisa, I too was picky. Extremely. Unlike Julisa, I was vanilla.

"That's a steep price for a night off," Julisa started to counter, eyes shining with interest.

But out of nowhere, the club's owner swooped into our space. "Get to fucking work! I don't pay you to gossip."

Thankfully, my hands were busy, just like Callie's. We continued to pour as the owner looked on in disgust. It wasn't unusual for Karlgrad to spend the weekends here, rubbing shoulders with important guests and making our lives miserable.

Not five minutes later, Diamond sashayed up. "I just worked the floor before I go on stage, and daaammmnnn!"

The dancer dropped the basket of snacks on the end of the bar. She tossed a flirty look to Karlgrad, but the owner was busy tapping on his phone. Without noticing how one of his dancers was acting, Karlgrad wandered away to catch Kevin. From the look on the owner's face, I didn't pity the manager.

"Those don't go there," I muttered, nudging the complimentary junk food we passed out to the tables.

Diamond ignored me.

"Good crowd?" Julisa leaned against the counter, flirting shamelessly. It was no secret she wanted Diamond.

And the dancer made her work for it.

"Why are Russians so cute? Black hair, blue eyes...ah!" Diamond moaned. "I could eat them both up!"

Julisa grumped about how Latina women were far more beautiful, and while I would have loved to back my friend up, I was suddenly standing still, martini glass suspended from my fingers.

While STYX was owned by the branch of a Russian mob, I doubted Diamond was talking about them. She would have used their names. No...she was talking about *other* Russians.

A phantasmal touch skated across my skin, sending prickles and chills to race over my body. My heartbeat doubled. A shaky breath whispered between my lips.

I peered out onto the darkened floor. The lights overhead were dim, and the strips of L.E.D.s on the floor weren't powerful enough to shine over more than the paths they illumined. Thick shadows cloaked the booths and hid the tables. I didn't see them. But that didn't mean they—*he*—couldn't see me.

It was illogical—it was silliness! But I swore I could *feel* him.

Blinking rapidly, my rational side sprang to the surface to bitch slap the rest. The crown prince of the Vlasov Bratva didn't know where I worked. There was no paper trail connecting me to this job.

Plus, he wouldn't come into Karlgrad's territory.

That thought squashed the fantasies swirling in my head. I hated that I thought of it, but it was true. Mobs stayed away from each other so blood wasn't spilled.

Besides, I had no reason to see Dimitri again. Unless I learned anything more about the assassination plot, life needed to go back to normal. That meant no contact. I didn't have friends...or lovers.

Warmth bloomed deep in my core. It had been there, smoldering, simmering, or spiking, ever since I made contact with the bratva prince. My body was in complete defiance with my rules.

"You're dribbling the shaker over the floor!" Karlgrad fumed, coming up behind me to snarl in my ear.

I jumped, which only made the glass shatter.

"That comes out of your pay," he snapped. "Get to work! Diamond, backstage. Now!"

Gritting my teeth and refusing to let the boss make me feel bad, I cleaned up my mess, made drinks, and stayed impossibly busy. I kept stealing glances toward the floor, pleading that the Vlasov heir forgot about me.

Just like I need to forget about him....

I slept. And slept some more. Not having to work tonight, I didn't move until my bladder screamed at me. After washing my hands, I tapped on my phone. I went back to bed, but forty minutes later the door announced the food delivery service.

I trudged to answer and slipped the driver a twenty. She beamed!

I'd heard from friends that third party food delivery drivers made shit for tips, so when I decided to be lazy and order myself a meal, I made sure to tip well. Although correlation was no grounds for causation, the next shifts at STYX were always heavier tip nights for me in return. Tell me karma didn't exist!

The chicken biscuit sandwich reminded me of my childhood trips to the southern United States to visit my paternal grandparents. Oh, it brought back memories. I licked my fingers and put the second away for lunch. They didn't do biscuits after ten, and I preferred those to the buns at lunch.

"Laundry, I said I would do you, but...." I frowned at the pile on the floor. A trail of clothing led to the bedroom.

On a whim, I'd bought one of those small washers from a sketchy website, since the apartment didn't have an in-unit washer-dryer. Plus, my work clothing wouldn't survive in the ancient machine on the lower level. Best money I spent that day.

The piles of dirty clothes stared back at me. *Le sigh.* The sooner I got it done, the sooner I could spend the day doing other things.

Pushing myself into action, I thanked the universe that I had separated everything the night before. My panties and thongs went into the portable washer first and I set up the drying wrack by the fan. Soon the space would smell like fresh lavender soap.

Going into my bedroom, I kicked shoes out of the way. There was a used coffee cup and I winced.

"I really do live like a slob," I said to my reflection as I sat. It had been my New Year's resolution to keep the apartment more tidy. I kept my tiny home clean-clean. The problem was a lack of storage and organization. But there was no point picking up when I was bone-deep exhausted from pouring drinks. It had been years since I had a maid, and I didn't regret it one bit. It would just be nice if the clothes would hang themselves back up when I was done with them. Or the dishes washed themselves while I was gone.

Clearing my throat, I began warmups as I arranged my filming station. Black out curtains closed, and the candelabra of black tapered beauties for my camera to look at were lit. My viewers couldn't see my face, and there was never an end to the snide comments about that. I might have a high six figure number of fans, but I couldn't risk letting them catch a glimpse of me.

It's necessary.

Today, I selected a song from memory.

The world faded away. From the lockbox of memories, I pulled a vivid image of the past. I remembered the rolling hills of Switzerland, the foot of the Alps. A girl begging her nanny to play Sound of Music, with her red braids flapping against her back. The smell of wildflowers came from the ghost of bygone days. The warm sun and the chilly wind created a delicious combination.

I tipped my head back and let my heart steal the music. The notes shot high, and I held the sound, channeling my inner Julie Andrews.

The words of *Do-Re-Mi* filled the apartment.

I swore I could feel the June sun on my long, bright braids.

And then, I clicked the off button. The filming stopped. I fell into the trap of swirling memories, staring too long into one of the flames. Out of the vortex of heartache, misery, and even pain, there was happiness. That was why I'd sang that beautiful song, even though it wasn't my typical style. The nostalgia was too strong to resist. Now that I'd indulged it, it was a struggle pushing back the baggage that hitched a ride.

I rubbed my arms. "That's it, the next piece needs to be something different."

Something that didn't bring up memories of a childhood traveling Europe.

I didn't listen to the acapella piece.

Instead, I chose a song about diamonds being a girl's best friend. I changed the tune and carried the rhythm well, even without music. When I was done, I relistened to the style. It was good! The DIY foam boards that I put around my room really had improved the quality of filming. I saved the song as a draft, planning to upload it this evening.

Ten more songs, and I had enough videos drafted for the week and then some. My days off were Mondays and slow Wednesdays. But lately, I'd been called in during the middle of the week. The men of the city were frequenting STYX. They packed them in and expected us to make craft cocktails on a budget.

Stupid. My bosses were stupid. And downright mean. They made Julisa cry before last night was over.

Blowing out the candelabra, I pushed my way through the dark to find the wall switch. I lost too much time thinking about last night.

How I couldn't find the Russian, and when I asked her, Diamond didn't know who she'd seen. And they were long gone when she finished her act and I could ask her where they'd been sitting.

There were so many Russians in the city that it was no doubt improbable that it was the Vlasovs. Plus, Diamond couldn't tell Ukrainian from Romanian, Polish from Russian, or even French from Italian. She was lucky her last sugar daddy bought her the newest set of tits.

"Time to rest my voice before tonight," I muttered, turning on the lights. I wished I had something sentient to talk to, but alone in my apartment, it was safer this way.

Chapter 7 – Laurel

"You know how the time flies. Only yesterday was the time of our lives. We were born and raised in a summer haze." The words skated across my tongue and flew into the crowd. The sounds didn't need the microphone stuffed in front of my face. The meaning boomed into the audience.

It was bittersweet. Per my specific request, no one saw me. The spotlight hit the front of the stage. The silhouette of my dress illuminated in the glow. My face was covered in shadows. The last eight years of living this new life were not going to be wasted on a fleeting moment of glory where the thunderous applause hailed me as a queen amongst the stars.

Right hand pressed against my chest, I poured my soul into the music. It didn't matter if one person heard me or a sea of people. This was my outlet.

No one could take it away.

So long as no one discovered the singer in the shadows.

"I remember you said, 'Sometimes it lasts in love, but sometimes it hurts instead,'" I repeated the last line, and let the notes linger on my vocal cords, forcing them out and into the void.

It was my final song of the evening. I paid tribute to the great musicians of this century, always throwing an Adele and a Celine in the mix. It had been three weeks since I'd sung this particular song. It felt right.

A beat of stillness lingered over the lounge. They were unable to see my face, but it was also hard for me to see much of the audience. It started as a murmur, the collective sigh rushing around the space. First one set of hands clapped, quickly joined by others.

"Thank you, you've been very kind. Goodnight, Kat Klub!" I rasped into the microphone before spinning and disappearing to the side.

The blue satin rustled around my legs as I hurried into the dressing room. With a quick slide of the zipper, I pulled the dress open. A fist rapped against the door.

"Shoot," I muttered. "Just a second!"

"It's Derek," the man called.

That was even more reason to hurry. Just like last week, and the weeks before, he had a habit of arriving right as I was changing. Gritting my teeth, I pulled the gown off and slid the trouser shorts over the fishnet stockings. A black shimmering blouse went on top, and I pulled on heeled booties. With a flip of the lock, I let the entertainment manager in with a flourish.

"You were *fabulous*," he gushed.

I gave him a careful smile. "Thank you, Derek."

He reached out, trying to clasp my hands. I turned sharply, gathering my things and pretending not to see him attempting to make contact. I wasn't imagining the attention. It was obvious what he wanted. Not only was I uninterested in the skinny boy with a manbun, I didn't want anything to affect this gig.

It had taken half a year to land it!

That hard work wasn't going down the drain because someone wanted to bone me.

"You really should think about letting the patrons see you," Derek said, stepping into my personal space.

Every fiber of my being wanted to push him, give him a good hard shove onto his ass, but that would never work.

"Derek, if I've told you once, I've told you a hundred times," I drawled, letting Southern sass in my tone cover up the rougher New York accent that would sprout when I was truly incensed. "That's nonnegotiable. I need to protect my privacy."

"What if I said there was a producer in the crowd tonight?" He leaned against my table, waggling his blond eyebrows.

His words needled. I wanted to itch my chest where the skin prickled. "I would tell you that I'm uninterested at this time. I would ask for his contact information, and I'll think about it."

Derek held a business card between his fingers. When I reached for it, he pulled it back. "Come have a bite with me, and I'll give it to you."

I had to bite my tongue so as not to say anything stupid. Shaking my head, I grabbed my dress bag, backpack, and purse. "Have a good night, Derek."

"Oh, come on, here," he relented, pushing the card into my palm. He curled my fingers over the piece of paper. "But I do want to have a bite of dinner with you someday."

"I have to go." I pulled away from him.

"Brunch tomorrow? Or lunch!" He stepped in front of me, blocking my exit.

My breath hitched. A cold sweat broke over my skin. I pinned the man in the doorway with a look. "I have to leave, Derek."

He's not blocking me.

The inhale didn't quite fill my lungs.

I can get past him.

"Come on, Laurel. I'm crazy about you, you have to know that." The words that came out of his mouth belonged to him. But the slithering, slimy, squelching feeling unlocked a vault of memories. The suddenness of the past rushing out had me stumbling back.

Taunts and jeers swirled around me.

A deceptively charming face that hid rough hands crowed triumphantly. Phantasmal hands bruised my flesh, reached for my throat—

Rapidly, I whipped my head back and forth. *Craig's not here. He doesn't know where I am.*

Those words repeated until I believed it. But it didn't change the current, although somewhat less nightmarish, situation. Derek saw the pause as an opportunity to advance. I gathered my wits and tried to wrestle with the blend of past and present.

Throat dry from singing, I couldn't speak properly.

Derek seized the moment and grasped for my hands.

"Don't touch me!" I gasped, jerking away.

Surprise flashed across his face. Instead of repenting or apologizing, his hazel eyes narrowed. "You don't have to be such a bitch about it."

Why were all guys the same? Refuse them and it was my fault? I squeezed my eyes closed, trying and failing to handle the situation.

"Derek, please, I'm being a professional. My love life is nonexistent at the moment. It's not you. I'm just not dating right now." Great, now I was apologizing for being hounded.

I clenched my jaw, wishing I was brave enough to punch him.

"I see how it is," he said, voice icy.

A shiver skittered over my skin. "Goodnight."

I pushed past him, making a beeline for the exit. As I rushed to where my rideshare waited, I realized I'd dropped the business card with the producer's name. Settling into the backseat, I let out a sigh. Too bad. It wasn't like I could perform anyway. But it was nice to know I had the options.

Chapter 8 – Dimitri

Feet planted shoulder distance apart, I stared at the far wall. I forced the calm through my veins. It would only be worse if I argued.

"You had one job," the pakhan snapped. "This is inexcusable."

"I understand, sir." I swallowed. Any reason or explanation stayed buried deep inside.

"Here I thought you were beyond making mistakes like this." My father pushed around papers, a sigh of pure disgust coming from inside. "Igor told me this would happen."

Igor is a fat idiot. "Emil was late with his squad."

"Did you just make an excuse?" Those words froze in the air.

Bracing myself, I said the only thing I could say. "No, sir, just stating fact. By the time appointed for the drop, we were discovered."

My father pushed to his feet, coming around his desk. "Your numbers this month were by far the best. But it seems that you still have much to learn about running this organization."

Like making sure the other captains do what they're supposed to? It was useless to argue. But that didn't stop the thoughts from popping into my mind.

"You should be grateful I'm going to allow you to be my heir. If your performance was any record, it would go to Emil or Igor." My father stopped in front of me. I pinned my gaze over his head. There was no point looking down at the boss and expecting mercy. I was a soldier, like all the others. Just because I was blood didn't mean I was treated differently.

I'd earned the position of captain by right of conquest. Few saw the work behind it, only the blood relation to the boss. That meant I had to outdo older heads like Uncle Vasil and Igor, while competing with the ruthless Emil. At least Uncle Yaroslav was dead. There would have been no beating that scheming bastard.

"Our organization lost a seventy thousand deal because you couldn't cope with a change in circumstance. When you realized Emil wasn't going to show, you should have adapted. Instead, you lost us the product." The pakhan punctuated the statement with an uppercut of his fist.

Only...tonight the pakhan was armed.

The brass knuckle cracked into my jaw, and my head snapped to the side.

Iron filled my mouth, but I knew better than to spit.

"Fix this—recover the product," the brute in front of me hissed.

Straightening I nodded. "It will be done, sir."

"Dismissed." My father turned on his heel and returned to his desk.

Red tinged my vision as I made my escape. I left the boss's office and marched down the hall. I didn't see anyone or comprehend my surroundings until I was in my room. Going to my sink, I spat the blood and examined my teeth. I hadn't lost one tonight.

I could have stopped the blow, but that would have been mutiny. The frequent abuse had lessened into occasional bouts of physical discipline. My father's displeasure always came with a taste of pain. Yet even he was smart enough not to push me. Not after what happened the last beating he'd given me.

That had been years ago.

Not that sending me to the hospital and crippling me for life would have stopped him beforehand. It was only after the fact, when Vasil pointed out how the others would see the pakhan as unhinged if they knew he beat me regularly to purge the weakness.

I might be strong enough to fight off the old man, but the real possibility of banishment was stronger than the pain of a throbbing jaw. The bratva was my life.

And someday this empire would be mine—someday soon if the cancer in the pakhan's lungs had its way.

Something seemed to pulse in my pocket. Just like a second heartbeat. I reached into my jeans and my fingers skimmed across the piece of plastic. I grit my teeth. I had to find close to a hundred thousand in illegal booze before tomorrow. There wasn't time to be normal.

But there was time to haunt.

Stopping behind an overflowing trash container, I took up my position deep in the shadows. It wouldn't be long now, and the employees would leave the club. Here in the cold, quiet of the night, I turned my thoughts upward. I pulled out the small icon of the saint and began to murmur the prayers taught to me as a child. Peace swept through me. It was a good thing heaven didn't look on my works to buy an entrance pass. Still...I wasn't a good man. All I could do was believe in the higher power to save me when the inevitable end came.

The door banged open, and my damned heart leaped.

There she was. What started as a mystery turned quickly into an obsession. I hadn't missed a night, trailing after her through the dark.

"Because, Derek, I just don't date," she insisted, and I realized she was speaking into her cellphone.

A frown carved across my face.

"Yes! I want to continue and—"

Laurel began to storm down the street, listening to whatever the person on the other end of the line was saying.

My steps were hard as they followed.

At the mouth of the alley, Laurel stopped short. She surveyed the night-bathed street, showing situational awareness.

Good girl.

Of course, she missed the one being lurking and watching. Not that she had anything to fear from me. I was there to observe, nothing more.

"Fine, lunch would be good," she conceded.

I stilled. My heart thumped double. Red tinged my vision, and I blinked hard.

I couldn't believe I was hearing this.

The hell she's having a lunch date!

"Noon, at La Belle Vie," she confirmed, before she stabbed the screen of her phone and dropped it in her purse. A long breath pushed from her lungs. My fingers itched to reach out and brush across her coat.

"Noon. La Belle Vie," I mouthed. I would be there. Only an act of God could keep me away.

After nights of watching, after hours of research, this was the first real clue into her life. And not one that I liked.

Laurel began to walk along the sidewalk in the direction of her shitty apartment.

Saints! To look at her, one would think she was born into a royal house. The way she carried herself, the way she moved. It came naturally. Never had I seen a woman more graceful, captivating, and confident as this one.

But there was something missing. Something didn't add up. She didn't belong to the criminal underworld, nor to the subsection of strippers, hookers, and cash. Yet here she was.

Why does she have to be so beautiful? I wet my lips as I tracked her every movement.

Her heels clipped across the pavement. She crossed right in front of the alley where I waited. I drew in a deep breath as she passed. A knot formed in my chest, and I took a deep gulp of the icy night air.

Slipping from the alley, I kept twenty yards behind her. She never heard me as I ghosted from shadow to shadow. Part of me wanted her to know I was there, if only so I could hear that voice again. That gorgeous fucking voice.

It was safer this way.

To Laurel's right was the empty lot where the rubble of an old building was covered in dirty snow dumped from the plows. Because of the frozen mounds, I didn't notice the movement until it was too late.

A figure emerged from the mess and stumbled into Laurel's path.

Blood roared in my ears, and I rushed forward.

She didn't scream or try to run. She stopped, and in an even voice, said, "Excuse me, but you're in my way."

The man inched forward. "Come on, honey, give us a kiss."

"How vile." Something flashed in Laurel's hand as she lunged.

The man cried out and fell, twitching. Laurel drove the heel of her shoe into his palm, moving it back and forth.

"Pig," she snarled.

Diving, she put another charge from her taser into his throat. And then, she straightened, running her gloves over her coat. With an elegant step over his body, as if it was a minor obstacle and not someone who wanted to hurt her, she continued to walk down the street.

A deadly queen of the night.

Admiration swelled in my chest. She didn't need a dark knight watching over her. But she had one, regardless.

Stopping only long enough to snap the neck of the man, I tossed his limp, unwashed body into the snow heap. "It was your own fault, bud. You should never have approached her."

There wasn't time tonight to draw out his death. It was quick and painless—more than he deserved.

Hurrying forward, I caught sight of Laurel's black coat disappearing into the lobby of her apartment building. Because it wasn't in the greatest of neighborhoods, I trotted around to the service entrance, forced the door open, and took the stairs two at a time. I cracked the fire escape door and watched a tired Laurel emerge from the elevator.

I held my breath as she approached her door. For a moment, the light fell over her just right. When she disappeared, I lingered for a moment longer.

"What am I going to do with you?" I asked, rubbing my jaw.

Her closed door gave no answer.

The next, most immediate step was clear. Tomorrow, I would crash her lunch date. She would see me. She would *speak* with me. That thought sent a buzz stronger than any liquor racing through my blood. Whatever happened after would be determined by how things progressed at the lunch. But one thing was for certain, I wasn't letting her fly away. No matter what plot she was involved with, she was mine to play with.

That dark and twisted part that pulsed deep in my chest, almost wished she was involved with some scheme against me. How else would I snare her, make her my pretty little captive?

Chapter 9 – Dimitri

There had to be sandpaper in my eyes. A yawn cracked my throat. I flexed my hand, and my whole body shook. We'd been out the whole night recovering the shipment, and now when I finally had my cousin alone, his attention was divided.

"Look at these for the dessert table," Daniella beamed.

Kazimir stared dreamily into his fiancée's eyes as she tried to show him a tray of tiny sweets in delicate white paper cups. "Good enough to eat," he murmured.

I groaned. He meant her, not the treats. Her blush confirmed it.

"And I want Jasha Popov on that list," I growled, cutting through the sickening wedding planning.

Kazimir cut me a hard look. "Why him?"

Daniella plucked something brown and gooey, darting around my cousin to shove it between his lips. "Can you two stop waging war for ten minutes? I have to get the final decision to the caterer."

Wedding crap—it was anyone in my immediate family talked about.

It had them frantic, running about and the details kept changing every five minutes. And yet, even though they were rushed and racing, they all seemed so damn happy. *Too fucking happy.*

Kazimir swallowed and gave me a sympathetic look. "We can finalize the hit list later."

Abandoned by the one I was counting on. "I have to go anyhow," I clipped out. "I'll be back in a couple of hours."

Kazimir narrowed his gaze. "You just got here, and there's a shit ton of work to be done. The pakhan wants this wedding to make a statement to the bratva."

The flick of my lighter punctuated my next words. "I'm not the idiot about to tie the knot."

"You're such an asshole. You're never going to find happiness with an attitude like that."

"Fine by me." I walked past him.

"I change my mind! I curse you, Dimitri Aleksandr! I curse you with finding happiness. May it be strong and make you weak at the knees so that you can't stand under the weight of it."

I couldn't believe he'd used my middle name. No one used my middle name now that my aunt was dead. The best slap was not to respond to his jab. I pushed through the apartment door and descended to the parking garage below.

The cold cut through the swirling in my brain. Clarity descended in its wake. This had always been my destiny. There could only be one king of the pride. The others could have lives and be happy. At the end of the day, their pakhan would bear the responsibility of the organization on his shoulders, while sitting alone on his throne.

Their current boss was a leviathan. So long as he didn't eat them, they could exist securely under his rule. Well, mine would be different. It was possible to be feared and loved, and while fear was better, it wasn't without the counterpart.

I might be the spawn of a monster, but I didn't resemble my father in the slightest. Hell, I barely looked like him.

But that didn't mean I wasn't a monster.

I stabbed the ignition for my truck and tore out of the parking garage. From Kazimir's building, it was a ten-minute drive to the restaurant, which was part of the reason I wanted to go there in the first place. Help him with wedding prep? Yeah, I couldn't believe he bought that either.

We still had a long list of soldiers who needed to disappear. I was discretely cleaning house, disposing of the opposition before I took control of our bratva. But if Kazimir was too busy playing happily ever after, I had other matters to attend to.

Like the fairytale snow princess.

This compulsion to destroy her dinner plans had nothing to do with tender feelings toward her. I wasn't anything like the puppy-eyed man I left with his bride. There was only one emotion driving me, and too many secrets fueling it.

I stepped into the bistro, taking in the scope of the space in one quick glance. There were two entrances plus the back hall that led to the kitchens and no doubt out the back. I chose a seat on the far end where I could see the whole dining area.

Pulling the baseball cap over my eyes, I picked up a book. The waitress came over and took my order. She didn't seem the least bit shocked that I only wanted a green tea.

I guessed the wiry man in his late thirties was the target when he stepped into the restaurant. He sat at a table and was facing me. When Laurel walked through the doors a few minutes later, it took more control than I cared to admit to sit still, to not look up—to not intercept her.

As I predicted, she glided to the table I suspected was her date. That frothy white blouse accented her curves. The buttons teased where I knew her gorgeous breasts hid. I fisted my lighter in my lap, ignoring the tight seam of my pants.

How a woman could turn me on so easily was a saints damned mystery.

It was as if the path between the tables was a red carpet. Laurel walked directly toward the man, pulled out her own seat, and folded gracefully into it. Already tempted to shoot the man for looking at her, I wanted to punch him because he hadn't pulled out the seat for her.

To make myself feel better, I drew my gun out of my coat and set it in my lap.

There were few customers, but I still couldn't hear what was being said. Reading the body language told me that Laurel wasn't comfortable. Her shoulders were drawn back, and the muscles of her back were wound tight. The only moment she relaxed was when the waitress came to take their order.

By the time their food came, I was out of my mind crazy. The wiry man was a spaz. He kept jerking around, unable to sit still or stick with a facial expression to save his life. The table between us left, and then the conversation was loud enough to carry to me.

"I want you to come out with me Saturday night," the man insisted. "There's a club you need to check out. I know the owner. Maybe...." He reached out and traced over Laurel's arm. "Maybe we could get you an audition."

"Let me see if I'm hearing you straight. You are blackmailing me for a date?" Laurel all but snatched her hand away. "I don't date, Derek."

"What is it about me?" the man spread his arms wide, volume rising.

"It's not you," Laurel insisted. "I don't do relationships."

Not yet, a dark voice countered in my mind.

Of course, just because part of me was obsessed with this woman, didn't mean I could act. I would only bring danger to her doorstep. It would be better for her if our paths didn't cross again.

And yet, here I was, unable to stay away.

The dead man caught my eye from under my cap. I let him feel the full weight of my displeasure. He deflated instantly. His lip curled in a sneer right before he looked away.

It was time to have a little fun. I angled my gun, flicked on the laser pointer, and aimed it at him. I started with his hand, making the red dot dance where he was sure to see it.

Unfortunately, he was too enamored with the beauty sitting across from him. I couldn't say I blamed him.

"You're jeopardizing your future at the Kat Klub," Derek said frostily.

Bingo....

"I came to have lunch with you," Laurel insisted. "To work something out."

This conversation was nearing its inevitable end. I was ready for it to reach that conclusion more quickly.

Maneuvering my gun, I trained the sight on the man's torso.

"You thought this would do?" Derek exploded. "No, Laurel. I want a proper date. I want to take you out on the town, show you off, and screw you for a couple of hours."

"Derek—" Laurel pointed at his chest. "You have something on you."

The man looked down and caught sight of the red dot. He looked back up, gaze locking with mine. I wasn't smiling. When his gaze dropped to what I held in my hand, he jumped up, chair knocking over, and attempted to scramble for the door.

I moved faster.

In one smooth move, I holstered my gun under my winter jacket before reaching to grab the man around the throat. "I think you owe the lady an apology, jackass."

"Dimitri!" Laurel was on her feet, staring between us.

My fingers tightened. I gave him a hard shake. Derek's face was turning a delicious shade of purple. Words garbled out of his mouth.

"They're going to call the cops," Laurel hissed, coming over and placing her hand on my arm.

The contact sent a jolt of electricity through me.

I momentarily forgot to breathe. I looked down at her, soaking up the expression on her face. It was part insistent, part relieved.

"Let him go. He's not worth it," she said in that tone of authority.

"If that's what you wish," I released my hold.

Derek swayed and stumbled back. He clawed at his throat, coughing hard. His wild gaze darted about. "You know, for a second there I believed you that you didn't date. But now I know you're not only a liar, but just a big fat slut," he spat.

Chapter 10 – Laurel

My fingers fisted, and I threw a punch. It connected with Derek's nose. I was rewarded by an explosion of blood.

"Ouch!" I pulled my hand back, shaking it hard. My thumb pulsed. The skin on my knuckles burned.

Dimitri shoved the cabaret owner over and growled, "Get out of here."

Conscious of the eyes on us, I sank into my seat.

"You'll regret this!" Derek promised.

I sighed. This peace offering lunch had gone from bad to worse. Once Derek cooled down, I would talk to him and straighten this mess out.

Dimitri watched Derek until he left, and then the mobster went to the waitress and manager. Whatever they said in hushed tones, he came back with a cloth full of ice and a plate with something savory on it.

A ham and cheese quiche. Part of the lunch I ordered.

"Let me see," he said gently, squatting in front of my chair.

I let him take my hand. Gingerly, he pressed the bones and joints. I clenched my teeth so as not to wince.

"It's not broken." Was that relief in his voice?

"What are you doing here?" I breathed, not that the adrenaline was giving way to clear thinking.

Dimitri jerked his chin to the table behind me. "I was reading a book and having a cup of tea."

"You've never been in this bistro before," I countered. A sinking suspicion hung heavy in my voice.

"Now, how would you know that." Dimitri looked up at me, something dangerous dancing in those sea blue depths.

I didn't want to admit how much I liked looking down and seeing this vicious, dangerous man crouching before me.

I tipped my chin up. "I come here more often than I care to admit. It's *my* turf. You don't come here."

But you do go to the club across the street. It was one that the Vlasov Bratva owned.

Dimitri took a seat from a different table and sat right in front of me. "Who was he?"

The direct shift in conversation caught me off guard. "A business associate."

Those piercing eyes narrowed. "You were on a lunch date with a business associate?"

I shook my head hard. "It wasn't a date." Why did everyone assume that just because you shared a meal and had a conversation, it meant you were into someone? "I was attempting to renegotiate a deal. You can see how well that went!"

In my distraught state, I flung my arms and smacked my sore hand against the table. The jolt of pain was blinding. My eyes pricked, and I drew in a sharp breath.

Dimitri growled. It was a low, purely animalistic sound. He snatched my hand, placed it flat on the table, and repositioned the cloth of ice on it. "Keep that on, will you?"

I smirked. I couldn't help it. Here was this gruff, monstrous bratva prince acting gentle. "Okay, mobster. Whatever you say."

He huffed. "Eat."

I picked up my fork. It was awkward and unsteady to cut through the crust with my less dominant hand. The bite ended up crumbling off the tines.

"Give me that," Dimitri snapped. He plucked the utensil from my hand before I could blink. Expertly placing a bite on the fork, he brought it to my lips.

"I never knew you were a lefty," I teased.

"Eat," he repeated.

I did as he commanded. While I chewed, I didn't break eye contact with him. The mobster didn't look away either.

"So...you don't date," he murmured.

I nodded and swallowed. "I don't. Relationships are too messy."

"I agree."

Now what is that little pinch in my chest all about? I should be agreeing with him. Commiserating over the fact that having to do the whole relying on another person was just more work than it was worth. I shouldn't feel bad, or sorry, that he was of the same opinion as me. I should be jumping up and down with joy to find a like mind!

Shoving the tightness away, and refusing to give it a name, I grinned. "So there's no Mrs. Bratva in your future."

Dimitri shook his head. "But if I did find one, I would fall to my knees, because she'd be a saints-damned queen."

"That sounds like the type of treatment women should be lining up to compete for," I teased before accepting another bite of food.

"The throne is cold and lonely. They wouldn't have what it takes to brave that with me. I'm better off alone."

Sad! The romantic in me bled for him. She begged me to consider the job application. Just to prove I could do it. "What a bleak outlook. You're probably right, but damn, way to bring down the mood."

"Because it was sunshine and roses before this conversation?" He inclined his chin to my hand.

I rolled my eyes.

"Did you just roll your eyes at me?" he whispered, leaning closer.

I snapped my gaze to his. "Maybe."

He drew in a long, deep breath.

"What are you going to do about it?" I dared, because I just couldn't resist.

"Since you're not mine, nothing."

Party pooper. "Oblige me. Tell me what *would* you do?"

"I would take you over my knee for being such a brat."

My mouth popped open in an O. The muscles of my core contracted. Heat tingled between my legs. I should not like that thought. I should be insulted!

And yet the thought of his palm cracking over my ass....

Oh, hot damn.

Realizing I'd been quiet too long, I protested, "But there are all these people! I didn't take you as an exhibitionist."

Dimitri slid a slow glance around the space. "What people, Laurel?"

That was when I noticed we were all alone.

"How did you—? What did you—? What!" I stammered.

"This is the only way to take a woman like you to lunch." He lifted another bite of quiche to my lips. "You want to know what I would do? I would make you the center of my attention, and no one else gets to see the things we do."

The air felt thinner, harder to draw into my lungs. My heart beat frantically as wild thoughts ran away with themselves.

Pull yourself together! I gulped hard, shoving the swoony feelings away.

"But how did you make them leave?" I insisted.

The corner of his mouth twitched, but he didn't smile. "I believe the saying goes: Where there's a will, you'll find a way."

"Close, but not right." I tapped my free hand on the table. "You paid them off, didn't you."

Dimitri only watched me.

"That's a shit ton of money," I breathed, sitting back into the chair.

The mobster brought another bite of quiche to my lips.

As much as every fiber of self-preservation screamed at me that this was a bad idea, that I should end things once and for always, I couldn't help but feel that it would be hopeless. Useless. *Impossible.* I was on Dimitri Vlasov's radar, and he wasn't done with me.

Didn't you always dream of this? Although that snide inner voice was right, I couldn't help but admit that reality wasn't always better than dreams.

When the last bite of quiche was done, I cleared my throat. "Thank you, Dimitri. This was probably the best lunch I've ever had."

He dipped his chin but didn't say anything.

"But we can't keep seeing one another."

"I know." He lifted the ice pack and looked at my hand.

Those two words sent a sharp pang through my chest. I wanted to yell at him that I'd changed my mind. That I would be interested in doing this again sometime.

Instead, I pressed my lips into a tight line.

"Next time, keep your thumb tucked here." He demonstrated with his own hand.

"Who says they'll be a next time?" I countered.

The corner of his mouth twitched. "With a girl like you, there's always a next time."

"You're probably right. And I knew not to put my thumb into the fist."

"Right. But also don't have it too high." Slowly, he took my uninjured hand and curled the fingers, before placing the thumb over the side. "Like this."

"Thank you."

That sea blue gaze studied me for a lingering moment. "You're welcome, babe."

My insides melted. I shifted in my seat, but I couldn't look away.

"I have to go get ready for work," I said finally, breaking the moment. Dropping a twenty on the table, which more than paid for lunch, I pulled out my phone and ordered a rideshare. It was a luxury to drive the few blocks, and I should have saved the money, but I had a sneaking feeling that if I walked, Dimitri would either come with me or insist on driving me. I needed to create some distance before something more could happen. "Goodbye, Mr. Vlasov. Try to stay out of trouble."

Dimitri rose, pulled back my chair, and held out a hand to help me to my feet. "You as well, Miss Gundry."

Butterflies burst into a frantic storm in my stomach.

The mobster followed me out of the restaurant. He waited silently until the rideshare arrived. Hand on the doorknob, he paused. "You know I paid for lunch, right?"

I nodded. "But if I didn't leave the twenty, it would have been a date."

"I know. That's why I let you." He held open the door. "Until next time, Laurel."

There can't be a next time.

I swallowed those words. They would only be a lie. The ultimate conclusion was that I would see Dimitri again. I knew the risk when I contacted him, and that was why I stayed off his radar for so long. Now, I could ride out the attention, wait until he grew bored and moved on—

Or else be swept into his world. That was an outcome I needed to fight, even if I knew it was a losing battle.

Chapter 11 – Laurel

A gust of wind shot down the street.

I blessed whatever foresight I had to wear Stella McCartney clogs with my acid washed pink jeans. My feet were warm, my legs were covered. I hefted the garment bag over my arm and rapped on the back door. It was ten after seven, and I shifted from foot to foot. It had been a good day off. Unlike Friday, I actually finished the laundry and hauled the delicate dresses to and from the dry cleaners. I wriggled in my new top, a bargain from the REALREAL. It was spandex, lime green. The fashionista I followed on TikTok wore a latex one, but if they made that for women of my size, I had yet to find it.

The rest of my outfit was on point. Even if I was the only one to see it, I dressed for no man.

Frowning, I banged my palm into the metal. I was a few minutes early, so that explained the locked door. But this was my usual gig—Wine Wednesdays. The cabaret knew to expect me.

"Come on, bud, I'm freezing," I grumped, shifting an uneasy look up and down the street.

Before I could knock a third time, the crash bar pressed on the inside and the door swung wide. I jumped out of the way, beaming up at the bouncer. "How you doin' this evening, Joe?"

"Can I help you, Miss Gundry?" The man's face was an unreadable mask of professionalism.

Unease trickled down my spine. I shook it away, refusing to let that negativity infect my evening.

"Joe? It's Wednesday. I'm scheduled to sing," I laughed, holding up my garment bag.

"You're not on the list, Miss Gundry," Joe said, and there was a twitch in the corner of his mouth.

"That's not.... What do you.... Huh?" I blurted out. Tension radiated over my muscles. It settled in my stomach, forming a hard knot.

"Derek said you weren't on the list anymore." Joe began to close the door.

My pulse doubled. This had to be some twisted joke!

He said I would regret it.

"Now wait just a minute!" I shoved my hand into the door.

The weight of the thing made me grunt.

"Take it up with Derek," Joe muttered.

My voice softened. "Please." *This is my outlet!*

I needed to sing. I needed to be *heard.*

His façade cracked and a flash of pity came through. "I can't do anything."

"Let me just get out of this cold and speak to Derek." I tried and failed to pull the door open.

If I could only see the entertainment manager, I could fix this. The fact that we hadn't connected on the phone now made sense. But Derek wouldn't slam the door in my face! Not after I straightened things out with him.

But the bouncer was in the process of pushing me back. "You'll have to call him. He said not to bother him with this."

The reality of the situation hit me. This was all because I wouldn't date the little prick.

"I'm playing 'C'est si bon' just for you." I shifted the weight of my tote and the garment bag. Joe always took his lunch break in the wings so he could catch part of my set. Eartha Kitt was one of his favorites. Mine too. "Joe, please. Let me just talk to him."

"I'm sorry, but there's nothing I can do." And with that, the door to the only singing gig I had closed.

Another gust of wind whistled through the alley. This one cut to the bone. Without this outlet, I was just a faceless voice on the internet. When I sang at the cabaret, I could feel my words affect the audience. There was a raw connection when my voice touched them.

The crappy feeling of loss morphed into an even shittier feeling of low self-esteem.

I conquered that crippling emotion once by starting a brand-new life where it didn't have a place. But just because I forced it into a cage, didn't mean the demonic little whispers weren't constantly in my mind.

"How dare that little shit stain make me feel powerless," I sniffed, looking up to keep the moisture from gathering in my eyes and ruining the carefully applied makeup.

Knowing he should never make me feel inferior and actually having those feelings were too different things. Anger seasoned despair. The need to escape overwhelmed the urge to cry. Affirmations and positive manifestations were only bandages when the scars they covered ran this deep.

I needed to change the way I felt on a cellular level. A hit of dopamine would give me the strength to force the soul-sucking emotional minions into their cages once more.

"What can I have that would make me feel good?" I hiccupped, starting to trudge back down the alley. On a strict budget with a reserve only for clothes and makeup, I didn't have the cash to splurge. If only I'd opened a credit card and—

I stopped short. *"Up to half my kingdom."*

I had credit. Not the traditional kind, but still!

Pulling my bottom lip between my teeth, I ran through a list of things I could have. New clothes. A car. A better apartment—or condo so I didn't have to make payments.

Jewels?

Would that make me feel better? Or would I still be the same girl in hiding struggling to repair the damage from the past?

No, I needed something stronger. Something that would fuel my inner goddess. She'd been battling the toxic waste trying to poison my heart for so long. All alone, and exhausted. What would build her up? What would give her a moment's peace, a recharge? A breath of fresh air!

Pulling my hand down the length of my throat, I let out a low groan. It had been so long since....

"Oh no! *Oh no....*" My insides clenched.

I knew what I needed. The only thing that could make me feel good.

"He could give that to me." I wrapped my arms tightly around my chest.

That would open a whole new level. One I couldn't conquer. But...I could sneak into the palace, take what I needed, and escape. I didn't have to be trapped in that dungeon or play the campaign.

One night with the prince would rid him from my system.

"Really?" I deadpanned. "You can ride the prince and just vanish? Life goes back to normal?"

With a beautiful memory of the forbidden, yes! I could carry that with me to my grave.

"I want him to screw my brains out, not date me," I hissed. "He could give it to me. Couldn't he?"

The manic little laugh through my head tried to smother me with instant doubt. After all, how could a handsome underworld prince want someone like me?

"Stop it!" I hissed. I was just as good as any other woman. And Dimitri *owed* me!

Pulling my confidence around me like fucking armor, I chanted nonsense in my head to drown out the noise. My phone was out, fingers tapping at the screen. Without looking where I was going, I raced down the sidewalk and turned at the corner right as the rideshare pulled to the side.

There was no time or space to catch my breath. I drummed my fingers against my thigh, emotions running impossibly high. The garment bag crinkled on my lap. I dropped a look to it.

The poor gown might as well have a chance to shine, even if it wasn't on a stage!

"Don't look in the rearview if you value your eyesight," I warned, as I shimmied out of my coat.

The driver frowned but muttered an agreement.

Pulling the cerulean beauty over my head, I managed to remove the spandex top underneath. It wasn't the first time I changed in the back of a moving vehicle. A soft laugh expressed gratitude to my past.

Ten minutes later, I popped onto the curb in front of the Vlasov fortress.

I didn't even have to ring, the door opened, and a guard gave me a clipped nod as I hurried forward. It seemed I had access to his home. An improvement to last time.

"Is Mr. Dimitri home?" I panted, stepping through the side door.

One of the guards was tapping on his phone, but the other answered. "He is, ma'am."

That was all I needed to hear.

The guard huffed to keep pace with my hurried steps. I chugged up the ramp and bulldozed through the front door, which the guard had raced ahead to open.

Standing in the foyer, my brain caught up to my impulses. The clinical feel of this building snapped some sense in me. What if Dimitri was busy? What if he...said no?

Dammit! That little voice was still spewing venom.

And the poison was working.

I clutched at my throat, suddenly overwhelmed with the insanity of the situation.

I spun on my heel, ready to dash away. "This was a mistake," I croaked to the guard.

Confusion bloomed into wariness as he faltered.

Yes, I no doubt seemed insane. Men didn't do well with heightened emotions in women. I really couldn't bring myself to care.

Taking a step forward, ready to push past the guard, there was a noise on the landing above. If my gaze hadn't flickered that way, if my heart hadn't started to gallop at the presence...but they did. And I stopped short. Dimitri stood at the top of the stairs. He was shirtless, black sweatpants hanging low and the waistband of his boxers clinging to the cut expanse of his hips. Ink artfully covered the tanned canvas. My gaze roved, memorizing shapes and swirls.

The sight of that body rooted me in place. Heat flared low in my belly, and I swallowed past the lump in my throat.

"Laurel, what's wrong?" he growled, padding down the stairs two at a time.

I shook myself. There was no way this would work. It was official. I'd gone crazy. "I just popped in for a chat and—"

The excuse was lame. *I should go.*

There was no way he would give me what I needed. I mean, he could *give* me exactly what I needed. Look at him! That body! It was better than warm cookies, Christmas Eve, and caroling.

"You can go, Toli," Dimitri said to the guard.

When the door closed, I jumped slightly. "I'm leaving, sorry to bother you," I stammered, shaking my head and trying to force my body to move.

Desire screamed at me to get closer to the walking sex-on-a-stick that was the Russian mobster.

Dimitri jumped the last steps and bounded into my personal space. He grabbed my upper arm, searching my face. "Did something happen? Are you alright?"

I stared up into his sea blue eyes. They were smoldering. He was looking at me. Really and truly looking. The intensity in those depths tripped me. My lip wobbled. "Yes and no."

Leading me gently to the steps, Dimitri lowered me down. "You came to me?"

I nodded, chewing on my bottom lip. "I thought you could help."

His lips twitched. It was as if he were trying to smile but didn't know how.

That might possibly be the saddest thing I'd ever seen.

"I'm glad you did." His voice was low and gravelly, as if rocks grated against his vocal cords. He slid his touch over my gloved fingers, plucking each loose. The slow, methodical movement entranced me. Heat radiated off his body, and a woodsy clean smell wafted off him, a dangerous combination. "What can I do for you?"

Lulled by his dominating masculine presence, the words I'd held back tumbled out of their own accord. "You said I could call in a favor. Anything. Well, I'm here and I know what I want."

"What is it?" he pressed, something dark simmering in his eyes. "It's yours, all you have to do is ask."

The words came out as the barest of whispers. "Make me feel good."

When he didn't speak right away, I withered under the gravity of what I just asked. If he turned me down, if he laughed at me, if he didn't like my body—

Dimitri pounced. He grabbed my face with both hands, and his lips crashed into mine.

Chapter 12 – Laurel

Dimitri kissed like he was famished. His mouth crushed against mine, his hard, beautiful, dangerous mouth. I melted into the kiss, a soft sigh whispering through my mind. One hand slid along the back of my head, plunging into my hair.

With his other arm, he slid me close. The kiss went on and on. There was a desperation behind it. *As if he needed to feel good too.* His touch silenced the doubt nagging in the back of my mind. I couldn't breathe. I would happily suffocate if it meant more of that devouring touch.

So caught up in the act, I didn't hear whatever noise the mobster must have caught. Because he broke away, head snapping in the direction of the hall.

"Come on," he said hoarsely, hurrying me up the stairs. "You can tell me exactly what you need, and I'll give it to you."

My insides convulsed. "More of that," I panted.

Dimitri shot me a look, full of blistering, unwavering intensity. "Done."

By the time I gave any attention to my surroundings, I realized I was lost. The narrow halls looked the same. We took two—or was it three?—turns. The lights, the paint, and the floor were all sterile. It looked like an insane asylum from the olden days, door after door on white walls. I tightened my grip on the mobster's hand. He squeezed me, and then we were pushing through a door at the far end of the hall. Dimitri threw it closed and flipped a deadbolt.

He deadbolts his room.

Before that could formulate into a proper thought, his mouth was on me again.

Breathing hard from the speed, stars clouded my vision. Dimitri's hands were everywhere, plucking my hat off, pushing my coat off my shoulders, his touch skimming up my bare arms.

"Saints, you feel as good as I imagined," he rasped. He sounded as turned on as I felt. "Twirl for me, baby."

I blinked.

But he didn't have to ask twice. I swished the material of the silk gown, letting the yards and yards of fabric flutter around me as I did a slow turn.

"You came to me, dressed like that?" He reached out and pushed a lock of my hair behind my ear.

A moan stuck in my throat. His voice was hot! His body was hot. The look in his eye alone set a fire raging through me. He made me *burn*. And he'd barely touched me. Barely begun to kiss me.

"Come here," he said hoarsely.

I moved into his space, and he wrapped his arms around me. It wasn't the tightness that bothered me, but rather the thought of them moving lower.

Maybe I wouldn't have to tell him what not to do. Maybe he wasn't into dominating.

Yeah, right. Lions devoured lambs. It was basic nature.

Trying to dispel the suffocating feeling, I greedily touched his chiseled chest. The smatter of hair was soft. I gripped his ass, enjoying the flex of those muscles. There was not one inch of him that wasn't honed sharp and hard.

He ground his hips against the fleshy swell of mine. Yep, all of him was hard.

Holy Hannah, he's huge!

My fingers itched to reach beneath the waistband and fish out that erection.

But something pulsed through me like a shockwave through water.

This wasn't going to work. Not without ground rules. There was one thing I had to say, and then I could really see what he was like.

"Dimitri," I whispered against his lips. He groaned, his kisses moving over my jaw and down my throat. "Do whatever you want. I have no limits, except—"

"Yes?" He stilled over the sensitive patch where neck and ear met. Each hot exhale tormented the skin, and I struggled to focus.

"Don't trap my hands."

This was it. This was where the curtain was pulled back, and I would be laughed at. Such a good joke.

Dimitri pressed a swift kiss against my pulse and pulled back. His gaze blistered, piercing into me and trying to root out something deep and personal. Something I wasn't going to give him. "That was a very specific request."

"It's just a little thing." I searched his gaze. "Anything else, but not my hands. Okay?"

There was an agonizing moment where he didn't speak. Didn't move. When he finally nodded, a rush of sweet relief washed through me.

I let out a long exhale.

"So...anything else is game," he murmured, bending to move his lips along my skin.

I groaned. "I'm willing to try, yes."

"I won't let you regret that." He pulled my head back and covered my mouth with his.

I melted. All the negative energy drained out of me. I could trust him to make me feel exactly what I needed, because he was already doing that.

Dimitri dropped to his knees, reaching under my bright blue skirt. I sucked in a sharp breath as his palms skimmed up my legs. I shook. Trembled. The anticipation made me feel nothing but alive.

Those great paws ran over my blue cheetah print, boy-cut panties. Dimitri groaned. "I need to see these."

The purely masculine tone sent a rush of heat between my legs.

"I can't wait," he choked and sank to his knees. He pushed the skirt back. "Oh, baby, that's the prettiest sight I've seen in a while."

He grasped the backs of my thighs and buried his face between my legs. He inhaled against the satin cloth, his nose skimming back and forth across the sensitive slit. It was primal. He was more animal than man. A shiver broke out along my skin.

"Just a quick taste." He ripped the panties down. And then, he was French kissing between my legs.

I soared, rising further and further, until I was lost in the stratosphere where there was nothing but delicious heat.

"So damn good." His voice was full of appreciation. He pulled me closer, hooking a leg over his shoulder to create better access for his tongue.

I shuddered. If this was only for tonight, I was going to enjoy each pulse of pleasure. I was going to soak the feel of him into my very bones.

Muscles tightened deep inside. Each slow lick, each pause to suck...and those teeth! They nipped playfully.

Not expecting it, I jumped. The skirt tangled with my legs. Balance was ripped away! My arms windmilled.

Dimitri shot up, not only steadying me, but *lifting* me.

"What are you doing?" I gasped.

"Taking you to bed," he growled.

"You can let me walk, I'm heavy," I protested.

The snort of derision rumbled through his chest. "It will be a sad day when I can't carry someone as beautiful as you to my bed." With little effort, he tossed me onto the mattress. "Off. All of it."

I tugged at the side zipper while kicking my clogs off. Dimitri waited, watching me with a smoldering gaze. My pulse ticked up in response. Breaths came hard and fast into my lungs.

Pausing, I gripped the cerulean bodice. The full weight of what I was about to do sank into me. He didn't seem to be reluctant. I hadn't caught a trace of acting in his movements or features.

Did he really want this?

A sudden wave of shyness came over me.

Dimitri's eyes darkened. "Are you depriving me of the sight of you, baby?"

I cleared my throat. An excuse stammered between us.

"Doesn't matter. You said your hands were off limits. Now...show me." He gripped the hem of the long skirt and tugged.

I released my hold so as not to rip the material.

The breath in his lungs left in a ragged rush. "Fuck—" He dropped over me, a fist on either side of my legs. "You will never hide this from me again."

There will be more than once? Electrocution shot through my veins. He meant tonight. Right? I could get on board with that...but only for tonight.

Dimitri sank his touch into my thighs and ripped me forward in a vicious tug until my feet were barely on the edge. "I'm going to need you to be a good girl and come on my face. Okay, baby?"

My insides contracted, and I couldn't form a coherent answer. Dimitri knelt before me, hot mouth covering my pussy.

I whimpered.

It felt so damn good. His mouth claimed me, those lips demanded submission, sought my heat, and pulled the pleasure from every fiber of my being. He devoured me like I was his last meal. But he didn't rush. He savored. He didn't hold back but feasted.

Those unforgiving hands spread my thighs wide. The muscles and tendons screamed in protest. I tipped my hips into him, rocking against his tongue.

"That's it, baby," he moaned as he shoved two fingers into my hot channel.

My hips bucked as a breathless cry left my lips. This was exactly what I needed. He didn't hold back. His fingers curled and stroked, pushing in and out of my heat.

"Look how wet you are, Laurel."

Oh, gods! That wet sound was me.

But Dimitri didn't stop. Neither did I.

I clutched the bedding over my head. My body arched and writhed. He sucked and kissed my pussy, working his touch deeper inside. It took seconds, and pleasure soaked into every fiber of my being.

The orgasm sent a spasm through me.

Dimitri pressed his mouth against my clit, and if I didn't know better, I would have said he smiled. He curled his fingers once more, and then his touch was gone. He rose up and prowled over me. Hovering there, he lifted a strand of hair and ran it through his fingers.

He tipped his head to the side, before looking back up to me. "Are you naturally red-haired, Laurel?"

My sex-drenched brain couldn't form an answer, so I only nodded.

"Why would you hide that?" he wondered, fingers combing through my hair. He lifted his hand and let the strands float down around me.

The bratva prince lowered his mass, settling his body over me. It was surprisingly comfortable. His arms caged me. Not touching, just resting on either side of my head. I was trapped under him. Except...they felt less like restraints and more like protection. I swallowed past the sudden tremble in my throat. I couldn't get comfortable. I couldn't grow complacent.

I couldn't spill my secrets.

"Laurel."

"Yes?"

"Your hair. Why would you cover it up with raven when you're a red bird?"

I stilled. "I—I have my reasons."

He nodded. "I see. Well then, I'll have to earn them, I guess."

Before I could tell him that was never happening, his hands grasped my head, holding me in place. His mouth found mine. He kissed me hard. Hungrily. I tasted myself, and my muscles clenched.

I was ready for more. I was *never* ready for more.

As if he sensed it, Dimitri reached between us, sliding his fingers against my pussy.

"Do you think you can cry out for me again, little bird?" he rasped. "Little...red-bird."

I nodded.

Dimitri moved to the bedside table and fumbled around. "Come on, I know I have one."

I slid my hand along his ribs, noting the puckered skin as opposed to the mottled colored skin underneath the ink stains. Scars and...bruises? My chest pinched. *Oh, Dimitri.*

That was the life of crime, I supposed.

Dimitri ripped the foil, rolled the condom over his twitching cock, and then came back over me. He grasped my right hand and lathed a sexy kiss over my pulse at my wrist. I let out a wordless exhale. He brought it around his neck.

"Hold on, baby, I'm about to give you exactly what you need."

A delicious shudder rolled through me.

The crown of his cock rubbed against my still sensitive clit. I gasped, arching into his body. With a dark chuckle, Dimitri slid his length down until the head pushed against my entrance.

His voice tightened. "Ready?"

I nodded.

One powerful thrust and he buried himself deep inside.

My abs contracted at the sudden invasion. I stretched and burned, but I took him. He seemed to know how he affected me, because he paused.

"Good?" he ground out, forcing the single word through his teeth as though it pained him.

"Don't hold back," I smiled, my voice breathless and panting.

"Oh, pretty one, you tempt me to insanity." His hips pulled back and snapped forward.

And then, he fucked me hard.

His tongue pushed into my mouth, mimicking the furious strokes of his cock. He kept one hand at the back of my head, while the other touched me everywhere. Pinching my nipple. Kneading my ass. Skimming across my middle.

I held onto him with arms and legs as he drove into me, hips pistoning faster and faster.

"Right there, baby, right there," he growled against my lips. "Give. It. To. Me."

I couldn't have answered if I wanted to. I was already doing what he wanted, opening myself to him, letting him reach places no man had ever touched. I was spread wide. I was stretched to my limits.

When I tipped my hips back just a fraction more, Dimitri let out a long, deep groan. That noise was drenched with pleasure. And I made him do that. Me. My pulse skipped in response. Sheer delight flooded my veins.

"You came on my face, now come on my cock." He sank his teeth into my bottom lip.

I surrendered with a breathless cry.

There was no resisting the pull. He drove me to the edge, and as he sucked my lip, I exploded. My release was a series of firecrackers, bursting through my body.

"Laurel!" he gasped, pushing impossibly deep and stopping. "Oh, baby, you're so damn tight."

"That felt amazing," I whispered, threading my fingers through his hair.

Dimitri looked up at me, his lashes thick and heavy. He studied me with an intensity so powerful that I didn't think I could stand its weight any longer. "You do that so well."

Warmth spread through me, soft and velvety. Suddenly self-conscious, I hid the unexpected reaction with a smirk. "I should go eavesdropping again, gather more information so you owe me another favor."

His tone turned deadly serious. "This isn't you calling in your favor."

"But I—that's why I came here tonight," I protested.

He shook his head. "Not when I wanted it just as badly. It can't count."

He wanted it.

Relief swept through me. I knew he hadn't held back but hearing him say it only solidified the truth. This hadn't been an act. Dimitri had wanted me.

Just as badly.

Wow.... A rush of some unnamable feeling shivered through my body. My insides clenched.

A groan ripped from him at the end of that sentence. "Ah! Laurel, do you know what you do to me?"

"Um?" Words failed me.

"You nearly ripped my dick off just now," he said, pushing his hips forward.

I groaned. "Oh."

Dimitri took my mouth again. This time, the kiss was slower. Explorative. It wasn't tender, and I could feel the hunger raging in the background. But he held it in check. It was as though he wanted to savor me.

When he finally pulled back, looking down at me through hooded gaze, I knew I needed to make my escape.

Or I'd be caught by this wild beast. That wasn't what I came for. Never would another person catch me again.

"I should probably get going," I whispered, drawing my fingers down his cheek.

Dimitri let out a long sigh. "I have to meet my cousins. Otherwise...."

That heavily muscled shoulder lifted in a shrug.

But it was the look in his eyes that tightened my stomach. I had to get out of here. "It's okay," I promised. About to add that I would see him around, I stopped. My inner goddess was satiated. I felt *good*. I needed to stick to the second half of my plan and cut ties.

Dimitri nodded. "Wait here."

He pulled away. I stretched out on his bed, eyes fluttering and gaze on the ceiling. So what if he knew about my true hair color? It wasn't like he would ever know the reasons behind that.

Something warm and wet pressed between my legs.

I cracked an eye and watched the great beast of a mobster bending over me and cleaning our mess.

"I hope you won't be too sore," he said quietly. "I shouldn't have been so rough with you."

I shivered. "Are you kidding? That was incredible."

"Until next time, then." He held out his hand.

I scurried to collect my dress. I had never had sex like that. And I knew without a shadow of a doubt no one else would compare to the bratva prince. But this needed to be a onetime thing. The metaphorical itch was scratched. This was done.

The weight of Dimitri's gaze as he tracked my every movement was damn near predatorial. I gulped, knowing I was fooling myself that this monster was done with me. I'd just offered him a taste. His expression along with the hunger from that last kiss said he wasn't sated.

He would want another encounter.

As would I.

Chapter 13 – Laurel

One hour and I could start cleaning up. Less than half the tables were occupied. It was fine by me to have a slow night. Tipping my head back, I stretched my neck and reached into the sink to rinse my fingers. Whoever thought blended drinks in fruit bowls was a good idea was an idiot. While they were fun in principle, we weren't equipped to deal with those kinds of drinks. The experiment was a disaster, and I was telling my manager that it wouldn't pay to do this on a busy night.

If Kevin listened or told the owner, that was an entirely different matter.

A sultry island beat pulsed through the club. Diamond shook her tassels and bootie. The backup dancers shimmied in the background. Bright feathers swished in the light. I gulped a breath of stale air and winced. This theme night was supposed to draw guests into the establishment. It hadn't. The club had been dowsed with a fake citrus spray, and there were tropical scents plugged into most of the wall sockets. The stench was overwhelming.

As I took the next drink ticket out of the printer, I caught Beck moving in our direction.

"Cookie, table eight." She snapped her fingers.

Shouldn't that be your job? She was the floor manager after all. Customer complaints should have been hers to handle.

"What happened?" I slid my apron off and adjusted my top.

"Nothing, they just wanted the busty barmaid to serve them," Beck said with a roll of her eyes.

"Gross!" Callie mouthed.

It was so unusual for her to comment or gossip that I couldn't help smirking. Forcing my tired bones to fake some pep, I glided over to table eight. It was a booth, heavily shadowed. Peering into the darkness, the stench of sweat and BO wafted to meet me.

I forced a smile. "What can I get you, hun?"

"Well, don't you sound just as sweet as you look," he drawled. "How 'bout some sugar, sugar?"

Great, one of those. "Sorry, no can do," I laughed, but didn't feel it. "My job is to make the drinks."

And if he wasn't a gentleman, I had my methods for making him fall asleep. It was rare I used the emergency pills I kept tucked in my inner pocket. But they were there, ready to be slipped in the drinks of obnoxious men.

"Karlgrad said I could have my pick," he said in hushed tones. "I pick you."

My stomach dropped. That wasn't right. The bratva who owned this joint was very careful to do everything above board. There weren't even rumors that the Russian pimped girls out.

"That's not how things work around here." I planted my hands on my hips. "Now, I'm happy to make you a cocktail on the house for the misunderstanding but we have a strict no touching policy."

"Really?" he challenged.

Warning bells peeled in my mind. I needed to get out of there! My foot moved back just as his hand shot out. That firm grasp clamped over my wrist.

Fear spiked through my veins. *No. No!* I struggled for my next breath.

The man yanked me into the booth.

Fight—I had to fight him. I kicked out. Platform pump connected with shin. The man hissed but continued to pull me into the booth.

I looked around desperately. None of the bouncers were paying attention. Neither was the floor manager. Callie couldn't see into the shadows of the floor. And the music was so loud that my scream would go unheard.

But I had to try.

I opened my mouth.

A sweaty palm clapped over it. I bit. The man cursed, wrenching his arm back. He was lightning quick, but time seemed to slow. Through the suffocating panic, I watched his palm descend slowly. A shadow moved in my peripheral. Something in the distance roared. Focused on the palm descending on me, I braced for the impact. The pain would be fast, and then I had to fight with everything I had.

Only...the blow never came.

I pitched forward, suddenly free. *Run!* There was no pause. Every muscle worked in unison to make my escape. I wouldn't be caught, I wouldn't be trapped. Never again. Heart in my throat, I scrambled out of the booth, but stopped when I heard the low pitch of a different voice say my name.

"Laurel, stop," the voice repeated.

The darkness shifted. Gone was the terror. The panic was banished. In its wake was only the sound of that voice, the indomitable presence. As if pulled on a string, I turned to see the true monster of the underworld lowering the slumped form of my would-be attacker to the table.

My body, however, hadn't caught up to my mind. The flight mode suppressed the sensory data before me. A dozen seconds passed before I gave myself a little shake.

He was here.

How was he here?

The prince of the underworld held my gaze. Through swirling chaos of noise and overwhelming stench, reality snapped back into place.

"You can't be here," I hissed. "The Mikhaylov Bratva owns this place!"

Dimitri continued to study me. There were a thousand questions struggling to form, but under his gaze, I felt still. Calm rushed over me. I was...safe.

"Thank you," I breathed.

Dimitri inclined his head.

Another bolt of panic jumped through me. "You have to get out of here!"

"Are you okay?" he asked, in that annoying habit of his changing the subject.

I blew out a breath. "I will be."

His gaze notched up in intensity. "What does that mean?"

I shook my head. "I'm not sure how to deal with him." I jerked my thumb at the unconscious man. "They don't tolerate harassing the staff, but this...this was different."

This guest seemed to have mob clearance. Which meant anything I said would be dangerous.

"He won't bother you, Laurel." Dimitri's voice was so steady, so calm.

I almost felt reassured. "You'd better get out of here; you've done enough."

"You first. I'll follow when I see you behind the bar."

When I remained rooted in place, he reached out. But his fingers curled into a fist, and he lowered his hand before touching me.

"It's going to be okay," he rasped. "I'll take care of everything."

I blinked, because what else could I do? Every bodily function was still heightened. From past experiences, the shaking would start next. But until I came down from the strained emotions, I didn't have complete control over my body.

"Laurel, look at me."

My heart thumped double. "I am."

"Yes, you are now—good." Dimitri pointed to the bar. "You're going to go back. If anyone asks, he just wanted to ask a question about the bourbon selection. You know the selection, right?"

I nodded. "Yes," I breathed.

"You're going to finish your shift, and you're going to go home. Okay?"

I swallowed hard. "Okay."

"Good—good girl." Dimitri flattened his hands on the table. "No one is going to know what happened. None of this will reflect on you."

But...when he wakes up.

Fear flashed through me. A shudder ripped down my whole body.

"Laurel! Hey," Dimitri insisted. "I've got you."

Those had to be the most foreign words in my vocabulary. No one had me. Even before, when I had people in my life, they didn't have me. There was no support. In fact...they'd enabled it.

My body shook again from another shiver. *Shit.* The shaking was going to start in earnest.

Food. I needed food.

There was still another—how long had I been here? The dancers were starting their final set.

It was almost over! I could clean up and reset the bar stations. I could leave.

"Thank you," I murmured.

Dimitri only watched me, silently but steadily. Leaning on his tangible strength, I pushed out of the booth and walked along the lit path to the bar.

If my hands shook while I began the pre-closing activities that we could do before guests left, Callie didn't comment. The floor manager never came back to confirm the customer had been taken care of. I hated her for it. Even if she didn't know about the special request, the preferential treatment, it was the fact that she wouldn't have stood up for me.

Without being obvious, I kept shooting glances into the sprawl of tables and booths. If Dimitri left, I didn't see it. But he must have because as we were spraying down the mats and filling the mop bucket for the floor when Kevin flew through the back doors, growling in Russian to his boss on the other end of the phone.

There was a body in the alley with a broken neck. The name was meaningless to me, but the player was a special guest of the Mikhaylov Bratva visiting from New York.

Chapter 14 – Laurel

The need for food didn't ebb with the passage of time. Instead, it raged internally. My stomach was gnarled like an ancient oak. It pinched and cried for relief. There was only one type of sustenance to be had in situations of extreme physical turmoil, and the one place that was open this time in the morning was a couple of miles away, more than I wanted to walk.

When the rideshare dropped me at the diner, I hustled inside. The shaking hadn't stopped, but I was steady enough to climb up on one of the stools at the counter. A griddle ran along the back counter and the menu was a blend of simplicity and perfection. Sally's Kitchen was a lot like the Waffle Houses that dotted the southern states. Except, Sally's had pancakes instead of waffles.

"Well, you look positively wrecked, honey," the waitress cooed.

The cook shot me a sympathetic glance.

I winced. "Rough night."

It was the understatement of the year. Dimitri had been at *my* work. I suspected he'd been there that one time, but Diamond never mentioned the cute Russians again, so I let it go. It was insanity for him to be there. And to kill the special guest? I shuddered again.

"Here's some coffee, Laurel, honey," the waitress insisted, handing me a fresh, steaming cup. "Short or tall stack?"

The door chimed behind me.

"Tall, definitely tall tonight, Rita." I clasped the mug between my fingers, letting the heat leach into my skin for a few moments before I reached for the metal pot of cream and the sugar shaker.

I couldn't bring myself to look and see who else came into the diner. Since there were already several vinyl booths full of tired workers and souls struggling to prevent hangovers, I didn't think much of the newcomer coming in right after me.

I stared into the black, glossy surface of the coffee. The wisps of steam curled along the top before springing eagerly into the air. The aroma was strong. It was definitely a pleasant change from the stench of island night.

Too late I realized my skin was prickling in warning. When a deep voice rumbled beside me, I jumped.

"Is this seat taken?" Dimitri asked.

I slapped my palms over my chest, breathing hard as I looked up.

"Sorry," he added, something much like pain flashing through his eyes.

"Are you following me now?" I gaped.

Dimitri seemed to be waiting for my answer, so I swept my hand over the seat. "Welcome, have a squat."

"Thank you, and not exactly." He folded his tall frame onto the stool. Plucking a napkin from the silver dispenser, he handed it to me.

I frowned. "How are you not following me?"

"Your coffee spilled."

Rolling my eyes, I snatched the napkins and turned to dab the mess. "I'm not accustomed to being snuck up on," I said hotly.

"Are you angry?" he murmured, leaning forward.

A long breath escaped my lips. Was I? It was hard to say. If I was, the root of the emotion was self-directed. I knew better than to show up on the radar of the bratva prince. The first time was understandable. It was the other night, when I let myself choose me and connect with him on an incredibly intimate level.

It opened a whole new door.

And no matter how many times I told myself it was a one-time thing, I knew they were all lies.

Case in point, he sat next to me. He'd *killed* for me tonight.

"When did you snap his neck?" I blurted out.

Dimitri's brown arched, and he shot a look to where the waitress was taking the order of a slurring customer. "The moment I laid hands on him."

I swallowed hard. The normal reaction to witnessing cold blooded murder was not...relief. "Thank you, Dimitri. No one has ever done that for me before."

There was a moment's pause where something monumental passed between us. I felt it. I saw it reflected in him. But whatever the name or even the meaning was, it was impossible to say.

Instead of answering, the bratva prince pushed to his feet. He moved across the restaurant, stopping to speak to each table. I missed the first one, but at the second, I caught him leaving a stack of bills. My eyelids peeled back so wide that the balls threatened to fall out.

There wasn't a chance to protest. Everyone packed up and cleared out of the diner in seconds. The waitress, who was immediately joined by the line cook, protested. Rita was a good soul. She shot me a worried look.

I raised my hand in a small wave. "I'm fine, Rita."

Pursing her lips, she pulled her purse from under the counter and hurried into the back. "An hour," she said as a parting shot.

The cook followed her, counting the stack of bills in his hand.

When those sea blue eyes turned back to me, I met his gaze with a shake of my head. "This is becoming an expensive little habit of yours, mobster."

"I have few expenses, and my savings account is plump." Dimitri removed his wool dress coat and folded it over the stool he'd been sitting on. He placed his suit jacket over it. Slowly, he unbuttoned the cuffs and pushed up the sleeves of his dress arms. My gaze was glued on the action. Such a simple gesture, but it made my pulse race.

The bratva prince rounded the counter and started to grab items. He was in the process of clearing the hot griddle, before the actions clicked in my brain.

"You're *cooking*?" I gasped.

"Is that so surprising?" he countered.

Yes. But I used his subject changing tactic to pry for the thing I actually wanted to know. "Why were you at STYX?"

Dimitri balanced the flipper against the edge of the griddle. "You haven't called."

"I don't have your number."

"You could have asked for it." He looked sideways at me. There was something slithering through those sea-blue depths.

It sent my mind scrambling and flipping backward. "I don't date, mobster."

"Neither do I." His answer was quick.

So quick that it stung.

"Then why would you want to see me?" I demanded, my voice holding more of a bite than I meant it to.

He looked away. "I don't know."

"I smell bull."

"I don't," he insisted as he went to the fridge and pulled out several containers. He proceeded to throw strips of bacon on the griddle as well as some veggies and ground sausage. When he squirted egg over the top, flipped it with skill, and put cheese on it, I couldn't help but be impressed. Once he squirted the pancake batter on the other side, he turned. "I don't know, Laurel. But I can't fucking stay away."

Surprisingly, that made sense.

"I've been fighting coming back to see you too," I said quietly.

Instead of smiling or reveling triumphantly in the admission, Dimitri seemed to harden.

Something sharp stabbed my chest. I didn't like seeing him like that. "You had the night off then? No mob business?"

"I had work," he admitted quietly.

I gestured to the diner. "And?"

"I blew it off." He turned back to the griddle, flipped the pancakes, and finished the omelet.

Those four words ricocheted through my mind. "You—you blew it off?"

Dimitri inclined his head. "Yes, that's what I said."

My bottom jaw landed somewhere on the floor. All I could do was sit there and gape at him.

"Why?" I stammered.

There was the smallest of shrugs as he scooped pancakes off the griddle, plated them, and then turned. "You seemed shaken. I needed to make sure you were okay."

"Yeah, I was," I whispered. "That kind of incident usually doesn't go down like that. We kick those handsy guys out. But," I sighed, "whoever he was, he was there per the owner's special request."

Dimitri's voice hardened. "Hunting, I know."

I unloaded several packets of butter onto the pile of pancakes before drenching them with blueberry syrup. "If they knew you were there—"

"They didn't."

"Dimitri." I dropped my palms against the countertop. "You were lucky *this* time."

"And the time before." It wasn't a smirk, but there was a definite twitch in his lips.

"I freaking knew it. I knew you were there," I muttered and stabbed the fluffy goodness. The first bite sent an instant hit of sugar through me. I moaned.

Dimitri was in the process of taking a bite of his omelet when he stopped.

Realizing what I'd done, I gave him a shy smile. "This is really good," I said after swallowing.

"Thanks," he whispered before inhaling his food.

We ate in a comfortable silence, both famished. I kept eyeing the bacon on the side of his plate. Finally, I snatched one and gobbled it. I felt the distinct weight of his look, but when I smirked up at him, he was on his phone.

"I'll order you a ride, and then I have to go." Dimitri slapped the phone onto the countertop.

My heart tightened. I wasn't ready for this to end. But I had to say what came out next if there was any chance of getting it out. "This has to be goodbye, mobster."

The muscle in his jaw tightened.

"There are too many reasons, and besides, I think you know them already so there's no need for me to point them out." Why were these words sticking in my throat? It had to be the pancakes and not drinking anything to wash them down.

His voice was hard. "You're right."

I nodded. "I don't want to be."

Silence pulsed as we finished our last bites.

I couldn't stand the strain pounding between us. But there was nothing to say. This situation wasn't going to improve! I had to stay in hiding. Being alone was the only way to ensure my safety. And Dimitri? He would run a criminal empire one day.

Still, I didn't want to part on a bad note. Reaching out, I grabbed his hand. He started, sucking in a sharp breath. I grinned. "Hey, mobster, why don't you give me your number so if I find any more relevant gossip, I can let you know."

Placing my phone in his hand, I soaked in the contact with his skin. *This is it. This is all you get, Laurel.*

Once his number was in my phone, that was it. Coats on and back outside. The headlights flashed at the other end of the street. Dimitri went to stand by his truck, pinning the oncoming vehicle with a hard stare. In his hand was a lighter. He flicked it open. A flame danced in the cold winter night. And then, with a clap, it shut.

My eyes tracked the repetitive motion.

I approached the sedan and used my preapproved password to confirm it was my driver. I opened the back door only for it to be shut. I started, but Dimitri leaned in, one arm on either side. My breathing accelerated. I tilted my head, moving into his space.

But then I pulled back with a hard breath.

His gaze searched. There was a wild energy pulsing around us. One touch, and we would fall—down and down. Dimitri leaned forward, inching closer and closer. He was ready to embrace the fall. Could I follow? I wet my lips, suddenly craving him. Blood roared in my veins.

But it was his turn to stop. A shuddering breath escaped him. "I can't."

Emotions choked in my throat. "It would be too hard."

Clenching his jaw, he pushed away from the vehicle. Violence shimmered around him. A colorful litany of Russian curing growled from him.

I felt the exact same way. "Goodbye, mobster. Stay safe." *Stay alive.*

Before I could get any silly notions, I escaped into the sanctuary of the sedan and told the driver to go.

Chapter 15 – Dimitri

Igor harrumphed as we surveyed the snow-covered streets. "The roaches could be in any of them. There's no telling which storage units they're hiding out in."

Due to a sudden death match with our enemy, today would show if the Vlasov Bratva was worth its salt. If we could stand a chance against a bigger, more powerful crime syndicate. I sucked in a deep breath. My head space was clear. The battle lay before me, and a dark buzz slithered through my veins. The monster deep inside roared, beating his sword against a shield. Generations of warriors brought me into this world, and I was born ready for situations like this.

"We have a wedding to get back to," Luka urged. "Let's just raze the whole complex to the ground."

"No, it has to be intersection by intersection," Kazimir said quietly, and Igor hummed in agreement.

How hard that statement had to be, since he was due at the altar, I couldn't imagine. He was choosing the bratva over his wedding. I blew out a long breath. How many of these other soldiers would do the same? That was loyalty. Beautiful and simple.

Painful and costly.

"Call the pakhan and Vasil with an update," I commanded. The Zippo flicked open and closed in my right hand. The fingers on my left itched for my weapon.

"Emil says there's a warehouse in the back," a soldier commented, from where he stood a ways away with a walkie talkie.

Cellphone towers were slammed. There would be no calling the police. The few cops we had in our pockets would do their damnedest to prevent any officers from being dispatched. But we weren't the only organization with law enforcement on the payroll.

"Any movement?" I worked my jaw back and forth.

"He doesn't say."

Of course, he didn't. "Go figure out what's back there, Kaz. I don't want any surprises while we're in the middle of exterminations."

"Pakhan says we're cleared to go," Igor said, smacking his meaty hands together. "When you're done, Kaz, come join me on the eastern side."

My cousin slid a look between the captain who had been our direct superior before I was made captain. "Dimitri?"

I gave him a short nod. "I've got Luka. Let's finish this quickly and get you hitched."

"Yeah, before his bride realizes there are a lot more attractive options," Luka smirked, nudging Kazimir in the shoulder.

"Knock it off," I snapped.

Kazimir cut me an annoyed look. He didn't need anyone to jump to his defense.

But when it came to this particular marriage, my feelings were strong. It wasn't as though we'd given Daniella a choice. A sharp pain stabbed in my chest, twisting at the thought of threatening a woman. However, she was crazy for my cousin, so the circumstances of their rushed nuptials weren't too taxing a burden.

"Dvum smyertyam ni byvat', adnoy ni minavat'," Igor saluted me.

One can't have two deaths, but you can't avoid one.

A beautiful and old proverb.

Igor always knew what to say. He might be aging and thickening around the middle, but he was a good leader. All four of my cousins had done long rotations under his command.

"I still think we should just blow them to high hell and get back to drinking," Luka grumped.

"Shut up." I scrubbed my face with my hand and forced my head space to focus on the task at hand.

Each of us four captains held a squad in position surrounding the area. Emil was toward the south, and Boris was close to him. Igor and I remained at the north and east. Our instructions were to clear the storage units, killing all Polish mobsters. There would be no quarter.

For my assault plan, my squad was divided in half. The first group would advance on the building while the others hung back to provide cover and backup depending on where we needed it.

Seven storage buildings didn't seem like a lot, except the interiors held a hundred units per floor. There were three floors per building. Each floor was divided into smaller sections, which meant to sweep a building we were looking at a maze of units, any number of which could be a trap.

Luka's idea of blowing them up sounded better and better. Especially when he promised it could look like an underground gas leak. My hesitation was that it would cause too much media coverage. When all the dead bodies with their weapons were found, the police would turn to the Feds.

The pakhan agreed with this.

My father and his brother were waiting in a van a few blocks back. No doubt he had his map out with little toy pieces carefully crafted for such situations. Updates would fly to his command center. He watched over such skirmishes with hawkish focus.

It's just another test. You're good at these.

"Igor should be to his position." I frowned at my watch.

"We should just go already," Luka muttered.

I pinned him with a hard look. "This time, Luka, you won't rush ahead," I said with a bite. "Stay with your group."

The baby cousin rolled his eyes. The only one of us he listened to was his older brother. And even then Kolya had to work some kind of dark magic to keep Luka in line.

"He just wants to keep up with you big boys," Aunt Dolya used to say. She was a good mother. The only maternal figure I had, in fact.

I stopped short, running my hand over the lighter in my pocket. I hadn't thought of Aunt Dolya for...months? She'd died a decade or more ago. It nearly broke Vasil, and would have if he didn't have the boys. What made me think of her? It wasn't just the way she quipped about us playing together. Her voice, her mannerisms as she gently scolded us, came to mind.

The words repeated once more. The tinkling laughter of my aunt rang through my head. And then, with sudden clarity, I realized why her ghost made an appearance.

She had flaming red hair.

"Dimitri! They're firing on my squad," Igor yelled through the walkie talkies.

Reality snapped into place. Bullets scattered the ground a few feet in front of where I stood.

The saints damned pollacks. They'd drilled holes in the side of the building!

"Luka," I called. "Grab an armored truck, put a brick on the gas, and let's ram the rolling door."

We needed to see if there were booby traps behind the main access points.

"Fall back, we're storming the first building. Hold the perimeter, but watch for surprises," I barked into the walkie talkie.

Luka swung a forest green truck at the rolling garage door that led into the first pole building.

That was his brother's truck.

Kolya was going to kill us. Murder us in our sleep. We would wake up choking on poison, unable to breathe properly with that quiet, contemplative face staring down at us.

Oh, saints. My eyes fluttered closed and a short prayer whispered from my lips.

"Do you happen to have a brick lying about?" Luka laughed out the window.

"Tie the steering wheel to the headrest," I barked, jumping in the back to grab a toolbox.

"I'm cutting the breaks," Luka chirped.

"Do that last." I heaved the box down and laid it across the floor peddles. Luka handed me a bungy cord and we secured the wheel. I put the vehicle in drive and the engine revved. The snip of the sheers, and I jumped down just in time. The truck lurched forward, barreling down the empty path.

Bullets riddled the glass. If the Polish were smart, they would shoot the tires.

The truck crashed into the rolling door and a mild explosion thundered through the air.

"The doors are rigged," I warned into the walkie talkies.

Kazimir cursed but responded that he understood. Emil's clipped answer was less colorful. Igor was radio silent. I looked to where the captain was supposed to be positioned. A plume of black smoke choked into the sky.

"Drive my truck to the door," I barked. "We'll unload next to the building. They shouldn't be able to shoot down at us. Those holes aren't big enough."

Luka whooped. The bulletproof glass was good for small rounds, but it was unclear if our enemy had armor piercing shells.

We loaded into the vehicle and Luka gunned the engine. Once we were alongside the building, safe from their bullets, we swarmed into the interior. Streams of frigid water from the ceiling poured on the fiery mess.

Warning pulses trickled in my mind. As the soldiers fanned out and gunfire erupted, I pulled back and contacted our leader. "Pakhan, the fire suppression company."

I read the tag.

"Nardini," I gave the name. "Make sure they don't get signaled and come."

"Smart," Vasil huffed. "We're on it. Good luck."

The stock of my semi-automatic pressed into my shoulder, I pushed into the interior of the structure. "Mind the corners!" I shouted as two soldiers fell.

We were losing men left and right, and we hadn't even crested the stairs.

It was exactly what we expected, a sudden death match.

The rolled door behind me snapped up.

My bullets found them before they could even aim. Four of the Lazarowicz crew dropped.

Opening the door to the stairwell, I groaned. It was too open. Several of our soldiers scooted to a stop beside me. They were looking to me. Always to me. I kept my mask of control over my features and gave them a tight nod. They wouldn't see unease on my features. Touching my breast pocket, I advanced. The saints would protect me, or they would greet me at the Pearly Gates.

There was a shout above.

I flattened myself against the wall as bullets rained on the ground.

One ricocheted off the wall and bounced over the toe of my boot. When the fire paused, I moved. Discharge flashed on my barrel. Three pops, and silence.

"Move, move!" I commanded the soldiers at my side.

They darted up the stairs. Gunfire erupted at the top landing. Someone groaned.

I bounded over the last step and joined them at the door. One of my men clutched his leaking shoulder. "You, stay with him," I commanded a capable looking man. "You three, with me."

We pushed through the door, taking out the Poles who emerged from storage bays. I turned the corner, cleared the hall, advanced, and turned again. It felt like hours, but in reality, it was a short onslaught. As I turned, a cold chill swept over me.

I was alone.

Leaning against a section of the concrete wall, I gathered my breath. The rapid pop of gunfire sounded down the end of the hall.

But I caught the hurried rush of footfall from the path I'd just come. One of our soldiers rushed me. He held his gun pointed at my heart.

"Umri, predatel'. Umri seychas!" *Die, traitor. Die now!*

I looked him dead in the eye. "Feodor, don't do this."

He fired at my chest.

Pain thudded against the muscle. There would be a wicked bruise there tomorrow. Nothing more.

I sprinted forward. The flash in his eye told me he realized his mistake.

"Always shoot for the head," I growled, colliding with his form. Our shoes scuffled against the floor, but I overpowered him. I forced the gun away, pushing his finger into the trigger until the clip emptied down the hall. With a jerk of my hand, I dislocated his elbow.

White hot pain lanced my thigh.

Motherfucker! "Did you just stab me?" I hissed, wrapping my hands around his throat.

He moved his hand to strike again. I loosed my hold long enough to catch his other hand. The satisfying snap of bone filled the air.

Feodor howled.

"Care to explain why you're attacking *me* and not the Polish?" I demanded, scratching his throat with the blade.

"Fuck you," he spat.

"Wrong answer—" The knife slid along the shell of his ear.

Instead of crying out he *gurgled.*

I frowned at him.

Foam frothed at his mouth. He had a false tooth. I lurched back, the warning peeling through my mind. This wasn't simply a murderer. This was an assassin. One of our own men.

"Not a very good one," I grunted, hauling his ass to the side. The clean team that would gather the bodies would no doubt notice there wasn't a bullet hole. While his body was still warm, I fixed that problem with one well-placed round. The blood leaking from the wound in his head helped wash away the poison spittle.

I scratched my mouth against the back of my arm and walked away from the scene. The rest of the top floor was swept clean. Rejoining the others below, we prepared to take the next building.

"The groom is going to be late," Luka smirked. Smeared across his cheek was a splatter of blood. He'd been playing with his knife again. "How pissed will Dani be?"

As long as Kaz made it in one piece, I didn't think his bride would mind, but I didn't deign to answer. I grabbed a packet of QuickClot from the pack on the front seat of my truck and doused my thigh. It wasn't deep, didn't ache. I wouldn't let it stop me if it did.

Scanning the faces of the men before me, I couldn't chase away the feelings of isolation. There was an unseen foe lurking in our midst, and I couldn't trust a single soldier.

"Let's go," I barked.

Chapter 16 – Dimitri

"They might as well surrender!" Luka whooped, springing down the staircase.

Blood covered him from head to toe. It was as if he'd stepped under a crimson shower. Drops fell from his ten-inch Bowie knife. They splattered on the concrete in a steady rhythm.

"Do I even want to know what you did?" I breathed, jerking my chin to his form.

My baby cousin shrugged. "No Poles on the second level."

Shaking my head, I stepped to the doorway and peered out. "Pakhan, we've secured the second building."

Dark was fast falling, and the temperature dropped. Something was off. The otherworldly warning rang from the marrow of my bones. Snakes writhed in my gut.

"Meet with Igor and take building number six, while Boris and Emil finish four and start on seven," Vasil instructed from the command center.

The battle wasn't won yet, and we'd taken heavy losses. However, the confidence in my uncle's voice told me he and my father felt good about the situation.

Must be nice not to hear the cries of the dying.

"Copy that," I ground out.

Raking a hand over my head, I dug my fingers into the back of my skull. A long breath left my lungs feeling tighter. The chaos seemed never-ending. This was the most violent fight we'd ever participated in. For an absent moment, my heart went out to the military who dealt with this regularly. Criminal skirmishes normally were small, contained, and swift.

This was hell on earth.

A rushed conversation took me out of my head.

Turning, I saw Luka standing off to the side. He was speaking rapidly into his phone, the permanent smirk wiped off his face. "He'll never forgive you!"

A stone fell in my gut. The snakes hissed and churned. Sickness that had nothing to do with my spinal injury crept up my throat.

Luka clipped out a farewell *to his brother.*

Dread slithered through me. My breath caught in my throat. "I thought the cell lines were downed."

"Satellite." Luka pinned me with a look. "Kolya's in town. We have to find Kaz."

My voice turned deadly. "Did you tell your brother we were in the middle of a saints-damned battle?"

Kolya had been out of town for weeks. He was hunting the filth operating sex rings while we combatted the Polish crime syndicate that protected them.

"They have Kazimir's girl," Luka said in a volume barely above a whisper. There wasn't a drop of humor, even his dark variety, in that statement. "And Nadia Petrova is hurt. Hurt bad."

Those words brought a tremor over our whole squad. All eyes turned to me. The weight of the decision threatened to crush me.

"I'll tell Kazimir in person," I told them. "Luka, inform the pakhan. The rest of you join Igor. We stay the course unless we hear differently."

"You can't go in there!" I roared, shaking Kazimir's shoulders.

The wild look in his eye told me he didn't hear a damn word I'd said.

I cut a look to our cousin, who stood helplessly by. There was no funny comment or inappropriately timed quip from Luka.

"The bastards have her as a hostage," Kasimir said, voice raw and the texture of gravel.

I threw up my hands. "We have two more buildings to clear, Kaz. We don't even know where they're moving her."

"She's my person!" Kazimir roared, and I stepped back. The beasts he kept leashed were right there, under the surface. "They want me. I'll cut them down for touching her."

"We have work to do!" I threw up my hands.

"She's everything, Dimi. Can't you try to understand that?" my cousin growled, hot breath right in my face.

"So let's blow up the buildings and have done with it," Luka said quietly.

Even though we stood a little apart from the others, I risked a glance. Their gaze darted away, looking at anything and everything else. But we were the sole focus of my squad.

Every word I said, every move I made was subject to their scrutiny. I should be with Igor, organizing the advance. Instead, I was dealing with this crisis.

"How small can we make the explosions?" I asked under my breath.

Delight sparked in Luka's gaze. "As small as you want."

The pakhan was going to kill me. He'd expressly forbidden explosives. But if it would relieve the pain in my cousin's face....

"We just have to clear the buildings, Kaz," I murmured. "We'll wait until we find out where they've taken her. Okay?"

Kazimir's phone rang. He stabbed the button, not even acknowledging my decision.

I bled for him. I did. If I felt this helpless, unable to quell the fear radiating from him, how much more did he feel?

But I would be burned alive before I showed it.

"Johnny tracked her phone. She's in the warehouse," Kazimir breathed, spinning on his heel. "She's there."

He lifted a trembling finger. Where we stood near building six, where Igor was already preparing to storm, the warehouse was barely visible in the deeply fallen night.

"Kolya is on his way," Luka choked, holding up his own phone.

I flicked a glance at him. There was more. Something he wasn't saying. "What?"

"Nadia...died."

With a bellow, Kazimir strode forward.

I rushed into him, taking him to the ground. His fists swung wide, but Luka jumped to help. Together we pinned the writhing beast of a man.

Kaz....

The skin of his face was bright red. Spit flew from his mouth as he strained against our hold. Nothing we could say would make him surrender. But we had to try.

"You can't go running into the warehouse! They'll shoot you on sight, you idiot," I seethed.

"I have to reach her," Kazimir bellowed. "Dimitri, you don't understand."

"I understand—"

"No! You don't. You have no fucking feelings," Kazimir spewed. "I can't let them hurt her."

"Kazimir," Luka bit out. "Stop."

"You're a mad idiot, and Dimi is cold as ice, but please, please don't punish me. I *love* her."

It was the crack in his voice.

That sound split my own chest. The storm of feelings I kept bottled tight swelled to the surface.

I opened my mouth, but only a croak came out.

"They're falling back. They're falling back!" Emil's intel rang over the walkie talkies.

"Cut them down!" I roared.

We needed to go.

Our soldiers scrambled into action. Yards away, between the storage buildings, the sound of heavy gunfire rang out.

"It's our duty to finish this." I clapped my hands around his vest and hauled him up. "It's almost over."

Kazimir didn't hear me. His wild gaze cut back and forth. It was like holding a wild dog. There was only one thing on his mind.

His duty is there. With sparkling clarity, I knew that if I let him go, he would charge into the warehouse.

My grip relaxed. If Luka saw me go soft, he didn't comment.

The moment my hands weren't on Kazimir, my cousin ran to his love.

"If I ever lose my head like that, shoot me," I deadpanned to Luka. He grunted in agreement.

Chapter 17 – Dimitri

I sat on the back patio, perched on one of the godless statues my father kept back here. Marena sighed and stretched on the cold ground. I tipped back the cup of spiced wine, wishing it was something harder.

"She's everything, Dimi. Can't you try to understand that?" Kazimir's words played over and over.

Mercifully, he wasn't shot as he ran into the warehouse. The other miracle we owed to Kolya's sharp shooting, giving us an opening to rescue Kazimir.

Kolya....

It was a miracle Kazimir hadn't shot him between the eyes when the story came out that Kolya could have attempted rescuing Daniella, but instead had tried to save the heavily bleeding Nadia.

"Protect my cousin," I whispered to the heavens.

Kolya had stayed at the party only long enough for food and a quick chat with me. So far, he was the only one who knew about the assassination attempt on me in the first storage unit. I would tell his brother and Kazimir later. After I told my cousin my news, and he contemplated without answer in that silent way of his, we'd feasted on the rewarmed wedding food Signora Barone and the catering company prepared.

I snorted into my glass, draining the last of the beverage. "What a way to start a marriage."

It was hard to believe a few hours ago, both bride and groom had lain bleeding on the concrete floor of the warehouse.

And yet, they'd been able to cut the cake, insisting that the wedding *had* to happen.

Setting the wine glass down, I looked to the clouds. The night was filled with turmoil and unrest, the sounds of the city magnifying off the thick dome above.

Across the excuse for a lawn, the plaintive howl of one of the hounds raised high, breaking through the thick night air.

Marena sat up, stretched, and looked between me and the kennels.

"Hmm, girl, I hear them."

As was his custom, the pakhan gave pieces of his enemies to his favorite hounds. The half dozen dogs had an appetite for human flesh. It was a practice I forbade with Marena. It made the dogs too unpredictable, in my opinion.

Tonight, and for the foreseeable future, my dog would sleep in my room. Someone had come after me, and I wasn't risking being caught unawares.

"This doesn't make you a pet," I warned her.

Hopping off the statue, I padded through the night to the kitchen door. The only guards here were those on duty, posted at the front and back gates with someone in the tower to monitor the sensors and cameras. Every other Bratva soldier was at Vasil's. They would celebrate long into the night. The party wouldn't be over before dawn, even though the bride and groom were making gushy eyes and ready to leave when I'd slipped out.

Having enough of the constant energy of other people, I'd walked home, needing the fresh air to clear my head.

Part of me was hoping my unknown enemy would send another attack. I begged him to try again.

No such luck.

The fight still surged in my veins, fueled by a turbulent energy I couldn't quell. For the others, tonight was done. The calculations in my mind wouldn't cease. I had an unknown enemy. We had crushed the Poles, which no doubt already sent a shockwave through the underworld.

"It's just beginning," I muttered.

Hand on the metal knob, a keen sound stopped me. I turned back to the backyard. The skeletal branches clacked as the winter wind blew and the flutter of wings ghosted through the space. A two-part whistle, ending in a fast trill, cut through the yard.

I only needed to hear it once to spot the songbird. Not a student of birds and wildlife, I knew two things for certain. Songbirds didn't come out at night, which meant it was much later than I thought. And second, such a beautiful cardinal coming to this desolate backyard was nothing short of a sign.

Turning away from the door, I jogged to my truck, which sustained little damage in the destruction of the Lazarowicz crew. Opening the door, I whistled for Marena. She looked between me and the seat, confused. Normally, her only method of transportation was being crated in the bed. But I didn't have time to grab one from the kennels.

My heart thumped a wild rhythm.

"Place," I barked in the obscure language I used for my dog and me alone.

Marena obeyed, good dog that she was.

Blinking through the windshield, I asked myself if I was coherent enough to drive.

"I had one glass of wine," I murmured. "And no sleep."

The second was the worst problem. But I could sleep later. There was no rest in my room. No...there was something more important. Pushing the ignition, I threw the vehicle into drive and took off down the road.

I had to see her.

Twelve minutes later, and three red stoplights that I didn't stop for, I was at her apartment.

"Stay." I held up my hand in the signal.

Marena rooted her tush on the seat and looked ahead.

I barreled from the truck, not bothering to lock it. I pitied the fool who tried to carjack my ride.

Taking the stairs two at a time, I sprinted to her door. The copy of her key was hot in my hand. It seemed to have a heartbeat of its own. I'd stolen the original from the building management and made myself one for a moment such as this. I entered her place, breaking the flimsy chain that held her door. As if that piece of cheap metal could keep me out. Already knowing there would be a mess of clothing, books, and random stuff on the floor, I picked my way to the back where her small bedroom was. In the seconds it took to collect my breath, I asked myself one last time if this was the right thing to do.

It was.

Laurel came to me when she needed to feel better. Now I was the one having a bad night.

Stepping over the threshold was the closest thing I had to a spiritual experience. Time stopped. The air around me held its breath. A charged, trembling energy thumped in a steady rhythm—one that mirrored a steady heartbeat. Ghosting the bed, I crossed myself. Any unholy spawn such as myself had no business in the presence of something so beautiful as this otherworldly princess. And yet, I pulled the blanket down, revealing bare skin. Heat pulsed in my groin. She was mine, no matter how much we denied it. No matter the lengths we went to fight it. The pencil-thin strap of her sleeping gown had slipped down her shoulder. Time slowed as I reached out and brushed the tips of my fingers down the smooth expanse of her arms.

Laurel shivered.

That vibration was contagious. It trickled up my wrist and settled deep in the pit of my stomach.

Touching her was my new favorite thing. How had it taken days to do it again? And that intoxicating scent? Rich, dark berries that beckoned me closer....

I wanted Laurel.

Wanted her badly enough to risk scaring her half to death.

The poor thing didn't have a damn clue what kind of monster she'd attracted, how watching her was my obsession. After her first abrupt appearance, I'd needed to know everything about her. It was a compulsion.

And then, she'd raised the stakes by appearing a second time.

"Make me feel good."

Those words haunted my dreams. They played like an ancient lullaby when I was awake.

Laurel came to me—*me!*—because she needed what I could give her. She wanted to feel better, and she came to *me.* There was no way in hell I was going to write it off as a one-night stand and ignore her life. Not after having such a taste. The trouble was, she'd practically shut down. That was the opposite of what I wanted her to do.

But it made sense. I should run from her. My life was dangerous, and enemies could follow me here. There was no protection for her as an outsider of the bratva, and my actions would be limited if she was threatened.

Truthfully, it would be easier to slit my own wrists than leave.

"I need you," I whispered. "Make me feel good."

As my fingers trailed back up her arm, those nipples tightened under the material of her satin gown. It was too much. I gave in to the temptation. Reaching out, I rubbed my thumb across one pert peak.

Laurel sighed, her lush frame stretched. I could see just enough to know her thighs clenched tight.

I would turn over every cent in my offshore accounts to have those thick legs wrapped around my face, squeezing me that tightly.

I suppressed a groan. My dick was iron hard.

How to wake her—that was the question. I wanted to rip back the covers, push up her sleeping gown, and bury myself in her. The trouble was, she'd offered herself once. But she hadn't tonight.

Pressing the alarm on my key fob, I folded back into the shadows as the horn blared. Laurel stirred, sitting up. Her fists rubbed at her eyes as she stretched, one arm crooked and the other flung wide. It was quite possibly the cutest thing I'd ever seen.

Flinging the blankets back, she slid her feet into a pair of furry heels. They weren't as high as the ones she'd worn before. I watched in wonder as she navigated the space, half asleep, in heels, and didn't break her neck.

And then I was treated to the sight of her round ass swaying under the royal blue fabric as she flicked on the bathroom light.

While the door was closed, I considered my options.

The best was the one where I could touch her again.

So I ghosted to the closed door. When she opened it, I grabbed her. "Don't scream, baby, it's just me."

The shrill squeak died under my palm. Her hard breaths fanned my skin. Those cinnamon eyes shone bright in the yellow glow of the light.

"That's it," I murmured, pushing my hand along her cheek and cupping it gently.

"You could have rang," she breathed. "I would have put on something—" She lifted her shoulder and shrugged. The strap fell down again.

"I had to see you," I admitted. "Are you mad?"

The corner of her mouth quirked up and she shook her head. "Why did you come, Dimitri?"

"Because..." I breathed. I could do this. I could admit it. I was already here. She was already awake. But the words choked in my throat. Something else came out instead. "Because you needed me."

She let out an incredulous laugh. "That's a stretch. I got my fix, mobster. Debt paid, slate wiped, one and done."

Something dark and violent sparked in my chest.

She held up her hand, that regal flash demanding my silence as she finished. "We agreed over breakfast that there can't be anything between us. We need to stay out of each other's lives. We agreed...we agreed that was goodbye."

It was the hitch in her voice.

That was all the courage I needed.

"No, it wasn't." I stepped into her. "I knew you needed me tonight, because I needed you."

Snatching her hot, lush body, I plunged my hand into her hair. The other became a band of iron across her lower back as I crushed my lips to hers. The kiss was savage. Demanding. *Pleading.*

I broke away, breathing hard. "Tell me to go and I will."

Her eyelashes fluttered. There was a heartbeat. One long, agonizing heartbeat where I didn't know what she would say or do. And then, heat sparkled in her gaze. Skating her hands over my black button up shirt, she fisted the material around my shoulders and brought me down to her mouth.

I drank her in, wrapping my arms tight around her. Relishing one calm moment before the storm. The kiss turned rough. Her lips were hard and insistent against mine.

The rest of our bodies took that as their cue to act. My dick throbbed against my slacks. Laurel's body brushed against mine, as if it knew. In a frenzy of hands, we pulled the buttons from my shirt. The garment flew across the room. Her hands struggled with the belt around my dress slacks. I moved to help, but she smacked my hands away.

Surprise made me rear back slightly.

Did she just— *Really, sweet one?*

Laurel drew the belt through the loops. Her gaze lifted to mine, and she folded the leather in half. Running it through the palm of her opposite hand, it was as if she were holding a weapon.

"What are you doing with that?" My voice was gravel, hard and without mercy.

Chapter 18 – Laurel

"You broke into my home," I panted, unable to draw a proper breath. My body was one big live wire. I buzzed with need. Heat pooled between my legs, and if he didn't take care of the ache soon, I would combust.

"Hmm," Dimitri murmured, the sound rumbling deep in his chest. "Do you really think you can fight me off with...that?"

I didn't.

"You weren't invited," I bristled.

He plucked the belt from my hands. "Tough. Admirable, but tough."

I fisted my hands at my side. "I can't have you breaking in here at all hours of the night—or day!"

The long, lingering look he drew down my body scorched my skin. "You didn't tell me to go."

"But we need to talk about this," I insisted. "We need ground rules."

"Your hands stay free." Dimitri lifted the belt, moving it back and forth. "Everything else, however, was on the table. Including nocturnal visits."

The belt snapped. I nearly fainted.

What did I get myself into?!

And why didn't I want to get myself out of it?

"Take it off." There was no mercy in his voice.

I reached for the delicate négligé.

"No." Dimitri gestured to his pants.

I arched a brow. There was a terrible beat where I tested his limits. Something dark shimmered around him, as if the violent energy he clearly was struggling to keep contained was ready to explode.

But I wasn't scared of him.

Dimitri Vlasov, you've met your match.

"What if I take it back? Said I was lying, and you should go." I tipped my chin up. "And we never, *never* see one another."

My pussy screamed at me. The greedy little kitty wanted to be gorged, and from the tight outline of Dimitri's slacks, he was more than ready for me.

He moved so fast, I didn't have time to react. His hand reached out and gripped my jaw, while the other caught the back of my neck. Behind me, the belt clattered to the floor, but the sound was covered by the snarl coming from the underworld prince. "Do you know what happens to liars in the bratva, baby?"

I didn't dignify that with a response.

His grasp tightened. "Well? Do you?"

"You're telling me you've never lied as part of your job?" I countered, wishing my voice wasn't quite so breathless, hoping he couldn't see the excitement in my eyes. And if he slid his fingers between my legs? Ha! My body would betray me so damn fast.

He leaned forward, hot breath fanning over my ear. "Secrets and lies aren't the same thing."

The mobster took my mouth again. I was glad he was here. He...needed me. Me.

There was no breaking free from his forceful hold. If I was telling the truth, I didn't want to. Part of me knew Dimitri wasn't good for me. He proved it by breaking into my apartment. I needed to stay anonymous and alone, yet this prince just waltzed in here, invading my hideaway. But the rest of me? Oh, there were church bells! Fireworks and parades!

Unhooking the slacks, I slid the zipper down. The heat between us blistered hotter than a flame. His cock was iron hard, and it pushed against the boxers.

"Look at me."

I snapped my gaze to his, feeling the collision all the way to my bones.

Dimitri stared down at me with a fierce insistence. Covered in shadows, his face was dark yet beautiful. "Are you sure you want this? No lying. No half measures."

He could force me. He could capture my hands, hold me down, and take what he came for. Knowing that he was the kind of man who would never do those things broke the argument that he was bad for me.

I hoped he read the submission in my eyes.

Just to be certain, I sank down. Dimitri released his hold only enough to allow me to fall to my knees. Slowly, I inched the material of his slacks down his thighs. My palm covered part of his cock, and I squeezed.

My voice was hoarse. "I want you, mobster. I want you more than anything right now."

Dimitri gripped me and tossed me onto the bed as if I weighed nothing.

"I'm not going to be gentle, beautiful." He prowled over me, like a predator ready to take the kill. Instead of running, I spread my legs. "I'm going to fuck you hard."

Need licked between my legs. "Yes," I moaned, not disguising how turned on I was.

Those powerful hands gripped my négligée and tore the material. I gasped, attempting to sit up. The protest turned into a moan when his mouth covered my nipple. Sweet relief rushed through me.

I grabbed the back of his head and pressed him tighter. He sucked the sensitive flesh. Sucked hard. I flexed my thighs, encouraging him to rub where I needed him most. My nails scored a path down his back until I reached the material of his boxers, which I snapped to get his attention.

Dimitri growled, pulling back and wrenching the fitted material down. His cock sprang out, bobbing and swelling. My mouth watered to look at it. He ripped a foil packet open. Where he'd pulled the condom from, I didn't know, but it didn't matter because he rolled it on and lowered himself on me a second later.

Every fiber of my being buzzed in anticipation for more.

But instead of offering me the sweet relief I needed, the rotten man took his sweet time swirling his tongue around my nipple.

"Dimitri," I panted and rolled my hips suggestively into him. "I thought you were going to fuck me. Roughly!"

A dark chuckle blew over my breast. "So impatient, sweet one."

I tapped his shoulder furiously. "Dimitri! I need you."

"Music to my ears, baby." He pulled my knees up, bending them around his hips. I realized my heeled house slippers were still on and made to remove them. Dimitri's hard touch clamped around my ankles. "Don't."

A protest croaked from my throat.

"Don't you dare, beautiful." He slid his touch up my calves, sending electrical currents coursing straight to my pussy. His fingers slipped between the wet folds. A shudder of pleasure sent me convulsing. "See? You *do* need me."

I rolled my eyes. "How do you play poker if you don't bluff?"

"Easily."

His finger was replaced by something bigger. Much, *much* bigger.

I sucked in a sharp breath.

"You like that, baby?" he growled.

"Fuck me already," I hissed, angling my hips closer to what I wanted.

Dimitri gripped his cock firmly in his fist and lowered himself. "Are you watching? Are you going to see how your slick cunt takes me?"

There was no time to enjoy the show. He thrust forward, pushing the head of his cock deep inside. I moaned, stretching around his hard length.

Dimitri pulled my arms around his neck. It was as if he were letting us both know where they were. Free and unrestrained. He dropped over me, an arm braced on either side of me.

As his hips set a furious pace, my legs widened, welcoming the intrusion. He thrust into me without forgiveness. All I could do was hold onto him tightly.

Could something this good be bad for me?

I appreciated the defensive side coming to argue in favor of this. Truly! I would hear her reasons out. But at another time. I didn't date, and this session was practically back-to-back to the one earlier this week. I was going to make the most of it.

Just in case the inner defense attorney lost.

I could get used to this cock. That thought sent a shudder through me, tightening my muscles.

I wriggled my arm, cupping his face and bringing his mouth to mine. There was a spice to his taste. I slid my tongue into his mouth, clashing against his.

This encounter felt more like a claim than a merciless booty call. It was something about the way he touched me. Despite all the hard edges, there was a gentleness to him. And that...did things to me. Something was happening between us, but my lust-drenched brain couldn't figure it out. I surrendered to it, so long as there was more of this—more of *him*—I would gladly submit to whatever was happening here.

Dimitri lifted my hips, rocking deeper. I was full, so perfectly full. Pleasure sizzled through me, the fuse lit and ready to explode in my core.

"Please," I whimpered.

"What do you need, beautiful?" Dimitri's hips snapped and his cock thrust inside me without mercy.

"You, I need you, Dimitri," I cried, my muscles already tightening around his cock.

"Then take me," he growled, driving into me with a punishing strength.

I did. Oh, universe help me, I did!

The fuse shortened. The pressure in my muscles built.

"I can feel you." He nipped my neck. "Take it. Take what you need, baby."

His words ricocheted through me. I clasped him tight, barely summoning enough strength to meet his thrusts. The combination of our hips rolling against one another did it.

I cried out. Pleasure exploded deep inside.

"Listen to how you cry for me, redbird. That's it, beautiful. Sing your song. Tell me how much you need me."

The sounds coming out of me weren't even human. Dimitri was my rock, and I clung to him as wave after wave washed through me.

"So saints damned tight. You're so—" he couldn't draw enough breath. His whole body jerked against me. A soul-shattering groan clawed up his throat as he released himself, offering me his body.

Chapter 19 – Laurel

Dimitri pressed his lips to mine. This kiss was slower. Gentler. *Reverent.* I sighed into his mouth and deepened the kiss. His hands tangled in my hair. A swipe of his tongue and my insides clenched.

Drawing back with a sharp hiss, Dimitri's voice turned tight. "Stop that, or I'm going to take you again."

I arched a brow and smirked up at him. "And that's a bad idea, because?"

With a growl, he scooted back, grabbed my hands, and pulled me up with him. "Come on, let's go clean you up."

Our hands threaded together, he led me to the bathroom while sliding the condom off his still erect cock. I looked at my torn négligée in the mirror. A sigh welled in my throat. "This was one of my favorites."

"Send me a shopping link, and I'll purchase you a new one," he said, dropping the condom in the trash and reaching to turn on the tap. Surprise flashed through me when he reached into my cupboard and pulled out one of my shower steamer pellets.

It was almost as if he knew....

But that wasn't possible.

He looked at me then. "What's with the frown?"

"You broke into my apartment."

"Is that a question?" He cocked his head.

Shaking mine, I reached for a claw clip on the vanity. I had to break contact to capture my hair in a twist on top of my head. There was no way I was wearing my polka dot shower cap in front of him, so this would have to do.

Dimitri studied me for a moment before moving behind me. He undid the messy clip. My hair tumbled about my shoulders.

"Hey! I don't want that wet, it's not washing day," I protested.

Those hands, which could feel so hard on my flesh, gently ran through my hair. He clasped a lock, rubbing it between his thumb, index, and middle fingers. That look in his eye could only be considered mesmerized.

Dimitri dropped the strands, piece by piece.

Both hands smoothed over the raven mass, and he tamed it back before twisting it and clipping it much more nicely on the top of my head.

"The black is pretty. It makes you look like Snow White," he said softly, pulling the torn garment from my shoulders. Squatting, he slid each slipper from my feet. Stray touches ran up and down my calves, behind my knees, barely touching my thighs. I shivered. "But I'm curious about your natural color," he added in a whisper, placing his lips against my leg.

I shivered again.

Dimitri rose behind me and drew me back into his hard mass. "Either way, you're stunning, Laurel."

"Thank you," I laughed, not really feeling the confidence I normally radiated. I was naked and on display in the glow of the bathroom light.

"You don't have to believe me for it to be true." His lips found the sensitive spot below my ear, and he pressed a kiss there. "Come on, I don't know how long your water heater lasts."

I let him pull me into the scalding spray.

Where I wasn't allowed to do a damn thing.

Expertly, Dimitri squirted my triple berry body wash onto the luffa and lathered a purply blue-tinted foam. The smell of ripe summer fruit mixed with the eucalyptus steam, creating a decadent scent.

I watched in fascination as the mobster pulled one and then my second arm high. He scrubbed the skin in long, sure strokes. As he worked his way down, pausing only to caress the more sensitive areas, I swore my body glowed.

No one besides myself had paid it this level of homage.

Dimitri looped the luffa on his wrist and with soapy palms, massaged my ass. When his touch inched toward the center, I sucked in a sharp breath and pitched forward. He caught me. But as he did, he slid soapy fingers through the seam.

A shudder ripped through me.

Whoa!

"Tell me, sweet beauty, is this a virgin hole?" he growled.

I dropped my gaze, seeing the ferocity blazing in his sea blue depths.

"Ah, so it's never been touched." Satisfaction made his lips smile. "I can read it in your face."

His finger rubbed over the puckered hole a few times. My inner muscles clenched tight.

When he pulled back, moving the luffa down my thighs, and calves, before washing my feet, I realized I was panting.

This man seemed to enjoy my body. My big beautiful body that I was told was wrong all my life. The body that my mother and her friends forced me to keep unnaturally slim. The body I freed here in Chicago, letting it grow and change shape as it needed. I loved it, and this man seemed to adore it just as much.

That realization made my insides all tingly.

I would deal with the implications later. For now, I just enjoyed his attention and devotion.

My mind reeled as he rose, took down the shower head, and rinsed me. After fisting his cock a few times with the soap, he shut off the faucet.

"What about you?" I protested, my voice scratchy and rough. I cleared it, but that did nothing to bring back my sanity.

Dimitri shook his head. "This is about you."

He stepped onto my fuzzy aqua foam mat and grabbed my matching blue towel. He wrapped me tight while grabbing a smaller one to dab himself. He disappeared into the bedroom and came back wearing his boxers and carrying my cotton robe.

I shrugged out of the towel.

"Wait." Dimitri reached back into the cabinet over the sink and took out my body lotion.

"You *have* been in here before," I gulped.

Dimitri flicked a glance up. "I think we both know the answer to that."

"Why, though?" I pressed, shivering slightly as the cooler lotion prickled over my thighs.

Pulling back, Dimitri rubbed his hands together, warming the lotion. "I wanted to figure you out."

That was an odd way to put it. Snoop? That I could understand. Search for a potential threat? That fit his MO. But figure me out?

"Am I some kind of mystery?" I laughed.

"Yes." The simple admission cut the mirth right off my tongue.

Dimitri made short work of applying the lotion. When my skin was well hydrated, I was wrapped in the robe and plopped on the end of the couch.

"Such service, I could get used to this," I teased, wriggling deeper into the arm. Reaching for a blanket, I tucked my perpetually cold toes under the covers.

"You will." The sorrow in his voice snapped my attention to the mobster.

Chapter 20 – Dimitri

"What?" Laurel scrunched up her face.

Letting out a long breath, I sank into the sofa. My fingers traced over the puckered royal blue brocade. "There's a good chance you're in danger. I would like to figure out a way to protect you."

"Oh," she said, sounding deflated.

My gut flipped. This wasn't what I wanted. Not by a long shot. But the pieces were already moving.

"You took a huge risk coming to warn me," I rushed to explain. She had to understand exactly where we stood. "Your face is known to my men. Whoever is trying to kill me has contacts on the inside."

"What happened?" Laurel sat up straighter, keen gaze pinning me. She deduced something happened.

A short laugh shot through my mind. How damn incredible was that? I had been careful to keep the wrath out of my voice, to keep my words neutral. And yet, she just knew. Knew that something was wrong. I had never met anyone who could understand like she did.

It was...nice.

My voice stayed even. "I was attacked."

"By one of your men," she finished for me. Those delectable lips twisted back and forth. "So it's begun."

I nodded. "You were right. I can't trust any of them."

The small smile played on the corner of her mouth. "Most of the time I love being right."

I bet you do. "I wanted to make this thing between us a regular thing," I admitted.

When she dropped her gaze, I leaned forward and snatched one of her hands. Gently, I pulled it onto my lap, turned it over, and began tracing the lines and grooves in her flesh.

"I would have said no," Laurel confessed quietly.

An ache panged in my chest. "Why?"

Laurel lifted a shoulder. "I don't date."

"I would have convinced you otherwise," I promised.

Look at us. Talking in hypotheticals.

I came here knowing she was something I shouldn't have. But I was on the fence about that decision. Now that she told me I wouldn't have been able to have it anyway, I pushed off, jumping into the abyss.

What if I could have her? I mused on that. It was entirely possible that I had been quick to dismiss this thing working. And the fact that she didn't date? Well, now I just wanted to convince her otherwise.

"The bratva wouldn't protect a girlfriend," I mused, brushing the tip of my finger over each of hers.

"Or a mistress," she smirked, giving me a naughty look.

I stilled. A dark current jolted through me. Reaching over, I cupped her face, my thumb rubbed against the delicate skin under her eye. "You would never be that."

"Why not?" she countered. "Some of the most beautiful and powerful women in history were courtesans or favorites. I've always been fascinated by them."

"And the other powerful women were wives," I said with a stronger bite.

"Well, I can't be either, so what's the point in discussing it." Laurel let out a long yawn, stretching her arms above her head. "Do you want me to make you some breakfast before you go? The only morning food I have, though, is toaster pastries. Otherwise, it will have to be a sandwich. But it's closer to midnight than dawn, so that still counts."

She continued to ramble, but an idea flickered in my mind. She needed protection, and I would give her that. But what if—

It was mad. Utterly crazy! But, oh, so damn good.

My phone rang in the other room, cutting off the barely formed idea before I had a chance to speak it. "A sandwich would be lovely. I'm going to answer that outside and check on Marena, but then I would love to have breakfast with you."

Laurel blinked rapidly. "You left your puppy outside!"

Kicking off the blankets, Laurel bolted off the couch. Surprised, it took a precious three seconds to react. I bounded after her, but she was already through the front door.

"Laurel!" I hissed.

"You left the poor thing out in this cold!" she snapped, bare feet slapping across the dirty laminate hall.

"The truck was warm when I left," I protested.

"That doesn't matter! She's all alone, out in the cold—at this ungodly hour!"

"She's a dog," I hissed.

Laurel shook her head violently and ripped open the stairwell door. Admiration shot through me. Damn, she was a quick one. My feet connected with the cold metal steps.

"Get over here," I snarled, lifting her and precariously balancing on the top steps. "Quick kicking or we'll both tumble."

"The dog!" Laurel continued to wriggle. "The poor puppy!"

Her ass ground against my front. It was like a shot of caffeine to my half-awake dick. He hardened instantly, greedy for another taste of this snowy beauty. The scent from her berry soap was strong. I groaned.

Bouncing her hard in my arms, I strode back to her apartment. Only when the door was closed, did I set her down.

"You will *not* do something so reckless again," I warned, pushing her back into the wall. "I won't have you going outside—barefoot no less!—in the middle of winter."

"Spring is a month away," she sassed.

The look I gave her was downright thunderous. She bit her lip, trying and failing to keep back the smirk. "That must be what your enemies look like, right before you off them. How very scary, Mr. Mobster."

"Don't test me," I warned.

Those lips pursed tight. "Why not? We're not an item. We barely know one another. If I want to go outside to rescue a poor, neglected animal, then I'll defy you!"

"You?" I pressed my body into hers. "Defy. Me?"

"Yes, I do," she said gleefully.

I whirled her around, crashing her front against the wall and pinning her upper body under my arm. I hooked a leg around one of hers.

It wasn't easy. Laurel writhed and squirmed. She wasn't petite, but that was an incredible asset. She wouldn't break easily.

I wrenched up her robe and let loose a series of swift, stinging blows with my palm. Her bare ass, lily white, bloomed with red from the sharp contact.

Laurel froze, her inhale caught in her lungs.

"Do you still defy me?" I demanded. My own breaths came quick and hard.

Her voice was tight when she let out that one, little, yet cataclysmic word. "Yes."

I unleashed my hand against her ass. I spanked her. The loud snaps of the rougher flesh connecting with the softer echoed through the tiny apartment. They were accompanied by the bursts of lush sound from Laurel's throat.

Her cries were music to my ears. Sweet, erotic music. My dick was iron, and he begged to be unleashed.

"Sing, little bird, sing all you want, it isn't going to do you any damn good," I whispered.

She was gasping for air. "I still defy you."

The overwhelming need to tie her to my bed, to claim her with a fierce predatorial need saturated every brain cell in my body.

This ass was mine.

This body will be mine.

Breathing hard, I ran my palm over her bright red skin. I needed to punish her, dominate her, force her to submit. But claiming such a beauty would take time.

Lowering the robe, I turned her, leaned my leg between her thighs, and found her mouth.

Holding her head in place, I kissed her savagely. If she didn't know already, the way my mouth consumed her told her this was far from over.

The answer I found on her lips was a dark defiance. She was ready for the challenge. Now it was simply a matter of getting her mind on board with my plan.

"Now would be a good time to make us breakfast, redbird," I murmured against her mouth. "I can help you when I come back."

"You're getting the dog?" It might have been inflected like a question, but it was phrased like a demand.

"Only if you say please," I smirked.

Laurel jerked but couldn't move far because of my hard grip on her neck.

"I'm waiting." My gaze dropped to her swollen lips. A smoldering pause ensued.

A short huff left her nose. "Please go get the dog, and I'll warm *her* up something to eat."

That wasn't what I was looking for, but I would take it. "She has a very strict feeding schedule and isn't hungry."

"She's a dog. They are always hungry," she protested.

When I didn't move, Laurel gave me a hard shove. "The truck will be freezing by now!"

I winced at the shrill volume. "No, it won't," I said flatly and released her.

Laurel hurried to put a few steps between us. She shook out her robe before rounding on me. "I can't believe you."

"What?"

"Spanking me. Like a child!"

"Naughty women earn them, too."

Shaking her head, Laurel pointed a finger. "Go bring Marena in this instant! Leaving her is terrible and cruel. This isn't a good neighborhood and—"

"And yet you live here?" I countered.

Laurel narrowed her eyes. "Your phone rang again."

This back and forth was going to continue until I brought the damn dog inside. With a strangled growl, I moved to the bedroom to collect the rest of my clothes.

But not before catching the sparkling smile on Laurel's mouth. It was radiant. Triumphant. With a flounce, she skipped into the galley kitchen.

I fisted and flexed my fingers. Had there ever been a woman this—

This—

Infuriating?

Intoxicating?

I drew in a deep lungful of air. "Enchanting," I whispered.

Standing in only my slacks and combat boots, I watched Marena rush about the dirty hills of snow. Relocating Laurel out of this neighborhood was an added reason to claim her. But…it wasn't like she would be safer with me. I blew out a long breath. It wouldn't be right to bring someone as sweet as Laurel into the underworld.

At least with me, she would have protection.

Stabbing the screen of my phone, I redialed my uncle.

"Dyadya, what is it?" I clipped, into the phone the moment he answered. "I missed several calls from you."

Vasil sighed. "I'm back at Mayo. With your father."

A chill ran down my spine. They were in Minnesota. "How bad?"

"He collapsed shortly after the bride and groom left. Chiara and I were able to manage it so no one saw. We took him to St. Vitus's, but the hospital staff said it was bad. They called for an immediate transfer, and he was airlifted to Rochester."

Time stilled. The cold street warped into a bleak reality.

"His heart won't take much more. If they don't get the numbers stabilized, he could be looking at hospice," Vasil continued.

"That means…." I couldn't finish the thought.

"Call my sons and Kazimir. Gather those most loyal to you and seize the crown, my boy."

It was how Vasil always called us. His boys. It warmed me—no. It grounded me to hear it this time.

"He'll shoot me if he pulls through and finds I've usurped him."

"He's not pulling through," Vasil murmured.

I refused to believe it. Not out of affection for my father, but something much worse. Something I didn't want to name. "We'll say that he is away on business as we did the last few times."

"Dimitri, you can't avoid it forever."

It wasn't an aversion to seizing the throne.

The ghost of beatings rippled over my muscles. Vasil didn't know how bad it was. There was one thing I was truly afraid of. And if this wasn't the end—because my father had been given six months minimum—he would likely kill me for warming his seat.

"We give it a week, and that gives my cousins and me time to move," I decided. "Understood?"

"Da, pakhan," Vasil assented and hung up.

A short breath whistled through my teeth. Marena came running, even though it hadn't been meant for her.

Chapter 21 – Laurel

The moment the door clicked shut, I sagged against the counter. "Holy shit balls."

In the shiny microwave window, my reflection stared back at me.

Sex drunk. That was the only description for the flushed cheeks, the wild eyes, and the untamed mane.

"That can't happen again," I protested.

The woman looking back at me frowned. *Why?*

I let out an exasperated breath. "I don't get close to people. I'm *hiding.*"

The reflection blinked several times.

My heart rate refused to slow, and my palms were sweaty. Heat pulsed between my legs. I knew damn well what that spanking had done. It wasn't so much the physical contact as the dominating nature of the bastard doling it out.

Hands on my temples, I ran them back through my hair. "It's going to come down to me running and replanting my life."

A frustrated growl hissed through my clenched teeth. That was a tomorrow problem. I marched to the fridge and began riffling around. There was muenster, thick cut ham, and—

"Oh, hey! I have eggs," I chirped. "Breakfast sandwiches it is!"

Pulling the sourdough from the farmer's market from the breadbox, and the fresh churned butter from the same vendor from the counter, I set to work.

The whole time, a tune ran through my head.

Every time the sex drunk fairy raised objects, arguments, and attempts to reason, the prosecuting attorney shut her down. Yes, I had turned the voices in my head into fairies, because I felt all light and fluttery.

And I had the biggest imagination of any person I knew.

"If I want a man, then I will get a man; but it's not one of my priorities," I sang.

If you want the man, then you should get the man; Dimitri's the kind you make a priority.

"I was in my zone before you came along; I don't want you to take this personal. Blah, blah, blah. I be like nah to the ah to the no, no, no." This time my voice was loud. So much so, that my next-door neighbor thundered on the wall.

I winced.

There was no zone, unless you mean dry spell. It is very personal. Blah, blah, blah-blah! Screw that. You should say yes!

"All my ladies listen up, if that boy ain't giving up," I whispered the lyrics, swinging my hips and dancing as I toasted the bread with cheese in one skillet while warming the ham in another.

"You shouldn't let him go! You can lick your lips and swing your hips all you want, girl, but you've had a crush on Dimitri for years. Years!"

The song died on my lips.

Memories surfaced from eight years ago. Dimitri walking through the park. Him stopping to visit. That...smile. Now he barely smiled. He didn't laugh.

An ache pulsed in my chest.

After getting on my feet, I tracked my mystery hero down and found he was the son of a notorious kingpin. I watched from afar, always keeping tabs on what happened with the Vlasov Bratva. But I never ventured to their doorstep. I barely had seen glimpses of Dimitri in the last eight years.

And now, he'd rocked my world—twice.

Not dating other men made sense. My true identity had to be kept hidden above all else. My secrets were precious and not worth sharing.

But Dimitri could be worthy. He could...protect me.

I wrapped my arms around myself, suddenly chilly. I would be putting him in danger if I did anything with him.

"He's already in danger," I breathed.

And he thinks he put you *in danger,* the inner witch cackled.

The doorknob turned.

When the door opened, the hound warily stepped inside.

"Hi girl, remember me?" I crouched, holding out my hand.

She froze. Those black eyes pinned me.

"She won't hurt you," Dimitri muttered, moving across the apartment. The ratty carpet separated the cracking linoleum and marked where the living room ended and the kitchen began.

"I know she won't." I opened my palm, and the lunch meat flopped across my palm.

Slowly, one foot in front of the other, the beast approached.

"What breed is she?" I asked, watching the floor and focusing on my breathing. The dog training book I read was very specific about this part. The dog needed to not feel threatened, and not facing her was a good way to indicate that with body language.

"Rhodesian Ridgeback."

I knew nothing about that breed.

"Come on, Marena. Let's be friends, hey girl?" I smiled encouragingly, even though I wasn't making eye contact.

I was rewarded when a long, warm tongue licked up the piece of food ever so gently. I lowered my hand. The wet snout followed, sniffing the skin.

Careful not to make a sudden movement, I pulled the container off the counter. The oven roasted turkey smelled good. I pulled another piece free and held it out. Marena gobbled it up.

"One more," I laughed softly.

This time, I lifted my gaze, keeping a broad smile in place. The dog inched forward, taking the offered slice.

I reached to scratch my fingers under her chin.

The short hair was softer than I expected. "Such a good puppy," I murmured.

Rising, I replaced the container in the fridge and wiped the slobber on my robe.

Dimitri stood at the window, staring into the street. He had a Zippo in his right hand and flicked the lighter open and closed. The steady beat was the same tempo as my pulse. I crept forward, conscious that I had a four-legged shadow trailing after me.

"Hey," I asked quietly, fingers itching to touch the mobster's back. "What's up?"

"Nothing."

"Bull. Your mood changed drastically since you stepped outside."

His dark head lifted and dropped in one slow nod. "My life is not my own."

"Oh, that sounds existential." I stepped around him and mimicked his stance, feet shoulder distance apart and stared out the window.

We remained standing there. The silence was thick, and it felt like a living thing. If this was goodbye, that would be best for both of us. I needed to cut this fast-growing addiction off.

No matter how much I didn't want to.

"I have a proposal for you," Dimitri said quietly.

His voice broke through my inner verdict, and I jumped.

He shot a side glance at me.

"What's that?" I tried and failed to ask calmly. He didn't need to know I was so easily startled.

"You're good at eavesdropping."

My shoulders relaxed, and I laughed lightly. "Oh, that. Yes, yes I am."

"Could you help me?" Dimitri turned, looking down at me with such a smoldering intensity.

It dawned on me what he was asking. "Listen in on conversations? To find who put the hit on you? Sure! But I doubt they'll meet again at the STYX, but I can sure give it a try—"

He cut me off. "No. I want you near me. Helping me."

I frowned. "Why don't you say what you mean, then. Enough with these short answers."

"Move in with me. Be my eyes and ears. Help me destroy this threat, because if we don't, the bratva could fall." His voice grew harder at the last statement.

"Move in with you?" I repeated. "How is that supposed to work, exactly? I'm not joining the ranks of criminals. The bratva won't protect an outsider."

Dimitri uncrossed his arms and took a step forward. "You won't be an outsider, Laurel."

"I'm not turning criminal," I insisted.

Those great big hands flexed and fisted. "That's not what I'm saying."

"So say what you're saying!" I threw my arms wide. "Please, for the love of life, just tell me what you mean, mobster!"

"Marry me."

The apartment was deadly silent. There was only the buzz of the electric stovetop droning from the kitchen. Even the heater wasn't running to fill the space. My heartbeat, on the other hand, thumped loudly. Blood thundered through my ears.

And then, I laughed.

It started as a choke, a great belching hiccup. Marriage? To Dimitri Vlasov? Oh heavens, forefend! The laughter spilled out of me, turning into a rambunctious cackling.

"I'm glad the idea of marrying me has you in such high spirits," Dimitri growled.

"It does!" I gasped for breath. "Can't you see us playing at house? Me in heels and pearls, cooking your supper—oh, shit!"

I dashed into the kitchen. The toast was hopelessly burnt.

The sight of charred bread soured my mirth. Flipping it out of the pan onto the counter to cool, I ground my molars as I reached for the loaf of bread.

Marriage.... Was he insane?!

So why does that excite you to your core? the devious inner voice taunted.

I slathered butter on the fresh slices of bread, turned down the heat, and dropped them into the pan. As I grabbed the cheese, I shot a small look across the apartment.

And locked eyes with the bratva prince.

Air stuck in my throat. The steady intensity in his gaze sent a wave of something through me. It was part lust, but something more. Possessive maybe. I didn't shrink under his gaze.

"Do you want any help?" he offered.

I shook myself and changed the topic. "Say I did marry you? That's a pretty big leap from twice sleeping to death do us part. What if I snore? What if you leave the toilet seat up?"

"You don't and I won't."

The cheese slices dropped haphazardly on the toast. "That's so not the point!" My hands flew to my hair, and I glared at him.

"What is the point?" he ground out, stepping forward. That predatorial gaze focused on me.

Any prey would have quaked with fear. But queens were never prey, and I was damned if I was anything less.

I brought myself up to my full height, which without my heels wasn't tall compared to the mountain advancing on me. "I am never getting married."

Dimitri loomed in the entrance of the galley kitchen.

I held his gaze for a beat longer, before I reached for the eggs and a third skillet. *Now, if I can just crack and baste these without breaking the yoke.*

"Is it me or marriage in general?" The question was soft, and there was something almost vulnerable under it.

I focused on the eggs, and once they were beautifully placed in the hot skillet, I placed a dollop of water over them with a lid. Marena, who'd done a complete inspection of the apartment, trotted over. She sat beside Dimitri. That long, red tongue ran across her jowls.

"It's not good, but maybe to you, it is," I muttered, reaching for the burnt toast. I tossed it and rounded to face Dimitri. "I don't want to be tied to someone. I had a very bad experience, and it's left the idea of marriage repugnant to me."

"So think of it as dating." Dimitri stepped forward. "I want more of you. Take you out on the town; wine you and dine you. I want to come to your bed and not worry about an enemy tracking me to your doorstep."

Dimitri shot a glance to the side and sighed. "It doesn't have to be permanent."

Marriage in name only. I worried the inside of my cheek. I focused on plating the breakfast, on carefully removing the eggs from the pan. Once the sandwiches were built, I presented him with a plate.

"We could have the marriage dissolved if the going got rough?" I clarified, searching his gaze. "No lengthy court case, just a simple 'we're done?'"

"If things didn't work out, yes." He swept his hand. "I think you could be an asset, Laurel. And if this is the only way we can be together, the relationship status doesn't matter."

"You're next in line for succession, aren't you?" I mused, breaking the yolk so the runny golden goodness saturated my sandwich.

My coffee was never black, but my eggs were always runny, and if I had a car, it would be fast. Just like the boy in the book I loved....

I chuckled at my random trail of thought, before dismissing it and focusing on the conversation at hand.

"I am."

I couldn't believe I was considering this! All my reasons for staying single, friendless—a lone wolf! They all vanished at the idea of more time with Dimitri.

My hero. Oh, shit. I couldn't let him die. I had to do anything in my power to keep him alive, didn't I?

"So catching the culprits behind the assassination attempt is imperative." I took a bite of the food and moaned.

Dimitri's hand froze partway from his mouth.

"What?" I garbled around the bite. "It's deww*li*cus."

Unable to stand the fire in his gaze, I dropped mine to the dog, who'd licked every last burnt crumb from the ground. The poor thing. If for no other reason, living with Dimitri would enable me to provide better food for the poor critter.

I swallowed and cleared my throat. "Alright. A fake marriage. No one will suspect your ditzy little bride of snooping for possible assassins."

"Ditzy?" Dimitri held up his sandwich. "Clever. Sharp and wicked smart."

"Pshaw, if you're going by the food, I have you fooled," I laughed. "I can make a few things well, one of which is boxed mac & cheese. Otherwise, I'm no great cook."

"I meant that you discovered the threat and came to warn me without hesitation. But this food is good. Damn good," Dimitri said, and although there was a smile in his voice there wasn't on his face.

What would I have to do to make you smile? Really and truly. He would look devilishly handsome with a grin.

And laugh! Oh, I bet he could laugh.

"What's so funny?" he asked, narrowing his eyes.

Not wanting to tell him that I thought he was handsome, because too much flattery of a husband could go to their little heads—I'd read that somewhere—I changed the subject.

"I have some conditions," I asserted with a bob of my chin.

Putting the last bite of sandwich in his mouth, Dimitri nodded.

"I expect monogamy," I clipped in my most businesslike manner. "I'll be exclusive to you, and vice-a-versa."

Dimitri reached out and cupped my face. "Done. My turn."

I gulped. "Okay?"

"It has to look real. We'll say we're madly in love—instantly so. Can you play the part of moonstruck bride?" While his face remained serious and somber, there was a faint twinkle in his eyes. As if he was capable of feeling mirth but hadn't the slightest damn clue how to express it.

"Oh, can I ever?" I gushed. My accent turned a bit southern as I added, "Darlin', you're gonna find me so smittin' with you, that everyone will believe I love you more than cornbread on a Sunday."

The shock that reverberated through his face was priceless. I would give my Alexander McQueen embellished clutch to see it again.

I would never really. That clutch was my prized possession.

But the look was half awestruck horror, and part uncomprehending daze. I might have been able to knock him over with a feather. My fingers itched to reach out and give him a little shove to try. Then again, they were covered in melted butter, yolk, and cheese grease.

Dimitri shook himself. "I suppose that will work. So long as they believe this isn't fake, we'll be safe." The poor man's voice was unsteady! "Is there anything else?" he added, cocking his head.

What else? There had to be more!

I could ask for the moon, and he might give it to me.

Let's try.

"You're not getting out of this easily, mister mobster. Even if it is a pretense, you're going to do it properly," I smirked.

Dimitri gave me a cautious look. "How do you mean?"

My lips turned up in a devious grin. "I want the works. Down on your knee, big—super expensive—ring, and flowers. Lots of flowers."

"Consider it done," he breathed, and then, his lips were on me again.

He tasted of breakfast and sin. A lethal combination.

The kiss had me melting. His warm, hard body molded against mine. It was both a claim and a surrender. I gave in to the madness. Why not add a new chapter to my life? Mob wife? I could always run and start a new life when it was over.

Until then, I could spend a few nights not being alone.

Sinking my teeth into his bottom lip, I tugged gently. "Great men need queens. Make me yours and we'll own this town."

A rough breath, part laugh, and part disbelief huffed from his chest. "You're something, Laurel. Are you sure you can handle being Bratva?"

How different was it really from the life I was born into? I held his stare. "Absolutely."

"I'll make you my queen," he promised, pulling back. "But first, you'll be my princess."

And just like that, I was unofficially engaged to the future boss of the Vlasov Bratva.

Chapter 22 – Dimitri

Looking over the selection of stones, Kolya shifted his weight. There was only one exit into this vault, and even though I wasn't as spatially bothered as my cousin, it made me uncomfortable too.

But Corwin Blau was the best in the business. None of these stones were on the market, which meant we paid a more direct price. He sold to select customers from his black-market stock, while keeping the stones out front at a below market price to attract buyers.

"So…you're pretending to have fallen in love," Kolya huffed in Russian. Disbelief rang heavy in his voice.

"I didn't invite you along to have you criticize me," I growled and pointed at a blue-tinted stone. "This is a diamond? Not a sapphire?" I asked in English.

"Yes, sir," Corwin assured me. "The color blue comes from trace amounts of boron that contaminate the crystalline lattice structure."

That was a lot of words to say it was in fact a diamond. "This one. Do you have it…bigger?"

Kolya let out a low whistle. "Maybe you *are* in love."

"I'll check in this case, but I believe I do." The jeweler ambled to the side.

Kolya shifted again.

"We're almost done," I murmured.

The cold look in my cousin's eye promised death if I pointed out his discomfort again.

Corwin set the new stone in the center of the white gold setting. Two smaller blue diamonds flanked the main stone. Not as rare as red, blue diamonds were still harder to find. But after being around Laurel, I knew it had to be this. No other stone would do, and a dazzling pure diamond was likewise out of the question. The jeweler set the ring in a holder and swept his palms outward in presentation.

The breath caught in my chest. The muscles swelled. Time slowed. That was the ring.

"I'll take it. How quickly can you fix it?" I asked.

"How soon is it worth to you?" the jeweler smiled. The bastard knew he had me.

"If you can set it before dawn, I'll double your rate."

"Done." White teeth glittered in front of me.

We shook hands, and then Kolya and I pushed through the exit. A visible shift in his body language told me the sheer relief he felt. He scanned the back alley before venturing out. It had been a week since the ordeal with the Polish, but there was his new, shiny truck. He'd already modified it.

Sliding into the vehicle, I ran my fingers over the dash. "You said you needed to talk. Time to spill."

My older cousin had picked me up from Club MØ, where I'd been working with the overly irritable club manager. If the meeting had continued, I would have punched Ilya in the face. It wasn't his fault that our clubs had been raided and it was hell to deal with. But his pissy, short temper wasn't doing us any favors.

"Kolya?" I ground out.

"I'm going back hunting."

I jerked in my seat. "You killed the filth responsible for the kidnapping and murder of the Barone girl."

One by one, Kolya had tracked the sex ring members responsible for Kazimir's wife's sister's death. The vengeance was completed when we destroyed the Polish mob protecting them here in Chicago.

"Daniella's information only touched the tip of the iceberg. The trafficking rings go so much deeper than the Chicago outfit." Kolya ground his teeth, focusing his piercing stare through the windshield. "I'm not asking Uncle Matvei's permission. But I am asking your blessing."

That was more words from Kolya's mouth than I heard in a typical day. A long, winding breath blew from my lips. "Of course you have it, you bloody idiot."

Kolya gave me a clipped nod. "If I don't take out more of the roaches, they'll slink back into Chicago in a month."

"And all the fighting with Lazarowicz will have been in vain," I surmised. "What help do you need?"

"None." Kolya shook his head.

The wraith was going back to hunt. I would have pitied the vermin he was going against—if they weren't buying and selling unwilling human flesh. The fire in Kolya's eyes was more emotion than he ever showed.

Clapping him on the shoulder, I murmured, "Dayut byerih, ah byut – byeghig." *If you're given something, take it, but if you're being beaten – run.*

It was a humorous turn of phrase that meant to seize the day. Unless it was dangerous.

It was my way of telling Kolya he could handle the challenge. It would take the apocalypse for the wraith to break a sweat. Even then, he would fight to the death.

"I'll contact you when I can." Kolya parked in the alley behind Club MØ. "And Dimi?"

"Hmm?"

"Don't let my brother touch my truck."

I snorted. "I'll do my best."

Hopping out of the vehicle, I went to the back door and pounded four times against it in a designated rhythm. The bouncer opened to me. Bathed in the glow of Kolya's taillights, I entered the club.

A vibration came through my pocket.

My heart jumped as I pulled the phone. Sure enough, it was Laurel.

It had been nearly a week since I'd seen her. Chaos had erupted in the ranks. One of our shipments was confiscated and a club raided. My father wasn't even gone a week and we were falling apart.

Redbird: Goodnight, mobster.

I wasn't sure I could recall the exact moment I discovered that nickname, but it fit.

"Sweet dreams, baby," I whispered. If everything went well, it would be her last night sleeping alone. She just didn't know it yet.

The suite at the Hilton was overflowing with flowers. No detail was left to chance. Daniella flitted around like a butterfly, chattering and teasing Kazimir.

And my cousin took it—with a fucking smile on his face.

"Why's she here?" I clipped in Russian.

Daniella narrowed her eyes at me. "Because, prick, some girl agreed to be tied to you, and she deserves all the happiness, even if this marriage is unreality."

"Fake," I corrected her Russian, and pinned Kazimir with a glare. "No one can know it is fake."

"No one will know," he confirmed in English. "The four of us are the only ones who know, cuz."

Kazimir didn't ask for permission to tell his bride, which was something I was going to have to remember going forward. Apparently, this groom wasn't going to keep secrets from her.

I would practice no such thing in my marriage. I would keep whatever was necessary for Laurel's protection.

"It's too bad lilacs aren't in bloom for a few more weeks. They would have made this place come alive," Daniella sighed.

I grunted. There were so many saints damned flowers, especially the blue ones.

"We'll see you around ten, solnyshka," Kazimir murmured, kissing his wife's head. "You have your gun?"

Daniella nodded, popped onto her toes, and smooched her husband. I turned away, pulling Luka with me.

"Best of luck abducting your woman," Daniella called after me. She still wasn't my biggest fan, and I couldn't say I blamed her.

"Thank you." I meant it. The words even sounded sincere.

That tight smile my cousin-in-law gave me might have been the first. One thing I'd realized while we prepared the room was that for Laurel's sake, it would be best if I got along with Daniella. My bride would need someone to talk to, a friend in this macabre life. How I would convince the woman whose husband I beat to a pulp that I wasn't hell-spawn, I didn't have the faintest idea. Pushing that thought aside for now, I ventured into the night to collect my bride.

Chapter 23 – Laurel

"As I said, sir, we don't have that brand of tequila. I can recommend a similar silver style at a comparable price," I repeated to the customer. He and his group took up the biggest table, which was front and center to the stage. Their hair was gelled to look wet and slick, but no doubt was helmet hard. A cloud of imitation Polo mixed with fake Dior hung thick.

The customer shook his head, glazed eyes rolling about in his skull. He couldn't fathom that I didn't have that brand. Precious had been unable to talk him down. The waitress had been close to tears when she came to the bar to ask for help. Big, old fat crocodile tears. She pleaded that we knew the brands of alcohol better, so why shouldn't we talk to him?

It was a coin toss between Julisa and me, and here I was arguing with a drunk. It was a Friday night, and we were already short staffed behind the bar because Saffron called in sick, which meant Callie was waitressing.

Now, my head ached. I sucked in a shallow breath through my mouth.

"You're not listening," he barked. "I want the Rey Sol Tequila Anejo and it's not a silver, it's a gold."

Two minutes ago, he'd called it by a different name and told me it was a silver. Customer service, especially in the food and beverage industry, was hell. Were there good tips? Most nights. Were the majority of customers agreeable? Sure. But when a drunk couldn't keep his booze straight....

It was time for him to take a little nap.

"Let me make you a mojito on the house," I offered, blistering him with a smile. "Top shelf—secret, one of a kind batch. All organic agave."

The fat fool preened.

Yeah, you're getting well labels with water. And my secret ingredient.

As I hurried away, drawing deep breaths into my lungs as I cleared the vicinity, I plucked one of the roofies from my pocket. I was such a merciful bartender. The drug could be something far worse if I was malicious.

"How was it?" my coworker asked, tossing me a sympathetic look.

A groan was my only answer.

"Yeah, I should have been nice and taken him from you." Julisa plumped her tits and rolled her eyes.

"His cologne!" I moaned, dropping my head against the bar top.

"Oh, Dolly P, do you want an Advil?" she offered.

I nodded.

A string of excited, badly pronounced Spanish spewed from that center table as the first dancers came to the stage. The table was a bunch of frauds who didn't speak the language. Why they were pretending to use it was anyone's guess.

Pouring the ingredients into a silver shaker, and slipping the pill into the mint to muddle, I whipped up a quick mojito with well tequila, which even here was expensive.

I took it to the table, not waiting for Julisa and the Advil.

The fat bastard grabbed it off the tray, body swaying. I glanced at where Diamond shook her tassels as she shimmied against the pole, front and center on the stage. Two other dancers twirled behind her. I needed a little of their energy to make it through the night. The customer took one sip and spewed the drink over the table.

"What the hell is this?" he railed. "I wanted the private collection of Reposado's tequila!"

Le sigh. Those Rohypnols weren't cheap. I beamed, keeping my smile broad. "I'll bring you another round." *And double the dose!*

"No! You're not listening." The drunk snatched my wrist.

A bolt of adrenaline shot through me.

I couldn't draw a steady inhale. Warning bells pealed through my mind. Words choked in the back of my throat. I knew on some level this was just an upset guest. But the past mixed with the present in a suffocating blend of panic.

"Please let go, sir!" I finally managed to say. I yanked my wrist. He was surprisingly strong. But it wasn't the pain of his grip that had my heart jumping into my throat.

Just breathe. Just breathe! I tried to pull away.

I couldn't move. He trapped me.

The sounds muted. My pulse doubled. Air stuck, unable to pull into my lungs.

"Please," I whispered. "Let me go."

Fight. Fight! From the corner of my vision, my tray lifted from my hands as if by magic, and swept around, ready to clock the bastard in the face.

The man crumpled to the floor, crying out.

"You're a dead man," a new voice thundered. The dark promise broke through the rising panic. I folded into that shroud, coming back to my senses under the shadow of its protection.

The tray connected with the man's face again, and again.

I blinked. The vise around my wrist was gone.

I sucked in a deep breath. Focus, I needed to focus!

"Dimi, not here, cousin," a voice warned in Russian. "Let me get his ID, you take care of Laurel."

There was a fumbling. I stepped back, resisting the urge to rub my eyes. The sounds of the performance blasted, immediately louder. The scent of the bad perfume smacked my senses like a semi-truck. I shook my head, clearing the last fog of panic.

The first thing I saw was a mask of black wrath on a bent shadowman. Dimitri, it was Dimitri. He was here. He saved me—again. My heart did a double beat.

The bratva prince was standing over the drunken guest. The serving tray was broken in multiple pieces. I gaped. Blood. So much blood!

There was a snap, and the drunk screamed. And then strong arms were around me, shepherding me toward the back entrance. Two shadows drifted after us, but I couldn't force my overstimulated senses to acknowledge them right now.

Julisa stepped out from behind the bar, her chocolate eyes wide. "Dolly P, baby, what happened?" she exclaimed.

Dimitri started to move me away, but I pressed my fingers on his arm. "It's okay, she's my friend."

"Here, here. Take these!" Julisa dropped three orange pills in my hand and held out a bottle of water.

"I'm afraid I'm going to have to ask you to leave," Karlgrad menaced, barreling through the crowd for our group. The club owner was ready to explode, judging by the purple color of his face.

I was mid-swallow and struggled not to choke on the pills. *Oh, Universe, no!* He was going to fire me for sure! I couldn't afford to lose this job. There were nights I pulled in a grand or more in tips.

One of the twin shadows broke from our side and intercepted the club owner.

"Karlgrad, how wonderful to see you again," the cheerful voice boomed. The man wore a white tee, suntanned arms covered in ink, and jeans that did nothing to hide the tight muscles of his legs. "How's Yakov?"

I'd never seen the boss blanch. Karlgrad was practically pale.

"Luka! I wasn't expecting you," he stammered.

Dimitri tightened his grip on me. I sagged into his touch, enjoying the comfort. But on the other side of the bar, Ms. Beck worried over the drunk who was blubbering like a child. His equally tubby friends were blustering about suing. They'd dropped the fake Spanish accents.

Julisa ignored the floor manager's signal, which meant Beck had to grab her own ice.

Beyond us, the night went on as though nothing happened. The dancers did their acts, teased their flesh, and eventually showed the goods. Men drooled. Their escorts pretended to be enthralled by their behavior. Did none of them notice the patron getting his face pulverized and...arm broken? Yep, his arm was definitely hanging at an odd angle.

Maybe other guests had noticed, but none moved to act. And now that the show was over, they swiveled their attention to one another.

It was laughable.

"It turns out your *patron* insulted one of ours, Karlgrad," Luka said lightly.

No...not lightly. The feathered way he preened and laughed was an act. Behind that lurked a vampire—and he scented blood.

I shook my head, and the throb only increased. Me and my damned imagination.

"Not possible." Karlgrad puffed up his chest, trying and failing, to look down at the Russian. "Cookie has had a thorough background check—our kind of check."

"Look how good that is," Luka laughed righteously. "Your intel ain't worth shit, boy."

Karlgrad blanched.

"Now." Luka clapped his hands together and rubbed them. "I suggest you get that filth out of here before we take matters into our own hands. I can only keep my cousin at bay for so long. And you know how he gets when he's incensed."

Reality swayed. Pressure pulsed behind my eyes. The knot in my stomach tightened. Leaning into the comfort at my side, an unfamiliar luxury, I tugged on Dimitri's shirt. He bent instantly. "Yes, Laurel?"

"Take me home?" I breathed.

"Done."

When I said home, I hadn't meant with him. And I sure as hell wasn't expecting the Hilton. I hadn't packed extra clothes in my backpack, and there was cola spilled on my left pant leg, making the rayon stick to my thigh.

But the moment we pushed through the double doors of the suite, my pulse skipped. Countless flowers welcomed us with a warm embrace, enveloping us in the bower of blooms. Emotionally drained, I struggled to keep myself together.

A lithe blonde woman skipped into view, rushing to hug the second shadow. Having kept tabs on the Vlasov Bratva for years, I knew this was one of the cousins, but I couldn't keep them straight. They hadn't said his name in the drive here.

Luka brushed past the couple and walked to the kitchenette. He plucked a muffin from a wicker basket. An honest-to-goodness, big, handled basket with checkered cloth covering the muffins. I gulped. What kind of fairytale did I fall into?

"You must be Laurel," the woman beamed. "I'm Dani. We're going to be cousins-in-law!"

"Um, hi Dani," I started, but looked to Dimitri for guidance. Did she know?

"They all know," Dimitri answered my unspoken question, glowering at the group. "These men are my cousins."

"I'm Luka, the handsome one," he called out, before shoving the rest of the muffin in his mouth.

"This is Kazimir. He's mine." Dani slid under the arm of the other brute. "We got married last weekend."

I gaped at her. "Last…weekend?"

"Mhmm!" She grinned at me. "Our anniversaries will be close!"

"Events have escalated," Dimitri said carefully. "If we're going to do this, we need to do it now. There'll be no more sneaking around. It's too dangerous."

We were getting married? Now? I frowned at my ensemble. This wasn't how I pictured it. While the ibuprofen tried to kick in, this was overwhelming. A new ache pulsed behind my eyes. At least they knew about the deal to be Dimitri's fake wife, so I didn't have to pretend to be the blushing bride. I couldn't exude the level of radiance that this willowy woman did.

I nodded. "I still want my proposal," I said for his ears only.

With a sweep of his hand. "Here it is, beautiful."

And then he sank to his knees.

Standing there, in dirty work clothes, with a fricking headache, I looked down at the most dangerous man in the whole of Chicago. This wasn't real. This wasn't…real, was it?

Dimitri clasped my hands. "Laurel, I have never gone down on my knees willingly. But for you, I'm kneeling here, promising to be faithful to you, so long as we're together. There will never be another. I'll serve you with my hands, support you with my body, and protect you with my life. Marry me."

I closed my eyes and took a shuddering breath. *"Marry me."* It wasn't a question, it wasn't sweet or tender. No…it was a command.

But what had I expected? This was a bargain. All of this so we could keep seeing one another, with the addendum that I would help him catch a killer.

Dimitri pulled my left hand ever so gently. "Marry *me.*"

"I will." It took more effort to deliver those two words than any rhetorical speech I'd memorized for the debate team growing up.

Soft lips pressed against my wrist. The same spot where the bastard at work had grabbed me.

I tugged my hand, wanting to hide the area. Dimitri didn't let me go. Instead, his touch slid back and forth over my knuckles. There should have been panic at having my hands captured. Instead, the calming motion had this crazy effect on me. I felt better.

The sharp stab behind my eyes lessened.

I blinked down just in time to see Dimitri slide a *huge* rock over my ring finger. I gaped. The stone was cushioned by two more, all three the palest tint of blue. Expensive. That gorgeous ring had to be downright expensive!

Dimitri rose, never letting go of my hand. "Are you ready?"

I must have nodded, because he signaled to his cousins.

"I drew the high card, so I'm the one who got ordained." Luka bounded over, skidding to a halt and standing before us. Crumbs dusted the front of his white tee.

I had to catch myself from laughing. This was surreal, the whole evening. I was going to wake up any minute and find I'd passed out at work from low blood sugar, hitting my head in the process.

"Just a minute, just a minute!" Luka set a second muffin down on the circular table beside us.

"Luka," Dimitri snarled.

"I have the whole thing planned out!" he protested. "I even have a phelonion I stole from Saints Peter and Paul."

"He robbed the church," Kazimir muttered in the background. "Of course, he fucking robbed the church."

"Go get the outfit, Luka," Dani encouraged. She bit the smirk back and tossed me a wink.

Dimitri actually bared his teeth, but Luka was already disappearing to the coat closet. He came back with a red cape, heavily embroidered.

Luka intoned, sweeping his hand. "We are gathered here on this most auspicious day to witness the union of this man and this woman. We must remember, above all else, that we have power over our minds—not outside events. Realize this, and you will find strength in your union. Humans have come into being for the sake of each other, so either teach them, or learn to bear with them. Do this, and strife shall never cloud your relationship."

Something downright lethal pulsed off Dimitri. It was pretty obvious his cousin easily got under his skin. I drew the tips of my fingers over his forearm. As ridiculous as this whole thing was, I realized I couldn't wait to find out what happened next.

Clearing his throat, Luka addressed our group. "Does anyone have objections as to why these two should not come together?"

There was a pause.

And then our would-be minister added, "Beside the obvious is that it's a sham—therefore unnatural. Probably unholy. Definitely has the potential to fall apart."

"Luka! I swear, you're dead if you don't cut it out," Dimitri snapped.

I squeezed his hands. "He's not wrong."

Dimitri swung his gaze to mine. I smiled up at him. Electricity clashed between us. It might be a sham, but this live wire was real enough. After a minute the cousin rambled off a bunch of religious stuff in both English and Russian.

He actually chanted a portion, and I couldn't help humming along. There was something cathartic about the rhythm. I should really spend more time listening to monkish soundtracks.

Stopping suddenly, Luka turned to me.

"Laurel, do you take this man to be your lawfully wedded husband, in sickness, in health, or in whatever mobster shit goes down?" Luka queried.

"I do." And I did.

The pseudo minister repeated the same variation of the question to Dimitri.

The bratva prince met my gaze. Sparks crackled where our skin touched, and my pulse beat a touch faster. "I swear it on my heart's blood. I do."

Those words stole the very breath from my lungs.

"Then by the power vested in me by the internet gremlins, I pronounce you husband and wife," Luka beamed. "Now, give her a ten second Frenchie."

Dimitri's searching gaze lingered on me a moment more. I parted my lips, ready for the touch of him. Anticipation shot through me, better than any shot of alcohol. When my groom didn't move, I wet my lips.

His gaze darkened as it fell to track the motion.

"Everyone, out!" Dimitri said quietly.

There was a pause, and a pin could have been heard falling in the silence.

Dimitri turned on them. "Are you deaf?"

"But the cake!" Luka wailed.

"There'll be cake at the party tomorrow," Daniella rushed to console him. "We can go out for coffee and dessert, though. Kaz?"

"Party?" I breathed, looking at the departing trio. Luka wore his robes and munched on the muffin. Kazimir was guarding his wife, but Daniella turned to call out goodbye over her shoulder.

"We'll see you both tomorrow! Congratulations, Laurel. He's a...keeper." Was that a flinch in her smile? The door was falling closed, so it was hard to say.

Chapter 24 – Dimitri

With a big sigh, Laural pulled away. She wandered to the kitchenette and found a bottle of water. I sensed she needed space, but that was the last thing I wanted to give her.

"Why did you take those pills?" I asked quietly.

She tapped her forehead as she drank.

I searched her pinched expression for any sign of lingering pain. "Did they work?"

Gulping hard, she shook her head. "No, but this might."

She plucked a muffin, tore a piece, and popped it between her teeth. Watching her mouth, heat stirred in my groin. Her little pink tongue darted out to lick as another bite found its way between those pillowy lips.

"These are so good!" she moaned around the next bite. "I'm starving."

"You're hungry?" How did I not think of that? I'd been so focused on the evening, but it was the simplest of all the details that slipped my mind. "We can order room service or delivery."

Laurel studied me as she chewed. "Giordano's is closed, don't ask how I know that. But what about a large cheese with sausage, anchovies, black olives, mushrooms, and green peppers?"

Yuck. "Why not regular old pepperoni?"

Laurel smirked. "I knew I liked you." She whipped out her phone and proceeded to tap away. "I am going to put green peppers on half though."

"Those can stay," I conceded.

She looked up at me from under her brows. "You sure?"

"Positive."

"Huh," she breathed. "Didn't take you for a veggie guy."

"What kind of guy did you take me for?" I stepped closer.

"I would assume you eat steak from a skewer and guzzle mead around the fire as you howl at the moon and pray to Odin—nope, for you it's Svyatovyy—but still, some war ritual could be as true as the next thing. In all honesty—" she set the phone down "—I don't know you at all, Mr. Vlasov. And as your wife, I should know at least the basics."

"What do you want to know?" I opened my arms, taking another and then another step forward.

"Favorite candy."

"Don't eat it."

She blanched. "Okay, strike one."

I snorted. "That's hardly a flaw."

"Yeah, we're going to have issues if you don't eat candy." She tapped a manicured nail against her lip. "Favorite song."

"Don't have one."

Her eyes widened.

"I *do* listen to music," I corrected. "Mostly rock and progressive metal."

"How am I not surprised?" Laurel mumbled. "Favorite position."

I stopped short. My ears *blinked,* trying to see if they'd heard her correctly. The pause thickened. And it wasn't the only thing. My dick sprung to attention, suddenly thick, hard, and pulsing.

"Well, I'm your wife now, that's definitely something I should know," she added, batting her eyes and feigning innocence.

Something inside me snapped. A carnal heat rushed through me, and I closed the distance in three long strides.

"I don't have one—" I snatched her hips and yanked her close "—yet."

I pulled her head back and kissed her.

It was such a simple thing. Touching every inch of her, molding my lips over hers. But the very connection washed away all the cares and turmoil of the last week. The need to constantly fight, to always be prepared, washed away. I simply existed, surrendering to this woman.

Giving myself to her mouth.

Pouring myself into the kiss.

Her moan pulled me deeper into the undertow.

"How long until the food comes?" I asked, my breath ragged.

Laurel waved a hand absently in the air. "We have time."

She claimed my mouth again. I fell, tumbling and dropping further and further, until I was completely lost. Her tongue slid against mine. The contact sent hot tendrils of fire searing through my veins. I grasped her jaw, holding her firmly as I plunged my tongue between her lips. Blueberries—she tasted like saints damned blueberries.

When she gasped and tried to move her head, I relented and drew my hand down her neck, feeling the elegant lines of her throat. I wrapped my fingers around it. My thumb brushed over her pulse. This level of control over her was intoxicating. Never had a simple kiss been hotter, made me greedier, and threatened to unravel my control.

The need to possess her, to taste all of her, especially *her* surrender drove me wild.

I scooped her up, and without breaking the kiss, strode across the room. Gently, I set her down on the floor in front of the bed. My hand splayed across her back, making sure she was steady on her feet before finally breaking the kiss.

Laurel gave her head a little shake. "I should probably take a shower."

I pushed the thick, black braid off her shoulder. "Later," I rasped and nipped her neck.

"Dimitri," she moaned. "I'm all sweaty and covered in bar juices."

"So?" I pulled at the hem of her sequin top, effortlessly sliding the halter shirt off her torso. My knees cracked as I crouched to peel off her slacks and shoes. Deep, red indentations marked her feet. I frowned at her wriggling toes. These shoes couldn't be comfortable if they left these marks.

"So I should wash up," she hedged, shifting her weight back and forth.

I rose, running my hands over every inch of her skin. Gooseflesh broke over the surface. The sight of my touch affecting her like this brought out the monster in me.

"Fuck, babe, I can't get enough of touching you." I slid my hand down her sternum, coasting along the planes of her belly.

A fever raged through me. I was going to possess her, take every drop of her pleasure, and give it right back.

Settling my hands on her hips, I lifted, careful to use my legs and not my back. I tossed her onto the bed. Those glorious tits bounced. They beckoned me to my next feast.

But first, there was something else I needed to taste.

Dropping to my knees for the second time tonight, I spread her legs and bent over her to run my tongue through the seam of her pussy. Laurel gasped. The sound was sweet music to my ears.

The second lick was pure bliss. The taste was all her, no fake soap or strange scent. The urge to do something primal, like bury my face in the delicious wetness consumed me. Not holding back, I licked and sucked to make her writhe.

Absolutely beautiful.

I slipped two fingers deep inside, curling them before drawing them back out. My tongue flicked against her entrance. Laurel tipped her hips up, inviting me to explore more. I ran my tongue along her length before I plunged my fingers deep inside. Her muscles clenched at the intrusion, but as I withdrew, her hips bucked in protest. I repeated until I left her panting, sucking on her clit the entire time.

Laurel pushed her fingers through my hair, pulling at me. "Dimitri," she moaned. "I'm ready for you."

I shook my head, scoring her gently with my teeth. "I'm not done, baby."

"But I need you!" she protested, voice barely above a whisper.

"Can't I enjoy my wedding feast a little longer?" I growled, nipping at her clit.

Air whistled through her teeth as she drew in a sharp breath. "Dimitri! I need your dick. Now!"

She didn't have to ask twice. "Well, when you put it like that, redbird."

I crawled over her, tugging at my clothes until I nestled between her legs, skin on skin. That connection was delicious. I slid my dick against her slick pussy.

With a curse, I reached for my pants.

Laurel's hand rested on my arm. "I'm clean, and I have the arm implant for my, um...girl stuff."

I stilled. "Are you asking me to take you bare?"

Laurel bit her lip and nodded. It wasn't nerves dancing in her eyes. Oh, no, it was excitement.

"Damn," I groaned. Reaching between us, I rubbed the tip of my erection against her sensitive clit. Her eyes nearly rolled into the back of her head. "I've never taken a woman bare, Laurel."

A shuddering cry exhaled past her lips.

Pressing her legs open, I leaned back. "This I have to see."

Fisting my dick, I drew the head down, down, slowly and more slowly. Laurel gripped the bedding, her knuckles turning white. She was breathing hard in anticipation.

As was I.

Right at her entrance, I pushed forward, but only an inch.

"Look at you, beautiful. Look how eager you are to swallow my cock." I inched forward again. When I drew back a small bit, her arousal glistened on the skin. I slid into her, inch by slow inch. "You're taking me so well. So damn well."

"Dimitri!" she whimpered, flexing and widening to embrace all of me.

I groaned and drove inside her.

My mouth claimed hers again, insistent and eager. She kissed me back every bit as hungrily. It was as though she was starved, and I was her next meal. I loved being savored. Being ravaged. It turned me on that she was as aroused as I was.

There was something wicked about her nails scoring a path down my back. I would never have let another woman mark me. But with Laurel? I wanted it all. Her claws, her teeth. Every feral piece.

These feelings, this...desperation, it should have concerned me.

There would be time to think of it later. I had to have her.

With every thrust, her pussy rewarded me with more slick heat. She shook, a chorus of gasps and whimpers a sweet reward. The wet sound pushed me to the very edge. But I would be damned if I was going over without her. I bent her knees and set a punishing speed.

One flick of my fingers against her clit and she came undone. A tremor consumed her entire body. it was utterly breathtaking to watch. My own release ripped from me in a powerful rush. With each tight spasm of her cunt, I ground into her, spilling myself into her—giving her what no other woman had ever taken.

Breathing hard, I pulled back. Hands on her thighs, I sat in such a way as to look between us.

Her words came out rushed and heavy with worry. "What are you doing?" she stammered.

"I want to take a mental picture," I whispered, not trusting myself to speak louder. "You're the first woman I've been inside without a barrier. I want to see us joined. I want to see—"

I pulled back slightly, and the mess leaked.

Laurel squealed, wriggling and trying to move away.

"No!" I rasped. "Let me look."

I dug my fingers into her thighs and held her in place. *Fucking hell. That's exquisite.*

"Are you looking at the—the stuff leaking out of me?" she squeaked.

"Yes," I growled. "It's my mark, redbird."

"That's so gross!" she wailed.

"No, babe, it's beautiful." I rubbed my thumb over the impossibly soft skin of her thigh. "I've put my mark in you. To me, that's sacred. I don't want to make you uncomfortable, but I want to enjoy this moment."

"Okay," she breathed, the air leaving her lungs in a whoosh. "As long as you're not grossed out."

I whipped my head back and forth. "Never. This is the most natural thing in the world."

I drank my fill of the sight. My dick remained hard and stretched her. When she finally relaxed, I flicked a glance to see her looking up at the ceiling, arms propped under her head.

For the foreseeable future, this woman was mine—all mine.

"Mrs. Dimitri Vlasov," she murmured, as if she was thinking similar trails of thought.

"The women generally take a feminized version in Eastern Europe, so Vlasova if that suits you. It's your way to claim the name and make it your own."

"Even better." She smiled, but her eyes were still pinched and her face was utterly tired.

Although there was still a deep, desperate ache pulsing through my dick and I longed to take her again, I needed to take care of her. With a reluctant sigh, I pulled free. The only consolation for leaving her heat was the sight of the stain widening on the duvet as more of the evidence of my claiming trickled out of her.

Gone for only a handful of seconds, I was suddenly overwhelmed by the weight of the responsibility I'd undertaken to protect this woman. But in contrast was the cloud-like feeling that nothing, no rule or command, could separate us. We had the final say over the next steps.

A warm, damp washcloth in hand, I returned to the nearly snoozing Laurel. I tossed her phone to her, as I sat on the edge of the bed and gently cleaned between her legs.

"How long before the pizza comes?" I asked.

"Fifteen minutes," she sighed.

I chucked the cloth across the room and turned back to her. "Do you want to shower before or after food?"

Laurel let out another long breath. "If I don't do it now, I won't want to after we eat."

I led her to the bathroom, cranked the water too hot—just how she liked it—and held the door open.

Something flickered through her gaze. "You aren't joining me?"

Dragging a long, lingering look down her body, I shook my head. "If I do that, we'll miss the pizzaman."

"That's not a problem," she smirked. She dropped a suggestive look to my twitching erection.

"Not right now, baby." It was more important that we took care of her, and she was clearly exhausted.

I snatched her wrist and dragged her to the glass door, meaning to give her a gentle shove into the spray I paused to check the temperature wouldn't burn. The sudden silence was my first clue. I snapped my gaze to hers and noted the roundness of those light brown eyes. Laurel was breathing hard, watching where my fingers curled around her wrist.

Dammit. I was a rotten bastard. I'd done the one thing she asked me not to do.

I lifted her arm and placed my lips against the pulse running on the underside. With my other hand, I drew my fingertips down the back of her arm before releasing my hold. "I'm sorry, Laurel."

She cleared her throat. "It's fine."

I didn't believe her, especially with that unconvincing frog in her voice.

"I only mind when we're having sex," she lied.

I bit my tongue so as not to call her out on it. Because the panic consuming her at the club had nothing to do with the physical contact between her and the drunk.

Whoever did this to you, redbird, they're dead. Just like the drunk at the strip joint.

Catching her hands again, I brought both to my lips. I didn't want to force her out of her comfort, but I wanted her to trust me. Needed her not to see me as a threat.

"Bathe," I ordered, flicking a finger toward the shower. I left the room before I gave in to temptation.

Chapter 25 – Laurel

I couldn't have asked for a better husband. In the aspects that he was attentive, considerate, even caring, Dimitri excelled. But I went to bed by myself, leaving him as he pulled out his laptop. When I awoke several hours later, I heard soft murmurs in Russian.

Wrapping the extra blanket around my shoulders, I padded to the door, peering through the crack to do what I did best.

I listened.

And what I learned was worth the effort.

The person was Alex. I assumed it was a boy, but when Dimitri said something in a feminine case, I stilled. My heart paused before galloping to a rapid beat. Whoever this Alex was, she'd been working closely with Dimitri, infiltrating the bratva soldiers. Dimitri questioned the loyalty of his men, and Alex was giving him names.

I memorized every last one. If any proved to be a threat, I would make it a point of seeking them out and bringing damning evidence to Dimitri.

I could do a better job than this Alex chick.

"I'm not jealous," I mouthed to myself.

The green spot in my chest simply laughed.

I spun the ring, the perfectly fitting ring, around my left ring finger. He promised me monogamy, and until he gave me a reason not to, I would believe him. But I would be damned if another woman took the glory. I was here to eavesdrop—to help him find invisible threats.

Dimitri ended the call and stretched. Although it was only a sliver, the muscles of his frame rippled and grew. A greedy little flicker sparked between my legs.

But instead of coming to me, Dimitri went to the couch. He knelt beside the sofa, pulled out a stiff piece of paper the size of a playing card, and bent his head. Low, melodic strings of poetry wafted.

No, not poetry.

Prayer.

Dimitri was praying, imploring the saints and the Holy Virgin to intercede on his behalf. He confessed his sins and swore he was heartily sorry for them. He begged for relief from the torment, and he rejoiced in forgiveness.

Shock rooted me in place. While there was a religious matriarch in my past, my family only attended as a social obligation, which forever turned me off from church. I believed that doing good produced good. But seeing the devout sincerity of this underworld monster struggling through his actions and horrified by life—yet his words sought the grace of a higher power—was beautiful.

When he was done, Dimitri stretched out on the couch, and from all appearances, went to sleep. I trudged back to bed, tucking under the plush bedding. It took longer than I cared to admit to fall asleep.

Blinking awake, I heard the door click shut. The delicious soreness between my legs confirmed the best dream I'd ever had was my new reality. Stretching, I peeped from the covers. In the other room, Dimitri thanked someone and shut the door. A rich scent wafted through the crack moments later, accompanied by the sound of rolling wheels.

Food. He had food!

I sat up, ready to scramble from the bed, when I stilled. The weight of the stone on my finger brought my attention to the obvious. Dimitri was bound to me.

My husband.

My *fake* husband, who I was dating—and helping stay alive. *Wow.* It was even more surreal in the light of day.

"What's got you so happy this morning?" Dimitri asked softly, his own mouth soft, albeit lacking a smile.

It might be crazy, the bargain we'd struck, but I had to admit, my husband was hot. Dimitri, a shirtless Dimitri, leaned effortlessly against the doorway. Tasteful pieces of ink decorated his torso. That expanse of man-bod had my ovaries popping like fizzy little candies.

I pulled the duvet over my body and stepped from the bed. "Just had a good dream."

His sea blue eyes narrowed. "What about?"

I smirked. "I'll tell you later. I want it to come true first." Curling onto the brocade chair at the shiny dining table, I rubbed my hands. "Whatcha got there?"

He pushed the tray between us and took a seat. "I didn't know what you'd want, so I ordered everything."

"Good! I worked up *such* an appetite. I'm half starved." I pulled at the coverings, mouth watering at the scent of breakfast meats and warm pastries. "I barely ate any pizza."

"I'm glad you have an appetite. I do too when I wake up." Dimitri slid an omelet with rye toast in front of himself.

I munched on a cinnamon bun and considered him. This was domestic. Oddly, I hadn't considered this portion of our agreement. We wanted to date, which was impossible, so we married. I forgot about the day-to-day activities in the excitement of the physical.

The silence was comfortable, filled with our quiet chewing. I grabbed a second pastry, eying his omelet. For the briefest of seconds, I wondered if what I was about to do would be weird. But I was here for the foreseeable future, and he was going to get to know me one way or another.

I tore a large bite of the gooey bun, reached over, and pushed it between his lips. The forkful of eggs, veggies, and meat hung suspended as he processed what just happened. I snatched the bite, lips pulling over the metal tines to catch every crumb of goodness.

Settling back in my seat, I watched him. The corner of his mouth twitched in the world's smallest smile.

Dimitri looked between his empty fork and me. After a moment, he chewed, swallowed, and then nodded. "That was...yummy."

That counted as a win.

"But if you want an omelet, I can order you one. You don't have to eat mine." There seemed to be an unspoken request there that I leave his stuff alone.

Ha! Too bad, what's mine is yours. He was the one who made the offer, and he hadn't specified this when we struck our bargain. But there was no way I was pushing the issue right now. I hummed and changed the subject.

"So this party, who's it for?" A faint buzz of excitement laced my veins. Did he plan a wedding reception for us? Was he going to present me as his wife to the bratva?

"Daniella has two kid cousins and a grandmother who lives with my Uncle Vasil. One of them turns eighteen."

That wasn't air whistling softly in the distance as my chest deflated. I cleared my throat. "When is it and what's the dress code?" I asked before taking another bite of my pastry.

"Tonight. Since I get away with black dress shirts and dark pants—either jeans or trousers—I'm not going to be much help to you there." He shot me a sideways glance. "But I'll give you Dani's number so you can ask her."

I swallowed. "Perfect!"

Chapter 26 – Laurel

The three-inch, silver sparkly heels were modest compared to what I normally wore. Hell, my entire dress was as well. It had been buried in my closet, something I didn't wear when I worked and since I didn't have social functions anymore, it wasn't necessary to have something like this. But I was so glad now that I did.

Being a shopaholic paid off!

I smoothed my hands over the fitted pencil skirt. At my knees, the mermaid hem flared into a ruffled hem. The bodice was high cut, with sheer lace to cover the rest of my chest to my throat and slide down my arms in long sleeves. I felt utterly feminine in the style, and the sapphire color was perfection.

It would have been the perfect dress...if this had been a normal birthday party.

While the hostess—the birthday girl's grandma—was all class and elegance, the guests were not. The mottled crew wore biker leathers or casual clothing. Tattoos decorated most of their bare skin. But it wasn't so much the way they were dressed as their manners. If I had been asked to write an essay, imagining being transported to the hall of a raider chieftain and writing five hundred words about his spring feast before pillaging the coastal towns and villages of Medieval Europe, this would have been something close.

Oh, how my mother or her socialite friends would faint if they saw this!

"Don't think of her," I chided myself under my breath. The past wouldn't ruin tonight.

I moved closer to Dimitri until a waiter passed with a tray of cheese puffs. I bounded after him and snatched four of the heavenly balls. Popping one in my mouth, I moaned around the dough. Gruyere cheese and Dijon mustard burst across my pallet.

"That's a noise I should be plucking from you," Dimitri growled into my ear.

I laughed softly. His warm breath tickled against my neck. Spinning in his arms, I pushed a cheese puff between his lips. "Try."

Shock crossed his features. He clearly never had a date like me at one of these bratva parties. Although, that wasn't saying much, because the men outnumbered the women by multiples. And from the looks the others gave us, it was a good bet that Dimitri *never* brought a date.

"These are divine, no?" I cocked my head.

His dark gaze slid down my body. I could have sworn I *felt* it draw back up.

"Tasty," he said quietly. "You're going to make this a habit, aren't you? Shoving things in my mouth."

Yeah, about that, when can we shove something in my mouth? I warmed. Practically sizzled. That thought was tantalizing. But I kept it a forbidden little secret.

"Is that a complaint?" I dared.

His voice thickened with a suppressed emotion. "When you take it into your brilliant little head to tease me, just remember what kind of a monster you married, Laurel."

There was nothing to fear from him. Not a damn thing. However, I decided that I might as well play his game. I tapped my chin. "You mean the kind who falls to his knees before me?"

"A gentleman takes care of his lady's *needs.*"

"Gentleman, huh? It felt more like a princeling falling to worship at the altar of his princess. But if you want to name the rose something else, it still felt as sweet to me." My soft laughter cut off anything else I might want to say.

The look on his face was priceless.

"Just wait until I get you alone," he promised.

I shivered.

We needed to change the topic before I combusted. "So, this is your uncle's home."

My hand swept over the richly colored stucco of the drawing room. Sliding pocket doors led into the dining room, which might as well have been a great hall in a castle. Like Dimitri's house, this was a converted industrial building. Unlike his place, however, this felt inviting. It was downright palatial, with a heavy nod to Mediterranean décor. The molding at the top of the drawing room had carvings in it. Lush murals added color and depth. And the furniture was sumptuous, tasteful, and well curated.

The moment I walked through the front door, I fell in love.

"I'm not sure how to answer that, since this is Vasil's house and you know he's my uncle." Dimitri studied me, as if he couldn't quite figure me out.

A smart-ass comment was on the tip of my tongue when a voice boomed in Russian.

"Dimitri! How are you, lad?" The speaker pushed through the crowd.

"Fuck," Dimitri muttered and stiffened. The softness was wiped clean off his face and his hard mask fell into place.

I wanted to gouge the eyes out of the person bold enough to interrupt us.

A rapid exchange of Russian ensued. I pretended not to soak up every word. Basically, the man was wondering where Dimitri's father, the boss, was. Dimitri deflected, utilizing excellent business tactics. I was quite impressed and had to turn away to hide the fact that my eyebrows jumped up in admiration.

And then the attention turned to me.

"Emil, may I introduce my wife, Vlasova." Dimitri spoke this in English, using my new last name, but not using the English *Mrs.* since it wasn't common to use that honorific in Russian. Why he left off my first name, I couldn't guess. But I took his lead, turned around, and dazzled the interrupter with a blistering smile.

"By all the saints!" Emil bellowed. "You married as well?"

A hush fell over those nearest. It spread out into the crowd, and murmurs rippled in its wake.

Dimitri's hand slid to my lower back. It might have been my imagination, but I felt the heat of it spread through the fabric.

I pulled myself tall and wished above all else I could check my lipstick post cheese puff feasting. And yet the other half of me wanted to speed through this part so I could track down the tray of soul-soothing pastries and commandeer the rest.

"I can't believe she's upstaging your birthday," Brittany whispered to her sister, the birthday girl, in Italian.

"I don't blame her so much as him," Camilla responded. "This has to be part of the reason Dani doesn't like the little prince."

I started. Cold washed through my veins. Daniella Vlasova didn't like my husband? Dimitri slid a glance down at me, but I ignored it. If the Barone sisters were whispering so loudly in Italian, it was unlikely the Russian understood.

I blessed my classical, private education for the ability to speak multiple languages.

Because someone wanted Dimitri dead, and I had my first suspect. And here I thought Daniella was nice. It made sense though; her husband was ruthless and strong. Maybe they wanted to take Dimitri's crown.

To stop the swell of gossip, Signora Barone clicked her fingers, muttered to the wait staff, and then signaled Vasil, Dimitri's uncle. He cleared his throat and gave a very moving toast.

At the end of it, he trailed off into a round of "Happy Birthday."

Pulled into the joy of the moment, I lifted my voice with the others to call out the age-old blessing on the birthday girl.

The words melted on my tongue. The notes filled me. My heart soared to the sky. I sang my heart out.

When it was over, I clapped loudly, swept up in the energy and happiness once more.

My hands faltered. A glittering darkness stared at me. It was as if Dimitri had seen the sunlight for the very first time, awe painted over his face. Desire crackled in his sea blue eyes. His hand gripped the window frame as if it threatened to break.

"Oh, yeah." My cheeks warmed, and I tucked a piece of hair behind my ear. "I can sing."

Chapter 27 – Dimitri

"I can sing," she'd said.

No—the people around us *sang*. Cows sang when it was time to milk them. Dogs sang when they'd found the scent of blood. But her? That sound was otherworldly.

Minutes had ticked by and my skin was still prickling with the sensation. The urge to scream at the crowd and demand their silence danced over the tip of my tongue. I would fall to my knees if that was what it took this beauty to enchant me with her voice again.

Redbird—how fitting.

We mingled with Daniella's grandmother and the orphaned baby of one of my most trusted soldiers. The child looked well, although to hear Signora Barone's account, it needed more prunes.

"I never grew up around kids," Laurel admitted, offering her finger for the chubby fist to wrap around. "She's awfully cute though."

The sudden impulse to see Laurel round with my child painted my mind. Blood rushed south, and my dick stiffened into iron.

So not the time, I growled at him.

Our marriage was fake. We were using it to protect her as she spent time with me, as she helped me find my would-be killers. The likelihood of it lasting was impossible. But what if...what if it was real? I rubbed my fingers against my jaw.

Damn, that *was* an idea.

"So Daniella adopted her?" Laurel cocked her head, keen gaze laser focused on the grandmother.

I frowned. Laurel had to be one of the most expressive people I knew. She used it as a tool to manipulate people with changes in her features. Just because I picked up on the trick, didn't mean I could read the intention behind it. There were times, such as right now, when I couldn't for the life of me puzzle her out. That smile was meant to seem friendly. But what lurked underneath raised caution in my mind.

"Oh, tragic story, we're still reeling!" the signora sighed. "Zoey's father died in early January; her mother passed this last weekend. She was such a strong lady, a terribly wonderful fighter. And to be shot in the back? Unfair. So unfair, I tell you."

"A fighter?" Laurel's voice pricked up a notch.

"We don't discourage women from our ranks," I explained quietly. "While Nadia was arguably our best, there are some feral ladies still left."

I gestured to the figures mingling out in the sea of guests. When I turned back to Laurel, her cinnamon eyes sparkled. A silent laugh bubbled in my chest. That eager twist of her mouth and the breathless excitement meant she was going to ask me something.

And I couldn't wait to see what it was.

She never got the chance, however. A frenzied whisper spread through the crowd. My gut twisted, and a cold sweat broke over my skin.

Vasil and I shared a look. His wide eyes told me that he hadn't expected this any more than I had. Steeling my spine and keeping a controlled mask over my features, I turned to face my father.

Although his body leaned on the cane, there was no other sign that he'd spent the week at the premier medical center in the Midwest. Why he hadn't paged that he needed a ride from Rochester, Minnesota, I couldn't guess. Unless...he wanted to surprise us.

He couldn't have picked a worse week to do so.

The pakhan made his way through the crowd, nodding to various greetings and exchanging small pleasantries. I took one step forward, placing my body between him and my bride. It wasn't meant to hide her, so much as to shield her from the storm I knew was coming.

"Demetrius." My father's clean-shaven chin bobbed. "I came here with questions, but it seems the answer is quite plain for those who have eyes."

I uttered a wordless prayer to the saints that he spoke in our mother tongue. "How do you mean, sir?"

"I see you've been otherwise engaged. That explains why our most profitable club was raided on your watch. You were too busy wetting your dick!"

Did he have to do this here? Laurel might not understand us, but every other member of our bratva did. Besides, this wasn't his usual style. Normally the dressing down happened behind closed doors. He wanted to keep a careful presentation to the soldiers.

My father must be irate to chastise me in front of the men.

I wasn't going to take it lying down. "I married her."

"Semantics. You didn't have my permission for that. It shows how incapable you are of running this organization." This time, at least, his voice was a low hiss. Only those closest could hear.

"Pakhan—"

"Save it, I'll deal with you later." My father stormed off, dogging down his brother. I pitied Vasil.

"That guy didn't seem happy," Laurel mused, fidgeting with her skirt. "Who was he? And what was that all about?"

The breath left my lungs in resignation. "My father is never pleased," I admitted.

"Oh! *That's* my father-in-law?" Laurel stepped into me, moving to lace her fingers with mine. "He doesn't look so good. Should he be out of the hospital?"

I snorted. "Try keeping him down. I dare you."

Laurel hummed under her breath, squeezing my hand. That slight pressure, the feel of her skin against mine—it grounded me.

"Come on, the cheese puffs went that way," she chirped and took off, dragging me with her.

I let her, knowing that hell was coming.

I left Laurel cocooned in my full-sized bed. The summons had come ten minutes ago, and I padded through the midnight halls of the house to the pakhan's office.

The door fell closed behind me with a click.

I didn't see the goons until they were on me. Roaring, I struggled to break free. But they pinned me to the floor. It took three brutes to do it.

"What is this?" I demanded, stretching to look at the pakhan.

Sitting behind his desk, filling an empty mason jar with noxious embalming chemicals, the boss didn't look at me. There was a frozen finger sitting beside the jar, another trophy he'd apparently collected.

"You disappoint me, Demetrius," my father observed. He flicked a cool gaze toward me, and then motioned with two fingers.

My father's henchman, a man with no soul, peeled off the far wall. This demonic sonofabitch was a faceless player in the underworld. Few knew he existed, and those who did prayed never to come upon him in the background.

I wrenched to the side. The soldiers holding me were strong, and they had a solid grip.

Ever since I was big enough to fight back, my father had been selective in his use of physical punishment. Tonight would be no different. The henchman plucked the chosen device for tonight's punishment off the pakhan's desk.

A chill ran through my blood.

A few weeks ago, I delivered a beating to my cousin. While I still loathed myself for having done it, at least that had fairness about it. Which was exactly why Kazimir didn't hate me. Rules were broken, and without rules, we were chaos. Crime and punishment, wrong and justice.

This?

It was hardly the same thing.

The goons stripped my shirt and the henchman advanced.

So tough! You think you're so tough, old man? The great and feared pakhan of the Vlasov Bratva needed three goons and one rotten bastard to dole out punishments. So tough indeed! The words died on my tongue, but I let them consume my eyes.

Placing the lid on the jar and screwing the ring tight, the pakhan rose to place the newest trophy with the others lining the shelf behind him. When he turned, my father's thin lip pulled back in a snarl. "Zakhar, begin."

The henchman lunged, the cattle prod extending like a foil in a fencing match.

White hot pain flared from my shoulder through my body.

I grit my teeth, but a cry gurgled up my throat and slipped past the barrier.

"You are so damn weak," my father snarled. "Getting involved with a piece of ass is one thing. But letting her into your life? Letting some bitch distract you so that the first week the reins are in your hands everything I built starts to crumple?"

"That's not what this is," I groaned, struggling to stay coherent under the steady stream of electricity.

When the smokey smell trickled from my skin, my father snapped for his henchman to stop.

The welt throbbed, a pain like none other.

"Give me one good reason I shouldn't shoot you and promote one of the other captains as my heir?" my father spat.

A million reasons bubbled into my mind. But there was only one that he would hear. "Because you groomed me to be feared as you are, pakhan."

My father grunted. "Half a mill, Demetrius. Half a damned million dollars lost because the club was raided."

And if Igor's fat ass had paid off the cops on time, they would have tipped us off before the raid. While Igor was my old captain, it grated that there was no mention of his mistake. His *costly* mistake.

It didn't matter the reasons, the pakhan held me responsible because it had been done on my watch.

"Get me my fucking money, Demetrius." The *or else* was implied.

I jerked against the hold of the men gripping me. "I'll get you the money."

My father's steely gaze swept over me. He gave a small nod, and the goons released me. I remembered their faces. They weren't prominent in the ranks, but I'd seen them around enough to know they weren't new recruits.

They were going to find knives in their bellies some morning. And Zakhar? The moment the pakhan's heart stopped beating, the henchman was the first person I would shoot.

I met the stare of the one person I couldn't bring myself to end.

"I'll find the money," I repeated.

Chapter 28 – Laurel

What a lumpy, dumpy bed. With a groan, I rolled over and stretched. A shiver ripped down my spine and I pulled the thin, cotton weave blanket over my body. I was alone. Sitting up, I flicked on the bedside lamp.

A dumpy bed for a dumpy room.

The other night, I hadn't noticed any of the ugliness when I'd been here. The paint was cracked near the ceiling. The floor was tiled and bare. It looked cold, and I hadn't stuck one piggy out to test. There were two roughhewn board shelves on the wall, not even painted. Stacks of books sat on their sides, but otherwise, there was no décor. The only furniture in the space was the spindly tri-legged nightstand, this uncomfortable excuse for a mattress on a metal base frame, and a singular dresser drawer. There wasn't even a closet, only a free-standing wrack with suit jackets hanging pitifully.

The bathroom was likewise sterile and unappealing.

"So this is your house, Dimi," I murmured.

The bathroom door banged open. I yelped, clutching the blanket to my chest as two black eyes pinned me.

"Hi, Marena," I breathed, melting back into the pillows.

The dog trotted over, placed her snout on the bed, and let her metronome tail thump against the air.

"I don't have treats, but you can still be my friend." Gingerly, I stuck out my hand. She licked it and I smiled. "Good puppy dog."

With a huff, I glanced around the space. This would never do. Marry a mobster because I couldn't date him? Sure, why not! Move in with him and become part of his criminal life? Yeah, what did I have to lose?

Exist in this frigid, asylumesque place?

Screw that.

Dimitri needed to let me decorate—probably renovate—or we were moving. As I hurried to find a sequined sweater and stretchy pants from my suitcase, the impossibility of the second option became apparent.

"Well, he's just going to have to agree to the first one," I told the dog.

Marena stretched out her front paws and leaned back into her butt.

"Oh! I get it," I laughed. "Downward dog."

With the hound at my side, hair brushed into a chic low pony, I emerged from the room.

The hallway was equally depressing. There were no windows, so the light came from the fluorescent fixtures overhead. The walls were white. The floor was white tile.

All the lack of color was going to give me frostbite.

Grumbling, I rounded the corner and nearly jumped out of my skin. Marena leaped forward, but I threw my arms around her neck and held the hound back.

"Miss, I didn't see you," the middle-aged woman gasped as she eyed the dog.

"Marena, sit." I tugged on the dog's collar. If she understood the command or the motion, the hound obeyed. If Marena chose to move, she wouldn't have much trouble knocking me over. But she didn't move, and she didn't take her eyes off the...maid? *Why the hell is she dressed like that?* "Hi! I'm Laurel. Sorry to surprise you, I didn't know there was anyone else up here."

The woman nodded, her black cap bobbing but it didn't fall from its place. She smoothed a hand over the traditional black and white ensemble. I was tempted to tell her the 1880s were looking to get their clothes back.

"We are fully staffed, ma'am," she explained quietly. "And there is always someone available should you need anything night or day."

It had been years since I'd had the luxury of house staff. It wasn't as if I was good at interacting with them either. They weren't my friends, a fact I learned the hard way. The few who were kind to me ultimately ended up losing their positions. Which meant loss of livelihood and bad recommendations so they couldn't work in service without relocating.

But my mother wasn't here. I could be friendly now.

"What's your name?" I asked the woman.

"Ania, ma'am."

"Well, Ania, I wonder if you have a moment to spare to show me where the kitchen is?" I gave her a winning smile and was rewarded when she nodded and began to move back along the hall.

I peppered her with questions and found out that there were coffee, bagels, and fresh farm eggs always stocked. It was awkward and jaunty holding Marena, but while I had some handle on the hound, I didn't trust her not to go tearing about.

"And what about her?" I asked, gesturing to the dog.

Ania gave me a quick look and then shuddered. "Mr. Demetrius doesn't keep her in the house unless she's with him. I can call the kennel master?"

I chewed on that. I didn't want Marena taken away, but I knew it was stupid to think I could control her. "Yeah, you'd probably better. When will Mr....um, Demetrius—" I choked on a laugh at the name. It was worse than my birth name! "—when will Dimitri be home?"

"Oh, he's here, ma'am."

I stumbled on the bottom step. Marena swung her head and pinned me with a look. I ignored her. "He is?"

"He's been in the gym all morning. But he won't want to be disturbed," Ania added.

Well, that explained the sheer mass of muscle that was my husband. As soon as I collected some coffee and sustenance, I would have Ania point me in the direction of this gym.

Frowning, I padded after her. "Did he say something?"

"Ma'am?"

"About not wanting to be disturbed," I clarified. Marena stuck out her front paws and let out a long, full-bodied stretch before she allowed me to continue stage walking her.

"No, ma'am."

Turning into yet another off-white, florescent-lit hall, a shiver rippled down my spine. "Then how do you know he doesn't want to be disturbed?"

"No one disturbs him in the gym."

I stifled a groan. Getting answers out of this woman was like prying open a tin can of soup without an opener.

In the kitchen, Ania placed a call on the wall phone. She was requesting someone to collect the dog. After hanging up, she loitered quietly in the background, only assisting me when I needed to know where something was.

Well, this isn't awkward at all.

I set to work making myself a latte. The percolator was the kind that cooked on the stovetop. In another life, I'd used this kind on my travels through Europe on the few occasions we were *roughing* it in the quaint villages off the beaten path. It took a moment to remember the tricks to get the thing cooking. The maid and the other female I assumed was the cook haunted the other side of the space, watching but not interacting with me. There were no syrups or flavors, but there was fresh milk.

The women said nothing, unfortunately. I was hoping they would whisper gossip in Russian for me to glean. But they were well trained. Eyes down, hands folded. Lips pressed tight.

While debating how to start a conversation with them, there was a noise at the metal door. Since there was no window, it was hard to anticipate who was coming. The back door banged open, and a man I assumed with the kennel master stepped inside, stomping his boots.

A low growl emanated from Marena. The dog stepped into me, bumping my leg and making me spill the milk I was heating on the stove. The man had an honest to goodness pole with a cinch rope.

"What's that for?" I demanded, planting my hand on my hip while continuing to stir the milk.

"Master's hound is a temperamental bitch," he grumbled in a thick accent.

Marena growled again as if refuting his claim.

I would be spiteful too! The size of that noose. And no doubt there were other methods for keeping her.

"Well, she's not bothering me, so I think we're good," I snapped, deciding I didn't like the dog caretaker. The man opened his mouth to protest, but I held up my hand. "You can go."

Looking at Marena, I arched a brow. "You better be good until we find Dimitri."

That long, thin tail whapped against the side of the counter. I tossed her a corner of the bagel, which earned me an appreciative bark.

After gesturing to a closed door, Ania scurried away. Clutching my coffee, I debated going into the space. "Just because she's half scared out of her mind...."

I gave myself a little shake. Dimitri hadn't ever been unkind to me. And if he was, I would tell him where to stick it. Fueled with delusional resolve, I pushed open the door. If the house was bleak and unwelcoming, the gym was hardcore and serious. Every inch was filled with equipment. There was a spa set up on the far side, and excitement flashed through me to see the sauna. While the walls were still white and bleak, the pads on the floor were black with blue speckles.

Marena began padding about, nose to the ground.

Metal clattered, drawing my attention to the sweating creature in the corner. His shirt clung to his skin, denying me a look at most of his gorgeous body art. I tiptoed farther. Dang but he looked yummy. He'd tasted me, and I barely had more than his mouth. I needed a proper taste—soon. Our gaze clashed in the mirror. Dimitri worked through his set, pressing the bar that was almost as heavy as me.

Instead of warming at his gaze, I faltered. There was something stormy there.

When he was done, he set it on the hooks and reached to remove his earbud.

"How did you sleep?" he asked.

My gaze ran over his body. He was breathing hard, chest rising and falling in rapid succession. "Alright, I guess."

Dimitri grunted.

"I'm just going to sit here, drink my coffee, and enjoy the view," I smirked. "If that's okay with you? Your housekeeper implied you didn't want to be disturbed, but I promise you won't even know I'm here."

And I'll clean up the drool when I'm done. I resisted the urge to fan my face, although I did cross my legs.

"That's fine," he rasped. There was a second where he continued to watch me. When he tore his eyes away, my chest clenched painfully. There was a stormy aura rolling about him this morning. It was ruining my raging lady-boner.

Dimitri hurried to snatch a shirt and threw it on. The brute force with which he took up the free weight made me wince.

Yeah, he definitely isn't in the mood.

To keep from going to him and pestering him until he spilled, I sipped my coffee. It was strong, which I liked. But it was bland and not sweet. It took a concentrated effort to choke it down. That kept me from bothering the raging beast.

That and wondering what happened to him.

I wet my lips and stole another glance. The volatile energy crackled through the room. Those muscles flexed and strained. beads of sweat ran across his skin. It made the tattoos look like they were crying. Heat simmered between my legs at the thought of kissing away those drops.

Setting down my almost empty cup, because I was completely unable to finish the last sips, I rose from the bench.

I felt more than saw his gaze track me to the open mat. My hair pulled into a low pony, I began to stretch. Arms above my head, I leaned to the left and then to the right. It had been four months or so since my last stint of yoga. Every so often I got the wild hair up my ass to begin practicing again. The last time only held my attention for ten days. But the time before that, over the summer, I'd gone for eight weeks and been the stretchiest I'd ever been.

It was a pity there was no one to share that with.

Now, however....

I bent forward in what I hoped looked like a graceful dive. *Hey! I can still touch my toes!*

Grazing counted as touching, right? It was a win for me!

That was huge, since there was extra winter fluff around my middle this year. I straightened, creating a slight back bend. The second forward bend, and the stretch deepened through my thighs. I jumped back into downward dog. First one and then the other knee, I gave light bends, waking up the muscles and encouraging them to warm and lengthen. The first complete sun salutation had me grinning triumphantly.

I could do this.

Moving back into prayer center, I sent a burst of gratitude to the universe for my beautiful body and the ability to move no matter how I was made.

I felt his approach. With my eyes still closed, I waited as the beast prowled closer. My heart pounded against my ribs.

And then his arms wrapped around my waist. Dimitri buried his face in my neck, inhaling deeply. "Thank you."

Unable to bring myself to form the words, I hesitated. I didn't want to spook him. Plus the hard press of his body against me felt nice. The moment drew on and on, until curiosity got the better of me and I croaked, "For what?"

"For not running out of here. I'm not the most pleasant of men." The load of that statement fell heavy on me.

Oh, Dimi.

He nuzzled against the side of my throat, pulling me into his body. A soft moan bubbled out of me. *I would do anything to take the pain away.*

"Do you want to talk about it?" I pressed, unable to help myself.

He laughed roughly. "I had bad news last night. To make a long story short, I need to find a large sum of money to fix the financials. If I don't, it could be a heavy blow to our organization, and it could bring unwanted inquiries."

"How much money?" I hedged, narrowing my eyes.

"Enough that I can't steal it without creating more problems."

Well, that wasn't what I was thinking. If he needed money....

"So getting it legally would be the best course of action?" I clarified, an idea tumbling through my mind.

"Preferably. But that's basically impossible for a criminal to do." He sounded hopeless.

My voice was barely above a whisper. "Will you be in trouble if you don't?"

Dimitri studied me silently. I read the answer in his refusal to comment.

"How bad, Dimitri?"

"You'll be safe, Laurel. I won't let this overflow onto you."

The organ in my chest banged painfully against my ribs. This all started because I wouldn't let him be hurt. I couldn't sit by and do nothing.

You know how to get the money, Laurel.

It was what I was born to do, trained since a child. The hours of education, the summer internships, and the social gatherings—endless nights rubbing elbows.

I could get him the money. But how could I explain my knowledge of the business world while keeping my past a secret? I wavered. It was such a simple problem!

For regular businessmen, it would be easy to find investors. Hell, my father was always doing that for his development projects. But Dimitri was underworld. Did investors line up to shmooze with him?

It could be fun to use that business mental muscle again. And...I could trust Dimitri. On some level. If I was careful. I married him, hadn't I? Me, who didn't have friends. I was saving him. That was a non-negotiable.

He can never know. The world I came from made his look like child's play. The polished men and the glittering ladies would give any criminal organization a run for their money.

He wouldn't find out.

I spun in his hold, bracing my hands on his still damp chest. The feel of those muscles was momentarily distracting. My index finger traced a path over the ink decorating his right pec.

"Like what you see?" There was almost a smile in that question.

I blinked up at him. "I can help you. But you have to promise not to ask how I know what I'm going to tell you."

Those sea blue eyes narrowed.

"I need your promise, Dimitri," I insisted.

"That's a very broad promise."

Shit, he was right. "Okay, well promise me this: If I withhold information, promise you'll respect my secrets and not push me."

"Curiouser and curiouser," he mused.

"Dimitri!" I smacked his chest. "Do you want my help or not?"

"I do." He snatched my finger, bringing the tips to his mouth. Those sea blue eyes heated. "I promise to respect you, Laurel."

"Thank you," I breathed.

"What's this grand scheme you've suddenly cooked up?" he teased gently.

I squared my shoulders. "What we'll do is find investors in your club. We can skew the numbers and forge the financials. You'll make up the difference easily."

"Investors? They won't want to invest in my businesses," he said resignedly.

"They will when I'm done with them. Hell, we can build a legal empire of clubs, venues, or any other venture your little black heart desires," I insisted, packing those words with every drop of determination. I might have fled from that world once, but I was still one of the best players when it came to the game of business.

"Investors will flock to you when I'm done with them. I know their type, I know how to hunt them."

Chapter 29 – Dimitri

While her excitement was infectious, her words sent the animal in me on edge. My grip automatically tightened around her. "You have ten seconds to explain before I go do some hunting of my own."

Just the thought of her surrounding herself with other men made my blood boil.

Laurel blinked at me in confusion. With a little shake of her head, she launched into a diatribe. "The rich like to get richer. You have to go to them and be flashy—that's why fishermen use shiny lures and tantalizing bait. We'll need capital, of course, but you've got that. So we donate and get noticed. Then we make appearances and all you have to do is talk to them. Oh! And the best part, because you're a vetted criminal—"

I snorted.

"—you're not above throwing weight into things. Bribes, blackmail, forced control, or anything else we feel is necessary to bend them to our will. Hell, it's probably going to be so much easier having you as a mobster. I'll show you! Does this make any sense or am I rambling?"

I studied her, letting those words churn in the already mushy pile of thoughts in my mind.

After peeling myself off the floor of my father's office, I'd come to my sanctuary. I hadn't wanted Laurel to see me like the tormented creature I was after an *interview* with the boss. A shirt big enough to hide the marks covered my body. They would fade and be lost in the tattoos soon enough. But...maybe instead of hiding, I should have gone to her. Not right away, of course. But just her presence, steady and bright, had broken through the torment. Normally that didn't happen until I pushed my body to the limits—or spilled a shit ton of blood.

A shudder rolled down my spine.

The pakhan had written me off. He made it clear my mess up wasn't to be tolerated. No doubt he contacted one of the other captains to fix this.

In contrast, here was this incredible woman who was ready to take action for me. Laurel hadn't counted me out.

"Well, what do you think?" She radiated a fierce determination.

I was immediately swept into her conviction.

I let out a low murmur. Her body shivered. "Let's do it."

Relief, closely followed by radiance, shone on her face. "And the capital?"

"I'll give you anything I can."

She nodded, and it was mesmerizing to watch the wheels working behind that bright face. But she stopped suddenly and cocked her head. "Why did you make it sound like a declaration of war just a minute ago?"

I barked a laugh. "Since you're keeping secrets, I wondered if your method for finding investors was of a less than savory variety."

Disgust washed over her face. She jerked back, but I didn't let her go. "Ew! No! I never have, nor ever will be a hooker."

I growled. "Good, because I would flay your John, piece by piece, while you watched."

Instead of scaring her, the little songbird warbled a laugh.

"I'm serious, Laurel. There will be no one else during our arrangement."

Her body shivered again, this time rubbing the ache in my boxer briefs. My fingers slid down the length of her stretchy pants. This had to be the most casual outfit I'd ever seen her in.

Taking a step forward forced her to take one backward.

"There will be no one else," I repeated, reaching between us to cup her pussy. It was hot against my hand.

Laurel's breath caught in her throat. "We already agreed on that."

We did, but what hadn't been said earlier was that I wasn't letting her go. Keeping her and keeping her safe was another matter. But I wasn't above a good challenge.

I squatted, pulling her pants with me. Laurel hissed and looked to the door.

"No one's coming. It's just you and me," I growled before sliding my tongue between the seam of her pussy.

Laurel gasped and clutched my head.

I flicked at her clit before sucking—hard.

"Dimi," she moaned.

"You're never to wear these pants in public," I warned, turning her sharply and pushing her down on the free weight bench. Business could wait. The monster inside needed a taste. "Grab the headrest."

She obeyed.

Her front lay on top of the bench, fingers gripping the edge. I stripped the pants, baring her sweet, glistening pussy. Dropping to my knees, I leaned over and ran my tongue from one end to the other, not stopping until I licked the entire length.

Laurel gasped loudly. "You can't lick *that!*"

"Can't?" I warned. "Baby, I just did."

Her stammering protests were cut off as I continued to suck and devour the entire length. Once she was soaked, which didn't take long, I ripped my own athletic shorts off and mounted the bench behind her.

"I don't like you telling me what I can and can't wear," she countered.

I ran my palms over her ass. "I dare you to wear them, Laurel. I would so love to see your ass glowing bright red."

"Caveman," she clipped.

My palm cracked against her delicious ass. Laurel reared, but I pressed my hand against the middle of her back. "I didn't tell you to let go of the headrest."

When she didn't jump to obey, Laurel earned herself another sharp smack on the backside. She hissed and arched, tempting and tantalizing. I ached for her. Still full of the endorphins from my workout and now given this beautiful image, I couldn't hold back.

I lifted her hips and drove into her in one quick thrust. The tight feel of her nearly sent my eyes rolling into the back of my head.

"Wrap your legs around behind me," I rasped, pulling her more firmly on my dick. I didn't think she had the muscle mass to keep them extended in a full wheelbarrow, but this modification suited me just fine.

With the limited mobility, I rocked into her hot, wet channel.

"This—belongs—to—me." Each word was punctuated by a driving thrust.

Her entire form shook. This angle allowed me to drive deeper and still give her what she needed. I continued to rock into her; the only sounds were her wetness and our hard breathing. When she didn't answer my statement after ample opportunity, I swatted her backside again.

Her pussy gripped tight in response.

It took everything I had not to blow my entire load right then.

"Do you hear how wet you are for me, redbird?" I asked between clenched teeth.

Laurel moaned.

"Look at us." She met my gaze a heartbeat later in the mirror. "Look how I'm fucking your wet little cunt."

"Dimi," she whimpered.

Her cheeks, free from paint and powder, were deliciously rosy. I found the change in her skin my new favorite obsession. Unable to stop myself, I spanked her ass again. Three swift strikes in quick succession. Her pussy convulsed with each swat. Her mewling cries filled the air. Red blossomed over her skin.

My sexy little redbird.

"Don't look away," I ground out, thrusting into her hard. "Watch me as I make you come."

As I spoke, I reached under her and flicked her clit.

Laurel melted. Caught in the wave of her orgasm, I couldn't hold back any longer. The convulsions tore a release straight from my control. I let her.

Her legs unlocked, and I helped her guide her feet to the floor. She braced her chin on her fist and continued to watch me.

"Who knew going to the gym could be so much fun," she confessed, trying and failing to hide the smile.

My lips twitched in response. "Come disturb me whenever you wish, redbird."

"Oh, that we can do." She peered around me. "By the way, that dog is unnaturally quiet."

"Speak," I commanded, and Marena started a series of vicious barking and growling.

"Quiet," I instructed.

There was silence.

"What language was that?" Laurel peered up into my face.

I paused. This woman, who'd flitted into my life, was asking me to reveal a secret. Marena was a weapon, molded into a killing protector who would trade her life for mine if required. I raised her myself and had been strict with her protocol.

No one, not even my cousins, knew what language I used. Nor could they replicate my commands—although it was comical to see Luka try.

I can trust Laurel. Snap decision made, I relinquished a thread of control, gave her a quiet answer, and then I went to the sink and fetched a stick of deodorant from the medicine cabinet above it.

"What was that?" Laurel grinned from ear to ear as she dogged after me. "I swear you mumbled something. But I want to make *damn* sure I heard you right before I give you crap for what I think you said."

Gripping the sink hard, I repeated it quietly.

"Klingon. Like the nerd language?" Laurel burst out laughing. "You're kidding."

"It's obscure," I said defensively.

"Are you a Trekkie?! Oh my word, I married a Trekkie!"

"I haven't seen a single episode of that show." Or many other shows for that matter. "It was a strategy."

My words fell on deaf ears. Laurel rocked back and forth, laughter bubbling out of her. I blew out a short breath, and my lips twitched ever so slightly.

"You'll learn it so you can control her," I decided and called Marena to my side. But there was no getting through to Laurel. She was far too wound up. I turned, rinsed my face, and combed water through my hair. By the time I finished, the righteous, musical sound had ceased. "Come on, let's feed you."

"Me or the dog?" Laurel grinned.

I arched a brow. "Are you hungry?"

"Depends what's on the menu." Laurel made a point of looking down my body, before slowly tracking her eyes back up.

Saints! This woman.

"Did you eat this morning?" I countered.

She shook her head and held up the coffee mug. "I've got fuel, though."

I grunted and led the way to the kitchen. Laying out sandwich items, which I'd requested be added to the grocery list, I began to make her a toasted deli sub.

Laurel scrambled onto the counter and perched beside where I worked. I had to focus on the food, or I would tip her back and dine on the one thing I really wanted.

"What does a typical day in the life of Dimitri Vlasov look like, and how will I fit into that picture?" she asked, head tipping to the side.

"When I'm not going out with my squad, or working on their tactical training, I'm holed up with the manager of my clubs," I explained.

"Ilya, right." Laurel plucked a slice of cheese, folded it, and began to munch.

I flattened my palms and pinned her with a hard look. "You know a lot about us, my little spy."

She nodded. "Enough, yeah."

Those two words were packed with a long conversation we needed to have.

"You'll need space to work on your...investment schemes." My fingers drummed into the countertop, before continuing to build the subs. "So, to answer your question, you'll come with me. When I'm not around, you'll have space at one of the clubs in a proper office." *So you don't have to be here, alone.*

Laurel nodded. "That works for me. Would I be able to come to tactical training?"

"Why?" I shot her a quick glance from the side.

"Gossip," she hissed. "Plus, I'm curious."

Of course, you are. But...that was smart. "We'll have to manage it, so your presence doesn't arouse suspicion."

Laurel nodded. "Oh, and I already met the cook and maid. They didn't say anything useful. Actually, they didn't speak at all," she frowned. "Don't speak unless spoken to."

The house staff were harmless, middle-aged sisters, and only Mila had been married once. They came every morning at five and left by seven at night unless the pakhan held a dinner for his men. However, my father preferred to host at Vasil's. The grandeur went over better there, and it wasn't like my father hosted much these days.

Before his first bout of cancer, there were parties here regularly. It was a little like flirting with a loaded gun if our bratva soldiers survived those evenings. Each party was like Russian Roulette, and sometimes the idiots even played that game. That was why the walls were white. It was easier to paint over the bloodstains than wash them. But then my father had cancer for the first time.

I stopped smoking the moment he told me—a decision he mocked me mercilessly for, even while the chemo made him sick all night.

"The only other staff you'll meet is Zakhar," I explained, stopping Laurel in the hall. "He's not a good man."

Although she continued to smile, the air surrounding her seemed to change. It seemed...forced. No, that wasn't right. Sad?

I screamed inwardly. My little bride was so damn expressive, but she was entirely unreadable.

Like an actress, or perhaps a chameleon.

"Aren't you all *bad* men?" she stage whispered, tone light and teasing, which didn't match the smile.

The muscles of my shoulder tightened. A pang shot through my upper spine and into my head, but I forced the muscles to relax. The last thing I needed was to trigger one of my headaches. My muscles were already tense from the encounter with my father and the ruthless workout I did. It wouldn't take much to irritate the already damaged nerves.

"We are," I ground out. "But the pakhan's manservant is demonic. Possessed. Steer clear of him." *I can't protect you from him.*

It must have been something in my tone. Laurel sobered. "I will. But can I expect much interaction with him?"

"I doubt it. When he's not hiding only God knows where, he's practically glued to my father's side, and the pakhan won't cross your path."

However....

"There's something I want to show you," I added, grabbing her hand and lacing our fingers together.

Slowing, I arched a brow and held up our joined hands between us.

Laurel swallowed hard. "Hand holding is fine."

Not sure I believe what you're tweeting, redbird. But she wasn't pulling, so I gently drew her along. Before reaching the kitchen, I guided us into a small antechamber. The space was stuffy and stale. I set Marena on guard before locking the doors.

Laurel smiled conspiratorially. "Whatcha doing there, mobster?"

I went to the far wall and opened the door to the furnace room. "I need to show you this."

Hurrying over, Laurel peered down the dark, damp stairway. "Ooh! Is this the secret door to the Enterprise, captain?"

I looked at the ceiling. Why?! Why hadn't I told her it was some obscure, dead language? "It's the furnace room."

"Not the dungeon?" she quipped.

"No. We keep prisoners in the far wing, where the thick cement walls dull the screaming."

Laurel nodded along. The smirk on her lips sent a pang through me. She'd been joking.

I hadn't.

"You don't believe me?" I crossed my arms.

"Oh, shit, you were serious!" She snapped her gaze to mine, eyes impossibly wide.

"Yes."

"You have a prison here!" she squeaked.

There was a small voice in my head screaming not to do this. To tell her I was kidding and force a laugh. But my world wasn't a fantasy novel with fun and games. I needed her to take this world seriously. The truth was the only way to keep her safe.

"I said no lies, Laurel. Just in case you get the idea to explore in that pretty little head of yours, don't. I don't want to come home and find you stuck somewhere you should never be."

That sobered her.

"Come on," I urged, hating that these conversations needed to happen.

We descended the narrow stairway. When we reached the bottom, I led her past the furnace, water heaters, and other pipes and electrical boxes.

"You can't tell from the outside." I counted the cinder blocks from the bottom up and from the wall over, and then I pressed the secret catch.

A portion of the wall swung open.

Laurel stumbled back. But it wasn't from fear. Her eyes, those gorgeous eyes, *gleamed*. "You have a secret passage!"

"I do. The pakhan, his brother, and me are the only ones who know." I leaned against the entrance and slid my hands in my pockets. The fingers on my right hand itched for my lighter, but I'd left it in the gym.

"This is so unbelievably cool," Laurel said, excitement dancing through her lyrical tone. "Finally, one redeeming quality about this creepy fortress."

"The term you're looking for is funhouse of horrors."

"Hold up." Laurel raised her hands, another one of her winning smiles plastered on her lips. "Did you just make a joke, mobster?"

"I wish I did," I admitted. "But no, the others call it the funhouse. They are creeped out, and it takes a lot to disorient hardened criminals."

It was exactly what my father intended for this place. It was a statement of power, strength, and horror. It lent to his image.

I hated this house.

"Anyhow, there are a series of tunnels to other access points on the property, one of them is the kennels to gain stealthy access to the vehicle bay," I continued, wanting to get the hell out of the basement. "And one goes to the street and a building that's been condemned. I'll draw you a map. Are you good at memorization?"

"Unfortunately," she sighed dramatically.

When I narrowed my eyes, she covered the comment with a smile. This one I didn't believe.

"I sing. I memorize songs."

Uh-huh, where's the rest of the truth, redbird? But I didn't push. "Good. You'll memorize the map, and we'll burn it. And I can't stress this last point enough. You can*not* tell another soul about this."

"Aye-aye, captain," Laurel gave me a mock salute.

"I'm serious, Laurel. The pakhan won't hesitate to shoot a threat—even you."

Laurel sighed. This time it was real. "I know your father is a real devil, Dimitri. His name is whispered on the streets with shudders of horror, and the religious folk cross themselves." She gave me a small shrug, and the world's smallest smile. "I'm just trying to lighten a gloomy situation."

A pang went through my chest, but I didn't understand that physical reaction or the emotion behind it. "Okay then, so long as you know how dangerous this really is."

"Trust me, I do."

I nodded.

"But why tell me?" She tipped her head, studying me.

I closed the distance, held out my hand, and waited. Laurel slid hers into mine after several heartbeats. Ever so slowly, I lifted mine and slid my touch gently to her wrist, never breaking eye contact with her. "You're not trapped here, Laurel. This isn't your prison. And should you ever need to, you can escape."

But I swear to you, I'll hunt you down. She wouldn't get far, not from me.

I placed my lips on her pulse.

A full body shudder rolled through her.

The moment my lips moved away, she tugged. I released her instantly. She took a step back, drew a long breath through her nose, and gathered her smile once more.

"Thanks for the tour. Now...do you think Scotty will beam us up, captain?"

Oh, fucking hell, what did I start?!

Chapter 30 – Laurel

"Oh! This one," I moaned, sinking into the mattress.

"How big is his room?" Dani looked down at me before sweeping a glance over the California king.

"Big enough, but absolutely empty." I bounced a little. "Oh, the lumbar support! Who would have thought that was so important."

Dani joined in my laughter.

"Get down here." I reached for her wrist and yanked her down. "See what I mean?"

Her moan was loud and sensual. "This bed."

"It will never fit in our apartment," came the surly response. It was easy to forget Dani's husband and his second in command, a dangerous looking man named Pavel, were here. They'd let us wander the mall, holding the bags of baby clothes as we pushed Daniella's adopted daughter around.

"Kaz, please," she insisted, flailing her arms toward him.

"No." The mobster glowered down at us. He had one hand on the stroller, which he rocked back and forth to keep baby Zoey sleeping. The paternal gesture should have been at odds with his seemingly dangerous appearance and the lethal energy he radiated. It wasn't. This monster looked like he was made for fatherhood.

"If I was you, I'd dump the apartment and get the bed," I whispered conspiratorially.

Dani nodded. "I'll work on him."

Pushing up, I signaled the salesperson who was waiting eagerly.

"I'll take this. Have it delivered by five o'clock tonight," I instructed him as I handed him my rewards Visa.

He hurried away.

"She sure is spending a lot of her new husband's money," Pavel muttered, to which Kaz let out a short breath.

I rounded on them, eyes narrowed. "I'll have you know that it's *my* money I've spent today. That makes it my business what I do with it. But if you're so damn nosey, I'll tell you this is my wedding gift to Dimitri."

"Buuurrrnnn," Daniella chuckled softly.

It was only as the men watched me in the aftermath of my outburst that I realized I'd answered their Russian conversation. At least I'd spoken in English. Maybe they wouldn't notice? My heart jumped about, banging into my ribs.

"Maybe Dimi will sleep better if he has a good mattress," Kaz said thoughtfully.

The salesperson came back with the tablet and my card. It was the perfect distraction to calm my racing heart. I filled out my information and the delivery instruction portion. Today had been going perfectly! I had Daniella eating out of my hand. Her cousins had whispered about her not liking my husband, and they had no idea I was onto them. I was just watching, waiting for her to slip.

And it was me who messed up.

"You're going to match the pricing of Bob and Fran's, who are retailers of this brand." I handed the tablet back. "Knock two grand off the price, please."

"It's already on sale." Confusion shifted through the salesperson's face.

"Yes, and it's your corporate policy to price-match all competitors." I waved the tablet insistently at him.

The salesperson deflated. "I can't authorize that."

"You can and you will." I gave him a blistering smile. "And I believe a bedding set with cool-technology pillows are included on purchases over three grand. So be sure to add those. I want the royal blue organic cotton sheets and that black ruched comforter."

Dani came up to stand beside me as the blustering salesperson scuttled away. "You are one hell of a shopper."

"Oh, I haven't even begun," I laughed. "But I've had my eye on these beds, just never had a place big enough for one. Maybe Dimitri will let me knock down a wall so we can make the bedroom even bigger," I mused.

"He has his hands full with this one," Kazimir said in Russian.

Pavel grunted in agreement. "Can't believe she just *showed up* one night."

I kept my gaze trained on the salesperson as he chatted with the manager.

"Do you know where they actually met?" Pavel asked.

It was obvious what the Russians were doing. They were laying bait, and I wasn't going to take it.

"I have my theories," Kazimir said, "but I need to speak to Dimi again. I'm not sure his bride is everything he said she is."

It was time to change the scales. They were suspicious of me? Well! I didn't trust them, either.

"Did your cousin have fun at her birthday?" I engaged with Daniella to prove I wasn't listening to the Russian conversation behind us.

"She did."

"I'm not sure Dimitri did," I admitted, flashing my own bait before her.

Dani's voice rose in a falsetto. "Oh? That's too bad. But I suppose Dimi had a hard time with his dad showing up unexpectedly."

I hummed. "Yeah, that sure was weird."

"Matvei didn't have to ruin the evening," Daniella grumbled quietly.

"I get the sense you don't care for the pakhan." *And you don't like his son.*

"I'm not his biggest fan, no." Dani flicked a glance behind her before adding in a whisper, "He's cruel."

"I've heard." I flexed my fingers, looking at the matte blue nails. They would keep another week before I needed a fill. "Like father, like son."

"So you think so too?" Dani cocked her head. "I thought you liked Dimi. That's why you agreed to help him?"

"Oh, he's a cruel bastard alright," I chirped.

"I'm glad you know that," Daniella stammered.

"Solnyshka," Kaz barked.

Apparently, he had been listening. And he chose to stop his Russian conversation about some book Pavel lent him to halt our hushed gossip.

I could have strangled him.

"Dimi." I tested the diminutive term on my tongue. "I'm going to have to start calling him that."

"It's cute," Daniella admitted.

The salesperson chose that minute to come back with the discounted pricing. He apologized for the delay. I thanked him. My extras were included, plus a restaurant voucher as their gift with purchase.

"Perfect! I got everything I wanted," I chuckled as we left the store.

"We're done then?" Pavel muttered.

Because it was in Russian, I looked at Daniella instead. "We got the baby clothes I was telling you were on sale. We got my mattress. The last thing was a dress for this weekend."

Daniella glanced at the sleeping little girl. "Do you know what you're looking for?"

"Well, I'll show you my favorite place if you promise to keep it a secret," I said conspiratorially.

That called to her inner shopper. She was frugal, and I liked that about her, but she also warmed to my discount shopping. It was too bad I was suspicious of her. I could actually see her being a gal-pal.

And I hadn't had one of those. Ever.

Dashing away the pang from the past, I stayed focused. I needed to corner Daniella in a dressing room, somewhere her husband wouldn't stop her from talking. I had a sneaking suspicion she would tell me things about Dimitri, feel the need to warn me.

That was how I would force her to admit she was opposed to him.

We piled into Kaz's truck and drove into the bougie, urban district. Miraculously, there was a parking spot. The men grumbled in Russian about going into a clothing store. But I was too busy explaining to Daniella that this was where I bought vintage and couture for pennies compared to their original prices.

Her eyes sparkled as we stepped into the used yet upscale clothing boutique.

"Laurie! You're here! It's been too long," Glenda, the co-owner, squealed in French as I wiped my ankle booties on the mat at the door.

"Hi, you," I gushed in response. "This is my cousin, Dani. We need formal gowns, something with a high neck and slit for her figure?"

When I turned, I caught the narrowed look from the men. I gave them a shrug. "There's a café next door. They have the best London Fogs and pastries."

"They do," Glenda added in heavily accented English. "Run away, gentlemen, while I help the ladies."

"We're fine," Kaz said tightly, adjusting his grip on the car seat carrier.

"I could use a coffee," Pavel responded at the same time.

"Great! I'll take a double Stella, large, with cream and cold foam. They'll know what that means," I said, offering Pavel a ten.

He shook his head. "It's on me."

"Thanks, dear." I squeezed his arm. "Dani? Want a coffee?"

"Oh, no. Thank you, though. I'm picky about my espresso drinks, and besides, I already had my max caffeine for the day."

Who has max caffeine intake? But the moment my brain asked it, two possible answers presented themselves. The first was that she was a dancer on a strict regime. The other had me glancing at her waist.

Which was cinched tight in the sweater and jeans hugging her willowy figure.

"The London fog with lavender can be made caffeine free," I offered, turning back to Glenda.

"You know what, that sounds good. I'll take one of those, Pav." Dani flashed him a grin and followed after me.

Kazimir didn't leave but stood like a sentry at the door. He cut a stoney figure, and I wanted so badly to point out that his gargoylesque figure was far more intimidating than Dimitri. But I bit my tongue, waiting for the right time to approach the subject again with Daniella.

"This Boston Belle might just be the thing," Glenda tripped lightly away to snatch a gown from the rack.

"Oh, the darling!" Dani reached for it but ripped her hands back. Her eyes became the size of saucers. "Something like that has to be too expensive."

"It's two hundred," Glenda jumped to say. "It was dropped off by a broke heiress whose grandmother left her only a trunk of clothes. She gave me the lot for change."

"How did you find this place?" Dani whispered.

"I'm good at finding a bargain. Clothes, furniture—I don't mind a project. And because I'm such a good customer, Glenda saves the better pieces for me."

"I'm so glad we met." Dani gently took the gown and held it before her body as she turned in front of the mirror.

"Me too," I laughed. "Even if I did marry a monster," I added in a whisper.

Dani grimaced. "He's really not that bad. They all have hard exteriors, but I'm convinced the insides are good."

I wanted so badly to believe she was sincere. To believe she wasn't involved in a plot against my husband. But I wasn't going to cross her off the suspect list. "You think they all have redeeming qualities?"

"You wouldn't have agreed to help Dimi if you didn't think so," she countered.

Touché. "I won't let anyone hurt him."

Daniella let out a short laugh. "Including his father?"

"Solnyshka!" boomed the voice from across the store.

Damn his hearing! Who had ears that good? "His father?" I mouthed.

Daniella slid into a changing room and pulled me with her. "Just watch yourself, okay? I would hate for anything to happen to you."

I studied her. It was a warning, but from whom was the threat coming?

Chapter 31 – Laurel

A delicious refill of coffee in one hand, while in the other, a dress bag with a satin gown in navy that would make it look like the midnight sky wrapped around my body, and I felt a thousand times better. It might have been a bust in fishing for information, but at least I'd laid some groundwork.

The cousins dropped me at the house. Holding my three purchases, I pushed inside the front door, where the warm feelings of the day were instantly squashed.

"It's you," my father-in-law sneered from where he stood halfway on the stairs, a lean, scarred middle-aged man behind him.

Something slimy slithered over my skin at the sound of that voice. I snapped my attention to the pakhan and offered him a friendly smile that I didn't feel.

"Good evening, sir," I greeted. "Lovely to see you again."

Cold, emotionless eyes ran over me. "What does he see in her?"

The man he spoke to didn't comment. Didn't laugh. Didn't *do* anything. He stood there, lifeless gaze boring into me.

I was struck with the sense that this being was devoid of human emotion.

"Well, I don't know why my son chose such a heifer," the pakhan snorted. "But if she's giving him the milk, who am I to argue."

Those words struck deep. My stomach flipped and I wanted nothing more than to pull my coat protectively over my stomach. At the same time, my defense mechanism sprang to the rescue and harsh words were on the tip of my tongue. But before I could challenge the mob boss, warning bells rang loudly enough through my mind that I paused.

He hadn't spoken in English.

Although it took every drop of my strength, I continued to smile as though I hadn't understood the jab. The pakhan and his emotionless shadow continued to descend, and without saying anything else to me, they disappeared out the front door.

I sprinted to the safety of Dimitri's room. Once the door closed behind me, my eyes prickled. I rubbed a hand across my suddenly tight chest. Air tried and failed to flow calmly into my lungs.

"He's a hateful old man." *I won't let him make me feel less. He doesn't have my permission to bring me down.*

I would keep telling myself that until I believed it. They were the words that drove me to the Midwest. They were the building blocks of my new life. I repeated them daily until I could reach for them in moments like this. Struggling through the turbulent emotions, I didn't pay attention to the bedroom. When something hard bumped against my legs, I yelped and jumped high in the air.

"Marena!" I gasped, slapping a palm on my chest. "You sneaky little ghost!"

She thumped her tail and nudged me with her nose.

I bent and scratched her head. "It's so hard to believe such a man parented Dimi."

That name. I liked it a little too much. Focusing on those warmer feelings, and the soft puppy under my touch, I pulled myself together.

There could only be one main character in my story. And it was me. I was the winner.

"Alright, puppy, let's not let the bitter old bastard make us feel bad, eh?" I patted her neck and rose. "Oh! I almost forgot, look what I got for you."

Hanging my dress bag on the rack, I pulled the bag with the other items off my wrist. Marena nudged my thigh.

"You smell them, don't you." I grinned.

Opening the cellophane bag and pocketing the twisty tie, I pulled one of the gourmet dog cookies from the bag.

Slowly, as if she couldn't believe it really was for her, Marena leaned forward. Her mouth opened, and she gently plucked the cookie. In a rush, she turned and trotted to the bathroom.

Hiding to eat her treat. Poor girl. She wasn't used to having things all to herself, if I was reading the body language correctly based on what I knew from the dog books.

I bustled about the room, hanging my coat and slipping out of my ankle boots. When Marena reappeared, licking her chops, I squatted down. "Come here, girl."

She trotted over.

Scratching around her thick, chain link collar, I fumbled with the buckle. When it was off, I massaged the fur and skin under the spot. Bringing out the final purchase, I held it for her examination.

"I liked the rhinestones, but those might come off easily. But this one has hand stitching in the leather." I began to buckle the new collar on. "Royal blue and russet hair are the best combination, don't you agree?"

Marena sneezed.

"Trust me, I know what I'm talking about." I finished and had to admit the new collar was much prettier. "Here, one more cookie and then I have to get to work."

She took the offered treat and scampered back to the bathroom.

Going to the bed, I folded the comforter and set it plus the pillows on Dimitri's dresser. It took all my soft muscles to lift the mattress. It might be full, but it was heavy and very old. Yet I managed to drag the damn thing into the hall. The box spring was next. And finally, it was a matter of dismantling the metal frame.

One of my nails chipped. An unfortunate casualty, but the battle was won.

Standing in the empty room and looking at the dust and debris collected under the space where the bed had stood, an idea popped into my head.

I looked down at Marena. "What if the pakhan wants his own son out of the picture?"

A chill rippled down my spine. It would fit the old man's nature. But two things challenged that idea. The first was that the pakhan would likely just shoot Dimitri in cold blood. The second was that he didn't stand to gain anything from such a move.

"Leave no stone unturned," I muttered. If I suspected the cousin and his new bride, I could also watch the pakhan.

Happy with the progress, I set off to the kitchen.

"Ania," I called, sailing into the space. "Where would I find a vacuum?"

The housekeeper gaped at me.

Mila, the cook, was slicing a beef roast. I snatched a slice of meat from the tray and munched on it while breaking and throwing pieces to the hound glued to my side.

"There has to be a vacuum," I insisted.

"What do you need it for?" the maid stammered.

"Cleaning." I took three deep breaths so as not to add anything else.

"Gold diggers clean?" the cook whispered in Russian.

I bit the inside of my cheek. So that was what they thought I was? Ha! It mirrored the reaction Kazimir and Pavel had at the mall. By not reacting, I hoped they would feel more comfortable to gossip around me in the future.

"Vacuum?" I insisted, speaking slowly and making pushing motions with my hands.

"This way." The wizened woman took me to the hall closet. The cook followed, watching from the door.

"Thank you," I said, plucking the Dyson from the space and enjoying their curious stares.

Chapter 32 – Dimitri

Long notes floated down the hall. I paused at the threshold of my room, where a vacuum cleaner blocked my path. Laurel sang something about the sky falling at the top of her lungs. The snowy beauty stole the very breath from my lungs. She could *sing.* Her voice lifted and fell, packed with emotion. The words conveyed more feeling than meaning. My guard dog pricked her ears and watched me, but my beautiful bride was oblivious to my presence haunting the doorframe.

Laurel smoothed the bedspread and nodded approvingly. As she turned, the song turned into a short scream.

"You two are going to steal all my nine lives!" she gasped.

"Two?" I narrowed my eyes.

Still breathing hard, she stabbed a finger at the dog. "Did you make a pact to sneak up and scare the living crap out of me?"

Avoiding her accusation, I asked, "What is my dog wearing?"

Laurel flicked a glance to Marena. "I understand the point of a training collar, but it looks like a torture device."

"She's a guard dog. A weapon." I rubbed my jaw.

"So? Now she's cute too."

"She's trained to kill on command." I let out an exasperated breath, knowing this was a battle I wasn't going to win.

Laurel arched a brow. "She can't kill with a pretty collar?"

I give up. I ran a glance down my wife's sensual, curvy body. "What's with your fancy dress?"

The light green material hugged her middle but covered little else. The straps on her shoulders resembled dental floss and the skirt was cut at an angle. The right side was long in a sharp triangle, while the left rested high on her hip.

It was not a dress to do housework in.

But that was exactly what this bombshell was doing. Her curled hair hung in a drape down her back and the paint on her face lent a fierce expression.

"Didn't you get my text about dinner reservations?" she snapped, propping a hand on her hip.

"I did, but I still don't understand why I have to offer the man a job at my club. The only one that serves food has bar food." I leaned against the doorframe and rubbed my chin.

Laurel rolled her eyes and waved her hand. "Proposed business expansion. That's what they're investing in, and they'll pay more than the expansion is worth. I'll explain everything on the way over. Oh, by the way, I'm rearranging our rooms. I can't sleep in a tomb."

Her sentence ended on a yelp. I snatched her upper arm and hauled her into my space. "Roll your eyes again, redbird. I dare you."

A smoldering pause ensued. Her hard breathing filled the silence, and my pulse ticked up in response. Her gaze dropped to my mouth. That pretty little red tongue darted out to wet her bottom lip before her teeth grazed the area.

"I would," she panted, finally dragging her gaze back to mine. "But we'll be late for dinner."

Saints! That challenge in her eyes was magnificent.

"With such a ridiculous husband, it won't be the last time I roll them," she promised softly.

I wanted to tell her to screw dinner. That there were far more important things.

But I was in hot water with the Bratva, and Laurel was working tirelessly to get me out of it.

"You're not going in that dress," I growled.

"Excuse me?" Laurel reared back. Indignation flashed across her face. It was hotter than the eyeroll.

The urge to push her down to the floor and fuck her mercilessly was powerful enough to consume every other rational thought. I had to fight to shake the feeling away. Even then, the mental image of her screaming my name was too strong to completely shatter.

My voice was strained. "Do you have a shawl?" I rasped.

I knew she put care into her clothing choices. If this was what she chose, she had a plan. That was all well and good, and I could respect it on some level. However, there was no way in hell I was letting those gorgeous tits fall out of the dress in front of other men.

The moment we were alone, however, those straps would be only too easy to pluck.

Her eyes narrowed. “Fine, neanderthal.”

I grinned. “It’s cute when you call me names, redbird. But just know I’m not above filling your mouth with something in punishment.”

Her mouth dropped open. “Well, if I knew that was all it took....”

I tipped my head and studied her. “What do you mean?”

“You— You—” She gulped. “You smiled.”

The words came out in a whisper.

“You *smiled*, mobster.” Her own mouth turned up in the brightest of glows.

I felt the flash of her attention to my toes. It buzzed through my veins. Stronger than any liquor, yet without the burn. Sending my heart soaring while keeping my feet on the ground. I would have to do it again if it produced this kind of reaction.

“Come on, we don’t want to be late,” I said, tugging her along. “And on the drive, you can explain what in the hell you’ve done to the bedroom.”

Chapter 33 – Laurel

Dinner was a success. The cook was flattered that we wanted him for a new, albeit secret, restaurant we were opening in one of the clubs. He apologized, but he said had a contract, which I already knew he would. The restaurant's back of staff would buzz over the news and word would travel fast to the owners. Mr. Lambcox was one of the biggest Food and Beverage guys in the Midwest. He owned many chains and franchises, but a thorough search showed that he had upscale establishments. He bought, rebranded, and rarely sold his ventures. We'd already made a sizeable donation to a charity the wife was on the board of. The groundwork was laid for Saturday night's gala. I could practically see the cheque in my mind's eye that this investor would make out to Dimitri.

There might not ever *be* a restaurant. But that wasn't the important thing.

One trap was laid, so it would be easy to hunt for more. I stretched in the elevator, feeling the weight of Dimitri's eyes on me.

"How did you know about this?" Dimitri jerked his chin. "How did you know specifically to play this hand? And how did you learn this game in the first place?"

I shrugged and told him as much of the truth as I dared. "I wasn't born into bartending at a strip joint."

"Hmm...." That sound was low and rich. It sent a rush of warmth skittering over my body. "I knew you were special, Laurel, but I had no idea you were able to walk in the world of business sharks."

It was a subtle kind of prying. I chewed on the inside of my cheek, watching him carefully. He wasn't supposed to be asking me questions. But I felt the need to give him something, even a small tidbit. "The males played the game of business thrones. My mother groomed me to play a more subtle but far more powerful version. One that women played traditionally for centuries." I paused and laughed up at the ceiling. "One I that I didn't think I'd play again."

"Whatever this game is, you're very good at it."

Warmth stained my cheeks, but I knew it wasn't visible with the makeup. I smoothed my hands over the beautiful dress. "Thanks," I mumbled.

"Hey, where's my songbird with her proud backbone?" Dimitri's fingers gripped my chin and lifted it.

Not wanting to admit that he so easily got past my guard, that wearing a mask around him was damn near impossible, I wet my lips. His sharp, predatorial gaze dropped and tracked the movement. It was scary to be back in this world even with a predator at my side like this Russian prince. I didn't need Dimitri to know how thin the veil was between my sanity and control. I didn't think he would turn on me, but because he held this strange power over me, it made it hard to trust him.

So I closed the distance and kissed him, effectively cutting off any further conversation about my past.

His tongue slid into my mouth, demanding and hot. I moaned against his touch. Circling my arms around his neck, I clung to him.

A sharp hiss of air brushed against me, and Dimitri pulled my hands lower on his trap muscles instead of the neck.

The ding of the elevator had me jumping apart. Dimitri stared at me with a hooded gaze. There was an unspoken promise there, and I couldn't wait to get home. *Such a handsome husband....* Grinning like an idiot, I fished through my handbag for my compact as we left the elevator.

Dimitri tossed his number tag to the valet, who hopped to attention.

"Oh, shoot," I muttered, double and triple checking.

"What?" Dimitri murmured, pulling me into his side.

"I left my compact on the table." I frowned, looking over my shoulder at the elevator. "It was an antique."

And one of the few items I owned that I paid full market price for, which made my klutzy mistake of leaving it so terrible.

"Stay," he commanded, pressing his fingers into my side before slipping away.

I watched him jog back to the elevator and press the button. The ride to the 65th floor would be short, but my heart pinched as I watched the doors slide closed.

Such a good husband....

"Husband." I played the word over on my tongue. "*My* husband."

Marriage was a business deal in the world I came from. Socialites chose suitable mates and family approval was necessary for longevity. That was why this arrangement never bothered me.

As I checked my lipstick in my phone's camera, a wide smile stared back at me. I wandered to the windows that acted as an exterior wall for the skyscraper's lobby. Downtown wasn't too busy, but there was something about the bleak, desolate streets that made me suddenly convulse with shivers. I pulled the coat tightly around my shoulders.

A flash of movement had me turning. A man pointed a camera lens at me and captured the look of outrage I gave him. I dashed for the revolving door, spun out into the street, and hollered at the man. The old New York accent came out strong, my tongue reverting to the world of my childhood.

The man took off running, black ballcap pulled to cover his features. Although on the opposite side of the street, I kept pace with him. And I did it in heels! We thundered down the sidewalk, until a nondescript car with tinted windows pulled alongside the cameraman.

He snapped one last picture before ducking into a car.

I snapped one of my own, catching the license plate number.

Huffing, I glared at the taillights. "Bastard."

I doubted the man was press. Paparazzi had a way of baiting. This one hadn't wanted me to see him. It might have had something to do with Dimitri. And it wasn't like I would have noticed the cameraman in the traffic when we'd arrived at the restaurant.

Turning and retracing my steps, I winced at how far I'd run. What had I been thinking?! Was I going to tackle the guy? Make him spill his beans? I wasn't a brute like the Bratva soldiers.

A sinking feeling pulled at my stomach. I huddled into my coat. *What if he was tracking me?*

It was possible my parents were still trying to locate me after all these years. But I'd hidden my trail so well. And I looked nothing like the girl that left the Big Apple.

No, it couldn't be that.

It had to be my Bratva husband.

A warning prickled my neck right before two hands shot out and grabbed me. I let out a high-pitched scream that was cut off by a foul smelling glove.

"What do we have here?" a voice cackled.

"It's so late for a pretty treat such as yourself to be walking the streets alone," a second male laughed.

The instinct to fight spiking in my veins was at odds with the cloying, suffocating memory of past horrors threatening to choke me. I struggled, writhing and lashing out. Kicking and flailing. I could have sunk to the ground, taking my captor with me, but that could have given him leverage to trap me.

"Get her in the van," the second voice urged.

Fight! I need to fight! I struggled. I bucked. I kicked my heels.

But my lungs didn't work. I couldn't breathe, and not because of his hand. My vision narrowed.

"She's heavy," the first whined, tugging me deeper into the alley. "Can't we just enjoy her here and leave her?"

"We're so exposed downtown," the second countered, but there was hesitation thick in his voice.

No. No! They were going to take me away. *I'm a survivor; I can fight!* I'd done it before, hadn't I? I could do it again. I would do it now! I reached deep inside, found the will to overcome, and I channeled it.

"Help me! She's bucking like those rodeo cows!" the man holding me protested.

There was a grunt from behind me. Satisfaction made my heart leap!

I focused on fighting the would-be abductors, instead of fighting the past. This was my enemy. Right here, right now.

My head wrenched to the side and my scalp screamed under the unforgiving hold of the second man.

"Let her go." The cold threat cracked through the air.

Dimi!

I struggled harder. My prince of darkness, if only I could reach him.

"I won't say it again. Let go of my wife," he said quietly, but the threat cut like a whip.

"It's one of the Ruskis," the man not holding me murmured. "Vlasov's men."

The crazed man giggled. Actually giggled! "We couldn't resist Ruski. What were you doing letting your prize wander the streets?"

"Laurel," Dimitri said, and then he said the word he used with Marena to lay down.

I obeyed.

My weight and the suddenness with which I dropped gave me the advantage. The man's arms slipped.

Two soft claps of thunder echoed through the alley. Gunshots. I gulped air, scrambling on hands and knees across the filthy, frozen pavement.

Two hard hands gently grasped me under the arms and hauled me to my feet. The anger rolling off Dimitri was tangible. But I didn't care. I was safe. I buried my head against his chest.

"If you hadn't screamed—" he began but stopped.

I was too busy rubbing my wrists, my forearms—my hands. They'd captured me. I couldn't move.

"Deep breaths, redbird. Come on, take a deep breath for me." Hot fingers brushed against my cheek.

The nightmares slunk to their boxes, and I relocked the lids once I was assured the new one joined them. The shaking stopped after several minutes. Somewhere close by came hushed voices, but I ignored the conversation. Besides, it wasn't in English, and it was on Dimitri's cellphone, I realized.

And then, Dimitri wrapped me in a tight hug.

Chapter 34 – Dimitri

I couldn't think straight. That man had his hands on her, his body pressed against her. *He was going to take her.*

My fingers tightened around the handle of my pistol. Laurel was mine. If I'd been thinking clearly, I would have kept the filth alive and taken my time with them.

"He had me," Laurel wheezed, gaze darting wildly about. "I couldn't get away."

The urge to scream at her for leaving the relative safety of the lobby bubbled up my throat yet again.

A choked sob escaped her lips before she pressed them tightly together. "I'm sorry, it's just…. I don't like being trapped."

And why is that, little redbird? Hmm? Who dared trap you? The anger ebbed and my gut twisted. I squeezed her close. "I don't ever want to see you like that again."

"Trust me, that makes two of us," she hiccupped.

Doors on a truck slammed and two bodies sauntered into the alley. I gave clipped instructions. The phantasmic forms nodded. The one was mute and the other spoke as little as possible. The cleanup crew set to work removing the bodies. There were few men my father held respect for. And the pakhan kept a healthy distance from the Igorevich Brothers. Their hair was the color of cream, and their skin probably hadn't seen sunlight in decades. But they were damn good at cleaning up messes. Loyal and quiet, I planned to keep them employed when the rule passed to me.

It was time to go.

I pulled Laurel from the alley. Back on the downtown street, light twinkled. Their cheery atmosphere was at odds with the blast of winter wind. Early March didn't bring reprieve from the bitter temperatures.

Gently as possible, I folded Laurel into the passenger seat. Once around to my side, I slammed the door. Laurel jumped.

"Sorry," I muttered.

"Dimi, wait." Her reddened hand came down over mine. The cold had instantly chapped her skin. I placed mine over hers to keep it warm. But she was talking again. "And that's why I ran. I think it has to do with the assassination attempt on you."

Dread pulsed through my veins. I swept a look around us. Kaz's technology company made trinkets, so there was no fear of a bomb. But a shooter? A sniper? *A knife in the back.*

Dammit.

I cranked the car into first gear and peeled from the curb. A horn blared, but I was already weaving around the evening traffic. Stabbing the Bluetooth screen, I dialed Kazimir.

"Yes?" The exasperated voice filled the car.

"I need you to run a license plate," I said and then explained the evening.

Kazimir let out a low breath. "I'll get dressed."

A feminine protest sounded. Weeks ago, I was disgusted at my cousin for being so wrapped up with a female. Now...I understood the need to be constantly naked and tangled.

"I'll drop Laurel at the fortress and then backtrack," I offered, giving them the chance to romp.

Clammy fingers threaded through mine over the gear shifter. I shot my girl a glance to see her shake her head.

"I want to stay with you," she breathed. "Please, Dimi."

There was nothing I wouldn't deny her. "Okay, change of plans, Laurel is coming with me."

Dani whooped in the background. Kaz gave me a clipped response and ended the call.

We drove in silence, but as I found a parking spot in the apartment's underground garage, I formulated what I wanted to say. I cut the engine, turned in my seat, and cupped Laurel's face in my hand.

"You don't have to tell me if you're not ready. But I'm going to need you to give me a name, so they never hurt you again. Okay, redbird?" I searched her wide eyes. They were nearly black here in the shadows.

"You can't promise me that." Her lip wobbled, but there wasn't a tremor in her voice.

"Yes, I can," I growled. "And no one is ever going to trap you again."

But she only shook her head. "He had his arms wrapped around me, Dimi. You were there tonight, but what if you're not next time?"

As much as I wanted to roar that there was never going to be a next time, I bit my tongue.

"You've got me now, and that's all that matters." She turned her head and placed a kiss on my wrist. "Let's get upstairs. I need a cocktail."

Dani poured a diet coke onto a healthy amount of rum. I watched curiously as Laurel accepted the beverage and drained the thing a few gulps. It was hard not to be painfully distracted by her throat working. Those crimson red lips clasped around the glass.

That gorgeous dress....

My pulse ticked up a few notches. *Saints, she's beautiful.*

"It's a stolen vehicle." Kazimir pushed the Bluetooth mouse away in disgust. He slid a look at the women, and then jerked his chin toward the windows.

Reluctantly, I followed him onto the balcony. "What?" I snapped.

"I don't trust your bride."

The words slapped me, and the wind chuckled as it played with the strands of my hair. "Excuse me?"

"She came into your life with the news. She wrapped herself around your finger. And now, she was the one who *saw* the cameraman?" Kazimir ticked the accusations on his finger.

"Unbelievable," I snarled, cutting my hand through the air.

Kazimir stepped into me. "You offered me the position as your second. I wouldn't be doing my job if I wasn't watching your damn back."

And then my cousin had the nerve to stab his finger into my sternum.

I swatted it away, grabbing a fistful of his shirt. "I will take your advice into consideration, but only because you're my second." I cut a look to the women who were jabbering in the kitchen, completely oblivious to the testosterone shitstorm brewing outside. "But if you threaten my wife, I'll end you so damn quick. Got that?"

There was a pause where only our breathing thickened the air.

"Damn, cuz, you like her."

"I do." I released Kaz and wrenched the door open. But before I opened it, I stopped, dropped my head to look over my shoulder, and murmured, "Thanks for watching my back."

"That's my job."

Unbelievable. My own cousin didn't trust my wife. He knew the deal, that she was here to help me catch my assassin. There was a probability in his claim, but I knew in my gut he was wrong about her. So damn wrong.

But until I could prove it to him, this would be a thorn in my side.

As if I don't already have enough problems.

We trailed into the kitchen, where Dani clapped her hands and did a little twirl. Kazimir pushed past me and captured her in his arms. "What's got you all excited, solnyshka?"

She beamed up at him. "We're taking Bratva soldier training."

"Like hell you are!" Kazimir crowed over her, but she struggled out of his hold.

"Nadia was a soldier, and you have other women in your ranks!" She flung her arms wide and leaned right into Kaz's face. "Why can't we?"

"You want to be a fighter?" I took the seat beside Laurel, not sure how she felt about PDA. Timeline-wise, we were fresh dating. But the patter of my heart warned me we were long past that. Still, I didn't want her uncomfortable.

"I don't want to brawl in the streets with your men." Laurel arched a dark brow at me, mischief dancing on her lips. "But yes, I want to be able to defend myself."

"I'll train you then," I agreed.

Laurel reached out, crossing the distance, and wrapped her fingers over my wrist. "Perfect."

"And you'll train me." Dani jerked her chin up.

I had to give it to her, she had no fear, not a drop. And Kazimir was known for making grown men weep before their one-way ticket to kingdom come.

In that respect, there was a big similarity between her and my bride. Both she-wolves amongst predators.

Chapter 35 – Laurel

Clicking on the website design, I finalized the plans for our restaurant expansion project. The brand evoked elegance on a budget. With the domain name registered and social media accounts saved, a trickle of pride slithered through me. We were actually going to open this place! The contractor would give us numbers, which we would fudge and present to investors as a larger sum. With some careful accounting, the money would make up for more than what Dimitri was replacing.

We could really do this. Not just the restaurant expansion. I told him we could build an entertainment empire—hotels, clubs, venues, and eateries.

I shot a glance to Dimitri. Would he go for it? There was only one way to find out.

"If the bratva grows, won't you need new places to wash money?" I reached into my brand-new backpack for the sustenance I brought to work today.

It took a heartbeat for the mobster to tear away from whatever he was reading. He glanced at me. "Sorry, babe, what was that?"

Warmth spread through my insides. Tearing open the package of sugary, fruity powder, I tipped my head back and poured some onto my tongue, ignoring the chalk stick that I was supposed to dip and coat.

That action caught his attention.

I swallowed, sighed, and met his gaze. "Instead of stopping with the update to the current club, why don't we also open a few more venues?"

Swiping a hand over his face, Dimitri let out a long breath. "The pakhan won't go for it."

"He doesn't want to grow." It wasn't a question.

But Dimitri nodded.

"What does the next pakhan think?" I tipped the rest of the sugar powder into my mouth.

"He thinks his wife is sexy as hell." Dimitri pushed away from his desk. "Come over here."

I shook my head, reaching for the swirled lollipop. The wrapper fluttered to the desktop, and I popped the candy between my lips. The weight of his glare burned. I popped my lips, before running my tongue over the sugar sweetness. A soft sigh escaped my lips. It had been a few days without candy, and I'd been in danger of going into withdrawal.

Something volatile crackled through the room.

"It wasn't a suggestion, redbird."

Slipping my feet from my clogs, I arranged my chair. With a smirk, I cut him a look, held his stare for a moment, and then rolled my eyes.

Dimitri shot out of his seat.

I timed it perfectly. I shoved my chair in his direction and bolted. The office door crashed into the wall. The slapping of my feet echoed along the corridor. Wild, reckless laughter rang through my mind as I darted around a corner. This had to be the first time in my life that I was so free.

As I dashed through the empty club, my heart thundered in my chest, a wild rhythm that echoed through the silence of the deserted corridors. The air was thick with the musty scent of sweaty bodies and spilled booze. It mingled with the sweet tang of desire that flooded my senses. The chilly brush of the forced air caressed my skin. Delight shivered through my veins, knowing such a dangerous beast charged after me.

The thrill of the chase drove me to run faster than I had run in ages. Each breath came in on a ragged gasp and needed force to exhale. The anticipation of the impending collision helped with my poor cardio skills.

The mobster was going to catch me. In fact, I was surprised I traveled as far as I did. I was near the front lobby of the club—the empty club.

There was only one place to go.

Spinning on a dime, I narrowly avoided the force of nature barreling through the swinging door. I squeaked and rushed into the dance hall. Dimitri tore after me.

I spun around, arms wide. "Safe! I win," I panted and popped the sucker between my lips.

Dimitri stalked forward. He ripped the candy out and his hard kiss replaced the sweet.

Caught by the mobster. Exactly where I wanted to be. Electricity crackled where our bodies were connected. It buzzed through my veins, leaving me alive, breathing hard, and delirious.

And soaking wet.

Who knew this primal side was such a turn-on? I needed this. Every inch of him.

I wrapped my arms around his neck, ready to pull him over me.

But Dimitri caught my wrists.

Panic sliced through the moment. *It's just Dimitri.*

He'd been making a point of touching my hands, my wrists, and my arms. He would kiss and caress, never capture. This time, he held them. "This is what happens when you tempt a monster, little songbird."

A whimper broke from my lips as I suddenly battled to breathe for a different reason.

Dimitri released one of my arms and reached out. "Lick."

I blinked. The tunnel I was fast falling down made reality sway. I couldn't comprehend what was happening.

"I said, lick." Something hard and *sweet* pushed between my lips.

My tongue flicked against the candy.

"See, you can obey." Dimitri pulled the sucker away. "Now *watch.*"

Trying, I focused on the colorful candy. It swiped against the inside of my wrist. The iron hold shifted to my elbow. And Dimitri's mouth latched onto the skin.

He sucked.

A sharp breath caught in my throat.

The panic drained, swirling away into the recesses, and it was replaced with need. Raw and desperate.

"I thought you didn't like candy?" The words came out with an audible tremor.

Dimitri straightened and stage walked me backward. Something solid crashed mid-spine.

"Suck," he growled as he shoved the candy between my lips.

Eyes glued on him, I missed the tell that he was reaching for me. The next moment I was in the air. My butt landed hard on a ledge. The bar top—it was the bar top. Instead of swallowing, I choked on the sugar and saliva as it trickled down my throat.

His voice was hard, packed with tangible darkness. "Swallow, redbird."

Heaven help me, I did.

The mobster yanked the faux leather pants and lacey thong down my legs. Cool air prickled the skin. But his hot touch skimmed up my thighs a moment later. Dimitri plucked the lollipop. His hand dropped. The slick candy rubbed against my exposed pussy.

My gasp felt as though I were inhaling fire. There wasn't a chance to protest that food didn't belong down there.

Dimitri's tongue replaced the sucker. He lapped the trail of sugar.

We might have agreed this thing between us was fake, but the raw chemistry crackling between us was real enough. It didn't matter how long this relationship lasted, I was going to soak up every minute of it.

I needed to tumble into the void, burn from the blinding pleasure we created.

"More. Please," I moaned.

He grinned against my pussy. "Look at your hand, redbird."

The sight of his fingers gripping my wrist sent a bolt straight through my chest.

Dimitri sucked hard on my clit. The pleasure was enough to dispel the rapid thumping inside.

"More," I begged.

Slowly, he drew my hand down. The sucker remained firmly grasped in his other fist. It wasn't the sugar he put on my inner wrist this time. It was me. He rubbed my wrist against my hot, sensitive pussy, before lifting my forearm and holding it in an unforgiving grasp.

A wicked smirk played on his lips. "You said your wrists were a limit. I'll let them go, apologize, and grovel for touching them."

"No," I whimpered. "You can hold them."

His grip vised on my forearm. "What else? Is this as far as you want?"

My head cracked back and forth. "No, you can kiss," I stammered.

Those soft yet hard lips pressed against my fingers, blazing a path down the palm before he stopped.

"Suck," I whispered. "Please, mobster."

His hot mouth clamped over my pulse. Dimitri sucked hard.

Heat flushed between my legs. I rubbed them together, desperate to relieve the ache.

Dimitri's tongue swirled up and down the tendon of my inner arm. He licked the entire length. Teeth scored the skin, lips caressed the flesh. Just before I screamed for relief, he shifted and lowered his body. That hot mouth closed over my pussy.

I sighed in relief. My head fell back, eyelids fluttering closed.

If his mouth worshiped my forearm, it devoured my pussy. Pleasure built, racing to find that much needed release. I bucked against him. My legs couldn't spread. I couldn't wrap them around his head. likewise, my body was trapped. I couldn't lay down, I couldn't open for him.

Needy, feminine noises trickled from my throat. It was right there, so close I could taste it!

"Dimitri," I whimpered, tipping into his mouth as far as I could.

"Yes, redbird?"

"Please?" I implored him.

"No."

My eyes snapped open in horror. His smirk turned into a low, rough laugh.

That was when I heard a distant voice shouting the mobster's name.

Dimitri tugged me off the bar top, catching me and setting me down gently.

"What—what!" I protested.

Bending, he pulled my pants back up my thighs. His hard grasp caught my chin, and he brought my mouth to his in a hard kiss. There was the hint of candy, but it wasn't strong enough to cover the taste that was all me. I flicked my tongue against his lips. A returning swipe of his own made the mobster groan.

"Ilya's timing couldn't have been more perfect," he said gruffly, pulling back. "Naughty girls who roll their eyes don't get to come."

If my eyes could shoot him, I would have unloaded a magazine in his chest. There would be hundreds of holes where the bullets sank into his flesh. Blood would spray, and I would dance in the mess.

"Hide behind the bar," Dimitri commanded, giving me a push to the opening.

"Like hell, I'm going to do that!" I planted my hands on my hips.

That was the wrong thing to say. Dimitri's hand shot out and clasped my throat. He didn't choke me, but it wasn't gentle. "Keep pushing me, redbird, and I'll make sure you don't come for the next week."

A violent protest bubbled up inside me. "How dare you!"

Dimitri chuckled darkly. "Your pretty little cunt is throbbing between your legs, isn't it?"

I pursed my lips. I might just stab him in his sleep. Not that he'd slept in the new bed I bought yet—but that was another matter entirely.

"In here, Ilya!" Dimitri boomed. He walked me back, forced me down, and slid his unforgiving touch back into my hair. "No other man, not even my best friend, gets to see you like this. Hot and sexed. That wild look in your eye is for me alone. Stay down, redbird."

And then he was gone.

His friend clipped out something harsh in Russian, as he came into the club's dance hall. Dimitri responded.

I was too angry to pay attention. Fuming! An explosion simmered under the surface. But—

The power of that man's command was strong enough to keep it at bay.

What the hell has he done to me? This strange control, it was a tangible thing, binding me. Making me obey. And—and—

"I don't hate it," I gulped.

"Did you bring the masks?" Dimitri asked.

I snapped my attention to the two men.

"Of course, I brought the damn masks. Five targets tonight? Dump them in Flannigan's territory?" Ilya rasped.

That man always sounded angry.

"No, six," Dimitri growled. "I want the idiot guard, Jasha, disposed of. He keeps looking at my wife."

"He's had it coming," Ilya agreed. "Six it is. If we can't hit all, then we'll save Anton for next week."

"Done."

There was a shuffle. "Aren't you coming, brother?"

"There's something I have to take care of quickly. I'm going to have Laurel sleep here tonight."

Ilya grunted. "Wait, hold up. Is that a lollipop?"

"What of it?"

"You *hate* sweets."

A dark chuckle crackled. "Not all sweets, apparently."

Ilya grunted again. "Meet you at the truck in five."

"Done."

There was a pause, and then Dimitri appeared before me. "I have to go."

Playing along that I hadn't overheard, I huffed. "Really?"

He nodded. "You can stay here, and I'll try to be back. But if not, there's a pull-out bed in my office."

I scowled up at him.

"And Laurel?"

"Yes?" I sassed.

Dimitri pulled me to my feet. His palm cupped my cheek. "If you play with yourself, I'll know."

No, you won't.

But the dangerous promise in his eyes warned me it would be a losing battle. "Where are you going?" I demanded, in an attempt to distract myself from the blistering ache between my legs.

"To take care of known bratva who dislike me."

The complete honesty of that statement sent a shock through me. "Oh," I breathed.

Dimitri nodded. "We've been slowly eliminating those who we know will cause problems when my father dies."

"Preventing an internal war." I nodded. "Smart."

His thumb rubbed back and forth under my eye. "Incredible," he whispered in Russian.

It was a struggle not to comment. "Shouldn't I go with you?"

Dimitri shook his. "Stay. Order pizza. Watch a movie. Sleep."

I looked around. The bar would open in a couple of hours. I hadn't bartended since this fake marriage. Maybe I could make a little pocket change. While I was contemplating the evening before me, Dimitri slid something between my lips.

"Suck, redbird." He leaned forward, his hot breath fanning against the shell of my ear. "Suck and know I'll have the taste of you on my tongue all night."

With that parting shot, the mobster hurried away. I was left standing there, gaping after him. Muscles trembling from the pent-up release. It might just be worth it to take care of the problem. But if I waited for him to come back.... I already knew how delicious it felt to be bad, but what if I waited for the opposite? Maybe, just maybe, I could be good. Just this one time.

Chapter 36 – Dimitri

The art of killing someone and making it look like an accident meant I had to force down my natural instinct. Which meant, I fisted my fingers at my side and fought down the urge to break Jasha's neck. The grunts and heavy breathing made it sound like a damn animal was in the next room. I felt bad for his date.

But then I stepped into her bathroom.

It was one thing to have a small apartment. Hell, I would even allow an eclectic mess. There was a line between cleanliness and clutter. The toilet hadn't been scrubbed in no telling how long. Toothpaste and heaven only knew what else was caked in the sink. A colony of black mold thrived in the crevices around the sink, toilet base, and most of the tub's caulk. A too florally scent filled the room, making me want to gag.

I wanted nothing more than to leave and bathe.

There was nowhere to stand but in the shower. The grime and scum made the surface slick, and I ran the risk of slipping. Bracing myself, I stepped inside, thinking of anything else. Counting the times his date called him daddy helped. She was either trying too hard or was using her pornographic performance to cover his rutting pig sounds.

"Noisy little fucker, isn't he," I snorted.

Ilya sent me a message, asking how it was going. I tapped a graphic one back, to which my only reply was silence. Moody fucker. Ilya had a good sense of humor, but it hadn't made an appearance in way too damn long.

There was a long, drawn out groan from Jasha.

The girl screamed.

Every muscle in my body jolted, ready to help. No woman should make that noise when they climaxed.

"Fuck! You're so good," Jasha panted.

The woman mewled. "Thank you, daddy."

I grimaced. What kind of man liked that scream?

There was a long pause. The smell of cigarettes swirled through the air. It only added to the filth of the place.

This was the gamble. If Jasha didn't come in here, I would have to escape without his date catching on. We could have trailed him after he left or been waiting in his car. But we needed his death to look like a heart attack. Too many of the bratva were mysteriously dropping like flies. Yet no one correlated it to the fact that every name on our list was someone who would oppose me and cause trouble when the pakhan died. We'd been strategic in the types of death, the locations of their demise, and the timing.

So Jasha's death needed to be a heart attack and it needed to be here, at the home of the woman he'd picked up from the bar.

Like clockwork, my target did the very predictable male thing of post coital urination. Stumbling into the bathroom, he banged the door behind him. He was wearing boxers. A small mercy. It was just wrong to kill a man while taking a piss. But I had a night to get on with. Opening the bottle, I poured Pavel's concoction on the rag I'd pulled from my pocket.

With his back to me, Jasha shouldn't have seen me coming.

The curtain must have flickered in the mirror. Because he spun around with a hoarse shout.

I lunged, soaked rag ready.

Our eyes locked. Recognition flashed in his, but was immediately replaced by a mixture of determination and caution.

His fists flew in a rapid onslaught. Weaving back and forth, I avoided the calculated moves. Unable to move past his guard in this small space, I circled him. All it would take was him calling out, the date dialing the cops or my father, and our mission would be discovered. The air between us crackled with tension, every movement a potential opening.

I saw my chance—a brief moment when his weight shifted just enough.

In a swift, decisive move, I closed the distance, my left hand gripping his wrist while my right arm snaked around his waist. He resisted, his muscles tensing beneath my grip, but I used the momentum to pivot my hips and throw him off balance. Our feet tangled as we grappled.

We hit the unwashed floor.

The impact sent a jolt through my body.

This close, the stench coming off his body was part booze, part sweat, both mixed with male pheromones. His dick wasn't tucked away properly. It flopped back and forth, as I struggled to pin his legs down.

"I can't believe I'll be the one to kill the great Vlasov prince," Jasha choked.

That was not happening! A bullet I would welcome, but not death by limp dick soldier.

With a surge of adrenaline, I slid my arm around him. My legs locked around his in a vice-like hold. I felt his struggles weaken, his strength ebbing as I secured my position.

I clapped the chemical infused cloth over his nose and mouth, praying I'd used enough.

Jasha wrenched back and forth. His fingers dug into my forearm, but I kept my hold. Even when I noticed his dick was no longer limp.

Gross....

Each thrash lacked the power before it. Victory was within reach, but I knew better than to grow complacent. I adjusted my weight, pressing down with just enough force to keep him pinned. His breathing grew ragged.

Finally, when he lay still, I pulled the needle from my pocket, jabbed it into his bicep, and depressed the plunger. The cloth had stuff to knock him out, but the needle had poison to stop his heart. If they bothered with a medical examination, it would look like a heart attack.

"It would have been so much easier to break your neck," I growled.

I released him and scooted out from under his body. A shudder rolled from my shoulders down to my knees. Of all the assassinations, I couldn't believe Jasha had put up a fight.

Ghosting from the bathroom, I saw the girlfriend scrolling on her phone in the dark bedroom. I slid from the apartment, closed the outer door quietly, and rejoined Ilya and Alex, one of our female soldiers, in the alley.

"It's done," I said tightly.

Ilya looked at his phone. "We'll have time for Anton after all."

But then I wouldn't have time to play with Laurel before church.

"He's stationed to guard the warehouse by Canal Parkway," Alexa said, leading the way to the nondescript vehicle we'd stolen.

Sighing, I slid into the front seat. Not only was my pretty little bird being edged, but I was in torment.

Chapter 37 – Dimitri

Laurel had been sleeping when I finally made it back to the office at dawn. I changed, attended early service at Saints Peter and Paul, and came back.

Lowering myself to the thin mattress, I slid my hand under the blanket. The cover slipped to reveal bare flesh. A groan strangled in my throat. Those gorgeous curves teased, tempting me to rip the covering and explore.

Berries and cream...she had it in a lotion, and her skin had been covered in the scent. So sweet, so tempting.

"Do you know what power you hold over me, snowy beauty?" I whispered.

My fingers found the slick heat between her legs. I stroked with two fingers. Her body shuddered, and she blinked awake with a gasp.

The way that lush body responded to me made me feel like both a fucking peasant and a saints damned king at the same time.

"Time to get up. The Signora is serving family dinner at noon—which is apparently the proper time to eat dinner," I added in my most businesslike manner.

Laurel stared at me. Her mental faculties were coming back online, and the moment she realized what I'd done, outrage blazed in her eyes. "I didn't touch myself!"

I flicked a brow. "So? It's time to go."

"You— You— You beast!" Laurel jackknifed up and stabbed a finger in my chest.

I caught it and sucked the digit between my lips. "I never said taking care of that needy little ache would be the first thing I did," I explained, voice rough and gravelly to my own ears. "Come on, I brought you a dress."

Laurel yanked her hand back. I let it go. She dug her fingers into her hair—and pulled hard. A suppressed scream shot from her.

"I should have just taken care of it myself!" she raged.

I chuckled darkly. "You wouldn't have liked the consequences of such disobedience."

Patting her arm, I nudged her off the mattress and directed her to the desk where a pretty blue dress draped over the surface. She snatched the material and stormed into the en suite bathroom, while I smoothed the blanket and returned the murphy bed to its upright position.

When she came out, hair slicked back into a side braid and wrath simmering in her eyes, she planted her hands on her hips. "Is the Signora planning to host a *formal* dinner?"

I tipped my head and frowned. "No, it's just the family."

Laurel stabbed her hands at her dress. "Then what the hell is this?"

I looked her up and down. My dick twitched against the zipper of my slacks. "I love that dress."

"It's a gown," she hissed.

"Well, you're not dressing for them." I crossed the distance and captured her chin. "You're dressing for me, my princess."

I kissed her protest. The hunger coursing through me threatened to drive me into a different track of action. It would be so easy to sweep the contents of my desk to the floor. To toss my beauty on the desk and take what we both craved.

But I held myself back with iron control.

"You look beautiful, Laurel," I breathed. In Russian, I added, "I was a bandit, hiding in the woods, and you stepped into my world, descending from your ivory palace to find me. You are royalty, you walk with the kings of old. And I am your humble servant, content to worship on my knees until you should deign to toss a crumb of your favor."

Those spicy cinnamon eyes narrowed on me. "If that was some grand plot to edge me to death, then know that I will come back and haunt you for eternity, mobster."

With that parting shot, she spun on her heel and left the office.

When the blessing was bestowed on the meal, we dove into the food. It wasn't just the immediate family. Our father's cousin's son Stepan was there, as were Pavel and Ilya.

The way the dishes were passed around, I scooped and served Laurel first. I doubt she noticed. A volatile energy beat through her veins. It seeped out into the air around her. I had to work hard to keep the satisfied smile off my face.

"Nonna, how many anchovies did you put in the dressing?" Dani gulped, pushing around her food.

"None, cara mia. You asked me not to," Signora Barone grumped. "Although why, I can't for the life of me fathom. You love your Americana salads."

The drone of conversation faded to the background as I placed a pile of pasta next to the salad on Laurel's plate. She began to eat. It was time to reveal the reason for me choosing that dress. Did I know it was a degree more formal than a family meal? Yes. Did I care? Not at all.

Especially when I slid my hand between the thigh-high slit and inched toward her center.

Laurel choked on her wine.

I didn't waste time teasing. My touch pressed against her clit. The small, firm circles offered the relief she was in desperate need of.

Laurel dropped her chin, dabbing her lips with the linen napkin. "Mobster," she breathed.

A terrible, dominating heat spread through my chest. My plan had been to punish her during the meal, but now I considered if I should make her come. Shooting looks at the other men around us, I ground my molars.

My snowy beauty wasn't quiet. The songs this pretty redbird sang were for my ears alone. I would be damned rather than have the others hear.

Tweaking her clit, I pushed my fingers deep into her channel. The liquid heat decided me. I pumped in once, twice, and then the words to excuse ourselves for a phone call were on the tip of my tongue.

Baby Zoey let out an ear-piercing wail.

"Let me get her a bottle," Dani breathed and scrambled from her seat. The one directly beside Laurel.

I had just enough time to snatch my fingers away before Dani thrust the baby toward Laurel.

"Here, hold her for a second, please?" Dani asked frantically.

Laurel didn't have time to answer when the tomato red, banshee-screaming babe was dropped into her arms.

The shock that wiped the constant smile off Laurel's face was priceless. My bride held the child between her hands like a struggling sack of produce that she was examining before purchase.

"Like this," I said, keeping the laughter from my voice. Plucking the poor little orphan from my horrified wife, I tucked the babe under my chin, holding her with one hand. "Holding her tight makes her feel secure."

I patted Zoey's back, murmuring low.

"How the hell do you know that?" Laurel hissed.

Ignoring the smirks from my cousins, I passed the child back. "You try."

Laurel pursed her lips so that I didn't answer the question. I smoothed her skirt and returned to my food. The steady patting of Laurel's hand strengthened and steadied as she gained a rhythm.

"You could sing to her," I said softly.

"I don't sing for people," Laurel snapped.

Maybe getting her so riled was a mistake. But I was loving this feisty, combative side of the snowy beauty.

Laurel's hand thumped, baby Zoey burped, and undigested mush spilled on Laurel's blue gown. My heart dropped to my stomach.

"Someone else take her," Laurel said slowly and calmly.

Luka rounded the table and snatched the child, who'd finally stopped crying. He snuggled the baby into his arm and began to hum an old, Slavic lullaby.

Laurel shot out of her seat and stormed down the hall.

"It's not the baby," I said to the family. "Laurel's in a mood because of me."

And it was time to take care of it. She'd suffered long enough.

"How am I not surprised?" Ilya muttered.

I smacked him upside the head as I passed his seat.

Teasing and riotous laughter followed me down the hall. I reached for the door of the guest bath, which was locked.

"Just a minute," Dani called, but the sound of vomiting sounded a moment later.

I frowned. "Is Laurel in there?"

"No," Dani gasped.

As I walked away, I debated texting Kaz that he was needed. But maybe my cousin-in-law didn't want him to see her like that. Since I'd seen my fair share of the insides of toilets, I knew I wouldn't like that either.

A sound at my uncle's study caught my attention. I poked inside and discovered the object of my search. Laurel threw back the shot of amber liquor.

"What's your poison, bartender?" I asked, closing and locking the thick wood door. Now this was what soundproofing was like.

Laurel pinned me with a look. "Scotch. But I'll drink anything."

I hummed, the sound grating against my vocal cords to sound more animal than man. As she watched me with a skeptical, laser focused gaze, I wet my lips.

Not speaking, I slipped out of my shoes. The slacks hit the floor and then my shirt fluttered after it. I jerked my chin at her. "Your turn."

Laurel arched a brow. "Maybe I don't want to play."

"One way or another, I'm finishing what you started, redbird." My boxers hit the floor. I stood there, a sacrifice ready for the snowy beauty to take.

Slowly, her fingers reached for the side zipper. She loosened the bodice, before pulling the gown over her head. I gripped my dick, slowly stroking the shaft. The moment she was free, she looked.

A short breath caught between her lips.

I stalked forward, the inner monster ready to stake his claim. Laurel didn't flinch. Her gaze tore away from my dick and pinned me. Need shone in those soft brown depths.

Those beautiful eyes...so familiar.

I snatched her into my arms and continued moving to the bookshelf.

"Wouldn't the couch be easier for you?" she countered.

I shook my head. "Easy has nothing to do with it."

Her backside connected with the ladder. I adjusted so a rung braced her ass and she wouldn't slip, but otherwise, I took her body easily. She was mine, and God made her just right for me.

"Hold on," I warned.

She spread her legs wide, and her fingers reached for the rung. I groaned. That instant obedience made me harder. The games were over, the need that pulsed between us was the only thing left.

We'd both had enough of touches. I brought us together in one hard thrust.

The connection brought a choked sob of relief from her.

If I could make a noise so sweet, so enchanting, I would have. But I wasn't a pretty songbird. I was a creature of the underworld.

I pulled back and sank into the maddening heat. Her tight little pussy was heaven. With each thrust of my hips, I drove deeper. She opened, taking all of me and squeezing me.

Laurel cried softly. A shudder rocked through her body, setting a fierce convulsion deep in her core.

I sucked in a sharp breath. "For the love of the saints, redbird, don't stop singing."

"Never," she panted.

Pleasure pulsed in my cock. Pressure built in my balls. Laurel moved desperately against me, her body craving the release the same as me. I leaned into her and found her lips. And crushed them to mine.

Every unspoken truth poured into that kiss.

"Good girls get to come. Don't forget it," I growled. "You may come for me, redbird. Come on *my cock*!"

That thick, beautiful body jerked. It strained, pressing back and opening impossibly wide. There was nothing holding me back. I drove into her over and over. More of that heartbreakingly beautiful song poured from her lips.

The force of her orgasm stole my release. Snatched it right from my iron control. There was no holding back. Heat crackled through my shaft, and my balls screamed as I came harder than I ever had before. Every drop of control belonged to her. She was the queen—that made her in charge.

Chapter 38 – Laurel

"Again." Dimitri's command barreled into my back.

I gulped, steadying myself. *I can do this.*

His hand came around my peripheral, and I struck. This time, I missed it completely. An elbow caught my throat. With lightning speed, hands captured mine. That unforgiving grip forced me close. I wriggled and balked. My last resort was dropping, sinking to the floor and letting gravity carry my weight.

Except Dimitri held me fast, unfazed by my weight.

My hands.

I couldn't move.

My pulse exploded. An invisible cinch tightened around my chest. Each breath was harder to pull into my lungs than the last. Dimitri had touched them before, but it was also sensual. There was arousal to distract. This time, it was during a simulated conflict, and the panic struck so much harder.

"Laurel?" Dimitri's voice was hard as iron.

Since my vision was narrowing, I closed my eyes and focused on drawing the next drop of oxygen into my lungs. Dimitri wouldn't hurt me! I knew that. But...but...

Shit.

"Shit," he echoed, releasing me instantly.

The inhale was a loud gasp. Hands on my hips, I bent and gulped air.

"Laurel, what's going on?"

I shook my head violently. "Again."

He began to protest, but before the words became sound, I threw my hand in the air. "I said again, Dimi. Let's go!"

A rumble of displeasure left his throat. "Fine."

His hand shot out. This time, I rounded on him. Left, right, hook, and jab. He blocked each until the last, because I made that jab a double. Both fists flew at his face. He only caught the right. The left connected with his neck.

His guttural cry chilled me instantly.

Dimitri pushed past me, and the bathroom door clapped shut with a resounding thud. A few mornings of self-defense lessons and this was the first time I landed a blow. The surprise kept me rooted in place until the sound of the sink couldn't cover the vomiting.

I sprinted forward. The handle was unyielding, and I crashed into the locked door. There would be a bruise there tomorrow. But I did it again.

"Dimitri!"

My breathless cry remained unanswered. Well...not entirely. The violent puking pounded through the door. I stood there, helpless and gasping as I watched the door.

Wasn't there someone I should call? I looked around, but no answer presented itself.

Eventually, a groan sounded. "Go away, Laurel. We're done for today."

"Let me help you." I rattled the door.

"Go..." he croaked.

"Dimi!"

No other communication came. I hopped from foot to foot. Did I call one of the cousins? Dimitri trusted them, but would he want me to contact them? I stroked the closed door. He was there and something was very, *very* wrong. I needed to reach him! But if he didn't want me....

Finally, in the pulsing silence, I left. If he needed to be alone, I could give him that, since there wasn't anything else I could do.

I didn't see Dimitri for thirty-six hours. Dani came to pick me up for the gala. When she didn't say a word about my husband, I wondered if she knew. *Where did he hide?*

The jab hadn't been that hard. But the physical reaction was instantaneous. A connection to the neck and Dimitri stumbled. *Stumbled*. The replay flashed through my mind for the thousandth time. I huffed.

"Something the matter?" Dani asked from where she sat in front of her cousin Cami's vanity. That cousin was filing her nails on the foot of the bed, her dark hair pulled back in a loose claw clip.

"Nothing," I breathed. If I trusted her, I might have confided in her.

If she was trustworthy, she would have told me where Dimitri was.

"There. The beading is fixed." Signora Barone fluffed the skirt of Daniella's dress.

The feminine energy was nice. Or it should have been. I wanted to throw my hands in the air and scream. Where the hell was my husband? Was he okay? And why hadn't he told me about his neck?!

Like you told him the reason behind your hands? The mental barb made me close my eyes.

In half an hour, we were dressed. Cami Joe, the cute now eighteen-year-old cousin, stared at us with doe eyes. "Belissime."

The Italian response was on the tip of my tongue when I swallowed it. "Thanks."

We descended to the parlor, where the Signora had cocktails and finger food. Dani shook her head at the drinks and hurried into Kazimir's outstretched arms.

"Explain to me how wearing this monkey suit is supposed to help us bring in money?" Luka whined.

Dani twirled. Her eyes glued on her husband's. "Who cares, so long as I get to keep this dress!"

It was a gorgeous Eloise gown with sleeves in Lino Weave. "Don't you love when you can find a bargain?" I laughed, wringing my hands.

"Apparently, the designer wanted ten grand, but Laurel found it for around eight hundred and nonna stitched the tear in the collar," Cami explained to Luka.

"I still don't know what that has to do with the need for strait jackets," Luka protested, tugging at his collar.

"Knock it off," I snapped. "You have legitimate businesses. Bring legitimate money into them—a.k.a. be businessmen. You go where the money is and you woo it into your corner."

"I thought it was a charity benefit," Kazimir said slowly. His narrowed eyes pinned me. Skepticism and suspicion laced his features.

Yeah, ditto, buddy. I don't trust you either.

I planted my hands on my hips and glared at him. For the sake of the cheerful Italian granny, I held back choice words. "It is. On the surface. Like your technology company. But the wealthy elites rub shoulders and make decisions behind the guise of good deeds. Some might believe in the causes. But the majority are there for tax write-offs, public image polishing, and back door deals."

"Noted." And then, Kazimir flashed me a slow smile.

"Laurel knows her way around the rich and famous. If she says this is the way, we do it," a dark voice said behind me. The confidence lacing that hard tone sent a shiver down my spine.

I spun on my heel. Blood jumped through my veins, and a smile split across my lips. Dimitri stood in the doorway, looking crisp and clean in his tux. When the corner of his mouth twitched, I dropped all reservations and ran.

He lifted me easily and half-twirled me.

I told myself I was putting on a show, acting the radiant bride just like Daniella.

So why did my pulse race, my heart leap, and my core clench greedily? Because I was such a good actress, I convinced my own body? That was what I would tell myself.

"I missed you," I confessed in a whisper. That, at least, was true, as was the next statement. "It was lonely last night."

"I'm sorry." It was all the explanation I was getting.

I didn't care. I was relieved to have him in my arms, and what I didn't tell him was that his presence steadied me to face the crowd that was my past.

Chapter 39 – Laurel

Dimitri swirled his drink in the cut tumbler. His calculating gaze swept the room. We'd talked to multiple businessmen, and I was the envy of several wives. There was a tangible buzz swirling about us. I could see the lines heavy with the catch. It was only a matter of reeling them in. The others were occupied in the distance, meeting people but also guarding us.

"We should really get you a downtown office suite," I mused. "Create a mother company with subsidiaries that operate on their own spaces."

That dark gaze fell on me. It *burned*. A delicious shiver raced down my spine, and my toes curled in my pumps. "You're turning me into a suit, wife."

I hummed in agreement. "You're clay in my hands, Vlasov."

"Hmm, we'll see about that." He set his still full cocktail down on a ledge, plucked the flute from mine, and laced his fingers to pull me along.

Laughing, I tripped lightly after him. We pushed into the employee only door. It was like jumping into a pool of cold water. I shivered again and moved closer to Dimitri. He pushed into one door but shook his head before I could grasp a clear view of what was inside. We headed to the next, and this time he pulled me into an unlit storage room. The door fell closed behind us, swallowing us in the dominating blackness.

"Dimi, what the hell—"

But the protest was cut off when he turned me and pushed me up against the wall. Those hard hands came down on either side of my face, fingers splaying into my hair. The air left my lungs in a whoosh. He caught the tendrils as his lips crashed into mine. One of his thick thighs pressed between mine.

Pinned by his body, head forced still by his touch, I was at this monster's mercy.

Something I'd been dreaming of the last few nights.

I ground against the hard muscles of his leg, making desperate little needy noises. Dimitri whipped his head back and forth, sharply breaking the kiss. His hand skimmed back into my hair, fingers tightening mercilessly in the strands.

"No, little redbird, here in the dark, you're not in charge. I might allow you to mold me like a fucking piece of putty out there. That's your world, you're their long-lost princess. But you belong to the dark. And it seems—" he forced my head back "—I need to remind you of that."

Tears pricked my eyes. The angle pulled hard on my throat, making each inhale a struggle. But my hands were free. If I told him to stop, he would. So I let him, because right now I wanted to surrender.

His hard mouth came down on my pulse. He sucked the tender flesh, and with the way I bruised, there would be a bright mark.

The twisted part of my soul was gleeful.

"It seems I need to remind you who's in charge." His teeth scored a path along the line of my neck. He bit the exposed skin right under the collarbone, carving a path of pain and pleasure until the dress stopped him. "Pull your skirt up."

Dimitri stepped back, creating distance between our bodies. I whimpered at the loss of him. But I obeyed, fingers scrambling to gather the material.

His voice tightened. "Reach between your legs."

I did. The lacey thong was one of my favorites, because instead of cutting into the softer parts, it lay flat. And it looked incredible. Skimming my fingers over the little bows and cut-outs, I waited.

"Are your panties damp?"

Oh! My nostrils flared. He wanted me *there*. I slid my fingers to the center. My touch trailed down where the proof of my arousal was evident. I nodded. "Yes," I rasped.

"How wet?"

"Very." My pulse beat double.

Dimitri hummed, the sound a deep, masculine vibration in his chest. He released me and took a step back. "Show me."

I blinked. The blackness of the room disabled sight. "You can't see me," I protested. "How the hell am I supposed to *show* you?"

A predatorial growl erupted from the bratva prince. "Put your fingers on that soaking, sweet pussy and show me how much you need me, redbird."

I gulped, and my fingers slid past the lace and into the dampness.

There was a tell-tale flick of metal, and the sole flame from Dimitri's Zippo bloomed to life. Wincing at the sudden brightness defying the dark, I turned away. But not before I caught the glint in those sea blue eyes.

Except...here in the dark, they were the color of the water right as a squall blew in.

"That's my girl," he murmured roughly. "See how your body craves this?"

Need smoldered, making my muscles clench and throb. I quickened my touch, rubbing tight circles over my clit, only dipping lower to bring more moisture to where I desperately needed relief.

"Keep touching yourself." Those words were punctuated by the sound of a zipper.

I dropped my gaze to his pants, where Dimitri was pulling out his cock. It was hard as iron, straining and twitching. My core convulsed at the sight.

Fisting the solid length, Dimitri stroked his touch up and down. Damn, but he was hot. That was a beautiful dick, large and thick, and his big hand worked over the veins pulsing with heat and blood.

"Look at me, redbird."

I snapped to meet his gaze. Those eyes were the darkest I'd ever seen them. Nearly black, with only the reflection of the flame to brighten them.

"We're going to play a little game. Ready?"

I nodded. "Yes," I whispered.

"You will not look at me. You will continue to touch yourself, and when you're close, only then will you lift your gaze as a signal. We'll see if you can earn the right to come." The corners of his mouth tipped up, but it wasn't a smile. Not really. There was too much dangerous, dominating control in the smirk.

We'll see about that. "Okay," I smiled sweetly.

"On your knees."

Warning prickled at the base of my skull. But I was already in too deep. There was no way I was calling quits to this game. I knelt.

"Suck." Dimitri stepped close but didn't touch me. It was up to me to take the challenge.

I scooted forward on my knees. The tightness and friction of the movement sent a wave of pleasure through my pussy. Licking my lips, I slid the head of his cock into my mouth. It felt as good on my tongue as I knew it would.

I moaned.

"That's it, redbird. Now show me how well you can suck on dick." His voice came out strangled and strained. "If you do a good job, I'll let you come."

I snorted mentally.

His hand snaked out and threaded into my hair. "Are you laughing at me, redbird?"

Pulling back, his dick made a popping noise as it released from my mouth. "Yes, actually, I am."

"Redbird," he growled in warning.

"What are you going to do? I come and then oops? You can't withhold my orgasm," I taunted, remembering so vividly the other night. I played nice then. It was unwise to poke the great, growly bear. But I was already playing with fire. And it was so much damn fun! I never wanted to stop.

"No, but I can take you to bed and fuck you over and over until you can't have another orgasm." His fingers forced my head up, so I was staring into the twin pricks of flame high above me.

"Ooh, punishment by orgasm, I might just disobey to win that prize." Stupid. *Stupid!* I should stop.

I was out of control. Delirious with need, and drunk on this exchange of power.

"Dammit, you'll be the death of me." He tipped my head back down. "Get to work, redbird, and don't you dare come until you're told. Now...touch yourself."

With the limited movement he allowed, I leaned forward and ran my tongue over his length. The slow circles I created on the tip mirrored my touch between my legs.

He fisted my hair, pulling it. "Quit teasing me."

Smiling triumphantly, I opened my mouth and took him—deep.

He groaned loudly, the sound drenched with pleasure. My heart skipped in response.

This part of our relationship was raw. Out there, amongst the others, we were fake, a show to manipulate. But this? This was real.

Dimitri had become something to me. There was a bond forged between us in the dark. He was a lover, someone I trusted to play sexy little games with.

I sighed happily. This cock tasted amazing. I eagerly swallowed every inch of the thick, velvety shaft. His balls were tight and heavy. No doubt they ached. I palmed them, squeezing and massaging. Dimitri rewarded me with a sharp hiss of air that whistled between his teeth.

I liked that sound.

No....

I freaking *loved* it.

So what if I was on my knees? If he was the one who would tell me when I could come? I had this mobster in my clutches and we both knew it.

I was soaking wet. I worked my touch through my folds, my pussy begging me to finish the deed.

"Ah, just like that. You're doing such a good job," he ground out.

Digging my fingers into that heavily muscled thigh, I opened my jaw wide and took all of him. Dimitri groaned. His fingers loosened, giving me the space I needed. So I fucked his cock with my mouth.

Fingers scissoring inside, I knew there wasn't much more I could resist.

I looked up, meeting his gaze. Dimitri stared back at me, expression unreadable. This was the signal right? to tell him I was close.

My tongue rubbed against the underside of his dick. I sucked harder. A scream bubbled up my throat, and I let it pour out of my gaze.

"You're so obedient, baby." Dimitri slid his hand from my hair. His touch cupped my cheek. His thumb rubbed under my eye. "Swallow. Every. Last. Drop."

I glared at him. My hips flexed, and my muscles clenched. Desperation flared hot.

His hand trailed down my throat. He didn't squeeze, but it rested suggestively there. "Be a good girl and swallow, redbird. Then you may come."

Taking a deep breath, one that would hold me to the end, I took every last inch of him. I swallowed him hard, sucking and gagging. It was rough and messy. But I was going to win this, dammit!

"Don't stop touching yourself," he snapped.

If I could have stuck my tongue out—

I pressed my teeth into his flesh.

He let out a strangled roar, his whole body jerking. Hot seed sprayed down my throat. I gulped, taking everything.

His voice was rough. His jaw clenched hard, and his voice tightened. "So good, babe. So damn good."

I know! I sank my fingers where I needed them most. My body arched. A needy whimper choked in my throat, unable to release past the thick cock still caught between my lips. I was too busy claiming my own orgasm to free him.

Dimitri hissed, no doubt sensitive. But I kept him in my mouth as I chased the pleasure.

"Come, now." His words gave me exactly what I needed. With a shudder, I came. Out of all the orgasms I'd ever had, it was in the top five. The pleasure crashed through me, consuming every fiber of my being.

My screams filled the room. "Dimitri!"

"That's it, redbird. My name—my name on your lips. Let me hear you sing."

Iron bands wrapped around me. His hands were everywhere, touching and caressing. They pulled me close, and I melted into his hard frame.

And then, he kissed me.

Only, as his tongue slid into my mouth, stroking in the same way his cock had moments ago, I realized this kiss was different. If I had to describe it, it felt like he was staking a claim.

I wrapped my arms around his neck. It was my turn for my fingers to dig into his scalp. His hair wasn't long enough to tug, so I reached for the crown and pulled those shorter strands.

Dimitri growled against my mouth. The vibration made me smile.

When he pulled back, we were both breathing hard. The realization snapped a moment later that he was also on his knees. I did that. I brought the dangerous mobster to kneel before me. I couldn't stop grinning.

"What are you smiling about?" he panted.

"You dropped your lighter. How can you see me smiling?" I demanded.

He placed a swift kiss on my mouth. "I can *feel* it, redbird."

Oh, universe, help me! I was falling. And the scary part, I wasn't sure I wanted to stop.

Chapter 40 – Laurel

After peeling off the floor and setting our clothes to rights, Dimitri helped me escape the storage room. He shielded me as we scurried to the venue's lady's room. I ducked inside.

The woman in the reflection looked thoroughly sexed, albeit not completely sated. I would have happily left the gala and gone to bed with my handsome mobster husband.

I grimaced. *Fake husband. Fake.*

I was here to help him find a killer, and now to help him with gathering capital. I couldn't lose sight of the end goal in the middle of the delightful twists and turns of the journey. Taking my clutch, which somehow hadn't been lost in the heat of the moment, I repaired the damage.

Stepping back into the hall, I noticed Dimitri was speaking with someone. The stranger had broad shoulders, much like an athlete. He wasn't as tall as the mobster, but he carried himself as an equal. Power radiated from his presence. It was the suit. It helped lend the appearance of strength.

Plastering a winning smile on my face, I approached. Dimitri met my gaze. The contact warmed me. I hated to break away, but I did, angling my body to greet the stranger.

The moment that handsome profile came into view, my heart stopped. I faltered.

"Laurel?" Dimitri stepped into me. His body moved to create a barrier between me and....

"Jack," I breathed.

The stranger, who was far from strange to me, turned. He did a double take. His chocolate eyes widened a fraction before that devilish glint twinkled. "Little princess.... Is that really you?"

He reached out, ready to pluck at a tendril of my black hair. Dimitri stepped into the billionaire, a snarl on his lips.

"It's Laurel Vlasova now," I said quickly, body reacting to the testosterone shit storm brewing. I placed my hand possessively over Dimitri's and tugged him into my side.

John Henry looked between us, keen eyes missing nothing. "I see. Well still...damn, *Laaurrrrel*. It's been ages."

He was mocking my new identity with a funny pronunciation. I hated him for it, but also because I could feel my mobster's blood boil. I gave the billionaire a tight smile. "It has."

With a chuckle, the billionaire touched two fingers to his head in salute. "Would love to chat, *Laurrrrel*, but I've got to run and take down a distributor who's skimming some books."

I shuddered.

John Henry sauntered away, grinning like the idiot he was.

I let out a long breath and sagged into the wall. I'd known this was possible, but I figured anyone I met from the old crowd wouldn't recognize me. Never in a million years would I have thought that particular billionaire would be here.

Just another cosmic curveball. Damn, the universe thought she was funny letting me bump into an old...friend? No. Acquaintance? More than that.

One of the good ones.

Dimitri turned on me. The knuckles of his right hand were white as he squeezed the life out of the Zippo. "How do you know him?"

I arched a brow, looking up into the mobster's stormy face. "I could ask you the same thing, Dimi."

"He does work with our family."

A rough laugh clawed out my throat. "Of course he does. Damn, little Jack Greene is all grown up and playing with the bad boys. Some things never change."

"Explain, now!" Dimitri's tone brooked no argument.

"I can't." I tossed my hands wide. "It's not something I want known."

"Laurel, I swear, if you don't tell me, I'll catch little Jack and pry the secret from his bloody lips."

I sighed. "No, you won't. You'll leave him alone if you know what's good for you. That boy's nothing but trouble."

Dimitri's gaze turned cold. "You know him well."

"Unfortunately." I pushed off the wall. That reminded me. John Henry was a manipulative sonofabitch, and I needed to make damn sure he kept his lips sealed. "I'm going to get a drink and find the others. Want anything?"

Dimitri's fingers snaked around my wrist.

My pulse spiked, but the panic stayed low, ebbing only at the edges instead of consuming.

Drawing his touch up my arm to hold my elbow, Dimitri leaned close. "Tell me one thing."

I started to protest, but he cut that off with a look.

"Was it him?" Dimitri lifted my arm so my wrist was visible between us.

I blinked. Of course, that was what he would think! The big, gruff beast of a mobster would jump to the worst possible conclusion.

"No!" I rushed to say, letting out a nervous laugh. "No, not Jack. He didn't know, although, if I would have told him, maybe he could have found a way to stop what was going on and—"

I stopped talking, clamping my mouth closed as the past crept up my throat, trying to vomit out.

Breathing hard, I fought back the memories. Dimitri simply watched me. When I felt I had a handle on things, I cracked a tentative smile.

"Tell me, baby. Who hurt you?" Dimitri's tone was nothing but gentle. However, if I listened hard enough, I could peel the layers back to hear black wrath roaring behind it.

I shook my head. "That's not a cloud that will darken the present. Now, I'm going for a drink."

I pulled away, and the mobster let me. Hustling back into the main event area, I looked around. The tell-tale cut suit stood out farther back, as did the head of dark brown hair. My feet never moved faster.

John Henry was talking to a pudgy, squat man with thick glasses. I glided right in between them and said to the trembling accountant, "Run."

He scurried away, legs peddling across the floor like a cartoon figure.

John Henry let out a soft peal of laughter. "Fuck, *Laurrrel*, I've missed you, girl."

He looked me up and down. There was masculine appreciation in the look, and I wanted to shake him for being such an idiot. I wasn't his, never wanted to be. But even he had to know checking out the wife of Dimitri Vlasov was idiotic. Suicidal!

"Jack!" I shoved his shoulder. "You have to keep my existence a secret."

"Tell me, little *Laurrrel*, does he know?" The billionaire jerked his chin back to clarify.

I saw Dimitri glowering in the entrance of the event area. He hadn't seen us, although he was looking for me. Avoiding his stare so I couldn't let it pin me, I rushed to say the rest.

"No, and it has to stay that way. I'm in hiding. Please, Jack. It's—" I pursed my lips, hating that I was literally begging at this point. "It's life or death," I hissed.

"You should tell your husband, *Laurrrel*."

I clenched my fists. "Stop saying my name like that, you twat wad!"

John Henry threw back his head. That rich, boisterous laughter brought unwanted attention from others around us. "You haven't changed a bit, my dearest Gisele."

"Don't say *THAT* name!" I gasped. "That woman is dead. Gone. Buried in the past."

"Not to hear your mother speak of it. But don't worry, *Laurrrel,* your secret is safe with me. I want to see how this plays out." He pointed at Dimitri, who stopped talking to his cousins and glared at us.

I pursed my lips.

The billionaire held up a finger and added, "You know, I take back my earlier statement. You've changed a great deal."

"Yes, yes, I know," I snapped, gesturing to my figure. "But I like me like this."

"Good. Don't let anyone take that away from you—but the way you look wasn't what I was talking about."

Dimitri chose that moment to charge over and basically toss me into his side. "What's going on?"

His voice was thunderous. He looked absolutely feral.

I had to take a moment to catch my breath. I *liked* him like this.

"I was just telling *Laurrrel—*"

"I'm going to murder you!" I seethed, but it wasn't convincing with the little laugh.

"—that I've never seen her so happy. She's changed, and for the better." John Henry met Dimitri's glare. The billionaire was cocky, brash. Idiotic. And too damn self-assured for his own good. A normal man would *fear* the mobster, especially if he was aware of the facts and knew exactly who Dimitri was. But not John Henry. "Now, if you'll excuse me," he added. "*Laurrrel* chased off my latest victim, and I wasn't done with him."

Without waiting for our goodbyes, the billionaire brushed past us and trailed after the bespectacled man.

"I don't envy that poor distributor," I said in hushed tones.

But Dimitri didn't say anything. The black wrath poured off him like a bad cologne. A soft sigh escaped my lips. It couldn't be helped.

"Please don't shut me out," I whispered.

And then, I held out my hand.

Dimitri stared at my open palm.

A tense moment ticked by, in which I wasn't sure how he was going to react.

"Come on, mobster, we're not done schmoozing," I coaxed.

Those sea blue eyes closed. A shudder rippled through his shoulders. "I hate that he knows you better than I do."

"He doesn't. He's the past. You—" I slid my hand into his, and my heart didn't explode, merely skipped "—are my present. So come be present with me."

I knew that statement wasn't enough for him, but he let me lead him away. The evening continued, and the trend of success skyrocketed. But there was a definite cloud hanging overhead. Nothing I did or said seemed to shake it. Which was a damn shame, because Dimitri didn't have the right to demand that piece of me. It was dead and gone; I'd survived.

Chapter 41 – Dimitri

My first society event was a raging success according to the radiant Laurel. *Or whatever her name is.*

I ground my molars. While I had been content to earn her trust and wait until she was ready to share her secrets, knowing that smug rich boy knew more about her story than me drove me mad. Was I being unreasonable? Probably. Did I care? Not one fucking bit.

Absently, I flicked my Zippo. The winter wind had an underlying warmth. Spring was coming, and the calendar said it would be a few more days before it was official. The gusts didn't care, however. They continued to howl down the street.

"I'm not ready to turn in," Laurel sang out, grabbing Dani by the waist and twirling her. I didn't miss the sharp way she watched Kazimir's wife. There was something going on there. It was yet another puzzle I couldn't figure out.

"Me neither," the other woman confessed. "I know I dance on stage soon, but I'm too wound up."

Kazimir scowled. I felt how he looked. The girls needed to get home. Whatever he planned do to with his woman, I didn't care. Mine? I wanted her to sit on my face.

"We could stay up for a nightcap, at least? Talk about the next moves for growing the Bratva?" Laurel addressed our group as a whole, but her eyes locked on mine.

"We can't go home; da and the pakhan are entertaining Igor tonight." Luka slapped his hand against the roof of the SUV we'd taken.

A sour flavor spread over my tongue. That should be a conversation I was part of. Vasil and I were going to have a sit-down.

"Let's go." I opened the backseat for Laurel, who planted a kiss on my cheek.

I caught her and pushed her against the side of the vehicle. Digging my fingers into her side, I bent and covered her mouth with mine. The lines of this strange relationship were blurring. This might have started as a fake marriage to create a plausible reason for having her near me, but we were so far past that.

I drank her in, swallowing her shallow gasps and moaning my own desire back.

"Are we good?" Laurel whispered against my mouth.

I sighed. "Am I mad? No."

"But you're frustrated," Laurel sighed, her hot breath a sharp contrast to the winter around us.

"You warned me."

"And you've respected my wish and haven't pried into my secrets." Laurel fidgeted. "I can see how much you want to."

Another man knows them. It was illogical. There were likely many people who knew. But I didn't know them. I knew John Henry. "I'm trying to let it go."

"Thank you," she breathed and leaned in for another kiss.

The horn of the SUV beeped. "The rich are watching."

"Luka's a dead man," Laurel growled.

A rough laugh barked from my throat. "I couldn't agree more."

Laurel reached up and brushed her fingers over my lips. "You're smiling."

"I'm with you."

She fucking glowed.

"This needs to be a quick nightcap," I warned.

"Okay, boss. Whatever you say." She laughed, untangled from my arms, and slid into the backseat next to Dani.

As I climbed into the driver's seat, I slid a glance to Kazimir, who was riding shotgun. "Where to?"

"Let's take the girls to the Little Italy. There is a pastry shop that starts baking at 11, and Dani has been begging to go," Kazimir offered.

"Will they let us in?" Laurel objected.

"The baker is a member of our former church. He'll give us first dibs on the sweet buns," Dani assured us.

I shifted in my seat. "Little Italy?"

"We'll watch the streets," Kazimir said resignedly.

If that was what the women wanted, it seemed we would drive behind enemy lines to make it happen.

Drowning out the chatter in the back, Kazimir and I spoke quietly about members of the Bratva who would be trouble when the eventual change of leadership took place. We had a running list, and last night, two street squad leaders had suffered accidents they never recovered from.

From time to time, I felt a pair of eyes on me. Luka wasn't paying us any attention. Leading wasn't his style. He was a blade, and I was damn glad for his loyalty.

But each time I caught the soft brown eyes in the mirror, I couldn't help but feel gratitude that I had Laurel in my life. It was almost as if she understood the terrible burden of ruling such a violent kingdom, and she lent me silent encouragement. It was too bad she couldn't understand Russian so we could talk about this together.

Not that Kazimir would appreciate that. He hadn't raised any more objections to my bride, but he wasn't her biggest fan either.

I sighed. This was my life now, juggling all the complicated pieces without a moment's rest. No wonder it aged my father.

I won't be like him. I was in so much better health, and I'd given up smoking the first time he had cancer.

Piling out of the SUV, we quieted. The girls hurried to the bakery where Dani rapped on the glass with her palm. I swept a look up and down the road. The apartments above the shops no doubt held the members of various Italian mobs. I didn't know who ran these streets and I didn't want to find out.

But the look on Laurel's face as she sat with a huge sticky pastry ten minutes later was worth the risk.

Luka sipped his coffee contentedly. He was positioned to shield the girls if shit went down. Sitting at a table a little ways away where we could watch the doors, Kazimir and I split something doughy and sweet.

"This was better than going to your house," I admitted to Luka.

"The pakhan's been spending a lot of time with Igor," Kazimir murmured. He didn't look at me as he spoke but watched the women.

"The fat captain is no better than a street soldier. A good one, but still. He doesn't have anything to do with the money laundering side. Why would the pakhan waste his time with him to fix this mess?" Luka huffed.

For being the most reckless of us, my youngest cousin was astutely perceptive.

"That's my question," I admitted. If Igor wanted a better seat than a mere captain, it would bode well for him if I was out of the picture. I pondered that. Would he be reckless enough to call a hit on me? It wasn't as if the position was guaranteed him if I was out of the way. Why would he take such a big risk? A hail Mary? Was he desperate enough to make that kind of power move?

It wasn't easy to ignore the sting in my chest at the possibility the unknown enemy might be my old captain. Betrayals were a part of life. I needed to get used to that.

"Igor," Kaizmir mused. "He was our captain before you rose in the ranks, Dimi."

I nodded. It was true. Vasil made sure that us three cousins worked every position of the Bratva. We'd started on the streets with Igor. The summer Kazimir joined our trio—having grown up outside of the Bratva—we worked with Vasil in laundering money. But after that, it was always the harder work of street warfare, gun running, and various other illegal ventures.

"That doesn't mean he isn't above reaching for the boss's chair," I agreed. "What I want to know is what Vasil thinks. His opinion will go a long way with the next chapters of the Vlasov Bratva."

"Da won't pick Igor. He's not an idiot. Fat Igor would sink the syndicate in months," Luka spat. "He's as equipped to lead as a neutered dog is to breed."

Again—Luka and his brilliancy.

We nodded in agreement.

Three synced beeps were followed by the tell-tale vibrations. I whipped my phone out, but Luka was already looking at his.

"You've got to be shitting me," he spazzed.

I tapped the sender's name and the call went through. It was answered a moment later.

"We're not on rotation tonight," I rasped.

Kazimir rose to pay the Italian baker.

"Igor said he was doing something important with the pakhan and that leaves you," Emil drawled through the phone.

He wasn't wrong. Borris, the captain in charge of more brute force situations, was tied up at the docks. If we lost a shipment because I wasn't available to step up with my teams, it would be another mark in my father's book.

"We'll be there." I ended the call.

So it seemed Igor was letting the other captains know about the pakhan's favoritism. I rose, fisting and flexing my left hand. Those fingers itched for a gun. Igor's sweaty forehead would make a nice target.

Laurel bolted to my side. "Who needs to die?"

I laughed roughly. "One of the other captains is causing trouble. And the other captain can't do anything right. He had *one* job, and now he needs backup. I should shoot them both and be done with it."

"You can't openly kill one without provocation," she hissed. "While the others would see it as strength, it will also breed mistrust."

I dropped my forehead to hers. The words tumbled out of their own accord. "How did I get lucky enough to find you?"

"Pshaw, it's just common sense."

"There's nothing common about you, Laurel Vlasova."

Her blistering smile looked absolutely delectable. I groaned. There was no telling how late we would be out tonight.

"Pavel will be here in five with a car," Kazimir informed me.

Which brought me back to the immediate problem. The girls would have to get home on their own. Kazimir and I seemed to reach that same conclusion. We shared a look.

I pulled Laurel to the side, where the security camera couldn't see me. "You go straight home. Take Dani with you."

Laurel started as I placed the cool metal in her hands. She looked down at the handgun.

"Do you know how to use this?" I pressed, kicking myself that we hadn't done target practice.

"Point and shoot." She nodded, lips pressing into a thin line.

"Don't aim at anything you don't want dead." I pulled her close and inhaled her hair. That fruity scent twisted something inside my chest.

"You be careful!" Laurel shook me with her free hand.

"Always. But this is a dangerous job," I deflected, trying to set her at ease. "I'm used to it."

Laurel shook her head furiously. "It's not the normal amount of danger I'm worried about. You don't know who is trying to trap you. This summons is out of place. I don't like this. Not at all. It doesn't *feel* right."

"My cousins will watch my back," I promised, not wanting to tell her it didn't feel right to me either.

Glaring at my cousins, Laurel huffed. I got the sense she wanted to say something but kept her mouth shut instead.

A roar of frustration clawed up my throat. Breaking apart, I stormed to the door and pushed into the streets. So what if the Italian mobs saw me? Taking deep breaths, I almost dared the little wops to come crawling out of their holes, just so I could punch something.

The others came outside in a suppressed rush of excitement. Dani carried three boxes of pastries the baker insisted on sending. Laurel cast a long, lingering look over me.

"Be safe, mobster," she repeated in a whisper.

"I'll see you tonight," I promised. *And you're going to give me something.* Just one, small secret. I needed it, more than I needed my next breath.

I watched as the girls piled into the SUV and watched the taillights disappear.

"Time to fight!" Luka cracked his knuckles.

I nodded. That was exactly what I needed. A good brawl.

Chapter 42 – Laurel

Dani rubbed her stomach. "I really need Pepto-Bismol."

"I know, I know!" I laughed, pulling into the 24hr superstore. The guys told us not to stop but go straight home. Well, we were already disobeying those instructions, because Daniella refused to go to the pakhan's house. Oddly enough, she also didn't want to go to Vasil's and be with her grandmother.

From the green color Dani was radiating, I could see she wasn't going to make it to her apartment either.

Taking care of her trumped the original order. Right?

It will have to.

Dani barreled for the pharmacy section. Hot on her heels, I watched her change directions and make a beeline for the bathroom. The sound of vomiting filled the grimy space.

"Just let me be for a few minutes," she insisted.

"Okay," I agreed and wandered out into the store. My stomach was restless too. But the solution wasn't chalky pink liquid.

After a quick stop in the pet section, I wandered to the food aisle, where my arms soon were full of munchies. I would drop Dani off, go back to the fortress, and plan social content. I'd neglected my channels in the rush of preparing for the gala. But that was just the thing I needed to take my mind off…everything.

I should be using this time to interrogate Daniella. She'd warmed up to me, and we were practically besties. I just needed to ply her with a little booze and loosen her tongue. She didn't like my husband? And he trusted her husband to watch his back!

I fumed. This captain Igor was next on my shit list. I needed to contrive a way to eavesdrop on him. That was a tomorrow problem. There would be no plotting tonight.

The beep of my phone sent my heart jumping.

But it wasn't my Bratva soldier boy. It was Dani, saying she was out in the SUV. Rolling my eyes at her, I grabbed one last bag of snacks. It had been forty minutes since we left the guys.

"Please let him be okay," I begged the universe.

My gut twisted. I ripped open the pack of strawberry ropes and started gobbling as I went to the checkout. Putting the shopping bags on my arm, I put my hand protectively in my coat pocket. Head down, I ventured into the frigid night.

I was so not built for this kind of weather. I belonged somewhere warm. Why didn't I flee to Cancún? I snorted. "Yeah, because I would have met Dimi on the streets there."

Mocking laughter stopped me in my tracks. There were a lot of cars out here for it being after midnight. But that didn't stop this group of punks from surrounding our SUV.

"You've got to be kidding me!" I hissed. Was this night ever going to end? And why was Karma taking such a fiendish delight in testing my sanity?!

I marched over, done with tonight.

Dani cut me a look and shook her head.

"Screw that," I growled. Anger boiled deep inside. I latched onto it, letting it fuel my movements.

I wasn't backing down.

"Come on, we just want to party. Come with us, pretty mama," one of the street rats urged, leaning against the window of the vehicle. His body practically dangled over Daniella.

"Hey! Asshole, get away from my truck," I snapped.

"Ooh! This one knows how to play."

I looked at the punk who'd spoken. Enough. *Enough!* "I'm really sick of prickish asshats like you thinking that you can bully women into doing whatever sick game you want."

As I spoke, I drew my gun.

A collective *oohing* and *aahhing* trumpeted around the group. There were five of them. And not a single one showed proper fear.

"I'm not asking again," I spat. "Leave."

"Only if you're coming with me, sweetheart," the one with blue tears on his chalky white cheek cooed at me.

I pointed at his junk.

He looked at his buddies for moral support, which they gave in terms of masculine notes of approval. Red tinged my vision. Why were the majority of guys such jerks?! Did they go to a secret class at school that taught it? I worked my jaw back and forth. I wasn't a damsel anymore.

I was a princess of the underworld.

"What are you going to do? Shoot me?" he mocked.

"Yes." I pulled the trigger.

A chorus of "Oh, shit!" rang out, but the retreating slap of their sneakers echoed on the pavement. The prick rolled around on the ground, moaning and whimpering.

"So much for loyalty," I gasped, my body suddenly shaking. The comfort candy threatened to make a reappearance.

"Laurel!" Dani sprinted to my side.

I shook my head, grabbed the first package of candy, and tore an opening in the package. The grape pellets hit my tongue, and I swallowed more of the nerds than chewed.

"We have to get out of here," Dani insisted.

I choked the mouthful and garbled around the candy. "He comes with."

Wrenching open the passenger side door, I put my bags onto the floor. Turning back, I rubbed my hands. "Between the two of us, we should be able to lift him."

Dani was tapping on her phone. "One of the guys at our tech company should be able to remotely erase the security footage."

"Oh, shit, I didn't think of that." I squatted and gripped the sobbing man. I couldn't lift him, so I dragged him to the trunk. On Monday, I was going to start working out in earnest. Living in the underworld meant I would have to be more physically active. And this little shit was scrawny! I should have been able to lift him.

Popping the trunk, Dani came around to help lift his feet. It was pathetic how strong the willowy ballerina was.

The man screamed when we dropped him in the trunk of the SUV.

I slapped his cheek. "This is nothing. Wait until my husband gets his hands on you."

We hurried to the front, and I turned up the stereo to drown out the noise. I ate my way through a can of chips and then turned back to the strawberry lengths. But as I turned down her street, Dani rolled the volume down.

"You can't have him escaping in our apartment," she warned.

"Um, how about I drop you, and then I'll go back to the fortress."

She nodded in agreement and that was exactly what we did.

And there goes the chance to pry the truth from her. I gunned the accelerator and headed into the night.

The shaking mostly stopped by the time I rolled through the front gate. I drove around to the vehicle bay, checked my phone, and when I still hadn't heard from Dimi, I sent him a message that I was home safe.

The screaming stopped, and I figured the punk had passed out. But I didn't want the other soldiers to find out I had a shot civilian in my trunk. So grabbing a box of biscuits, I hurried to the kennels.

Marena's tail began to wag double time when I appeared. "Kill some time with me, girl?"

I tossed her a cookie. The other dogs were noisy and frantic. Their vicious barking put me on edge. Marena prowled to my side and walked out.

Looking back, I felt bad.

So I retreated and dropped a treat for each of the other cages. I nearly lost a finger when the great black pincher lunged for the cage. I made sure to drop extras in his pen before hurrying away.

Once outside, I raced Marena back to the SUV. It was still quiet inside. I grabbed the ball and the launcher, pulling the plastic packaging off. Marena cocked her brown head and watched as I attempted to throw the ball.

She looked at the bouncing flash of yellow and then swung her head back to me.

"Don't you know how to play fetch?" I gasped, squatting to rub her head.

The whap of her tail was the only answer.

"Come on! Like this." I took off running, hiking my skirt to move.

The dog bounded after me but left it to me to pick up the ball. I frowned at her.

"You aren't good at being a dog, girl."

"She's not a pet," came the mocking response.

I smelled the cigarette a moment later. Peering around the tacky stone statues littering the cement slab meant to be a patio, I discovered a group of grizzled men. Locking gazes with the Bratva pakhan with two of his soldiers, I wasn't sure what to say. He simply stood by the back door and smoked. With the metal and brick framing his body, he looked like a terrible warlord from some steampunk graphic novel. Not a drop of warmth flickered from him, despite the fact that he was my father-in-law.

"No one touches Dimitri's dog," one I recognized as a gate guard sneered.

"I'm his wife. I can assure you, I have permission to...touch." My smile was part snide, part sultry. "And this is good for her training. Stimulates her mind."

I had no idea if what I said was true, but because I packed more confidence behind the words than I felt, I knew they'd buy it.

"Train? No, no. Just like everything my bastard does, he can't even train her properly." The jab was cut off due to a fit of coughing.

"I think she's a fine animal," I countered. "Lots of potential."

The hacking breaths turned into laughter. "Figures. A fat cow thinking a useless dog has potential."

The other men chuckled.

Because he spoke in Russian, I had to bite my tongue hard. *Careful old man, this cow has horns.*

My phone buzzed. I pulled it out and walked back to the SUV. There was no need to continue a conversation with the cruel men.

Conscious that he could watch me in the exposed expanse that was the backyard, I rounded the SUV to take shelter. It was Dimi.

He was on his way home—to me.

Chin held high, I continued the game for no other reason than I wouldn't cower before men who I wouldn't allow to make me feel weak.

Chapter 43 – Dimitri

I pulled into the fortress and pulled around to the parking bays, only to slam on my breaks. Laurel was tossing a tennis ball a few feet, racing to it, and doing everything in her power to get my Rhodesian Ridgeback to grab it.

Snapping my seatbelt, I launched out of the car. "What's this?"

"Dimi!" Laurel straightened and flashed me a grin. It sent a bolt of warmth straight through me. "Your dog doesn't know how to dog."

"You need to give her the command." I held out my hand for the ball.

"Damn it, Jim! It's not supposed to be this hard," Laurel laughed, hiking her skirt to hurry over. She looked a little like a wild bear, loping across the frozen ground. I wanted to peel that fur—fake fur, she was very adamant about that—off her and discover the temptress underneath the enchantment.

"That had better not be another Trekkie jab," I warned.

Laurel smirked. But the light feeling lifting my heart to soar sank and drowned in horror the next moment. Her skirt was streaked in crimson.

"What happened?" I closed the distance in two steps and wrenched her arm.

Her eyes widened at the contact, but then she looked down and began laughing.

"Who did this to you? Are you hurt?" I growled, giving her a hard shake. "Quit laughing, woman!"

Gasping, Laurel sank down. I clutched her close and kept shaking her. She swatted at me but then swiped at her eyes.

"Oh, too funny," she gasped. "Too freaking funny."

"No! Not funny." I grabbed her hands.

That sobered her instantly.

But she didn't pull away from my touch.

"Who hurt you, redbird?"

A crazed impulse surged in my veins. Someone was going to die! Where was my gun? I reached for it.

"It's not my blood," she countered.

I would decapitate whoever dared touch her. Burn their lairs to the ground! *Water the earth with their blood!*

"Dimi!" Laurel snapped, stepping into me. Her voice was plaintive. Despite my hold, she clapped her hands, forcing me to focus. "You're not listening. It's not mine. It's not my blood!"

My voice was harsh. "Then whose is it?"

"Please let go of my hands."

"Only if you tell me," I urged.

Laurel took a deep breath. She closed her eyes, and her hands shifted in my hold. I loosened my grip, but only slightly.

"Dani got sick, so we stopped at Wally-World for meds. She ended up puking her guts out. I grabbed snacks, but she was already at the car. When I found her—"

Laurel stopped and gestured at her clothes.

"What?" I snarled.

"Don't be mad."

"Can't promise that, redbird." My blood simmered. No...*boiled*. Someone was going to die. Just as soon as she gave me a name.

Laurel gulped, squeezing her gloved fingers tightly. "A group of hood rats were bothering Dani. They wouldn't leave, so I...um..."

"Laurel."

"I shot one."

I swayed. My head felt light. Shapes became unfocused. "You shot one?" I repeated in a whisper.

"I'm just so sick of nasty men thinking they can bully women!" Raw hatred laced her voice and hid something far more painful. But the agony was still there. "He had the chance to leave, but he thought we were just little playthings. I'm no man's plaything!"

A knot formed in my gut.

"Are you okay?" I leaned forward, clutching her cheeks between my hands.

She nodded. "As long as you're not mad."

"Why would I be mad?" I rasped. *I thank the saints you had a gun.*

Laurel lifted her shoulders. "Shooting random assholes isn't good for business. But!" she rushed to add. "Dani assured me that the footage was erased. The punks didn't have the wherewithal to take down our license plates, and the guy won't talk."

"Why not?" Curiosity tickled the back of my mind, despite the all-consuming panic at the knowledge my wife had been in danger and I hadn't been there.

"I—we! We hauled him into the trunk of the SUV. That's how I got all bloody."

I barked a rough laugh. "You what?"

Laurel struggled to her feet, gesturing eagerly at the trunk. "I figured I would save the pleasure of dealing with him for you. But...." She looked around me. "I didn't want the guards to snoop and find him. So that's why I stayed to guard the vehicle."

Words failed me.

"It's a good thing you weren't longer." She shivered. "It's not exactly barbecue season out here! It's fricking freezing and I have to pee."

Still at a loss for words, I wrapped my arm around her shoulder. Laurel wound hers around my middle and hugged me back. The heightened emotions pulsed furiously through me, and my mind raced so as not to be overwhelmed by them.

And then I remembered the would-be tough guy was in the trunk.

A malicious glee rose to suppress the other emotions.

"Come on, let's see how our guest is doing," I urged, tugging Laurel to the trunk.

She rubbed her nose on the back of her glove. "I don't think I can stomach torture. I know that's how you mob guys get your rocks off, but I don't think it's my thing. I'll go take a nice, long shower and doze off."

"That's just fine. You don't need to see what happens next." I spun her around, cupping her face in my palm. "I've got it from here, redbird."

"I know you do." Her voice was full of relief.

That trust, such a small instance of complete faith in me, but it meant the world. And it had the strangest reaction shifting through me. My heart beat double, thudding against my ribs. My chest warmed, and that heat trickled in delicious rivulets through my body.

Laurel watched me. Her intense focus was like a laser. I turned abruptly so she would see the truth. She didn't feel the same about me, and so I wouldn't admit how deeply she affected me.

I popped the trunk.

Laurel scrambled out from under my arm. She fidgeted with something as I took in the situation. *Ah, crap.* How was she going to take this? When I cut a look, I had to bite back a laugh.

"You can put the gun down, baby," I said as seriously as possible. "I won't let him hurt us."

"You don't know what he's going to do!" she insisted. "He'll be desperate."

"And you don't think I could handle him without a weapon?" I crossed my arms and leaned against the opening of the trunk.

"Dimi! Don't turn your back to him," she nearly shrieked, but her voice was so low it whistled through the night.

"Redbird, look at me." When she did, I let my lips turn up in one of the smiles I now knew she liked and reserved only for her. "Thank you for worrying about me, but in this instance, you don't have to."

She opened her mouth to protest, but I cut her off.

"He's dead."

Laurel blanched. She peered into the trunk before stumbling back several paces. "He must have bled out."

I murmured in assent. "And even if he hadn't, I can take a man bare handed."

Laurel threw up her hands, gun waving wildly about. I darted over and snatched it. We were going to have to go over some basic gun safety.

Breathing hard, she looked up at me in surprise. "I killed him."

A pang shot through me. Quickly, I turned her away. Putting a hand on each shoulder, I stared into her eyes. "You protected yourself and Dani. You did nothing wrong."

"I know that." She swallowed hard. "I wanted to kill so many people before. Always wondered what it would be like."

Worry flickered through my chest. "Let's get you inside. I don't want you going into shock out here. Okay?"

"I don't think I will." But Laurel let me pull her away. I closed and locked the vehicle.

"My snacks." Laurel rushed to the passenger side.

Unlocking the doors, I reached inside and plucked the bags. Not only were there enough snacks to feed a gaggle of teens, but there were many packets of dog treats. *She's spoiling the creature.* "How many of these did you give her?"

"Hmm, what? Oh, that...it wasn't all for Marena." Laurel hurried toward the back door of the fortress.

"What do you mean?"

"I gave some to the ones kept in the kennel," she said with a shrug.

Yet another surprise! First horror and then admiration washed through me. I was in danger of having emotional whiplash. The turbulent concoction needed an outlet.

A dark, wicked idea slithered into a plan.

"Didn't I tell you to leave the dogs alone?" I murmured.

The deep and rough tone had the desired effect. Laurel shivered.

"You're not very good at following directions—just like the command to drive straight home," I growled.

Holding up a finger, Laurel countered that one. "Dani was puking. She needed stomach chalk."

I ground my teeth. "Vomit comes out of upholstery."

"Ew!" Laurel squealed. "You did not just suggest I let her puke in the car."

This wasn't an argument I was going to win. Placing my hand on the back door, I caged her against the frozen metal. "Did I or did I not tell you to leave the dogs alone?"

"I did leave them alone." Her chin tipped up and defiance danced in her shadowed eyes. "I just fed them through the chain link."

"Laurel."

"What?" She grinned. "Technically, I obeyed."

"Am I going to have to put you over my knee until you get it through your head that these dogs are not pets?" I stepped into her, crowding her against the space.

And then she said the one thing I least expected. "It probably won't work, but we should try it anyhow."

My balls ached at the dare. My palm itched to connect with her creamy flesh.

The smell of Marlboro Reds ruined the moment.

Looking down, I noted the smoldering cigarette lying on the ground. Laurel noticed it too.

"Your dad is an ass," Laurel said quietly, toeing the butt. "I'm glad you stopped smoking. I used to hate seeing you light up beside your truck with your cousins."

I stilled.

Realizing her slip, Laurel snapped her gaze to mine. "It's no secret that I know you, Dimitri Vlasov."

And yet I don't know you. I'd told myself the emotions from the gala needed to be saved for another time. But since I was already worked up, they reared their ugly heads.

"How often were you there?" I asked quietly.

"Oh," she laughed. "Every few months. Over the course of several years." Laurel tucked a piece of hair behind her ear and adjusted her furry hat. "But I wasn't brave enough to act until it came down to life or death."

I let out a shuddering breath. "Aren't stalkers supposed to be creepy?"

"How do you know I'm not?" She gave me a tentative smirk.

I shook my head, clasped her face between my hands, and crushed my mouth to hers.

The kiss spoke for me. It told her I hated her secrets. There was a note of desperation, knowing she'd been in danger. It promised my devotion. And it asked for her patience.

Her lips remained silent. Like her smiles, they were beautiful, albeit unreadable. The only thing I knew for certain was her desire for me simmered, but that was only because it was on the surface. I couldn't reach past it for something more.

When we disentangled, because I wasn't going to take her against the industrial, metal door, we were both breathing hard.

"Heavens, that stinks!" Laurel moved away to stamp the cigarette.

It wasn't just a butt. It still had plenty of tobacco left. I frowned. That was odd. My father was so careful to put them out. Something was off.

"I'm glad you quit, but if you ever wanted to kick back with some bud, I would be open to that." Her words surprised me, momentarily chasing away the sinking feeling at seeing a wasted smoke.

"I haven't smoked that since I was a teenager," I grumbled.

"Well, the offer stands." She wrinkled her nose. "It's nice the house doesn't smell like cigarettes, though."

"The pakhan comes out here to smoke because it's the only time he gets fresh air." I ripped the door open and held it for Laurel.

Who gasped and covered her mouth with her gloved hands.

Chapter 44 – Laurel

After rushing to the hospital and having the pakhan sent back to the Mayo Medical Center in Rochester with a collapsed lung, we came home mid-morning simply beat. I could barely keep my eyes open. Dimitri tucked me into bed, and before I could protest that he wasn't joining me—*yet again*—I fell asleep.

It was impossible to tell the time from my surroundings. I rubbed my eyes and sat up. If I had to guess, it was shortly after I fell asleep.

I couldn't have been more wrong. It was early evening.

Scrambling out of bed, I found my phone plugged into the charger. Dimitri hadn't come to bed. But he answered my frantic text with one word.

Gym.

I rolled my eyes. Did he do nothing else? As I pulled the stretchy pants over my legs, another answer presented itself. The gym was his safe space.

Hesitantly, I knocked on the door.

"Enter," came the command.

"Am I disturbing you?" I called through the crack.

"Get that fine ass in here," Dimitri growled.

I hurried inside. The door closed with a clap behind me. "You didn't come to bed," I accused him.

He shook his head and gestured to the corner of the gym. "I waited up to hear my dad was stable; they repaired the leak in his lung. By then, I had a headache and laid down here."

Frowning, I wove through the equipment before I came to the...freezer chest. He was sitting in a freezer filled with cold water! His normally tan skin was beat red. It blazed and contrasted against the swirls of dark ink. My stomach flipped.

Social media had these ice baths, but I always thought it was a prank. "That can't be comfortable."

"It isn't."

"Then what the hell, Dimi?!"

A timer beeped, and the wall of carved muscle rose from the icy water. He prowled over. "I'm cold, redbird."

I stilled. An ache deep in my core pulsed.

Chilled fingers gripped my arms. "Warm me up."

I wet my lips and swallowed. "Okay."

Dimitri lifted me easily. He padded over to the blue mat and tore at my clothes as he set me on my feet. Once I was bare, he laid me down, spreading my legs wide.

"I've thought about nothing but licking this pussy since I saw you in that dress last night. I can't believe you made me wait so long," he growled.

"It wasn't me!" I protested.

"Mmm." The rough noise rumbled in his chest.

His face settled between my legs. He licked and sucked. I moaned, burying my hands in his hair. My hips tipped up of their own accord, moving with the rhythm of his tongue.

Dimitri pulled back with a curse.

I peeled my eyes open, gasping at him with a wordless question.

"I can't manage it this way." He flopped onto the mat, rolling me over.

"We can do something else," I offered, not really understanding, only knowing that I needed more—more of him.

"All in good time. I want to pound into your cunt until you scream my damn name! But first? I need you to ride my face, baby." As he spoke, he pulled me over him.

I straddled him, looking down. It was incredibly intimate, and so damn hot! But.... "You don't look good."

"I'm tired. I'm sore."

"So why don't we—"

"No." He pulled me down and drew a path through my pussy with his tongue. "You make me feel better. You take my mind off it."

"Dimi," I moaned.

"Ride me. Ride my face, redbird."

I lowered and tentatively rocked over his tongue.

"Come on, Laurel, you can let loose, babe."

Universe help me, I did. My thighs opened wider. I arched over him, gripping some metal bar in front of me. And then, I let go of the reservations.

I rode his face—hard.

His tongue flicked over my pussy.

Those lips that I adored kissing, French kissed my clit.

There was a real danger of melting from the pleasure. I whimpered. His mouth was wicked. I couldn't believe how good it felt.

Dimitri dug his fingers into my ass and hips, urging me to go harder. There was no holding back. I screamed his name and orgasmed on his face.

In a split second, he slid out from underneath me, pushed my forearms over the foam-covered bar, and yanked my backside against him.

"Hold the bar," he growled, sliding his thick cock against my pussy to coat it with wetness.

I gripped the brace with the waning strength left in my muscles. *That's it. Monday I start working out!*

Dimitri spread me and shoved deep inside with one hard thrust.

I groaned. "So full!"

"That's right, redbird." He pulled back. His hips cracked forward with a second forceful thrust.

We'd had sex. It had been full of passion. This? This was different. Dimitri said he needed me. And damn, he showed me just how much with the unrelenting way he fucked me.

I held on for dear life and enjoyed every damn second.

He buried his hand in my hair, snatching the cloth binder and freeing the raven locks. "This would look incredible if it was the same color as your pussy."

A moan escaped my lips. In this moment, if he asked me to change my hair back, I would. In a heartbeat. But he didn't.

He just continued to pump into me.

His unforgiving touch dug into my hips, and he snapped his own in rapid succession. But that hard touch inched down. before I could fathom it, his fingers rubbed my pussy.

"It's time to come on my cock, redbird."

His words held *power*. With a cry of delirium, I obeyed. My muscles convulsed, and the orgasm ripped through me.

Dimitri groaned.

Wave after wave of violent pleasure washed through me. I wondered if I glowed. Every fiber inside me blazed bright.

"You squeeze me so tight—" he rasped but speech failed as he thrust deep with a roar.

The purely masculine volume rebounded off the walls.

I soaked up the bliss of making the beast roar like that.

Chapter 45 – Laurel

Gripping my wrist, Dimitri tugged me up. We stopped only beside the rest station, where he wetted a paper towel and dabbed between my legs.

The tender way he patted my swollen pussy had my heart clenching with something foreign. I watched him, trying and failing to name the emotion.

But it was there. And it was assigned specifically to him.

"I have one more temperature therapy, and then we can grab a bite of dinner," he said, tossing the paper towel in the trash.

I nodded. "I'll join you in the sauna."

The end of that sentence inflected like a question.

Straightening, Dimitri wrapped his arms around me. "Thank you."

While part of me wasn't sure I deserved the praise, I took it. He smelled like the woods, cozy and safe. I drank in the moment, not ready to let him go. When he untangled us, I protested feebly.

"Come here, redbird." Dimitri pulled me into the sauna. After clasping the door tight, he dashed a cup of water on the coals. The pant of steam shot into the air. I echoed the noise and grabbed my length of hair, knotting them above my head.

To be truthful, I'd been waiting for a chance to enjoy the steam.

"Sit on my lap."

There was plenty of room beside him, but the thought of being nestled against him was too tempting. Besides, it wasn't a question. I obeyed. Secretly—something I would never admit aloud—I enjoyed when he gave me commands.

But only because it was him.

Dimitri trailed his fingers over my hair. "If I asked you a question, would you answer me?"

I considered that for a moment. There were so many secrets swirling between us. Did I dare give him one? It didn't have to be the whole truth....

"Only if I get to ask one," I agreed.

"Alright, you first then."

"Why do you practice temperature therapy?" I asked, calmed by the repetitive motion of his hand on my hair.

"I received a spinal injury. I get headaches. The therapy...helps."

It was a short answer, but it was telling.

"I had no idea, I'm sorry," I breathed.

Dimitri shrugged. "I don't like to let people know. It's perceived as a weakness."

"I can understand that." I brushed my fingers down his side. "Thank you for telling me."

Dimitri grunted. "Why did you dye your hair?" he asked in turn.

Taking a deep breath, I vowed to be brave. I could do this. I was *safe* with this underworld prince. But even as I wanted to trust him, old habits died hard. Only part of the truth came out. "I'm hiding. It's a layer of protection."

Dimitri nodded slowly. "You know you have a place here for as long as you want it. I'll keep you safe, redbird."

"I know," I breathed. My chest tightened. Emotions spiked, and I struggled to get my next words out. "But what if you tire of me?"

He pressed his cheek against my skin. His hot breath made it prickle. "That's not happening. If you want to leave, I'll let you go. But as far as I'm concerned, this is where you belong."

That was so much! We'd been together for mere weeks.

And yet, it made sense. It just...fit.

"Bound to a criminal organization?" I laughed incredulously.

"Co-ruling an underworld kingdom."

I sighed. *A daydream.* A castle we created out of clouds, sweet and intangible.

And yet, the question of what if pounded in the back of my mind.

Co-ruling was something I felt qualified to do. Hell, my very upbringing prepared me for something like this. While the path my parents steered me toward was considered respectable because it was legal, this crime world actually fit the ruthless ethics instilled in me since childhood far better. Being in the mob was honest. The monsters thrived in plain sight. And they didn't hesitate to end those who hurt them or their loved ones.

You are more than a bartender.

The inner encouragement went to great lengths to assure me. Could I do this? Could I…stay?

One look at the handsome profile and my heart fluttered with a resounding affirmation. This started as a friends-with-benefits situation. And now? There was definitely something more. I would be a fool to not embrace that.

While all these tumultuous thoughts rattled through my mind, Dimitri brought his hands over my backside. "I can't get enough of your ass. It's fucking gorgeous."

I wriggled on his lap. "Why, thank you. Thank you very kindly."

A strangled exhale came out of his mouth. "But how the hell is it so bony?" he exclaimed.

I laughed. "You're not the first person to say that."

The underworld prince stilled. Dimitri's eyes darkened. "Laurel…has anyone ever *touched* this ass?"

He ran his fingers through the seam to let me know exactly what he meant.

A bolt of white-hot lust spiked my veins. There was no way I should still be aroused. And *that*? That wasn't sexy.

My body begged to differ.

I wriggled against him. My inner muscles clenched. An achy need throbbed between my legs. I couldn't create the friction I desperately needed, but it didn't stop me from wriggling at him.

"Well?" he demanded, shifting me off his lap and reaching between my legs. He pulled wetness from my pussy and brought it over my puckered hole.

Just the touch back there was enough to make my insides clench.

"Nnnooo," I gasped. "No one, I swear."

"Mine," Dimitri growled.

He stood swiftly, sending me forward, and pushed me out of the sauna. The sudden opening of the door brought a rush of colder air. I shivered. My hardened nipples ached at the contact.

Before I could grasp what happened, Dimitri returned. He fisted his cock. The whole, powerful length glistened. The time to protest was now.

Any objection died on the tip of my tongue. Curiosity cut it off. Desire buried it deep.

"Coconut oil," he explained as he reached for me. "Bend."

I did.

"Hands on the wall."

These orders! Hot and swoony—and I didn't think I was someone who let others boss her around!

But here I was, bent and waiting for his touch.

There wasn't much room in this space. Dimitri resumed his seat. His fingers reached between my cheeks and stroked the *other* hole.

My pussy convulsed at the contact, even though she was being ignored.

"I'm going to take this virginity," he growled and pushed a finger inside.

I squeaked at the invasion.

"So damn tight, babe." Dimitri withdrew his finger and stroked the puckered opening. "Tell me to stop and I will."

This was a game time decision. I could tell him not to, and the experience would be lost. *Can I do it?* Did I trust him enough?

With a shudder, I decided. Why not give this to him?

"Take it. It's yours to claim," I rasped.

With a growl, Dimitri pulled me down. As I descended onto his lap, the head of his cock lined with my ass.

And then he pushed inside, filling and stretching what had never been touched.

I cried out, every muscle tightening in protest.

"Relax, I've got you," he promised.

"I know," I panted. "Now take me."

I was proud the stammer in my voice was minimal.

Dimitri lifted me by my hips and brought me down onto his length. It hurt. I would be lying if I said it didn't.

In the pause that followed, Dimitri's lips brushed over my shoulder. "You're doing such a good job, baby."

The encouragement helped me through the feeling of impossible fullness. I drew deep breaths into my lungs.

That wicked mouth kissed a path along my back. He sucked and caressed. Nipped and scored. I focused on his lips, letting the feel of them wash through me.

I *did* trust him.

It was obvious. I wouldn't have let him grow this close. I knew it when I accepted his offer to be his fake wife. I just couldn't admit it. Even now that was hard.

"There you go, nice and relaxed," he murmured against my shoulder.

"Mmmm," I agreed. Sweat dripped down my forehead. I swiped it away.

His palm slid around to reach my breast. He pinched the tightened nipple. The accompanying contraction deep inside chased away some of the ebbing discomfort.

Dimitri sank his teeth into my flesh. His hand kneaded the tender flesh. But when his fingers reached around to my clit, the delicious friction was enough to have me tentatively moving, testing—liking!

"I've got you. Hold onto me."

I rolled my eyes at the command, and his grip immediately tightened. I gasped.

"You're lucky I'm in a forgiving mood, redbird. Those eye rolls are going to catch up with you one day." His rough breath skated over my sensitive skin.

A full body shiver raced through me.

It left us both breathless.

There was a silent pause, and then he began to move.

I scrambled to grab his arms. They were slick with sweat, hot against my palms. I managed to grip his arms tight. He was an anchor. But he was also the storm.

His touch was relentless. Sliding against my pussy, his fingers played me like an instrument, and my body sang in response! I moaned as heat flared between my legs. The delicious kind that sizzled without burning. I squeezed my muscles to create more friction.

The steaming rocks hissed in the background. Our bodies were wet, sweat beading and dropping. The harsh gasps of each exhale sounded loud in the closed space.

Sitting on his cock, he did most of the work. As he drove into me, he licked and sucked, kissed and bit my back. I would wear his marks later—which was fine by me!

I whimpered, feeling the distinct tightening.

"Take it, baby. Take it all!" Dimitri growled.

He tweaked my swollen clit. Those fingers made tight circles, and a strangled cry left my throat. Pleasure pulsed, the muscles deep inside convulsing.

There was nothing remaining but the impending release.

"Look at you, redbird. You're so greedy. Look at how you work your hips."

I hadn't realized I was bouncing up and down on his cock. But I was. Taking everything he gave.

It was hot—too hot. The stones steamed. Our bodies crackled. Each pulse of pleasure was fire. The flames licked my veins, burning me from the inside out.

"I'm coming," I sobbed.

"Good. Good girl," he murmured against my neck.

"It's so much," I whimpered.

"I know, but you're doing so well. Just a little more. I need you to come for me."

I nodded violently, holding onto him for dear life.

"Come, Laurel. Now."

A strangled inhalation filled my lungs. The delicious throb rang deep inside as pleasure blinded me. My body arched, bent as if in the middle of an exorcism.

And then I was screaming my release.

Dimitri bellowed his own in an echo of mine.

Chapter 46 – Dimitri

Breathing hard, I held her close. Heat poured off our bodies, and there was no relief in the sweltering hot box. I couldn't make myself move away. What we'd just done...it was huge. Laurel gave me something no other man had claimed.

The feelings surging through me.... I was crazy for this woman.

Now to convince her.

I let out a slow breath so as not to sigh. Her reservations came from that dark chest of secrets. If I could only pry open the lid, slay her demons, and set her free. But she didn't want a hero.

Good thing I'm the villain in this story.

That gorgeous body shifted above me. There was a distinct wince, and Laurel stilled.

"Easy," I murmured.

Even though my dick swore up and down that he was ready for more, I knew that Laurel wasn't. Lifting her carefully, I snatched the paper towels that I'd brought and cleaned up the visible mess.

Her silence worried me.

I flicked multiple glances at her face, but she wore that unreadable mask. There was only one thing to shatter the façade. Pushing the door open, I pulled her out of the sauna. She stumbled as she hurried to keep up.

But she stopped short when she realized what I was doing.

"No!" She jerked away.

I smirked. "Oh, no, redbird. You're not getting out of the other half of this."

Laurel whipped her head back and forth. "Dimitri! No! Absolutely not!"

"Too late to say no, babe." I wrapped my arms around her and carried her struggling form to the chest freezer.

Popping the lid with my elbow, I mounted the short ladder. "Will you stop your wriggling? I'm going to slip and drop you." *Or fuck your sweet ass again until you submit.*

And that wasn't a good option. She would be too sore.

Laurel screamed at the top of her lungs as the cold water swelled around us.

I lowered my body, tugging her into me. The cold had the exact effect I hoped it would. Laurel's mask was gone, and anger mixed with indignation shone brightly. It made me smile to see it.

"See? Not so bad," I teased, nipping at her neck.

A violent shiver made her quake. "I hate you!"

Flipping her around, molding her body against me, and hooking her legs with mine, I pressed my nose to hers. "Lie to me again, redbird."

Laurel pursed her lips. "I can't believe you do this."

"Regularly."

"Why?" she wailed.

I shrugged. "Ice baths are good for you."

"The hell they are!"

I couldn't help it. I laughed, my sides shaking. Water pushed out the sides of the cooler and splashed Laurel in the face. As she watched me, some of the rage seeped away. The corner of her mouth even twitched.

"Tell me what you're thinking?" I gasped, trying to regain control over my breathing. I never laughed. Not carefree and light like that.

"That I might just let your cousin kill you," she seethed.

More laughter bubbled up. "My cousin? Nah...you've got it all wrong."

Laurel huffed. "For your information, I'm onto something."

I snorted forcefully. "Do tell."

Laurel tipped her chin up. "No. Not if you're going to mock me."

I reached up, cupping her face. "Tell. Me."

Laurel shivered again. "Only if you let me out of this godsforsaken bath."

"Five more minutes." I slid my hand through her hair.

"That long!"

I nodded. "Now...which cousin?"

"Kazimir."

Riotous mirth exploded from somewhere deep inside. I had no clue that I was capable of so much unsuppressed glee. But the delightful situation of having Laurel's naked, shivering body pinned against mine was the world's strongest propellent.

This woman makes me laugh.

I knew she was something special when she flew into my life, but every day with her only proved that to be true again and again. I pushed my fingers into her hair, pulling her head down to press against mine. Words that I couldn't say were on the tip of my tongue. I wasn't going to scare my songbird away.

"Kazimir is my second in command. I trust him with my life—as I do with my other cousins and a few of my men. He's not the one who put the hit out for me."

"You sound certain," she scoffed.

"Clearly the cold is making you grumpy. Come on then, spill. Tell me why I'm wrong."

Triumph laced her voice. "Kazimir's wife doesn't like you."

"She has every reason not to," I agreed.

Laurel reared back, but only as far as my hold allowed her to.

I swept a look over her. That pale, creamy skin was a delicious shade of red from the freezing water. I wanted to carve a path over it with my tongue. "Does that surprise you?"

When she didn't answer right away, I arched a brow.

Those rosy lips pursed. "If she doesn't like you, how can you be certain she's not a threat?" Laurel insisted.

"Because, liking me has nothing to do with survival." The words were a sharp dash of reality.

The clock on the wall ticked. Every few seconds, a shiver rippled through Laurel. We watched one another as the dark truth of our world spun a web of dire implications.

"If you...I mean, if the assassin succeeded, then Kaz and Dani would be in danger," Laurel finally said quietly.

I nodded. "Right now is a weird period of waiting. I don't have the reins, but I need to be ready at a moment's notice to seize the throne. We've quietly eliminated the most troublesome members, but until the bratva decides to back me or turn against my claim, I can only be so prepared."

Laurel lifted her hand and ran her touch over my head. I closed my eyes and tipped back into her touch. It felt good—so good.

"When you succeed, you're going to be the strongest organization in Chicago," Laurel whispered. "I can see it."

I clenched my jaw tight. *Stay—stay with me.*

Laurel cut a look to the clock. "It's been seven minutes!"

Reluctantly, I let her pull away. She clambered out of the freezer, and I surged forward to grab her elbow in order to help her. There were darker marks on her back, ones made by my mouth.

Damn, she marks well.

The beast inside purred at seeing her skin speckled from my kisses and bites.

Laurel wrapped herself in a fluffy towel. When she plucked one from the rack and brought it over, I leaned against the freezer's ledge. "Be truthful, temperature therapy isn't *that* bad."

Her eyes narrowed. "You're right. It's not *that bad.* It's fucking terrible."

That straight-faced reaction set me off laughing again. Laurel shoved the towel at me and turned sharply to dress. I hurried to follow her. I had fresh clothing down here. Hurrying to where she finger-combed her hair off her face, I leaned down to press a kiss against her throat.

It was hard to tell, but I could have sworn she sighed.

"Hungry?" I asked.

She nodded. I laced our hands together and, when she didn't fight my hold, pulled her down to the kitchen, a smile playing on my lips the whole time. This songbird was learning to trust me.

Chapter 47 – Dimitri

Wrapped in a hoodie, Laurel handed the final document to Ilya. The club manager scanned the paper and nodded slowly. "I like it."

Laurel beamed. I handed her a water bottle with electrolytes, and she took a tentative sip. Her skin was still flushed red from our self-defense exercises before Ilya came. As much as I would have preferred working out in my home gym, we needed the space of the fighting ring to work through some more advanced moves. I was so damn proud of my bride for getting up after every fall. And she was making progress!

However, if someone actually attacked her....

I hid my shudder by moving to take a seat opposite. Laurel had a long way to go before she could defend herself. I was taking her to the target range in the next couple of days. That would be her best bet.

"I like this," Ilya muttered. While we were the only ones in the bratva's gym, Ilya still spoke cautiously. "Won't this kind of unity bring unwanted attention?"

Laurel shook her head. The mass of tight, black ringlets bounced on her shoulders. "They won't be linked. Not all of them. Restaurant, hotel, club; linked. Clubs—plural—make them look like rivals. Make them compete. But we run the competition and make it dance to *our* tune."

"This will take capital." Ilya tapped his finger on the hand drawn notes Laurel made.

My wife cut a look to me. "It's not going to happen overnight. But I should say in five years, the Vlasov Bratva will run a large chunk of Chicago."

Five years. Those two words echoed through my mind. The organ in my chest jumped. My pulse doubled. My father had been content to make money from blood and carnage. He would have loved more power, but that came with risks. He was content with mediocrity.

I never had been.

But it wasn't until I saw it through Laurel's eyes that I believed in the empire the Vlasov Bratva could be.

"We'll start the ball rolling," I said, hoping she couldn't hear the breathlessness I felt.

"But quietly," Ilya added. "The old guard won't care for this. It was too damn bad your father survived the latest attack."

Laurel gasped. Her eyes darted between me and my oldest friend.

"It won't be long," I agreed. "We're ready when it happens."

"At least your bride doesn't look green," Ilya snorted in Russian. "Talk life and death to most chicks and they flip out."

About to tell him exactly how strong and capable my bride was, the gym door banged open. Pairs and pairs of soldiers rushed in to escape the chilly evening. I glared at them.

Laurel began to gather the papers, but I shook my head. "Hiding the papers would only make this look worse than it is."

"Dimi, you sure?" she breathed.

Ilya's look said he thought the same.

"Let him see," I commanded.

Their captain took up the rear. They set to work stripping into workout gear, cracking open cases of beer, and cranking the music to a thunderous bump.

"Doesn't Emil have a job tonight?" Ilya growled.

I nodded.

Seeing our group, Emil and one of the goons from his team came over. After greeting us, he plucked some of the papers off the worn and abused coffee table. A long whistle pushed past his lips. "You've been busy, Dimitri, my boy," the captain said in Russian.

Emil was only a few years older than me, and we'd been made captains within months of one another. I curled my fingers around my Zippo and refused to answer.

"You're just going to up and open another club?" Emil laughed incredulously, dropping the paper back onto the pile. "To launder money through?"

"It's a proposal. I'm bringing it to the captains and the pakhan."

"And here I thought you were keeping your daddy's seat warm," Emil teased.

"I got the money to fix *your* mistake. That qualifies me to concoct ideas for our organization."

Emil smirked. "Look at the little prince, already ruling."

My grip on my Zippo tightened.

Ilya pushed to his feet and took a step forward.

Laurel shot to her own, coming around and standing between them. She might not understand Russian, but she read body language. "Ilya, one more thing."

And then my delicate, fragile bride—because everyone was compared to Ilya—tugged on the soldier's arm. "I forgot to show you the hotel that goes with this."

Miraculously, her attention broke Ilya's. He turned his death glare away, and I didn't have to shoot my friend for murdering a captain.

I pushed to my own feet. Throwing an arm around Emil, I leaned in close. "I don't know what you're playing at, but if you go against me, you lose."

"I would never think to oppose the heir," he said, but there was something underneath, something...evil.

I released him. "Aren't you supposed to be down at the docks to receive a shipment?"

He shook his head and collapsed into a seat. "John Henry's crew was stopped by Canadians."

Laurel cocked her head. It had to be because the British name was understandable, even in Russian.

The far door banged open. Kazimir prowled across the space, pulling his gloves and coat off. He threw one look over the scene, and his blue eyes darkened. I shook my head ever so slightly as I sat back down.

"Looks like I'm free to hit the bag after my takeout order comes," Emil yawned and stretched, a feline movement. I shifted my weight to put more of my body between me and my bride.

"I thought we were sparring." Kazimir stopped at the edge of the seating area.

"We had a meeting with Ilya about some ideas." I jerked my chin at where Laurel spoke animatedly with my old friend.

Kazimir merely nodded.

Emil burped and tapped on his phone. "Food's here."

We waited for the pest to rise.

When he didn't, Kazimir growled. "Don't you have to go collect it?"

Emil shook his head. "She'll bring it inside."

"That's not the rules, and you know it." Fire leapt through Kazimir's eyes. "No civilians inside our training area."

"And how would she get through the gate?" I countered.

"With the gate code?" Emil drawled.

Saints, what a damn idiot. I might just have to shoot him one of these days. A bullet would be an improvement on his broad forehead. "Emil. Get off your ass, go outside, and get your damn food."

The other captain narrowed his eyes.

"It's the rules," Kazimir added softly. It would be a mistake to take his low volume for gentleness.

With a great sigh, Emil rose. "Alright, alright. Don't get your balls in a wad. Jeeze—would have thought you'd be a little less of a stickler than your daddy, Dimitri." Emil itched himself. "But I want to say one more thing. I've got ideas for this organization too. Lots of them. The wise man who'd be willing to listen to me would have my full support."

The captain didn't wait for my response before he sauntered away.

A palpable tension released.

"What in the hell was that all about?" Laurel murmured softly.

Kazimir shot her a look, before he took the seat cushion Emil had been sitting on, flipped them over, and sat.

"He's probing," I sighed and rubbed my eyes.

"The vultures are starting to circle," Ilya added.

I nodded. "Go check that he didn't let some delivery girl into the gate."

Ilya grunted but obeyed.

"Ilya's been so damn moody all winter," Kazimir murmured in Russian.

I wish he would tell me why. "He has. Today is the most he's spoken in weeks."

I found Ilya on a visit back to our family in Russia. I'd struck an instant friendship with him, and he'd come back with us to the States. His papers were fake, as were many of our soldiers. But ever since early December, Ilya had been off. Foul tempered, he'd picked fights, hardly participated in bratva business, and...hadn't been a good friend.

"Go figure it's her that's brought him out of his shell. If your wife needed a wild animal to do her bidding, she'd have it fucking eating out of her hand," Kazimir said quietly.

I both hated and loved my cousin's observation. He wasn't wrong. Laurel could move mountains. I just didn't want her moving anyone's but mine.

"That brings us to other matters," Kazimir said in Russian. "You're still keeping this ruse going."

I fisted my hand beside my thigh. "This needs to end, Kaz. Laurel is staying."

I can't let her go!

"We haven't confirmed who's out for your head, boss," he snarled back.

"It's not her." I crossed my arms and dared my cousin to contradict me. "And you let your wife go home with her—where Laurel saved her!"

Kazimir stilled. "What?"

Haha, well shit. The newlyweds weren't telling each other everything after all. "Ask your bride what happened at the Walmart. Ask her who saved her. My wife—my wife, who's not an assassin!"

"I'm inclined to agree with Dimi," Ilya muttered, coming back to join our group. "If she wanted you dead, you'd be rotting in a casket already."

If that wasn't the most accurate thing I'd ever heard.... Laurel wasn't physically strong enough to overpower me. But with her wicked sharp mind, I would drop dead and never see the blow that struck.

"I don't want to spar in front of the others," I clipped out, changing the subject but continuing in Russian.

Kazimir barked a rough laugh. "Couldn't agree more."

Ilya was busy saying goodbye to Laurel, and he gave me a tight nod as he passed. "Be well, brother."

"And you too." I watched the fierce soul weave through the crowd. "Call Pavel and have him bring Dani to my house. We can spar in my gym."

"Ah, hell no!" Kazimir shook his head violently. "Dani never wants to go to your place again."

There was a soft laugh. Or so I thought. When I turned around, Laurel was busy gathering the documents and bobbing along to the music.

I could have sworn I heard her laugh.

"Go home, be with your wife—and daughter," I added as an afterthought. "I'm taking my bride out to dinner."

I watched her face for even the smallest detail. I must have been hearing things, because Laurel made no move that she understood.

Holding out my hand, I caught her attention. "Kazimir's going home. We can go out."

Laurel blinked. "Don't you have mob stuff to do?"

I shook my head. "Nothing's on the schedule. And dipshit wasn't able to collect his transfer, which means he won't be calling for backup. I'm all yours tonight."

My hand bobbed in between us, insisting that she take it.

"What happened?" Laurel looked to where the two dozen soldiers were spread out, drinking and pretending to work out.

"Cargo didn't make it," I explained, enjoying that she took an interest in every aspect. But I could feel Kazimir seething as he barked into the phone to his second in command. "A vessel belonging to your buddy John Henry was detained. I would call him, but the prick has been ignoring my calls. My sources tell me he's out on the East Coast, so I can't ream him for not ensuring the cargo gets to us." *And beat him to a bloody pulp until he tells me about my wife's past.*

Was that relief on her face? It was hard to tell.

"I'm not sure I want to go out," she said hesitantly. "I'm all sweaty and greasy."

I took a step closer, moving my hand to where she could take it easily if she wanted. "Pizza at the house? A picnic? I'll even light a fire in the barrel on the roof."

Something sparked in her eyes. "There's a fireplace in the big room. But the animals give me the willies. No—let's stay indoors. How about a picnic in bed with a movie?"

"I don't have a TV in my room," I hedged, taking another step.

"I have a phone," Laurel countered. "But I have the distinct feeling that you don't like the bed."

It's not that, redbird. I'd stayed away to give her space. She'd come willingly into my dark corner of the world, but it wasn't her first choice. She wanted to stay hidden, stay anonymous. I'd waited nightly for her to ask me to bed. To make this more than just lust. Was this finally my answer? I held my breath, waiting to see what she would do.

Laurel slid her hand into mine. "Giordano's won't deliver to your castle of doom."

I pulled her close. "We'll pick it up on the way."

Laurel moaned, stretching out. Together, we'd polished off an entire *Chicago Classic* deep-dish pizza. I set the box, paper towels, and can of soda on the piece of wood that served as an end table. This room was coming along. Laurel had started painting the one end. A vibrant sapphire blue stared back at me. Black art accented the wall. But the furniture was still mine—old and dingy.

I hated it.

Damn.... This bed was nice. I pulled Laurel close, propping the phone on the pillow.

If anyone asked me what we were watching, I couldn't have answered if my life depended on it. All I knew was her. This beautiful, fierce creature in my arms.

"I can't let you go," I whispered in Russian.

Laurel pricked up, half rolling over to me. "What was that?"

"Nothing." I pressed a kiss on her lips. "I just have a lot on my mind."

Those warm, sensual brown eyes blinked up at me. "You can tell me."

Not without scaring you, sweet, flighty songbird. "It's too hard to say, beautiful," I began in Russian, taking the coward's way out. I pulled her into my chest, rubbing my knuckles up and down her spine. "I didn't believe in soulmates. But now, I'm starting to wonder if you weren't sent to me from heaven to guide me through the trials and tribulations of this world. I'm going to be a king, redbird. And I need a queen. But no other mortal woman will do. They aren't queens, but you have the making of one. A foreign princess, blown into my life on the midnight breeze."

Laurel shuddered.

"There's something about you. Some enchantment." I lifted her wrists and pressed them to my lips. "One day, you'll trust me. One day, you'll tell me the name of the man who darkened your life. I'll take delight in peeling him apart, piece by piece. Because no one should haunt your life.

"And if that means that someday, I need to let you fly away, with a heavy heart I'll open the window. But I am going to do everything in my power to make this a place you want to stay. Because I can't face ruling this pitch-black corner of the world without your vibrance by my side."

We lay still, my confession hanging between us.

There was part of me that wanted to feel foolish. I'd fallen and was mad—crazy. Insane!—for this woman. And she only saw me as her fake husband—her lover and business arrangement.

No, it wasn't foolishness. It was pain.

I need you to see me as more. I would fall to my knees and worship her every day if only I knew it would make her stay.

Laurel sighed. "Whatever that was, it sounded beautiful."

I smiled sadly against her head. "Just something I had to get off my mind. Thanks for listening."

She chuckled. "Next time say it so I understand."

If only I could....

"I have a question," Laurel yawned.

This time my smile was brighter. "You know the rules, redbird. Only if I can ask one in return."

She rolled over, clicked off her phone, and then snuggled deeper into my arms. "Why haven't you slept with me?"

My fingers drew a slow, sensual line down her side. "Today? I can remedy that."

Laural swatted my hand. "I meant sleep-sleep. I bought this bed, and you haven't been in it with me *to sleep*."

I splayed my hand over her hip. "You needed this to be fake. I wanted to give you space, redbird."

"Stay with me tonight?" she breathed.

It might be my ears playing tricks on me, but I thought I heard a catch in her voice.

"That was two questions," I teased.

Even though it was her profile, I caught the eyeroll. My fingers squeezed her ass cheek. "Never mind, my questions can wait."

I ripped her lounge pants off in a quick tug and spread her legs apart.

"Dimitri," she moaned, but her fingers clutched at my shirt.

My cock was out and in my fist a moment later. I slid a merciless tug up and down. Laurel's gaze hooded as she watched.

"Tell me you want me to stay," I rasped.

One black brow arched. "Or else?"

I lined myself with her entrance—

And sank deep into her heat with a powerful, unforgiving thrust. "Or I'm going to fuck you senseless until you're melting and unable to form a coherent sentence."

Those beautiful legs wrapped around mine and held tightly. "If I say I want you to stay, will you still promise to do the other?"

Pumping into her, testing and giving her a moment to adjust to my size, I growled. "Yes, my queen."

"Until the crown is on your head, I'm technically your princess," Laurel grinned.

I dropped down to kiss the smirk right off her, and then, I stayed with her. All night.

Chapter 48 – Laurel

There was something about the ballads of the 70's. The 60's had short, punchy, gut-twisting tunes. But the 70's? They sent my heart racing.

The Bee Gee's came through my headphones. I watched the screen, memorizing the cadence.

One drink of water, and then I pressed record. The camera focused on the single navy-blue silk flower and the yellow candle burning.

I fell in chorus with the three British icons. "I know your eyes in the mornin' sun, I feel you touch me in the pourin' rain, And the moment that you wander far from me, I wanna feel you in my arms again."

Where they kept the vocals mellow, not raising to higher notes, I broke from the normal. I could hit high. So I did. My voice soared as I belted the chorus. Once I added the instrumentals, I hoped it would sound like Celine singing the ballad. It was how I preferred to change songs, making them mine.

The words were universal. Music hit truths that every person could relate to. But the way I presented was all mine.

"'Cause we're livin' in a world of fools, Breakin' us down, When they all should let us be, We belong to you and me."

"Oh, wow," I gasped.

That hit differently.

Dimitri practically told me he loved me. He didn't use the words, but he'd said it.

"How deep?" I whispered. "I need to learn."

Drawing in a deep breath, I switched off the recording. I had enough material prerecorded for the next few days. And because it was my custom to release clips before the whole piece, I really had two weeks of content.

I couldn't finish. Not that song. Not...right now.

I need to learn. How deep? How...deep....

Making quick work of cleaning up my workstation, I backed up the recordings before powering down my laptop. The refrain played on repeat through my mind. The words warbled softly.

I flicked the light on—

And screamed.

"Hello, redbird...." Dimitri stepped away from the wall, his hand outstretched.

I glared at him, gasping for breath. "Do you *want* my heart to explode?"

"No," he growled, black brows knitting together.

Drawing in a deep inhale, I straightened. "You're a brat. A sneaking brat."

And then, I pulled away, but he snapped my arm and tugged me back.

"That voice. That fucking voice—" His lips crashed on mine. This kiss was hard. His tongue slid between my lips, and I melted.

His touch cupped my back, tangled in my hair.

I held on, using him as my anchor so I didn't fall.

We broke apart panting. "You have exactly five minutes to get in the car or we're not going anywhere," he rasped, gaze turning molten as it fell on me.

I stumbled back. He turned and strode purposefully from the door.

My husband had been listening to me. For how long, it was impossible to tell. Since the songs I'd recorded were cheesy love ballads, it didn't matter when he'd come in.

He'd been listening.

I scrubbed my hands through my hair. Music was my outlet. I'd turned to it this afternoon, sorting through the words of others to grapple with my own feelings.

With a sigh of resignation, I pushed to my feet. My molars worried the inside of my cheek as I changed into the sheer top and hooked a bustier around my waist. Blood red lipstick and compact in hand, I grabbed my Valentino clutch, leaving seconds to race from the bedroom.

Down in the entryway, Dimitri paced before the front door, eyes glued to his phone. But those sea blue orbs snapped to me when the clattering of my heels sounded on the stairs.

I was rewarded by his eyes widening.

Before he could speak, there was a knock on the door.

Scowling, he ripped it open.

A booming voice came through. "Dimitri! I can't believe I caught you at home!"

"I'm going out."

"Where?"

"Dinner."

"Aren't you on rotation for the exchange with the Sicilians?"

"Not until nine." Dimitri's voice could have cut glass.

"I needed to run a few things by you, but if you're busy...." The voice trailed off and a bristled head of dark hair stuck in the house. If the top was cut military short, the beard was wild and long. Sharp eyes took me in. A short whistle escaped the man's lips. "I see it's *important* work."

"Get the hell out of my house," Dimitri snarled.

"Your house?" the man repeated, punctuating each word. "I wasn't aware."

Dimitri shoved the man outside, closing the door. When I descended, slipped into my coat, and pulled the door open, I saw the taillights of an Audi.

"What was that about?" I asked, since the conversation had been in Russian. It was becoming complicated to pretend not to know the language. Especially when such amorous confessions took place in bed before my fake husband slept with me in his arms.

Such was the punishment for eavesdropping.

"That was Igor, one of the other captains."

The face and the name clicked. "Why was he here?"

"To be honest? I'm not sure," Dimitri said quietly.

"Well, if it felt like a check up to you, that's the vibe I got," I confided, linking my arm through Dimitri's.

His jaw tightened.

"Hey." I reached up and pulled his chin down. "Let's go have dinner, and then I'll be waiting to continue that kiss when you get back later tonight."

Confusion flickered through his eyes.

My pulse spiked. Shit. *Shit!* I wasn't being careful. So caught up with secrets, I'd slipped.

"You said you had work tonight," I added, even though he hadn't said much.

Pacified with my explanation, he nodded. I hated that my saving grace was the weight of responsibilities on his mind and the endless chess moves he played.

He wants me to be his queen.... Was that something I could do? Well, could and would were too different things. Queens were the most powerful pieces, and that was me. Being a bratva princess hadn't soured me to the idea of something greater.

I rubbed my wrist, watching the city still slumbering in the chill of winter pass by.

"I saw it in the window," Dimitri pointed at the storefront.

My heart pitter-pattered. The bougie boutique was on the same street as one of his clubs, and he'd thought of *me* last night on his way home.

"It's gorgeous," I rushed to say. "But it looks small."

Dimitri shrugged. "So we'll get the bigger size."

I sucked in my waist, but it was useless. "Dimi, this kind of place doesn't sell to women like me. I doubt they have plus size clothing."

The crushed look that came over his face was a punch straight to my chest. Growing up *different* accustomed me to that sad reality. In the 90's, plump kids weren't treated nicely. Mostly scorn and ridicule. Years in the socialite circles only stressed poor body imagery. The trauma my body had undergone to attempt to fit in—and still had never been good enough—would never be something I could escape. To someone like Dimitri, he didn't understand. How could he? His physique was Greek god worthy.

"But!" I sent a quick good vibe to the universe. "If they have a size big enough, I should be able to modify it to fit. And if I can't, Signora Barone is a maestro with needle and thread. Let's check it out."

Hope flared in his eyes. I ached for him. He was just trying to do something nice with no idea of the realities oppressing that kind-hearted action.

The moment I saw the thin-lipped shopkeeper, my heart sank. She was one of the old-fashioned idealists. I greeted her with a warm smile, but she didn't bother concealing her huff.

"I would like to try on the royal blue midi dress in the window," I said with confidence.

"Such a beautiful dress," the woman gushed. "I'm afraid it's not a good style on you, dear."

"Well, I'll take it anyway. In the largest size you have. That is the dress I want for the Johnson Benefit this weekend," I insisted, hoping she caved for Dimitri's sake. My skin was thick. I was used to this.

But the look in her eyes said she considered me barnyard fodder. The shopkeeper pursed her lips, tapping on a digital screen she'd pulled from her pocket. "Oh, I'm ever so sorry, that has been sold in the *largest* size."

"Alright, well thank you for your time." I turned.

And smacked into Dimitri's hard chest.

"Check again." He spoke above me.

"Dimi," I whispered.

The woman mumbled something about going to the back.

"I hate women like her, putting other women down. If she'd said it was gone, I would have let it go, but it's that she dared to make a comment first," Dimitri growled.

I pulled back. "Mobster." My mobster, coming out to play.

And the prey had no idea the monster she'd just provoked.

He cut a look to me.

"How hot are you?" I whispered.

"I'm not one to threaten ladies. But I have trained female soldiers for that." He clenched his fists.

"It won't come to that, but thank you for the consideration," I breathed, keeping back the laugh. Stepping into him, I rose on my toes. "I want to be one of your badass chicks."

Instead of laughing, Dimitri pinned me with a look.

I waited, unable to breathe.

"You'd be their queen, redbird."

He said it. In English. He said it for me to hear.

And I backpedaled mentally. I just—I just couldn't. "I have a lot of physical hurdles to overcome," I deflected.

"It's not impossible," he agreed. "You could do it."

The woman came out of the back with the dress. It was a size large. I held it up before me in the mirror. With extra material, I could modify it to be a few sizes bigger.

"We'll take it," Dimitri clipped out.

"It was reserved," the woman started to say. "I could special order you one, if the manufacturer deigned to sell you one."

"Too bad. Take my cash or don't, but that dress is coming home with us." There was no tearing down my husband.

I graced the shopkeeper with a sickly sweet smile. "Better do as he says, dear."

Ah, shit. I could do it. I could be a mobster—their queen.

Chapter 49 – Dimitri

"We should set Luka up with a date," Laurel mused, fingers tapping against her clutch. "He stands out by himself at the edge of the crowd."

Not looking at my cousin, I shook my head. "A word of warning, don't bring up women and dating around him."

Laurel tipped her head, her eyes shown. "Why?"

I lowered my voice, even though it was impossible for my words to carry across to Luka. "He hasn't shown interest in dating since his wife died."

Jerking back, Laurel stared.

"Quit," I hissed, tugging her deeper into the sea of people. "Don't bring it up with him. I only told you to warn you. He's been known to stab people when they talk about it."

"You have to tell me—everything!" Laurel tugged at my tux sleeve. "Now, Dimi!"

I sighed. This was not the conversation I wanted to be having, nor the place for it. "I'll give you the bullet points, but you need to swear to me that you won't bring it up. Ever."

Laurel mimed zipping her lips and throwing the key away. "But a wife? He's so young!"

"It's been eight—no, nine years." I let out a long breath. "Sasha was Nadia Petrova's sister, baby Zoey's aunt."

Those cinnamon eyes were the size of saucers.

I rushed to spit the rest out so we could end this conversation. "Sasha and Luka were childhood friends, and sometimes rivals. High school turned them into lovers. It was disgusting how they were always together, always sucking face—always *cute*. Inseparable. Sneaking into each other's rooms late at night. Like her sister, Sasha was one of our best female soldiers. So it was a competition between Sasha and Luka, always trying to one-up each other on jobs. They were wicked thieves, as well. He stole her engagement ring from a museum, actually."

Even though the memories were painful, a sad smile crackled at the images of the past.

"What happened?" Laurel breathed, enthralled by the story.

"Some Armenian gunned her down in the street. It wasn't a clean kill—"

"And she died in my arms." Luka appeared at my side, looking between us. "I wondered when you would tell her."

My heart froze in my chest, refusing to beat. He was still, deadly still. There was no jolly, joking exterior. The beasts beneath prowled, ready to spring. "Luka, I—"

"I guess that means you're officially one of us, now that you know our secrets. Welcome to the family, Laurel. We're all messed up." Luka gave her a clipped nod. "Now, if you'll excuse me, I'm going to take off. We've been at this gala far too long. And this monkey suit is making my balls itch."

Neither of us tried to stop him. Luka melted through the crowd. It took a long time before our silence broke.

"I had no idea," Laurel whispered.

"How could you."

"Well...he didn't stab us at least." Laurel gave me a hesitant smirk. "Come on, there's another couple I want to catch."

Part of me wanted to escape like Luka, but Laurel had put too much work into tonight. I snatched a cocktail off a tray.

This gala was more exclusive than the last. The rich of this windy city spent their weekends rubbing elbows and pretending to be charitable. Much like their type did in other bustling and influential metropolitans according to my bride. And we were using that predictability against them, hunting the wealthy in their natural habitats. Navigating the terrain came back to Laurel. She was marvelous—truly mysterious. She told me who was worth our time, how to entice them, catch their attention, and woo them into a business bed. Once they wanted to do business with my legal fronts, Laural suggested blackmail for me to acquire them. She was adept at finding rumors, listing them for us to follow up.

I let her lead in every way, content to be a shadow at her back. The moment anyone's gaze lingered, they met with my displeasure. Most laughed off my scowls.

Others rolled their eyes, falsely confident that they could circumvent my presence to reach my bride. I dared them to try. I would love to pummel any of these pricks in their smug faces. They thought they were so gracious to have a fancy meal for a good cause. Granted, some of the money no doubt reached those in need. But instead of wining and dining the elite, the funds could have just been sent direct deposit to the children in the medical wards and the event spared.

What did I know? I was only bratva and part of the criminal empires running the world behind the scenes.

I took a sip of my Manhattan and wished I'd grabbed a plain vodka. But that was too predictable. Laurel navigated us to yet another couple and used a wet headed stockbroker standing idly against the wall to mediate an introduction. Brian had far too much gel in his hair. He was useful for making the acquaintances of the gala, since he knew everyone but didn't seem to have friends. Laurel used that to her advantage.

The clever woman.

"That dress," Mrs. Olson gushed. "Where did you get that dress?"

Laurel smoothed her hands over the lacey material that fell to mid-thigh. "My husband found it for me, actually."

"I had that on reserve, in the largest size, and when I went to collect it, they'd said someone else bought it."

"How obnoxious for you," Laurel cooed.

"Well, that employee was fired for breaking policy, so I suppose that's okay," the stiff-lipped socialite harrumphed.

Laurel flicked a glance at me. "Fired for selling a dress on reserve?"

"Strange," I agreed, lips twitching.

From the look in her eye, Laurel knew exactly what I'd done.

"Should we grab fresh drinks?" Brian asked me, holding up his empty beer.

I might not know a lot about this world, but there seemed something intrinsically wrong with drinking from an aluminum bottle of lager. Even if the damn thing cost three times as much as any other establishment.

"I'll take a bourbon Manhattan, extra cherries," Mr. Olson instructed me. He inclined his head to my nearly empty drink.

The temptation to toss the remaining sips in his face was strong. Sliding my hand into my pocket, I stroked my lighter. *He didn't just demote me to waiter, did he?*

Laurel paused, turned a bright smile on me, and asked for a white wine. Her unspoken signal sent a wave of calm toward me. Begrudgingly, I accepted it.

Stalking to the bar, I took up a position at the far end. From there I could see the floor. Brian tried and failed to flag the catering crew working at the drink station. But my focus was snared by the four brutes in striped suits coming directly for me.

I let out a rough breath. *You've got to be kidding me.*

"You're on the wrong side of the tracks, cabbage eater," one of the men called out.

His compatriot elbowed him, gesturing to the crowd.

"Mr. Sarracino wants to talk," another said, but more discreetly. "Will you come to the business center? Quietly?"

The way they crowded around me left little choice.

A stillness washed through me. I took the last swig of my drink. The burn trickled down my throat, fueling the rage in my pulse. This was a risk, meeting members of other organizations. It was why Kazimir insisted on Luka and him coming with last weekend. Kazimir was out dealing with Igor's team on an import of weapons. And Luka...yeah, I couldn't blame him. He didn't deal well when his wounds were picked. I set the empty glass on the bar top.

What were four little men? I pinned the more courteous spokesperson with a hard look and gave him a tight nod. "I'll be right with you."

Turning to the stockbroker, who was completely oblivious to the predators facing off behind him, I clapped Brian on the back. "Tell Laurel I've gone to speak with an acquaintance. I'll be back in a quarter of an hour—" *more like five minutes* "—so please get them their drinks."

"What did Mr. Olson order?" Brian blinked up at me through his designer lenses.

"Brandy Manhattan. Neat and no cherries." Not one part of me felt bad for telling Brian the wrong drink.

Cracking my neck, I turned to follow the pack of dogs from the event room of the hotel. We took a back door, and the moment the metal fell closed and cut off the noise behind us, I stopped.

"I'm not coming with you. Tell Gino he can come down here."

"That wasn't the order." The poor soldier looked so confused.

Goon. At least none of my men would falter this badly.

"Are we going to have to drag you, Ruski?" the leader of the four menaced, stepping forward.

I arched a brow. "You can try."

The four matching smiles should have been a warning.

Something crashed into me from behind. Pain zapped up my spine.

Whatever struck me, hit the injured nerve. I swayed, vision immediately blurring. The floor rose to meet me.

A burp bubbled up my throat.

Shit....

Bile spewed everywhere.

The Italians cursed, jumping out of the way.

The uncontrollable retching continued, but after the first burst of nausea, the Italians grabbed me under the arms and drug me down the back corridor. Reality swayed in and out until I was dropped.

"What's wrong with him?" someone snarled, sounding far away.

Weak. Weak! I had to move. The Sarracino Famiglia wasn't on friendly terms with the Vlasov Bratva.

Me lying on the floor wouldn't endear them to us. No...they would see the future leader of the bratva as a slobbering, puking mess.

Get up now!

It didn't matter how much I screamed at myself. This happened often enough that I knew I was incapable of movement.

There was a crack.

A sharp scent filled the air.

Warbles of Italian sounded in frantic volumes. Another, and then a third crack exploded in various places. Through the blurred surroundings, I tried to focus. The chaos was indistinguishable. But...my leg felt funny.

Pushing onto my elbow, I tried to look at it. The pants weren't black. They were...orange? That wasn't right.

My head swam. The oncoming headache that followed the nausea was inevitable. I blinked, fighting back the blinding mental confusion.

"Oh, Dimi, shit!" a sweet voice sang. "Your leg! It's on fire!"

My heart doubled suddenly. I barely noticed the heat licking my leg, knowing my redbird was there.

More cracks exploded in quick succession.

"Roll over, you fool!" Laurel shouted.

The tell-tale ring of a silenced gun pealed.

Adrenaline forced back the migraine. Choking past the uncontrollable nausea, I pushed myself up.

"Dimitri! Your leg!" Laurel cried.

A bullet whizzed over my head.

It was followed by another missile. This one breaking and roaring.

Molotov cocktails—my little wife was throwing fucking Molotov cocktails.

I drug myself across the floor.

"Yeah, that's right, run cowards! Chitebbiv! E chitemmuort!" Laurel launched another bottle of burning liquid. "Touch my husband, and I'll kill you."

Strings of Italian argument sounded.

"Si, cap`e cazz! Correte! Correte, stronzi," Laural cackled.

A clip unloaded.

I launched into her, tipping her easily in those skyscraper heels. I caught her head, preventing it from cracking against the ground. The dry heaving mercifully stopped as I covered Laurel with my body.

The shouts faded.

Replaced by fire alarms.

"We have to go," Laurel panted, her hot breath fanning over my throat. "Dimi!"

I sucked in deep breaths, testing my reflexes. Adrenaline seemed to give me an edge over the damaged nerves in my spine. Grabbing her wrist, I hauled her off the ground. She scrambled for her clutch, which was on the metal cart with the unused bottles of vodka. I tugged her hard.

We ran.

Room key in hand, I beeped the scanner. Slamming through the back door, we ducked into the stairwell. Despite the blinding pulse in my head, I cut sharp glances up and down the space. An eerie silence whispered back. There was no sign of the famiglia. Not wanting to risk it, I hauled Laurel to the first flight. The sooner we were in the room, the better.

"Your pants are smoking," she laughed nervously and tried to lean down to pat them as we climbed.

I cut her a cold look I reserved for the worst offenders.

Chapter 50 – Laurel

"Dimi?" I breathed.

Oh, shit. He was pissed.

That glare was nothing short of terrifying. If it had been anyone else, I would have been quaking in my shoes. Although a shiver rattled down my spine, I pulled myself straight. He did not get to be mad at me. Not when I was still reeling from seeing him being drug away by the Italian mob.

"Do you want me to go down to the coat check for our keys?" I asked, gesturing to the doors leading back into the hotel's third floor.

Without speaking, Dimitri kept climbing. I huffed. This week I'd been more physically active than I had in years. It didn't mean I was equipped to flee up a damn staircase.

By the fourth landing, I was panting.

And on the sixth, I stopped short. My lungs were bellows, working the air in deep gasps.

"Can't," I managed to bite out.

Dimitri let out a sigh. He glanced at his leg, turned his head upward, and then sighed again.

"Stay," he growled.

I narrowed my eyes. He did not get to order me around! I glared at his back as he cracked the door open.

"You're welcome, you know!" I seethed.

Dimitri slammed the door closed. He crossed the distance in one step and pushed me against the railing.

I gulped.

"What were you thinking?" he snarled.

Resisting the urge to look down the six-flight drop behind me, I focused on getting mad. "Thinking? Thinking!"

I stabbed a finger into his chest. He caught it, and I slapped his hold with my other hand. When he grabbed that, I reacted immediately. I kicked him, putting my self-defense lessons to good use.

"Thinking!" I shouted over his groan. "I was thinking that some bastards had my husband. I was thinking that we didn't have weapons, because of the security checkpoint. I was thinking— I was thinking—"

Words failed me.

There was no way to adequately describe the panic I felt at seeing him limp and having an attack of sickness. That ghost of being defenseless threatened to make me cry even now.

"I fought back," I growled, pushing on him. "And you're welcome! Do you know what those men were saying? Since I know you don't speak Italian, Russio!"

"What?" Dimitri snarled.

"'We aren't getting paid enough to do this.' 'But we signed the contract.' 'Tell the don he escaped.' And there was more, but I was kind of busy lighting their asses on fire," I shouted.

"As they shot at you!"

Wrath sizzled under my skin. I kicked him again. "They would have shot *you,* mobster!"

Dimitri dug his touch into my side, pulling me hard against his body. "Don't you ever get in the way of a bullet meant for me."

And then, he dove.

His mouth found my neck. Teeth scored my throat. Lips sucked my pulse. Tongue French kissed my skin. The contact was fierce.

Dimitri poured his anger into it. I met him measure for measure, pushing under his clothes for flesh, climbing his body, letting him know how pissed I was that he was mad.

How much it hurt at the idea of losing him.

The hard length in his pants pressed right above where I needed it. Moaning, I ground against him, suddenly desperate for more. I needed to know he was okay. It was too scary.

Pulling back sharply, Dimitri looked daggers at me. "Oh, no, pretty redbird. You don't get to come. Not until you've been thoroughly punished."

I reared back. "Punished? *Punished!*"

A terrible smile curled his lips. Dimitri nodded.

I pounded a fist against his chest. "I saved your fucking life! They were there to assassinate you!"

"And you put yourself in danger," Dimitri snapped back. "I'm going to make you come until you shake. And then, I'm going to make you come again! And again!"

My insides clenched greedily, and warmth flooded my panties. "Punishing me with an orgasm? Oh heavens, it's so terrible," I mocked.

Gripping my chin hard, he pulled my face to his. The brush of his lips on mine was searing. But it was brief and left me needing more. "We'll see if you feel that way in a couple of hours," he warned.

With that dark promise, he picked me up, tossing me over his shoulder as if I were a sack of feathers.

Chapter 51 – Dimitri

Anger roiled through my veins. Laurel was my bride. Mine. Mine to protect, and I hadn't been able to do that. She had no idea how crazy she drove me—and that was on any given day! When she pulled shit like this, putting herself in danger, saints! I wanted to punish her. My palm ran over her gorgeous ass. The thought of how my handprint looked on her backside was almost enough to stop climbing the stairs, bend her over the handrail, and shred the dress.

I liked that idea far too much.

We weren't safe out here, however. On the fifteenth floor, I kicked through the door and marched down the hall.

"Where are we going?" Laurel hissed.

I bounced her hard on my shoulder in answer. This was supposed to be a night away. Something nice, a surprise stay at a fancy downtown hotel because I knew she liked it far more than the haunted brick monstrosity we lived in. At least the headache retreated. I was lucky. Spinal damage wasn't something that would ever go away. The symptoms were always there, waiting in the background to possess me. And tonight...*fuck!*

With the key in hand, I let us into the corner suite and locked the door. Stalking to the couch, I dumped my load, my precious, precious load, on the couch, before turning sharply on my heel and walking to the bar cart. Pouring three fingers of vodka, I swished the sourness out of my mouth before swallowing the booze. My legs shook from the exertion. I'd practically run up the stairs. They would be sore.

But that was a future problem.

The tap-tap of those damn heels sounded. I turned to watch Laurel move about the sitting area. Hunger rumbled deep inside, but it wasn't the kind that demanded food. No...I wanted to devour this fierce woman.

I took a step forward. "Take it off."

Laurel arched a black brow. Her lips twitched, a defiant smile playing at the corner of her mouth.

"I'm not playing games, not tonight," I warned.

A short laugh pushed through her lips. "Aren't we always playing games? Isn't this *whole* deal one big round of make-believe?"

Closing the distance, I grabbed the material over her chest. The sound of tearing fabric ripped through the space. What lay underneath was a skin tone body sleeve.

A growl roared from deep inside. I tore it off her, bending only enough to tug it down her legs. I didn't trust my head to do any acrobats.

Laurel stood there, naked and exposed. That proud chin stayed up in defiance. She wasn't going to submit, even as her body cried for me. It was evident in the damp spot on her cotton panties. Her nipples hardened instantly in the cooler air. My mouth watered to taste.

In a minute....

The snowy princess wasn't ready.

If her hands weren't a trigger, I would have bound them to her ankles. Instead, I released my belt. The leather snapped through the air.

Laurel didn't even flinch.

"I should leave welts on your pretty ass," I snarled.

She had the nerve to laugh. Her derision tinkled in the space between us.

Looping the end through the buckle, I dropped the noose over her head before she could react. *That* wiped the mirth right off her beautiful face.

"On your knees." I gave the rope a tug.

"What?" she gasped, anger making her eyes blaze.

I drew in a slow breath through my nose. "You put yourself at unnecessary risk. On. Your. Knees."

Laurel narrowed her gaze, lips pressed in a thin line.

"Redbird," I snapped and gave the belt another tug. None of this was to hurt her, I would sooner carve out my own organs and eat them. The small correction was purely a dominance tactic. Laurel wasn't hurt.

I saw the moment she decided to obey. Her eyes flashed but not in submission. She bent one leg. Kneeled onto the calf, before she repeated the movement.

Good. I turned and crossed the suite. Pushing into the bedroom, I sat on the edge of the bed. Only then did I look at her. "Crawl to me."

Her voice was high and full of outrage. "You've got to be joking!"

I didn't respond.

"Fine, if this is what you need to sate that cruel streak, I'll *play*," she seethed and began to shuffle across the floor.

My fingers curled into fists. *Saints!* This woman was maddening. She tested my limits like no other. "This is for you, Laurel."

"No, no it's not," she laughed. Mockery laced the delicious noise. "What I need is your cock. In my mouth, in my pussy—hell! I'll even take the back door again. But if taking what I want means this silly little show of dominance, then dominate me, mobster. Do your worst."

By all the saints, the rush of pure, primal hunger that rushed through me should have been enough to kill me.

As she moved closer, my beautiful snow queen slowed. The wait was maddening. Agony ripped through me. It took every thread of control not to reach out and pluck her off the ground.

Laurel stopped in front of me. That unreadable smile dazzled on her lips. "What now, mobster? Do you want your prize to sing for you or perhaps I should dance?"

I spread my thighs, a silent instruction as to what was next.

A dark, dangerous laugh made of pure feminine power and delight sang from her as she opened my slacks. When my dick was free, Laurel bent over him. That pretty pink tongue darted out and swirled around the tip.

"Mmm," she murmured. "But don't you want to hold my leash?"

My next words were a violent explosion. "Yobushki-vorobushki."

Laurel snorted.

I narrowed my eyes.

"That rhymed," she smirked.

My hand shot out, and I ripped the belt off her. It sailed across the room and crashed into the opposite wall.

With laughter on her lips, Laurel slid my length into her mouth.

I hissed at the sharp burst of pleasure. Sucking and swallowing, her head bobbed up and down. Damn, she did this so well.

I should tell her. "Look how well you take my cock, every saints damned inch," I rasped.

Her gaze flicked up to meet mine.

"Saints, redbird, those eyes. Have I ever told you how breathtaking they are?" She shook her head. "Right now, they're begging me to fuck you harder. Can you handle that, babe? Can you take everything I give you?"

I thought I could be slow, take my time. Draw out this...this punishment? No, it wasn't a punishment. The sight of her exposed and waiting was powerful enough that it nearly sent me to my knees.

Reaching down, I lifted her and spun us both onto the bed.

My lips found hers.

The kiss was wild and demanding. She opened, and I drove my tongue into her mouth. Laurel whimpered. Her mouth was eager against mine. The ache deepened, and my dick screamed with need. Nothing would do but her tight little pussy.

Spreading her legs, I sank into her. Moving in and out with a savage fury, I took her—hard. Laurel's slick heat wrapped me tight. Pleasure surged from my balls to the head. A flicker of hesitation stole into my mind that I was being too rough on her.

But it quickly vanished when she moaned and tipped her hips to take me deeper.

"Dimi," she panted.

"That's it, redbird. Say my name. Tell me to whom you belong." I buried myself deeper and deeper.

"You, you rotten brat!" Laurel arched. "You tell me that you can't stand the thought of losing me? Well! Let me tell you," she panted, "it goes *BOTH* ways."

My bruising touch dug into her thighs, forcing them wider, drawing one leg higher. That only made her buck her hips in desperation.

"Say that again," I growled as I claimed her with a brutal urgency.

She squeezed her eyes closed. Her head whipped back and forth.

"Eyes on me," I rasped, pinching her nipple and making her gasp.

Those heartbreakingly beautiful eyes snapped to mine.

A damn fire skated over my skin where her hands braced on my shoulders.

Fine, if she wasn't going to talk, I would.

"I burn for you, redbird. All day long. It doesn't get better when I come back to you."

Laurel sucked in a sharp breath.

“Now imagine if you weren’t there—” my voice hitched. I ran a hand over my head. “*Fuck.* I can’t even say it out loud.”

Her bottom lip trembled. “I’m here, Dimi. I’m here—and I’m yours.”

That was all it took.

With a violent twitch, hot ropes of cum exploded inside her. I roared, my voice loud and triumphant. It wasn’t my release that took her over the edge—hers pulled me over. That tight little pussy convulsed, and my redbird screamed her song.

When we came down from the terrible height, our rough, mingled breathing was the only sound to be heard. We both trembled, our limbs shaking in the silence after the storm. Beads of sweat trickled between the swell of her breasts. If her legs weren’t clasping me so tightly, I would have bent to lick away her body’s tears.

Shifting my weight onto one arm, I cupped her face and studied every beautiful detail. “I can’t lose you. You will *not* put yourself in danger like that again.”

I should have seen the warning spark in her eyes.

Chapter 52 – Laurel

The crack of my palm connecting with his cheek was deafening in the otherwise quiet room.

Dimitri was still pulsing inside me, and I'd struck him. I was so mad. Anger didn't even begin to cover what I was feeling. How dare he say that! How dare he tell me I couldn't, when he put himself at risk every single freaking day!

I glared at him, a thousand words fought to be the first to explode. The predator lurking behind those sea blue eyes watched me, waiting to see what I did. But I wasn't prey. I never had been.

Wriggling out from under him, I launched out of bed. I didn't bother covering myself; I was too busy storming around the bedroom. My fists silently stabbed the air. The hard, sharp breaths made my chest heave. I stomped a path to the windows, looking down below. This midnight kingdom was just as much mine as it was Dimitri's.

Why the hell couldn't he see that?!

Because I haven't claimed it.

Marching into the other room, I found the bar cart. I poured a healthy amount of amber liquid into a glass. Tipping it back, I let the smokey alcohol burn down my throat.

A hiss snaked between my clenched teeth.

And then, I whirled on my heel.

Dimitri stood in the middle of the living room, hands loose at his sides. A fighting stance. That tall, built frame casually proclaimed that he could take me, but he was prepared for my onslaught all the same.

Well, at least he was smart enough to know I wasn't going down without clawing tooth and nail. I marched forward, getting right up close and personal.

"That isn't fair," I snarled, my words accompanied by a stab of my finger into his chest.

His eyes darkened. "Life's not fair."

Oh, I could murder him!

Growling, I shoved him. There was no way my soft arms had enough power to move this mountain. But the sweep of my foot, timed just right, sent him tottering. His arms windmilled and I pressed the advantage. Dogging him, I kept pushing and nudging.

"You don't get it," I hissed, backing him further. "You don't get it, Dimitri Vlasov!"

"What?" he roared. "What don't I get?"

One more well-timed move and I shoved him onto the couch. Standing over him, I narrowed my eyes. A dangerous energy rippled from his body. His temper was thinning, and an explosion was imminent.

Good. That made two of us.

"I don't get to put myself in danger?" I repeated his words. As I spoke, I climbed over his body. It was probably the only reason he didn't interrupt me. "You don't get it. You're an underworld prince—you'll be the boss! I can't tell you to stay out of danger. But what I can do? Is stand by your side!"

I drug my pussy across the plains of his stomach. While most of our previous mess was on my thighs, there was no doubt a little between my legs. But most of the slick heat was me—all me and my desperate need to consume this man.

Something raw and desperate filled his voice. "I can't lose you."

"And I can lose you?" I cupped his face, rolling my hips.

Dimitri reached for me. But I wasn't having that.

"Hands behind your head," I snapped angrily.

Dimitri groaned. "Redbird."

I freaking loved that name. "We're in this together."

His gaze pinned me. The turbulence there made my chest clench.

"Don't make the mistake of putting me in a gilded cage for my protection. Where you go, I will go." I reached between us, took his rock-hard cock, and drove my pussy down on it.

A strangled breath roared from him.

"Keep them there, or I won't come," I warned. "And you promised me endless orgasms as punishment for saving your ungrateful ass."

"Laurel." The word was hard and strained. "I am *not* ungrateful."

I flexed my hips, taking him deeper. My pussy stretched to accommodate him. The delicious feel of his thick cock was part pleasure with a dash of pain.

"It *is* my job to protect you," he insisted, desperation shimmering in his eyes.

But I was desperate too.

I rode him hard, rocking and rising in turn. My breasts bounced in the air. The tightening in my core was nearly impossible to resist.

How I managed to avoid coming as I impaled myself over and over on his cock, I hadn't a damn clue.

I waited for the telltale sign that he was about to fill me. His body tensed. Each breath was tight and short. Right before his cock twitched, I lifted and didn't press back down.

Springing off his body, I tripped away.

"Well, that's that," I chirped, a shake in my voice. "This red birdy is going to fly free."

I took off but didn't even make it far. Dimitri, cursing violently in Russian, scrambled after me. He pounced, taking me down on the mattress. His heavy body pinned me. The air left my lungs in a whoosh.

"I'm never letting you go," he snarled, hot breath singeing my ear.

"Then don't cage me," I bit back.

Dimitri grunted. His hard thighs pushed between mine, forcing my legs open. He drove into me, keeping me trapped against the bed.

For the first time in my life, I didn't feel the cloying panic.

And it was probably because as soon as he started to fuck me hard, his hands found mine, and our fingers entwined. I was at the point where I craved every freaking piece of this man, even if it was his hands around mine.

Thrusting hard, Dimitri made my insides scream. "If it's either be with me or be away from me, you'll stand by my side, redbird," he growled. "But you're going to learn how to fight. I can't always be there to save you, and I need you to survive at all costs."

"Agreed," I breathed, sweet relief washing through me. He wanted me. *He wants me by his side!* The hesitation to tell him what was already written on my heart vanished. And the confession fell quickly from my lips. "I'm yours, and you're mine."

His fingers tightened around, through, and on mine. "You're willing to make this thing real?"

I couldn't leave if I wanted to. The thought of leaving and not knowing if he survived until after the fact would kill me. No...at least here, with him, I could do everything in my power to keep him alive. "It's real. This isn't a game."

"Say it," he growled.

I smiled shyly. "This is real."

My words were magic. With a low, rough cry, he released inside me. I took every drop, my throbbing insides clenching painfully around him. The heady act of mutual possession pushed me to the edge, and I followed him off, hand in hand.

In the wake of our simultaneous orgasm, Dimitri slid out of me and off my body. Those strong arms wrapped around me, and he pulled me close. Cradled in his arms, my face pressed against his hard chest and legs tangled between his, I caught my breath.

It was now or never. I whispered, "YA ne mogu bez tebya zhit'." *I can't live without you.*

Dimitri jerked back, staring hard at me with those impossibly deep sea-blue eyes.

I smiled, reaching between us and trailing my fingertip over his lips. "I'm done with pretending to be your wife," I confessed in Russian. "I want to be yours for real. And I think I already am, I just haven't been brave enough to tell you before this."

It took almost losing him for me to realize running was no longer an option. I was already in this. I was already his.

"Lyubimaya." *My love.* "You're my wife. From now until the day I draw my last breath."

Chapter 53 – Dimitri

"For these and the rest, I confess my sins. I am most heartily sorry for them, and sincerely repent of them. Help me, oh heavenly host, to walk a better path, and when I can't, bring me back to the holy body—"

There was the soft patter of footfall, accompanied by the swish of a blanket.

"I thank you for my bride, for my family, and the work you set before me. So let it be," I whispered.

And then, I cracked my eyes open and looked up into the radiant face of the woman who loved me back, even though she hadn't said those words.

Heaven sent you to me.

"Why do you believe?" Laurel tipped her head to the side. "You of all people."

I shrugged and pushed to my feet. Walking to her, I placed a kiss on her head. "My soul is sick. There is a Great Physician who can heal—even a black hearted monster like me."

"I'm glad you have that," she laughed softly.

Taking her hand, I led her to the breakfast spread, which covered the entire table. "Me too. Hungry?"

She nodded eagerly. I pulled out a seat and tucked her into the table.

It was cozy, sitting beside Laurel, who was wrapped in a comforter, and nothing else. A rare feeling of contentment spread over me. I'd been itching to get her out of the house. While the gym and now our room were sanctuaries, that cold, cruel structure where I'd grown up felt more unlike a dwelling and everything like a prison. Growing up, I told myself it was military strictness. How cool was it that I lived in a barrack like a soldier? But now I saw it for what it was: a shrine to my father's iron control.

"Pass the jam?" Laurel asked in perfect Russian. There wasn't even an accent. Granted it had a formal edge, but that suited her. She would have been one of the doomed aristocrats of the old kingdom.

Holding the little pot of sweet, sticky fruit spread between us, I pinned her with a look.

"So…you suddenly speak my native tongue." She blinked. Those cinnamon eyes watched me. She wasn't frightened. Oh no! My little songbird was calculating. "And German."

"Yes, so?" Laurel shrugged.

"Do I recollect correctly that you also yelled in Italian in the midst of the firebombs?"

Those fine shoulders squared. "What of it?"

I rose, lifted her chair, and spun it around.

"How many languages *do* you speak?" I pinned her against the breakfast table.

"Many." Her eyes shimmered.

"Makes for good eavesdropping," I conceded.

"It does. And we need to go on pretending I'm ignorant. Your bratva is more likely to slip up if they don't think I can understand."

Wise woman. Saints, she was incredible. "I'll agree to that. But why not tell me?"

There were things I'd said, things I'd wished I hadn't said in front of her. Things my men and others had commented on. She'd heard them all.

"I told you, I have my secrets." Her chin tipped up defiantly.

That was the one thing she said that could ruin this moment. My fingers curled. The knuckles whitened.

"I thought we were past that." *I thought last night broke the barriers!*

Laurel's eyes fluttered closed. "Demetrius Aleksandr! You have to be patient with me, meelyi!"

Loved one. She was telling me she loved me.

My anger deflated. "Kazimir believes you were sent to kill me."

"I know. And you disagreed." She smiled softly. It made her eyes sparkle. "It's only fair though, I mistrusted him and him me."

"I want you two to get along," I rasped, voice suddenly choked with emotion.

"Someday, but you can't force trust. I have a feeling it will grow, and when we are friends, our bratva will be an unstoppable force."

I pulled her up and crushed her into my body. Her simple admission, packed with belief and certainty, melted the stone surrounding my heart.

After a beautiful weekend spent in bed with Laurel, reality hit hard. The absence of the pakhan had the men on edge. I put out one fire after another. But I never thought my own men, those most loyal to me, would be the ones I would have to discipline.

The truck came to a hard stop. I snapped my belt and jumped out. Boris and I went around to the back, and I pulled the door open.

"If you touch me, I'll geld you," Ilya hissed.

My friend tried to descend from the truck. His knee caught, buckled, and Ilya plunged to the frozen pavement.

"Dammit, quit trying to be a hero, comrade," Pavel shouted as he leaped from Kazimir's big, dark truck.

Kazimir came around his vehicle and met my gaze. His eye was closing shut. Misha sulked behind him. It was supposed to be a simple evening drop.

While the others hauled the wounded through the kitchen door, I stopped in front of Kazimir.

"It's getting worse," my cousin muttered.

I nodded. "Ilya has turned damn near feral this winter."

"When did it start?" Kazimir scrubbed a hand over his face, as if the detail was just within reach.

"Sometime between cultural Christmas and Orthodox Christmas?" I couldn't quite recall. "He was the one who drove like hell to get your ass out of Flanigan's territory."

Kazimir grunted, his fingers ghosting to the thigh I knew was riddled with scars. "Yeah, other than the way it ended, that was a fun little stakeout. Ilya wasn't a rotten bastard then."

"No, he wasn't," I agreed. "It doesn't matter how it started, but that it can't continue."

"Beg to differ," Kaz snorted. "If we know the why of it, we can fix it."

"While that's true in principle, I can't have my soldiers brawling to the point that they're drawing guns on one another." I let out a long breath. "It doesn't matter what shit is twisted in their personal lives."

"You're going to have to discipline them," Kazimir spoke low.

That had been the reality running through my head the entire frenzied drive back. "My father would take a body part. I can't rule like that, Kaz."

The raw admission was a whisper.

"So don't rule like him."

I shook my head. "Even if he's weak, he'll hear about it all the way in Minnesota. I wish—" My mouth clapped closed. I couldn't finish that.

"Maybe he won't come back," Kaz encouraged.

But it was false hope. Even riddled with cancer and not having properly working lungs, my father defied death. Which meant his terrible reign continued.

"The beating worked for you," I sighed. "I don't want to stitch Ilya up, though, only to beat the ever-loving piss out of him and have the wound reopen."

Kazimir kicked his boot but stopped short. "Here's an idea."

I glared at his foot. Ice stayed frozen on a heavily shadowed patch of the landscaping right off the sidewalk. I arched a brow at my cousin. "Beat them with an icicle?"

Kaz gave me a withering, condescending look that I would have shot another man for. "No, dumbass. You need to instill discipline. So do things that build that."

"Bury them with ice?" Now it was just for fun.

My cousin brought his fist to his lips and blew on it, the exhale long and strangled. "Ice baths, dumbass. Ice baths."

I blinked. That wasn't the worst idea.

"Pushups. Run laps. Ice baths. Mile long treks—I don't fucking care which!" Kazimir swept both his hands wide. "You do other military level training techniques for fighting. I would have thought you of all people would have seen discipline as corrective behavior."

"That is why I have you." I gave him a tight smile. "There will still be times more severe punishment is required."

"So save the ugly stuff like losing fingers or ears for that," Kazimir said with a grimace. "Just don't put them in pickle jars."

A shudder ran down my spine. "First thing I do as pakhan is destroy that office."

Jerking my chin, I led the way into Vasil's house. We'd brought the guys here because it was closer than the suburbia house we used for medical situations. To my surprise, there was quite the group gathered in the kitchen.

The oldest Barone girl was sitting across from Ilya. There was a bowl of warm water beside her. "The salt will sting," she murmured, dipping her cloth in it.

Ilya shrugged. "It doesn't matter."

Laurel broke away from Dani's side and gave me an inquisitive look. "What the hell happened?"

"They got into a fight," I said without warmth.

"He was shot!"

I flicked a glance at Misha. "He was beating Misha to a bloody pulp. Didn't even try to stop the lad pulling a gun."

Laurel's gentle fingers reached and brushed my cheek. "Someone decked you."

I snorted. "Ilya's elbow."

My savage songbird gave the soldier a cold glare.

"And what is this?" The young Barone was asking the still bleeding soldier. She tapped her knuckle into the gold pendant, so small and delicate against Ilya's ink-stained chest.

"'*da mi basia mille*'" Ilya murmured. "Latin. Something about kissing."

"Catullus," Laurel breathed with a soft laugh.

Ilya cut a look to her. "What was that?"

I stepped up behind Laurel, making sure he felt my presence shadowing her.

"'Vivāmus, mea Lesbia, atque amemus," Laurel started.

"English," the soldier growled.

Laurel cleared her through, a condescending smirk on her lips as she shot me a glance. "Catullus was a poet, asking his lover to kiss him. It's a fascinating love story."

"I had to search the internet to figure it out. And you just plucked that line of poetry out of thin air?" Ilya responded skeptically.

"When you have to memorize and recite most of those poems, yes...you remember." Laural's tone could have frozen water. "Da mi basia mille—give to me a thousand kisses. It's beautiful."

"It was." And then, Ilya did the most incredible thing. He backed down. He gave the Barone girl a nod and she continued to wash his wound.

"The bullet went clean through." The young cousin looked up at me.

"Cami, right?" I bent over my soldier to examine her work.

"Yes," she said dryly. "And you're Dimitri."

I hummed. "Want to stitch him up?"

Her eyes widened. "Really? Can I do that?"

Dani breathed a protest, stepping forward. Kaz caught her and gave a small shake of his head. "But the doctor?" she insisted.

"I can do it," Cami asserted. "You and nonna made sure I could sew. And there was that summer we did hand embroidery."

The younger girl looked eagerly at her cousin.

"That's true," Dani conceded.

"Stitch him well. He has a boat to catch." I slid my hands into my pocket.

"Here." Signora Barone bustled into the kitchen. Her sharp gaze took us all in, and she tutted under her breath. "Davvero? Stupidi gli uomini."

Laurel snorted. She took the bottle from the signora, squirted the pungent liquid on a cotton ball, and pressed my side. I took a seat, bringing her between my legs. Blood ran south, and my dick twitched at her nearness.

"What about a boat?" Laurel pressed.

I cleared my throat. "Misha? Ilya?"

They nodded.

"Actions have consequences. You showed a lack of respect for each other and this bratva. We'll be taking a little excursion onto Lake Michigan. There isn't ice, but it's cold enough to teach you a lesson." I pinned them with hard looks.

Laurel dabbed at the swelling tissue around my eye, her own black brow arched.

"That's...merciful," Ilya breathed.

"We'll see if you think so after your ice bath," I said with a bite.

Chapter 54 – Laurel

The next evening, we came home from the club to find the pakhan back. With a little nudge and a soft whisper, Dimitri sent Marena and me up to our room. Instead, we padded to an unused space that was directly over the pakhan's office. Lying on the cold floor, I pressed my ear to the air exchange vent. The shouts carried through, but the words were lost in the air vents. I wrapped my arms tightly around myself and waited. The faithful hound lay curled beside me, dark eyes trained on the metal grate.

I couldn't be down there. My presence wouldn't help. Hell! It would probably make the old tyrant even more furious. But I could sit here and lend Dimitri moral support.

And then, everything fell silent.

Minutes ticked by, and when no more noise came through, I sprang to my feet. Marena scrambled after me. Silently, we tiptoed to the home gym, but Dimitri's sanctuary was dark and empty. Teeth worried my bottom lip. Looking over my shoulder, I stared down the hall. There was no noise from the office. The hound whined.

"I know, girl," I whispered. The truth was, I didn't know if I was brave enough to face the pakhan. It wasn't an aversion to going to Dimitri, but rather knowing that my appearance would make it worse. Knowing that the old, sick man had the power to hurt the one person I'd grown to care about.

Hatred for my father-in-law bubbled and simmered in my veins.

You could do it, you know.

My fingers curled into fists. It was what he deserved. Plus! It would free Dimitri. I could put him to sleep—permanently. But it had to be done so that in no way was Dimitri to be suspected. The easiest way to do that?

"Take the fall," I breathed.

I would have to confess to the murder. If the Vlasov Bratva ran a blood test postmortem and found the drugs, I would have to take full responsibility. Which meant I would have to flee.

“I don’t want to go,” I whispered to the hound.

Marena placed her chin on my lap.

The tightening of my chest was suffocating. I had the answer to stop the torment Dimitri so desperately wanted to be freed from. If it was as simple as killing the pakhan, he would have done it, wouldn’t he? No...I couldn’t bring myself to put the old man to sleep. Not if it meant there was a chance I would have to leave.

I’m being selfish.

I wrapped my arms around my chest. “I don’t want to be a loner, again.”

The chime of a text message dragged me from the bleak, swirling thoughts.

Big D: I’m going to the warehouses with the boss. Don’t wait up for me.

A long breath escaped my lungs. “Come on, girl, looks like it’s just us tonight.”

That long tail didn’t thump at the prospect.

I tried to obey. Back in our bedroom, I cleaned up and curled under the blankets. But tumbling, terrible thoughts barraged my mind and chased sleep away. When Dimitri crept through the door, I sat up and opened my arms to him.

He didn’t speak a word as he shucked his clothing, prowled forward, and crept under the covers. That solid, chiseled body curled into my curves as if I was his lifeline. He placed his head on my chest, and we lay in silence. The fact that he didn’t even reach under my satin teddy was a testament to how distraught he was. And it had nothing to do with exhaustion. His thick, hard cock pressed against my thigh.

Destructive thoughts toward the pakhan rapidly fired from my mind.

How could Karma be so unfair? The evil this pakhan did, the disrespect for his duty as a father was so apparent! And yet he was actively surviving a horrific terminal illness.

His time will come, I promised myself.

For anyone to torment a mind as strong as Dimitri’s, that man had to be made of pure vileness. It was noble that Dimitri hadn’t killed his parent. While I was grateful my villainous mobster husband had a moral code, filial respect, and a strong sense of duty, I desperately wished he would crack, and the monster inside tear down the evil that was his father.

Because...if he couldn't destroy that evil, how could I hope that he would someday destroy the one haunting me? Not that I wanted my past to cross into my future, but it was always a possibility.

I clutched Dimitri close while the swirling vortex of thoughts, worries, and desperate feelings consumed my mind.

Glasses chinked. Cutlery scraped. Mouths smacked. And all around us Russians boasted and chatted. Their voices rose and fell, bouncing off the frigid walls to shatter like ice. The five captains were having a lavish dinner with their pakhan. A wood table had been brought into the great room, and a fire was lit in the hearth. With the white walls and pale wood floor, the atmosphere defied the blazing heat. The dead animals, including the grizzly bear head, that decorated the walls created a grim, creepy atmosphere. Whoever thought candlelight would enhance the mood was out of their mind.

I knew it wasn't Ania. The maid followed instructions. This had to be the way the pakhan liked hosting, when he did it in his own home and not his brother's.

Two of the captains had trophies hanging on their arms. The stench of cheap perfume was nauseating. Vasil's fiancée was gracious and pleasant, but I had a sneaking feeling that Signora Barone had no more patience for the twin flavors of the month than I did. From the careful poise of her shoulders, it was clear she was on edge.

I bet she can't wait for it to be over, as well. Could I end the meal before dessert? Various ideas flitted through my head, and I smirked into my plate.

"My brothers of blood," Matvei chuffed, raising his glass.

For having a collapsed lung not a fortnight ago, he looked downright spritely. The Bratva captains lifted their glasses to their leader. Following Dimitri's lead, I did the same.

"The Vlasov Bratva is a name to be feared. I apologize for my absence, but I am proud of how well the two older heads kept this vessel steered true." Matvei nodded to his brother and Igor.

Vasil cut a look to Dimitri but didn't interrupt his brother.

Emil slapped his palm against the table and gave the equivalent of a *here-here*.

Boris, the only captain without a date, could have been carved from stone. He didn't even blink as he perched on his seat at the end of the table.

The pakhan continued. "The war with the Polish syndicate was swift, but it's brought fruit already. The remaining family members have asked for a marriage. They hope our shadow of protection will shelter them as they recover."

Matvei ended that sentence with a wicked round of coughing.

I knew the various mobs intermarried for gains or political matters. But knowing and hearing it happen in front of me were two different things.

"However, we've been blessed with the marriage of my son and the engagement of my brother." Matvei's glance shot daggers in my direction.

I met his glare and brightened my smile.

"Even if she is a fat cow, at least Dimi seems happy with how well she milks his cock," the pakhan joked in Russian.

Dimitri jerked. His wine sloshed from the glass.

I jabbed my fingers into his thigh under the table.

"Forgive me, father, I don't know what you just said," I rushed to say in English, batting my lashes.

In an added hiss under my breath, I added the command Dimi taught me for Marena. "Down."

Dimitri couldn't explode. Not here, not in front of the others. He needed their support to rule once the sick man died.

And he would die. There was no escape from the cancer ravaging his lungs.

"I said we were fortunate," the pakhan lied. "But our fortune will continue to grow when Igor marries the little Polish nun."

Cheers rang from Emil.

Boris harrumphed, a man of few words.

Vasil was silent.

And Dimitri boiled.

This dinner really *needs to end.*

I needed to get him out of here. The effort to keep the wrath contained made his body shake. If he disrespected the pakhan, it was over. Maybe that was what his father wanted. To push him. Whether it was to pave the way for his favorite, Igor, or just because the old man was a sadistic bastard, I didn't have the brain power to put forth a hypothesis.

I had just the thing. Snatching my glass with one hand, and something softer with the other, I rose, cup extended.

"To the happy couple!" I beamed, turning to Igor—and dragging the tablecloth.

The tapered candles wobbled.

"Oh goodness." I lunged and managed to knock the taper onto the cloth.

"You idiot!" Matvei shouted.

Signora Barone jabbered that it was fine.

The bimbos didn't bother to hide their snickering and giggling.

Emil called me a fat cow in Russian.

Igor and Boris were silent.

"I'm so sorry," I gasped, snatching Dimitri's chilled vodka.

The flames rose, as did my wicked inner glint of satisfaction.

"That's not water!" I faked horror.

"How stupid can you be?" the pakhan raged. Or he tried too. The excitement was too much, and he wheezed.

Pushing out my bottom lip, I made my eyes round and somber. "I didn't mean to. It was an accident, really." I faked a stammer.

Yes, old man. See me as weak. Underestimate me.

I will be the one sitting on your throne when you're cold in the ground.

"Cows can't expect to be anything more than milk," Emil chuckled.

I wanted to punch him. The words didn't hurt me. I had thick skin. But Dimi?

Crap! Bloody, stinking crap!

"I'm so sorry," I wailed. Faking tears, I rushed to the door, hands covering my face.

When Dimitri didn't follow, I panicked. It wasn't like I could call for him. And if he stayed, he would lash out. So I gracelessly tripped into the door frame. The pain that jumped up my side was real enough.

I cried out, gasping and cursing. On my hands and knees, I remained frozen, fake sobbing. It was the whimper that finally did it. Dimitri was there a moment later. His touch was gentle, completely contrasting the black wrath simmering in his eyes.

"Take me to the ice bath," I whimpered, needing to keep the act going. Moisture prickled my eyes as I rose. *Shit, that actually hurt!*

Dimitri scooped me into his arms. One of the trophy women made a nasty comment. Emil boomed with laughter. I tightened my grip around Dimitri's throat but cut a quick glance over the others. The Signora nodded discreetly to me. Clever woman, I knew I liked her.

Leaving the chaos and jokes behind, Dimitri took me to his inner sanctum. He set me down and with quick, efficient moves, undressed me. The lid on the chest freezer snapped open.

The dare was real. I frowned.

I can do this!

Slowly, I forced myself into the icy water. I had no intentions of staying long. Saunas were a yes. This thing was torturous.

The minutes ticked by. First five, then ten.

At the fifteen mark, when I could no longer feel my toes, I pushed out of the liquid. From the reading I'd been doing about ice baths, beginners didn't need to soak for such a long time. But I was hoping my perseverance earned me some of the mobster's terrible focus.

Dimitri didn't look at me.

Torn between needing to stay in the ice bath to keep him from leaving me and desperately wanting to go wrap my arms around him, I hummed a tune under my breath. When the song finished, I desperately needed to leave the cold.

My frozen feet hit the floor, and I stood dripping over the rubber mat.

An ache spread across my chest. I'd laid in ice for him. What more could I do to break him free of the toxic spell in his mind? Gritting my teeth, I went to the sauna and flicked the button. The heat began to stir.

"Aren't you going to hold me, mobster?" I breathed, because saying anything louder would make my teeth chatter.

Dimitri shook his head. Bent over the sink, he took hard breaths.

I took my sweet time pouring water over the steaming stones. When the sauna was hot, I approached Dimitri.

"Won't you come and join me?"

At my touch, his eyes snapped to me. It took everything I had not to recoil. It wasn't Dimitri looking out at me from behind those sea blue eyes, but a monster, angry and vicious. And that beast was in full possession of him.

Not a drop of fear slithered through me—not for my own safety.

But I had everything to fear for him.

"No one talks to you like that," Dimitri rasped.

"Dimi," I pleaded and flicked a quick glance to the door. He locked it as we came in but knowing that was all that separated us from the vermin outside sent a shiver through me. "You can't overthrow him. Not without causing a split in the ranks."

That lethal hand, one that could do terrible or tender things, shot out.

The mirror above the sink shattered.

With a yelp, I jumped and grabbed his hand. My strength wasn't enough to stop it from pummeling into the mirror a second time.

I wrapped my hands around his arm, using my weight to pull him down.

It was nothing.

For a guy who benched my body weight on a regular basis, that was no surprise.

"Stop! Please, just stop," I cried.

Hard breaths filled his lungs, the organs working like bellows. That mighty frame shook. The fearsome look in his eye promised death.

"Don't do this, Dimitri," I murmured. "If you kill him, your men will turn against you."

"I defy them."

My blood chilled. Those words were stronger than the icy water. I reached for something fundamental, some stroke of reason he might listen to! "Isn't patricide a terrible sin—"

"Then I defy the edict of the saints!" Dimitri gripped the sink and with a moan, ripped it from the wall. The porcelain shattered on the cement floor. Water spewed from the damaged pipes. "He disrespected *you*, Laurel. You! My redbird."

Before me stood a man possessed. For the first time in my life, I voluntarily whispered a prayer to a god I still wasn't convinced was there. But I needed something more powerful than the universe to help me. Good vibes had nothing on the black wrath swirling in Dimitri's volatile gaze.

"And what did I do?" he roared. "I sat there. I fucking *sat* there and respected his authority."

With a soul-shattering bellow, he turned and wrenched the chest freezer. It tipped. And then, it crashed. That wasn't a small freezer, because he fit comfortably in it, and there was no telling how many gallons of water were there.

My mobster...his beasts were unleashed.

I stepped into him, cold water splashing over my feet. "Please, Dimi. For me."

It was the wrong thing to say.

"For you," he agreed, to the opposite of what I'd meant.

Horror squeaked from my throat.

But Dimitri was already rushing from the gym.

My hoarse scream followed him, but he wasn't stopping for anything. I scrambled for my dress, thanking my previous self for choosing something that could be pulled on and off without zippers, buttons, or lacing.

The house was eerily silent by the time I emerged.

There was no noise coming from the great hall. Backup—I was going to need backup! Some of the other soldiers were in the rec room, waiting while their captains convened. It hadn't been long since we left dinner, so I counted on those bratva men to still be there. Peeking inside, I caught Luka's eye. I didn't have to call him or say a word. The cousin bolted up and hurried to me.

"Shit went down. Dimitri's gone mad," I blurted out.

Luka looked around. "Dammit, Kaz. Where the hell is he when you need him?"

Hearing the serious tone from the lighthearted Luka, I blanched. There was no need to answer the rhetorical question. Tonight was Dani's dress rehearsal for her ballet company.

"You have to help me, Luka. Dimi won't listen! We have to save him." The sob that came out this time was real.

Luka bounded up the hall. I sprinted after him. The door of the empty dining room banged open on its hinges. They couldn't have left. Which meant they were somewhere. We shared a look.

And then, we raced through the kitchens and into the backyard.

Where we found Igor puffing like a steam engine on a cigar while the pakhan was pushing one into his son's bicep. Two guards kept Dimitri in place. A third, that demonic henchman, had the noose of an animal control pole wrapped around my mobster's throat.

Cold air scraped my throat as I struggled to fill my lungs.

"Dimitri!" I screamed at the top of my lungs.

"Take her to Vasil's," my husband barked.

Arms corded with lean muscle wrapped around me. Luka *lifted* me off the ground and moved away.

I railed curses, but Luka bounced me.

"Stop!" he hissed. "Or it will be infinitely worse for Dimi. You can't save him from this. All we can do is hope the pakhan gets his jollies out."

Craning my neck, the horrific image of the pakhan raising his cane slid into place.

"He's hitting him! He's hitting his own son!" I gasped.

Dimitri jerked, but the goons holding him in place were unrelenting. I memorized their faces and promised them death. The pakhan wavered, stopped, and shook his head. He handed the cane to Zakhar.

With one solid blow, the henchman broke the fiberglass cane over Dimitri's body.

"No!" I wailed. Agony tempered with helplessness washed over me in a suffocating cloud.

"It's not his first beating, Laurel," Luka growled. "V zhopu! If I'd known he was going to confront his father—"

He let out a string of vile, colorful cursing.

"Let me go," I pleaded. "I can help him."

Hauling me onto his lap, Luka started the truck. He had to keep me there as he pulled through the gate and onto the night bathed road. "No one can help him."

Chapter 55 – Laurel

Kazimir walked through the door, Dimitri balanced around his side. Luka shot out of his seat to help. I stared—unable to move—at my mobster. His sea blue eyes were shut tight.

He's alive.

My heart stopped for about five seconds. And then, it began to hammer mercilessly against my ribs.

Dani squeezed in behind them. A vision in a pink hat, creamy coat, and vibrant fuchsia leg warmers, none of it matched her puffy eyes.

"I hate him," she breathed, running to me.

"Careful," Kazimir growled. "We don't know if Matvei has spies."

"Not in this house," Luka protested.

Meanwhile, I exchanged a quick embrace with Daniella before pushing her gently aside and moving to where Kazimir set my husband down on the puckered leather sofa. Dimitri fell over, eyes still unopened.

"Good, you have medical supplies," Kazimir said gruffly.

"Yeah, we're all set," Luka clipped out. "I even have one of Dimi's IV kits. Don't have a damn clue how to use it, but we can try."

"Cami's in bed, or I'd ask her." Dani chewed on her lip. "She would be the best to help us. She's really taking a liking to medicine. Should I wake her?"

Kazimir shook his head. "I can stab his vein with a needle. We'll just do a slow drip so the lines don't clog."

They set to work hanging a bag of liquid, prepping a vein in Dimitri's forearm, and giving him an IV full of vitamins and recovery stuff.

"It's too bad we can't pop some morphine in there," I said quietly.

Kazimir shook his head. "Dimi doesn't take painkillers. Won't even touch over the counter stuff."

I blew out a short breath. My mobster—the hero. "Do it. I'll take responsibility."

Luka and Kaz shot one another a look. Luka whistled an exhale between his teeth. "I'll make a call."

"Touch that phone, and I'll choke you," Dimitri hissed.

Snatching the bottle of witch hazel and a cotton ball, I crouched in front of Dimitri. I cupped his face, turning it back and forth while my chest ached. The vicious agony threatened to crack it in two.

"Sorry, Dimi, there's no ice bath," I teased quietly.

He didn't answer. His jaw clenched tight.

"He puked the whole way here." Kazimir crossed his arms.

That was when I noticed he'd brought a plastic lined waist pail to my side. "I don't care who hears me," I growled. "I hate the demonic sonofabitch."

"I hate him too. The pakhan did it to Kaz," Dani confessed, rubbing my back. "Here, put that antibacterial spray with lidocaine on his burns."

I took the bottle and unscrewed the lid before I shot her a side glance. "Really?"

She nodded. "Ordered him beaten, yeah."

"Yeah, that was brutal. Dimi did a number on you, eh, Kaz?" Luka thumped his cousin on the back.

I blinked between them. "Dimitri *hit* you?"

"Sixty-two strokes. By order of the pakhan," Dani menaced quietly.

So that's why she didn't like my husband. I blew out a long breath. That was going to take a bottle of wine and a box of candy to process. Since neither of those things popped out of thin air, I was going to have to content myself with shoving that thought away until I could fully deal with the trauma of the past when the present reality was terrible. Horrific. *Oh, so wrong.*

"That was different," Kazimir started to protest.

"It was not! It was unjust and disgusting." Daniella's voice cracked. Squeezing her eyes tight, she looked at the ceiling. "I'm sorry, Laurel. I'm so freaking emotional."

"You're exhausted from all the prep for the show this weekend," Kazimir comforted. He held his arms open.

I let out a short laugh. "Yeah, and being pregnant doesn't help either."

They froze.

Ah, shit....

I looked between them. "Did you seriously not know?"

"I wasn't going to tell him yet!" Daniella broke down. The tears fell in earnest, and my gut twisted full of guilt.

"Another baby!" Luka whooped. "Well done, Kaz, well done, old chap! In the words of a wise Frenchman—and I know that's an oxymoron—'Children need models rather than critics.' But you two totally have this!"

Everyone ignored Luka. At least the fact that he was finally rambling meant that he was in a better headspace.

"I thought it was obvious," I protested, hoping Dani didn't hate me. I was just starting to truly like her. "You didn't drink at the birthday party. And you puked your guts out at the Walmart. And at the last few family night dinners, you complained about your salads, your side dishes, and even the meat entrée. And when we were talking about which color to paint the end tables."

"Is it true?" Kazimir had eyes only for his wife.

Daniella nodded, rushing into his arms.

The tenderness between the two would melt even the coldest heart. For a minute, I wanted that. The excitement over starting a family. But looking back at my unconscious husband, the ugly truth about families stared back at me.

Not that I believed for a split second that Dimitri would lay a hand on any child of ours.

Unless they were choking. Then he would thump them and Heimlich them until they could breathe.

The manic laughter that bubbled out of me came from a place as crazed as it sounded. The happy couple looked skeptically at me.

I gasped for breath, waving a hand over Dimitri. "He and I came from such messed up homes. And we found one another. And—and—"

"And we're going to build a saints damned home that isn't a nightmare," Dimitri croaked.

I smoothed a hand over his head. "We are."

There was a moment of profound silence as my mind came to terms with reality. In that moment of peace, I realized beauty could come from brokenness.

When Daniella hiccupped, I turned to them. "Get her home, Kaz. She dances two shows tomorrow."

"Like hell you are," her husband growled.

"Kazimir Brian Vlasov. You will *not* tell me I can't dance. It's for...for...for Cady!" Daniella was full-on hysterical.

"Stay here. We have space, and Baby Zoey is already asleep in the dove room." Luka sprang to the door.

"Come on, let's go draw you a bath in the blue room," Kazimir encouraged.

"I'm dancing."

"Let's go to bed," he insisted.

Bickering, they paused only to tell us goodnight and that they'd be upstairs if we needed them.

"That's not a disagreement I want to witness," Dimitri chuckled darkly. But because his face was half swollen, it came out demented and garbled.

Sighing, I looked around Vasil's great library. It was either that or break down in tears myself. Focusing on the distraction, I noted the details of this cozy yet elegant space. I really did love this room. It was every book girly's dream, with masculine energy radiating from the décor. Personally, I liked the leather and dark wood, forest green and brass accents. Dimitri and I would definitely own a place like this. A glance at the ladder made me smirk. *And one of those.* We had to have a ladder.

"Can you...." Dimitri stopped.

I cut my gaze to his and brushed my fingers through his hair. "Yes?"

"Sing to me, redbird."

"Um..." I didn't perform where I could be seen. Never. But for him? I swallowed hard. "Anything in particular?"

"No," he whispered.

My eyes fluttered closed. I reached into the inner well and plucked a song at random from the 1960's. The notes rose to the surface, little bubbles popping into the world around me.

"When the night has come; And the land is dark; And the moon is the only light we'll see; No, I won't be afraid; Oh, I won't be afraid; Just as long as you stand; Stand by me..."

Dimitri moaned. "Redbird."

My smile grew impossibly wide. "So darlin', darlin', stand by me; Oh, stand by me...."

With a groan, Dimitri pushed himself up. One palm ground into his temple.

"Your head?" I breathed.

He nodded. "Keep singing. It...helps."

I poured my heart into the classic.

The words held truth. The sound of my voice carried feeling. My heart beat for this man, and my song let him know.

Dimitri slid his black button up shirt from his torso. He tore it to remove the sleeve over the IV. I reached to help, but he pushed my arm away.

"Sing for me, my little songbird. Sing...I beg you."

"Whenever you're in trouble won't you stand by me; Oh, stand by me; Won't you stand by," I finished.

"Again," the monster, beaten, bruised, and still bloody, demanded.

I cleared my throat. "When the night has come; And the land is dark," I began, letting go of any strand of embarrassment. This was my person. What did I need to be shy about? I knew I could sing, but it had never been encouraged.

Now someone needed it more than he needed to breathe. He needed me.

So I gave it to him.

I slid my dress over my head and crawled over his lap. Skin to skin, I held him. He pressed his head against my chest and wrapped his arms tightly around me. Absently, my fingers trailed over the nearest tattoo—a crooked wolf.

"Again," he murmured.

I started the classic once more. This time, the artistry failed. The words became a prayer. I whispered them between us, a poem of my soul to the man who was its other half.

Although I was naked, and he was shirtless, there wasn't anything overly sexual about the embrace. We were fragmented beings, put back together because of our combined strength. The skin-to-skin contact was a closeness we needed to strengthen the bond.

I pressed my forehead against his. "I am going to stand by you, Dimitri Vlasov."

"I'm so broken." Those three words tore from his very soul.

I shook my head back and forth. "If you are, then I am too."

"No, redbird, you soar."

I grabbed his hands, put them over my wrists, and drew in a sharp breath. "It's not impossible anymore for you to hold me like this—but it's you, Dimi. It's always been you."

"Laurel."

"Two brokens make a whole." I kissed his head.

Something rough choked in this throat. "I knew I was right making you my princess—and soon you'll be my queen."

"Tomorrow, we redouble our efforts to take your kingdom, my king." *One way or another, your father's reign is done.* No one touched what was mine and lived. And that was what Dimitri was—mine.

Chapter 56 – Laurel

"I know I've said it before, but welcome to the family, Laurel." Luka clapped my back.

The lone wolf found her pack. *Huh, what do you know about that?* "Thanks," I rasped and spit into the sink.

Fingers wrapped around the knob, I twisted. It wasn't locked. Relief mixed with confusion. What kind of mobster didn't lock his door while he slept? In a rush of self-preservation, I stepped behind the frame as the door swung open on silent hinges.

When nothing jumped out, I peered around the aperture. Moonlight carved a path through the thick darkness. A few shapes stood out, but it was the tall bay window that stole my focus. Or rather, the highbacked chair that was turned to observe the outside, while also keeping tabs on the interior.

The monster perched on the judgment seat swiveled to take in the intruder—me. Through the dark, a pair of glacial blue eyes stared back at me. "I had a feeling I might be seeing you tonight."

I swallowed thickly. He was expecting me? "I have a proposition for you."

"How's my big cousin?" The question cut me off.

"Sleeping."

"A mercy at last." A short laugh cut through the shadows.

Leaning against the door frame, I shivered. It couldn't be my imagination. But this bedroom was a good ten degrees cooler than the rest of the house. "I need your help."

The monster nodded. "Who do you want to kill, princess? The guards who pinned him down? The captain who watched? Or...are you going for the jugular?"

As much as I wanted to take out the pakhan, I couldn't ask this nephew to help. The glint in his eyes told me he was as bloodthirsty as I was. He would do it. But that would forever mark him as a traitor to his organization. Dimitri might be forced to discipline him, and the punishment for murdering a former pakhan would be certain death.

"I want to kill the henchman," I said softly.

A sharp grin cracked across his face. "I knew I liked you, my dear cousin."

Unfolding from his chair, the youngest Vlasov padded to the window and pulled one of the panes shut. Another shiver raced down my spine. This one was tempered by excitement.

"Is your husband going to wake up and raze my father's house to the ground when he doesn't find you?" Emerging from the dark, the shadows seemed to absorb into the man that was Luka.

"No, he's sound asleep." With half a rohypnol in his system. But to convince Luka, I added, "I left a note explaining that I had to run to the store for milk."

Rich, low laughter rumbled from the bratva prince. "Oh, he's going to be so pissed."

"Not if we hurry."

Luka tossed a set of keys in the air, as he closed his door. "Do you know where to find sweet old Zakhar?"

"I was hoping you did," I admitted, shifting my weight. These black sneakers were stiff, since I hadn't worn them yet. But they had a good grip, and I could sprint in them if necessary.

"It just so happens I do." Luka led me down the hall to a back staircase. I kept pace with him, hurrying into the freezing night. While the days were starting to rise in temperature, the night still reminded us that it was winter in the Midwest.

In the garage, we climbed into a nondescript, early 2000s Honda Civic. "Normally, I would take my baby, but she's easily recognizable." At my look of confusion, Luka pointed to a bright yellow jeep. "Don't you remember? We drove that here last night."

I shook my head. "You'd think I would have remembered riding in something so flashy."

"No, cuz, I wouldn't." Luka backed up, and then peeled out of the garage. At the gate, his houseguards let him through without comment. "Anyone who witnessed what you did wasn't going to pay attention to something as silly as the color of my Wrangler."

The Civic crept down the street, only to pause a street over from the pakhan's fortress.

"I know how to get in without being seen," I whispered. This was the one part of my plan that I wasn't confident about. Dimitri hadn't given me permission to tell his cousin about the secret passage.

"The tunnel from that condemned structure into the boiler room?" Luka swung a look to me.

Oh, well, that takes care of that. "Let's go."

At the doorless entrance to the seemingly sound building, I reached into the pocket of my yoga pants and produced a flashlight.

Luka batted it away. "Come on."

The night swallowed him, but when I took a step forward, I tripped.

"Steady on," he hissed, grabbing my upper arm.

"I can't see a damn thing," I snapped.

With a tug, Luka led me into the unfriendly blackness. One arm put in front, I seriously debated the sanity of my resolve. We walked for what seemed like ten minutes, but that wasn't true. When Dimitri brought me here, it wasn't far from the entrance. Luka stopped short and let me go.

Did I just go into a dark, abandoned building with the crazy Vlasov cousin?

The sound of metal twisting grated sharply. I jumped. Yep, Luka could bury me alive and no one would ever know.

"Ladies first," Luka chirped.

He had to guide me to the hole in the floor. Swallowing past the racing nerves, I descended the ladder. At the bottom, I stepped back.

"You can use the flashlight here, if you want," Luka said from behind me.

I sucked in a short breath. He must have been right on my heels to already be down here. Clicking on the flashlight didn't bring relief. The damp, stale, yet impossibly cold tunnel met me.

"Do you know how Dimitri damaged his spine?" Luka plucked the light and began to advance down the space.

I cleared my throat. "He's never said."

"Ah, well, if you didn't want to kill Zakhar already, you will after this." A manic glee bubbled from Luka's mouth. I padded after him, suddenly hanging onto his every word as we traversed the length of the secret passage.

"As you've noticed, the pakhan has always been physically abusive to his son. He believed his stern methods would mold Dimitri into the perfect soldier, one as cruel as he imagined himself to be. One that didn't feel, only acted."

"He failed," I spat.

Luka harrumphed in agreement. "Dimitri always had bruises as a kid. But it was one summer, when he was nineteen. The details aren't important, but he severely disappointed his father."

This story had one outcome, and still, I couldn't properly brace myself against it.

"Dimitri snapped," Luka continued. "He didn't fight back, but he defended himself."

"Oh, no," I breathed. My heart thumped painfully in my chest.

"Yeah. Zakhar, who'd been an enforcer at the time, happened to be passing by the pakhan's office. Or maybe he'd been eavesdropping. Either way, he pinned Dimitri down, and Uncle Matvei beat his son. I heard it was a wooden bat. Someone else heard it was a steel pipe." Luka paused at the door to the furnace room of the pakhan's fortress. "He broke a vertebra in Dimi's spine. The damage was something he ignored for too long, and when he finally had a disk replacement, the nerve that had been pinched was so damaged that now it's easily triggered."

I swiped at my eyes. Words failed me. But the horror was completely washed away. In its place was an overwhelming drive to destroy anyone and everyone who'd touched my mobster.

"There she is," Luka murmured. The smirk that tipped up his lips was nothing short of malicious. "Let's go kill the demon plaguing this family."

"Zakhar's death will also cripple the pakhan," I laughed roughly.

"An added bonus," Luka agreed.

Silently, we emerged from the secret tunnel and slipped through the empty, desolate halls. Luka led me deeper into the fortress than I had ever ventured. Dimitri's warning about not exploring had kept me to the main, inhabitable parts of the building. But clearly, Luka knew this place well.

As we turned down a second-floor corridor, our steps slowed. Eastern, mystical chanting droned through the halls.

"The enforcer is working," Luka chuckled. "Good, his room will be ready for use."

"The dungeon?" I whispered, not because we needed to be quiet, but because I couldn't speak any louder.

"You *are* good, cuz." Luka slid to a door and pounded his palm against the metal.

My heart jumped into my throat. A protest burped up my throat.

Luka only grinned, a blaze sparking in his eye.

The door ripped open, and Luka pounced. His fist cracked into flesh.

I fumbled with the gun in my back waistband. The safety flicked off, so I kept it pointed at the ground, my finger brushing against the trigger.

Soft thuds echoed from the room. The somber beat of the meditation track pulsed in the background. It wasn't Tibetan chanting. That I was familiar with, having spent several months trying meditation. But the noise was similar.

And in the glow of red lamps, it was eerie.

The dungeon was a long room with manacles on the wall. Still lumps of flesh dangled off two. Close to the door were stainless steel counters with various implements.

Luka's howl snapped my attention from the hall of horror.

Blood already permeated the space. The metallic tang twisted my gut.

But rational thought sprang to the front, and I realized rivulets of watered blood trickled over the floor toward central drains. These two happened to be rolling in it.

I pointed my gun. *Crap!* With a hiss, I raised the muzzle and pointed at the ceiling. I wasn't a good shot. The bullet would just as easily hit Luka as the henchman.

Tension vised around my muscles. The harsh sound of grunts and the clatter of the struggle filled the room.

I have to do something!

Desperation snapped me into motion. I rushed to the stainless-steel counters and shelves. Settling my gun on the spotless workbench, my gaze swept across the implements. From the back of my mind, knowledge I'd soaked up over time came to my aid. It would be disastrous to get close. So I needed something long and powerful. From the hooks hung a flexible looking rod with prongs on the end.

"Huh." I plucked it down. "This could work."

There was a trigger, and when my finger pressed it, the end buzzed. It would hurt. It was long. Spinning on my heel, I moved to the edge of the brawl.

Their bodies twisted and writhed in a desperate struggle. Metal flashed between them. My stomach flipped. Luka had a lethal looking black knife. The henchman? He had a scalpel. It might be small, but he delivered a swift series of slices. Luka's arm became a shower, spraying down on Zakhar.

"No!" I gasped, lunging.

And missed.

My heart hammered in a frantic drumbeat that threatened to drown out all rational thought. Fear clawed at my throat, threatening to suffocate me as I watched helplessly, my limbs frozen in a state of paralysis. Every fiber of my being screamed for action, for intervention, but the sight of the knives flashing in the dim light held me captive, a chilling reminder of the fact that I wasn't from this world of violence.

The dim light cast eerie shadows over the death match, distorting their figures into grotesque shapes. I pulled back at the last second. The prongs were just as likely to hit one as the other! I stood frozen over their forms. Luka managed to knock an elbow into the other man.

But Zakhar's eyes danced with malevolent intent. With a brutal thrust, the henchman reached around and sank the surgeon's blade into Luka's back.

Rage banished hesitation.

Time seemed to slow to a crawl, each second stretching into a pool of raw, desperate power. The room pulsed with the explosion of my inner violence. I might not have been born into this nightmare, but now I was thoroughly invested as one of its queens.

The forked end slipped perfectly between Zakhar's unclenched lips. My index finger squeezed the trigger with enough strength to crack the device.

Choking led to convulsing.

Luka instantly gained the upper hand. His black blade plunged through the left ribs.

"Stop the electricity!" he bellowed.

I dropped the torture device.

Luka ripped his blade away. "Genius touch with the cattle prod," he chuckled, ripping the stick from where it stuck in the back of Zakhar's throat.

In the sudden wake of the fight, the adrenaline had no more outlet, and my stomach flipped. "I'm going to be sick."

"Sink on the wall," Luka said, but instead of leaving me to stumble, he grasped me gently around the waist and hustled me.

As my empty stomach spilled into the basin, his steady touch brushed over my hair. "I've got you, cousin, I've got you."

With each retch, my throat burned with a searing pain, as if the very act of expelling the contents of my stomach was tearing me apart from the inside out. The muscles in my abdomen clenched and convulsed. The spasms wracked my body and seemed to radiate through my very bones.

Tears pricked at the corners of my eyes, hot and stinging. I struggled to regain control of my body. The violent reaction left me feeling hollow and empty, as if I were purged of every ounce of strength and vitality. And yet, even as I gasped for breath, I knew this was just an initial reaction.

The darkness inside me reveled in victory. That feeling grew stronger with each passing second. We'd done it! That demon would never haunt our family again. Dimitri was avenged. And the pakhan? Hopelessly crippled without his henchman.

When the sickness ceased, the sour taste coating my tongue left it acidic and bitter. I coughed. "We need to hide the body."

"Don't worry, I've got something better." Luka gave me a final pat and retreated.

Drawers wrenched open. Their contents shook, and the stainless-steel workbenches rattled. I rinsed and spat. Turning, I saw Luka pluck a glass jar from the middle compartment.

"Fill a bucket of water," he instructed.

The questionable stains in the empty five-gallon pail under the workbench made my gut flip yet again. I drew careful breaths through my nose.

"Not that much. Here." Luka traded me the cattle prod for the bucket.

I hung the device quickly, and then crept back to the scene of the execution. I was like the queen of hearts. *Off with their heads.* And this monster of the underworld jumped to help. Who would have thought the little socialite would grow into such a powerful fiend? I laughed roughly under my breath.

"Stand back. I don't want to splash you with this," Luka warned.

The henchman was covered in a white powder. Luka stood back and flung the water over the corpse. There was a retched, chemical scent. I pinched my nose, back peddling for the door.

Zakhar's leg twitched.

"Holy shit! Is he still alive?" I gasped, my heart threatening to pop from the surprise.

"I pricked his left ventricle, don't worry. He'll die." Luka returned the bucket to the shelf under the shelf.

I gulped. "What is that powder?"

"Something that reacts to water and turns into a nasty little paste. I saw Pavel disintegrate a rat with it once. I figured it would work just as well on a man," Luka chirped, herding me out of the dungeon. He hit the wall and the red lamps lining the walls blinked out.

"Kaizmir's Pavel?" I scrambled to wonder what that had to do with anything.

"Yeah, he's wicked good with science shit." Luka steered me along the dark corridors. "Anyhow, thanks for your help."

Just like that. As if I held a shelf while he screwed it into the wall. Not helped him murder a very bad man.

"Your arm!" I hissed.

"We'll wrap it in the car, and then I'll wake Cami Joe. She's pretty handy with a needle. Don't worry about it." Luka squeezed my traps just like I was one of the boys in the boxing ring. "Matvei is crippled! Long live Pakhan Dimitri!"

I shook my head. "I don't underestimate the old bastard for a second."

That dark admission held truth, because it was powerful enough to silence the crowing, crazy Vlasov cousin.

Chapter 57 – Laurel

Daniella was magnetic. She *shone.* While she was technically a minor character in the show, none of the others held a candle to her. The moment the curtain closed, Kazimir dashed from his seat. Beads of sweat ran down his temples and it was impossible to miss the blood returning to his previously white knuckles.

"She'll be fine," Signora Barone laughed from two seats down.

Vasil nodded to Dimitri, and they scooted close and began a hushed conversation. One of many they'd shared today.

It was tense. The pakhan hadn't issued any orders after what was considered Dimitri's act of insubordination. According to Vasil, it seemed as though the son could return, and the incident would be forgotten.

There was no way in hell I was spending a night in that horror house.

But I couldn't let Dimitri go there alone.

I stood to stretch, as did the signora. Patrons of the Lyric Opera House milled about, chatting about the local, amateur ballet company. Our seats were the best in the house, in my opinion. Front row, where we could hear the thud of the pointe shoes hitting the wood of the stage. Something about theater called to a deep, intrinsic part of my being. Ballet was only a close second to opera. I wondered if Dimitri would become a patron of the arts.

The signora beckoned to the stage. "Ti piace?" *Did you like?*

Ah, so she'd figured it out. My singing a lullaby to baby Zoey last night must have been the final clue that I spoke Italian. Clever old woman.

My palm slapped against my chest, and I let out a strangled moan. "Mi piace?" With a sweep of my arm, I beamed, "Bellisima, Signora. Ho provato una gioia così intensa che sembrava di poter toccare il cielo con un dito."

The wizened Italiana broke out laughing. "You speak like a native! So many Americans mess the grammar."

I shrugged, but the flippant comment on my tongue dried.

Above, in the prime box, his arm slung around a woman with platinum blonde hair, was a fiend I prayed never to see. Panic gripped my muscles. Air refused to fill my lungs. Scrambling to clutch the rail in front of our seats, the drive to flee accelerated through me.

But when the demon above turned in laughter to speak to the person at his side, that cruel brown gaze drifted in my vicinity. He looked away. But the moment recognition hit, he snapped those eyes back at me, and Craig recognized me through the disguise of ninety more pounds and jet-black hair.

A solid hand fell on my shoulder.

I yelped, but the surprise washed away as the familiar strength leached into me on a wave of my husband's warmth.

"Mobster, get me out of here," I rasped, struggling to pull enough oxygen to form the words.

"Vasil, find out who the bastard is in that box," Dimitri clipped in Russian.

I gulped. "Don't! He's too powerful."

"Go, uncle," Dimitri hissed.

"Dimi, don't." Panic swelled through my veins. Because in that moment I knew Dimitri had put the last piece of the puzzle in place. He knew someone hurt me, but never pressed for information even though my tangle of secrets drove him mad.

Well, now he had a target.

Why didn't I just look away?

Because when a nightmare appears in the daytime, it had the power to freeze its victims in their tracks.

Dimitri made to move. A warning bell clanged in my mind. I shook my head, forcing down the physical sickness.

I had to stop my mobster. The trauma would be there to grapple with later.

Right now, I couldn't risk the corrupt businessman putting a hit on my husband when there was already one active kill order. And that wasn't counting other mobs who would spend the rest of Dimitri's life trying to tear him down.

There was one sure way to stop sidetracking the ruthless bratva prince.

"Dimi, please," I whimpered. "Hide me. Get me out of here!"

Craig was on his feet, pushing through the door. He would intercept us in the lobby. I began to sprint when Dimitri grabbed my wrist, squeezed hard, and took off backstage where Kazimir had already disappeared.

"I'll get your coats!" Signora Barone called.

Dimitri clipped out thanks, and then we were pushing into the back section of the theater. I did it. We were escaping. Relief swept through my veins, panic and fear hot on its heels. Reality blurred. The world spun. The next thing I knew, I was in Dimitri's truck, and the tires were pulling us away.

Chapter 58 – Dimitri

Laurel clutched the bottle of water in her hands. I turned the heat to full blast, chasing away the winter night that had filled the truck while we were outside. My bride was breathing easier now, short and shallow breaths, but the nausea was gone.

I turned my body to the side, watching her across the center consul. The silence ticked on, but I was a patient man. It was time.

We weren't leaving this overlook until she talked.

As if she sensed the inevitable, Laurel sighed.

"Craig was the suitable choice." Laurel looked over the water of Lake Michigan. "He was old money from good breeding and had dazzling prospects."

But….

I knew the direction this story would go before she even said it. I stayed silent. This was her show. And she forced the words from her throat.

"It started with small things. I let them slide as long as I could, but the moment I'd had enough and stood up for myself, the dam broke. I realized too late that Craig was only holding back on the verbal and mental abuse before. So I ended it." There was a catch in Laurel's voice. Her eyes squeezed closed, and she reached out for me. I clasped her hand, tight enough so she knew I was there, but not hard enough that she couldn't pull free. "I told my parents. They brushed off my concerns and said in no uncertain terms that the relationship would continue. I said 'no' when he asked me to marry him."

Laurel smiled faintly.

I could see it now, her impossibly strong backbone.

"That was the first time he hit me," Laurel breathed. "I swore it would be the last. I went into my mother's room, and I pointed to the bruising tissue. And she brought me her cosmetic case. 'You're going to have to learn to hide those.' That's what she said to me. To her daughter!"

Laurel squeezed my hand tightly.

"He's dead," I promised her.

There was a strangled sigh. "The story's not over."

"Laurel," I breathed. "You don't have to—"

"I do. I'm done with secrets, Dimi." Laurel shifted in her seat, pinning me with a look.

How I longed for those words!

Now, I wished to erase their existence from both our minds.

Since that was impossible, I knew I had to do the next best thing. I didn't know if I was strong enough to hear it. But if she was strong enough to endure the memory…if she was strong enough to tell me, I could be strong for her.

"Craig was into abstinence. When we first met, I thought he was ridiculous. By the time we were engaged, I was grateful for those lines. At the rehearsal dinner, he drank more than usual. Nothing short of standing in front of our family, friends, and the entire elite society, telling them exactly what a brute the charmer was would have stopped the wedding. But—" She faltered. "I couldn't."

I rubbed my thumb over her fingers. "It's alright."

"No, it's not. I couldn't because what if they turned on me like my parents? What if they told me I was silly? That Craig was the perfect husband, and I was lucky to have him? I couldn't face that coming from them all. But they didn't have control over my story. I took off my ring and left the table."

Laurel laughed ruefully, bending and straightening her finger. "In hindsight, I shouldn't have provoked him. It would have been far more wise to slip away, and then dump the ring—or pawn it. But I couldn't resist the little jab. The subtle message that I didn't belong to him. That stroke of hubris cost me."

She stopped talking and took a sip of water. Her hand trembled. Some of the liquid escaped her lip. I reached out to wipe it away.

Her smile was tight. It was tired. *It didn't glow.*

"I will kill him, redbird."

Laurel's smile grew more sad. "The worst part wasn't him calling me a whore, slapping me around, or even when he forced himself on me." Although her voice grew quiet, there was a fire behind her words. "It was that if I could only free my hands, if only I could *move*, I could fight back. He would have killed me. Put me in the hospital and had someone *take care* of me. Ask me how I know that."

"Laurel...."

"Yeah, he told me. If I wasn't a good wife to him, he used to say, I wouldn't be anyone else's wife." Laurel's eyes blazed. "I tried to fight him that night, to make that happen. But he bound my hands with his tie."

She held up her hands.

We sat there in silence.

"He's dangerous, Dimitri." Her cinnamon eyes, impossibly warm, pleaded with me.

The muscles in my jaw hardened. "So is your husband."

Laurel whipped her head back and forth. "You don't understand. You get away with bad things because you skirt the law. He—and his cronies—get away with it because they *are* the law. They're untouchable. No one can stand against them."

I had been conceived, born, and raised as an enemy of the law. Fighting it was nothing new. And if it was the law that brutalized my Laurel, then it was the law that would burn for it.

But right now, she didn't need to hear that. Instead, I told her what she wanted to hear. "Okay, babe. I understand."

Relief washed through her. I moved to bring her close, but she shook her head.

"There's more," she huffed.

I grit my teeth, not sure I could stand more.

"I managed to flee that night. He passed out, and I stole three hundred bucks from his wallet. I fled. Bought a box of blonde hair dye, a tourist sweatshirt and shorts, and kept enough cash for a bus. No documents, no electronics—no trace."

A smile flickered on the corner of her mouth. She took another long sip of water. And when she spoke again, her voice was steady. There was no shake in her body.

"I came to Chicago, and I met you."

"And I forced you into my dark corner of the world." *Dammit, I'm no better than him!* "I didn't give you a choice."

"Don't you see the difference, Dimi? I would let you tie me up. I would let *you* pin me down. Because I'm free to fly away anytime I say. But...I don't want to. I want to build a nest here, with you."

"But I've trapped you," I choked bitterly.

Laurel shook her head, grin wide. "I haven't finished the story, silly."

I didn't respond, because I didn't think I could.

"When I got as far as Chicago, the money ran out. I hadn't been able to save enough cash, and I couldn't get back to my house to get it with all the wedding excitement. I sat on a bench in Hyde Park, wondering if by begging I could manage to make enough for lunch. It had been days, and the street rabble wasn't kind. They all had their turf, their corners to beg at. I didn't want to assert myself because I knew any police involvement meant I could be found by my family. But that day, I had the best luck. The universe finally gave me a break from all the shit."

I found myself holding my breath.

"A tall, dark-haired man was walking through the park. I was singing, hoping to have some change thrown in my used food container. He saw me, and I smiled at him. I was gross and hadn't taken a shower in days, but the man still came over."

My heart slammed into my chest. I knew this story. Just like...I knew those eyes.

Pulling up her skirts, Laurel crawled over the center consul and settled on my lap. There wasn't anything particularly provocative in the gesture. She didn't reach for my pants. It was a simple claiming of her rightful seat.

"He asked me to sing him another song, and he would pay me. I told him only if it was enough for a meal and a night at the shelter, with enough extra for—"

"For a new life," I whispered, the words clawing from the recesses of my memory. I reached out and pulled the clip from her hair. "Impossible."

"Not really. Meeting you was fate. Finding you again...that was all me." Laurel beamed.

"How? What?" I stammered. My fingers fucking trembled as they combed through her dark, thick strands.

"You took me to Gundry's Diner—I'm heartbroken it was torn down for the bougie apartment buildings, by the way. I always hoped to bring you there, to buy *you* lunch." Laurel ran her fingers along the side of my skull.

"Finish," I demanded, blood racing through my veins.

"You gave me an insane amount of cash. If I was actually a hobo, I would have OD'd within the hour." Laurel grimaced. "But I didn't. You also told the staff to feed me whatever I wanted. I ordered food for later that night, checked into a homeless shelter, and the next day found someone on the streets to make me a fake I.D. Ask me why I chose my name?"

"Laurel Gundry," I laughed incredulously. "The surname is explainable."

"You found me under a bay laurel plant." Darting down, she pressed a kiss on my lips.

I caught her mouth and didn't let her go. Hunger simmered under the surface. It reached beyond the scars and shone through the darkness haunting the truck cab.

Laurel squealed and pulled back. "I'm not done," she insisted.

Clasping her wrist, I brought it to my lips and placed a kiss on the pulse. "Finish," I growled.

She only laughed. "I watched you, you know."

A jolt of electricity shot through me. "I know, but *how*?"

"You said your name was Dimitri. I heard you speak Russian on the phone when you were walking up to me. I put feelers out on the street and found you. A bratva prince of one of Chicago's Russian mobs. A small but feared mob. As I worked as a bartender, hiding in the less savory parts of town, I kept my eyes and ears open. Every few months I would hear about you. I even watched you sometimes. Glimpses from across the street. Eventually, I even discovered where you lived."

"More powerful criminal organizations have tried to take me down, and you just...watched from the shadows?" Kazimir's warning echoed through me. I didn't believe Laurel was after me to kill me, but if she could so easily track me, who else could?

Laurel shrugged. "I was determined. And I think the universe helped me. Because it knew I had a great cosmic debt to pay."

I frowned.

Pressing her forehead against mine, Laurel finished, "You saved my life that day, Dimi. I became yours and you mine, even though we didn't realize it at the time."

"You could have said so when you came to warn me," I grumped. "It would have saved Kazimir thinking you were working for my enemies."

Laurel shrugged. "Call it self-preservation. I didn't want you to turn away from me, so I told you as little as possible. Plus...."

When she didn't finish that, I nudged her. "Yes?"

Laurel pursed her lips. "I was really turned off by the idea of relationships. While I had the biggest crush on you, anything more scared me."

That made too much damn sense now.

I slid my hands up her skirt, the feel of her soft skin driving me instantly crazy. When my fingers brushed over the curves of her hips and ass, I stilled. She wasn't wearing any panties.

The beast inside roared to claim her, but I remained motionless as she trailed her fingers down my dress shirt, each button plucked quietly free. She spread the material with agonizing slowness.

The teeth of the zipper sang as her deft fingers slid my pants open. Before she released me, Laurel reached to push the button for the seat to tip back. The electric buzz droned through the air. Once the seat was just right, Laurel settled over me and pulled me free in one swift move.

I sucked in a sharp breath.

Laurel rubbed the tip of my dick against her pussy. I groaned at the feel of the slick heat.

Bringing me to her entrance, Laurel lowered. Each painful inch was sheer torture. I simply held her, letting her take control of our pleasure. Her tight pussy stretched and opened for me.

The shuddering sigh that escaped her lips was reward enough for not hurrying her.

A desperate throb crackled through my length, settling root-deep in my balls where it became a tight ache. Laurel flexed her hips, settling tightly around me. She began to move and stars popped around us. My breaths became a ragged accompaniment to her gasps and whimpers.

Her fingers dug into my shoulder.

"Do you see how my cock makes you shake and tremble?" I rasped.

Laurel cried out. "Dimitri!"

"That's it, redbird. Sing my name. Let the world know who adores you."

It took every drop of my control not to pump into her. Those gorgeous tits bounced right in front of me, threatening to spill from the material. I was no doubt bruising her delicate flesh with how hard I held her.

"What do you need, baby?" I rasped.

"You," she choked. "I need *you*, Dimi."

"You have me," I growled. "The moment you come, you'll pull the seed with your tight little cunt."

Laurel whimpered, her movements faltering.

My control snapped. One hand holding her so I could thrust from below, I reached to rub small circles on her clit.

"Say my name, tell me who this sweet pussy belongs to?"

"You, Dimi. It's all yours."

I stared into her eyes, unable to look away from the storm I knew would crash through her.

Saints! She was the most beautiful thing I had ever seen.

"That's right, I own this. It's mine. You're *mine*, redbird."

A cry left her lips, and she dropped forward.

"Give me your breast," I growled. "Put it in my mouth."

She obliged my demand. I sucked on the tight nipple, flicking my tongue against the pebbled flesh. Wetness from her pussy coated my cock, my fingers slipping against her.

I snapped my hips and drove deep. Those inner walls clenched tightly around me.

As the release consumed her, Laurel arched her back with a scream. Her breast popped from my mouth. I groaned, following her and pressing my head against her chest.

The horn blared behind her back. Eventually, she collapsed against me. Each shuddering breath shook her whole frame.

I didn't have the strength to move us. Content to just enjoy her, I wrapped my arms around her. And we lay there until the sun broke across the horizon.

Chapter 59 – Dimitri

The whir of the engine droned in the background. Staring over Lake Michigan, I witnessed the most incredible sunrise in all my thirty-four years of life. The sky bloomed purple. The darker shades retreated and the lighter turned rosy, then red and orange. Laurel breathed softly on my lap. I trailed my touch up and down her spine.

When she stirred, I pressed my lips against her forehead. "Good morning, beautiful."

"What the hell? Did we sleep in the truck?" she yawned.

I pulled her close, burying my nose in her hair. Saints damned berries and cream. My dick twitched in response, an instant turn-on. But it was more than sex. There was a sacredness about the scent.

"There is a church service at nine. We would have time to change and grab a bagel before. If you want to come with me," I offered softly.

Laurel swallowed. Those warm cinnamon eyes watched me steadily. "Can a skeptic attend? Or will I burst into flame?"

I chucked her under the chin. "I won't let you burn, redbird."

"Okay. I miss the gospel hymns granny made us sing when we went to church with her."

Scratching my head, I hummed. "Um, what church did she go to?"

"Fifth Avenue Presbyterian Church in Manhattan," she chirped. "It's an old, famous one. But we went to the Southern Gospel services."

"Yeah, you're in for a culture shock, redbird. Saints Peter and Paul is very different. More...chanting than singing gospel hymns."

Laurel shrugged and wound her arms around my shoulders. "So long as I'm with you."

And then, her mouth found mine.

I took it with a moan, suddenly starved for her touch. My fingers raked over her body, soaking up the precious minutes until we had to leave. That mouth, that body; I couldn't get enough.

Laurel took to service like she did everything else, full of grace and poise, with an untamable spirit driving her. My queen—I would make her queen of the underworld.

Because my princess was already solidifying my reign.

I owed her my life, and it looked like I would soon owe my throne to her skill.

Stepping into Vasil's home for Sunday dinner, my uncle jerked his head to the side. As Laurel pulled the black lace scarf off her head, I leaned in to press a kiss on her forehead.

"Did I tell you how beautiful you looked, sitting in the pew, staring up in reverence at the icons?" I whispered, brushing my hand over her head.

"I would play the part of pious wife again." Laurel smoothed a hand over her high necked, lacey black dress. "I find the modest fashion and head covering a fascinating alternative. Like a gothic Victorian."

I snorted. "Whatever makes you happy, beautiful."

With a squeeze of her wrist, I let her hurry off to the Barone cousins. Daniella was dancing the matinee, and then one show this evening, so Kazimir would be absent from the meal. But Laurel seemed as comfortable with these younger women as she did with the one her own age.

I frowned, suddenly realizing how little I knew of my bride. Her story from last night filled the larger gaps, but how old was she? When was her birthday? *What's her favorite flower?* I knew her on the deepest and most intimate levels. But I needed to know the rest too. She was mine—all of her.

"What did you find out?" I clipped the moment Vasil shut the door to his study.

My uncle walked past the bookshelf ladder. The muscles of my lips twitched as dark, delicious memories flashed through. The modest, pious side of my redbird was fascinating. But underneath, she was wild and flammable. Her touch burned me in the best ways.

"Craig Snell, vice president of a media corporation. The Snell family holds shares in more than one media outlet. They're old money—one of the first printers in Colonial New York. They've got Snells in politics, business, and internationally they've married into the great houses of Europe." Vasil walked to the sideboard, opened the minifridge disguised as a cabinet, and poured a finger of vodka. He held it to me.

I remained frozen. "Corrupt, then."

"Yes. Very," Vasil agreed.

I took the chilled alcohol and downed it.

"And very, *very* well connected. If I stress nothing else, my boy, know that their family is not to be underestimated," Vasil added, dropping his hand on my shoulder and squeezing the muscles.

An ache shot through my nerves.

"Now...why are we interested in young Craig?"

"He hurt my wife."

Vasil let out a low whistle and took a swallow from his own glass. "Well, his days are numbered then, aren't they?"

I changed the subject. "Any word from the pakhan?"

"Your father is livid," my uncle admitted. "He wanted you to marry the Lazarowicz girl and unite with the Polish."

Unease slithered down my spine. "Then why make a show of bestowing the favor on Igor?"

My uncle shrugged. "His mind is twisting, Dimitri. It's going to get very ugly before the end."

I nodded. "And it will stay cloudy and stormy for months if not years after."

"Such is the price of the crown, my boy," he laughed.

"Do I just seize the throne, sir?" Although I was three inches taller and thus looked down at my uncle, it was with the utmost respect that I asked for his opinion.

Vasil let out a long breath. "I've always been loyal to my sibling and the bratva."

"But?"

"I don't condone patricide. But a hospice, with the best health care and high security, would be a kindness to my ill—very, *very* ill—brother."

I nodded. "Let's make that happen. I don't want him to suffer."

"Never that." Vasil grinned.

Luka burst through the door like a shot. "Dimi! come quick. Your bride is in big trouble."

My heart in my throat, I ran. "Where?" I barked.

Luka tore after me. "Sitting room. The pakhan is here and so are—"

I stopped at the door. "What the hell is going on?" I said quietly, menace tightening my voice.

"A blessed family reunion," my father chortled. The words turned into a cough.

And secretly, I hoped he choked.

Laurel stood behind an armchair. A tall, albeit portly man with grey hair barely covering the bald spots dogged her. A posh woman stood in the middle of the room, lips pursed tightly. And there, standing on the other side, effectively trapping my wife, was the rotten bastard from the ballet.

My words had startled the men, but they turned away, walking toward Laurel. With a yelp, she made to push the chair at the one and dove out of reach of the other.

"Stop!" I roared. "Lay a hand on my wife, and I'll break your necks."

"Young...man," the portly man sneered. "Do you know who I am?"

"I don't give a shit. I'm her husband and that's all that matters." I held out my hand, and spoke in Klingon. "Laurel, come."

She made no jokes at the sci-fi language, threatening in that secret way of hers to tell my cousins. It hurt that she was so frightened. I ground my molars.

Laurel sprinted around the man. The idiot was stupid enough to dive for her.

My gun was in my hand the next second. The shot glanced off his shoulder instead of going through. It was on purpose. I would make this man *bleed.*

"Demetrius!" My father roared. "He has blackmail on us. You can't kill him."

Laurel sprinted free, flew to me, and took shelter under my arm. I squeezed her tight. Her hard breathing fanned me. The frantic look in her eyes twisted my insides.

"Dimitri, put down the gun." My father's voice was a whip. "This is the CEO of Bartlet Enterprises, Mr. Bart O'Connell and Mrs. Françoise O'Connell."

"And that, young man, is our daughter, who's been missing for eight years." The portly man puffed his chest.

I swung my gun toward the other man. "And that's the man who raped her."

My bullet sailed past his cheek, clipping his ear and burrowing into the wall behind him.

"Will you cease!" the pakhan roared. "They offered a great reward for reuniting with their daughter."

"We have collateral," Craig said coolly. "If Gisele doesn't come home with us, the feds will raid this house and your other enterprises, and you'll all go to high security penitentiaries."

Laurel shuddered. Her face pushed deeper into the shelter, hiding from the threat.

Beautiful songbird, I have you.

Options of how to play this shifted through my head. Poking holes in these vile beings sounded like *ssooo* much damn fun. But that was immediate satisfaction. Furthermore, if they did indeed have dirt on us, the ramifications could hurt those I cared about.

Just because they don't die now, doesn't mean they won't later.

And I could have just as much fun with them later.

"How can *you* stand there and let this sonofabitch talk about taking your daughter when you know he's done unspeakable things to her?" I growled at the mother.

The woman didn't even flinch. "Gisele knew her place in society. It was a good match—"

"It still is a good match," Craig spoke over her. He clutched his leaking wound, face whitening and sweat beading on his forehead.

"—he was drunk and didn't know what he was doing. My daughter has a temper and no doubt needled him into a just rage, and—"

"Enough!" I shot her dangling handbag. "How dare you."

Staying within the shelter of my body, my redbird pulled herself straight. "You're right. I do have a temper. So you'll leave and never come back. It's Laurel Vlasova now. Bring the law into this, I'll tell them all your dirty little secrets before I go join my husband in prison. Because if that's where he goes, that's where I'm going too. No one is taking me away from Dimitri."

Luka quietly edged the room. There was a glint in his hand. I caught his eye and gave a small shake of my head. He didn't need to gut these people. If they disappeared, no doubt there would be inquiries.

No...when they died, it would be a whisper in the night that they never saw coming.

"Dimitri, you don't understand what they're offering. Divorce her and you can have the little Polish princess. I'll name you my successor," my father bargained.

I cut him a withering look. He was practically salivating, hands wringing tight.

You damned coward. "Laurel's last name is Vlasova—and that isn't fucking changing." Turning to the foul, cruel trio, I added, "Leave. There will be no cops. Laurel's told me everything. You come for her, and you'll find yourselves fallen from grace."

The portly man gummed his mouth for a moment. "Come, my dear, let's go. It's clear we lost our daughter and I don't know this fat drag queen standing here. You won't be hearing from us again."

"See that I don't." *But you'll be hearing from me.*

As long as that man stayed alive, Laurel was in danger. And as for killing the mother, I had female soldiers to do that. But Craig and Bart were mine to end.

"Let me show you out," Signora Barone intoned, tipping her chin in the air.

They followed her out, but the tension only thickened.

The pakhan banged his cane into the floor. "This is the final infraction."

A stillness fell over the room.

My father ripped his phone from his pocket. He stabbed the screen. Glaring at me, he placed it to his ear. There was a moment's pause. Laurel leaned into my side. And then.... "Igor," the pakhan clipped. "Assemble the men. I'm appointing you my heir to the Vlasov Bratva."

A wordless protest exploded from my wife.

I gripped her hard, tucking her under me. "As you will, pakhan."

Snorting in disgust, my father limped from the sitting room.

Vasil closed the door behind his brother and turned to me. "The joke is on him. Igor won't accept. Even if he doesn't get the Polish princess, he's pledged his support to you, my boy."

Relief washed through me, but it was short lived.

"Igor is the one coming after you," Laurel hissed, eyes darting to look out the door.

"How did they find her?" I demanded of my cousin.

Luka shrugged. "I guess they had connections too. Your father showed up with them, but from what he was saying, they came *to* him."

"I told you they were dangerous," Laurel muttered. "Now forget about them. What about Igor?"

"Igor's not the one who put a hit on him," Vasil said with a sigh. "We're back to square one on that."

"I meant to tell you after the ballet last night." I combed a hand over her hair. "I'm sorry, something else came up."

Laurel's shoulders dropped. But just as quickly, she pulled them straight. "We'll redouble our efforts then."

This fucking woman.... She came into my life and completely turned it upside down. And now...and now.... *Every time I look at you, I smile.* I needed to remember to show her. My lips turned up, and I flashed her a broad, full grin.

Chapter 60 – Dimitri

Kazimir bent over his foster brother's computer. Only the night janitors were roaming the halls of Neb. Tech., and they knew better than to disturb us.

"He hasn't got squat on you," Johnny laughed as he typed strings of code into his computer. "And he claimed it was a misfire with his handgun that grazed in his shoulder. The hospital stitched him up but allowed him to spend the night in his hotel suite. He has a nurse monitoring him from there."

So...my father silenced them. I had to hand it to dear old dad, he could be a sweet talker when he wanted. No...not sweet talk. Bargaining. I worked my jaw back and forth. There had to be a nice, fat incentive for the dirty businessman to keep his mouth shut about the bullet wound. Files flashed on the screen. With clicks of the keys, the programs sorted them into other programs to scan.

"I want his dirty business dealings publicized," I instructed.

"On it." Ellie, Johnny's wife, tapped on her keyboard. A bar with a percentage appeared on one of the many screens.

Luka knocked on the door. "The Waldorf Astoria. Their floor has private security, though."

He tossed a knife. It flipped double in the air, before landing hilt first in my cousin's palm.

"I'm in the mood for a good challenge." Kazimir smiled.

"I'll leave you to it." I nodded to Johnny.

"We'll text when it's done," Ellie called out before sipping her London Fog. Johnny narrowed his eyes on the screen, tapped on the keys, and gave me a half nod. While he was brilliant at code, he was only somewhat skilled at hacking. It was his wife that shone in that department. I doubted anyone knew that his wife was the world's most famous internet hacker. She played the part of office computer geek so well. Even her boss didn't know. Granted, Kazimir wasn't close to his foster brother for Johnny's protection, but Ellie guarded her secret. I only knew it because once I needed help and she was able to offer it.

In exchange, I bought her a cabin in the Great Woods of Wisconsin. It was completely off the grid, and they spent weeks at a time there, soaking up the ethereal aesthetics and peace of nature that couldn't be found on the screens, no matter how good the graphics cards were.

Flanked by my cousins, I left the office.

The scent of lavender filled the space. The pillow mist sat on the nightstand, and I wanted nothing more than to grab the glass container and bash it into the broad forehead below me. I took careful breaths through my mouth because that scent was going to fast become one of my least favorites.

Running my knuckle down the prickled cheek, I laughed darkly. "Wakey, wakey," I whispered.

Muddy brown eyes blinked up at me. Craig gasped, jackknifing up.

I sat on the bed, clamping my gloved hand on his shoulder. "I wouldn't do that if I was you."

"You touch me, and your organization is going under. I don't care what kind of leverage your father thinks he has. I'll end you," he spat, bravery flickering in those murky depths.

"See, that's funny," I breathed. "Isn't it funny, Luka?"

"Fucking hilarious," my cousin chirped. "He's already ended you, bra."

Bra? Really? What kind of cringey street slang was that? Sometimes Luka just didn't make sense.

"You haven't ended me," he seethed. "I'll fight you!"

"Really? You want to go?" I rose, lifted my palm face up, and curled my fingers in a come-at-me symbol.

The fool jumped out of bed, assumed a boxing stance, and surged forward. One foot faltered. With a gasp, Craig stumbled. He clutched at his wounded shoulder, shaking the sleep from his head.

Only...it wasn't sleep.

I held up the empty syringe. "This is better than you deserve. But I had to make it look like heart failure after your *accident* cleaning your gun."

"Poison is so underestimated. They call it a woman's weapon—and while I love a sneaky wench, I think it discredits them. It's the cunning that counts," Luka prattled.

I rolled my eyes. Why he couldn't be upstairs with Alex, taking care of the O'Connells, I didn't understand. Instead, Kazimir volunteered to do the dirty work of creating a perceived murder and suicide with our best female bratva soldier. "The more you move and elevate your heart rate, the faster the poison will destroy your heart."

Craig clutched his chest.

"If you can make it to the hospital, you might just survive," Luka cackled.

Craig lurched for the door.

I stepped in his path. "How do you like feeling trapped?"

"Move!" He shoved against my chest.

I hated that he was a big man. I could just see it, him pushing Laurel around. Especially since she said she used to weigh so much less, starving herself to fight back the pounds.

"This is hard for me," I growled, gripping his jammies.

What kind of saints damned loser wears silk jammies?

I gave him a little shake.

"Careful," Luka warned.

"He's right," I snapped. "I have to be *oh so careful* with you, when really, I want to lock you up and torture you for days."

"Until your mind is warped by pain, and that's the only thing you know. You'll come to love it, because it will become your existence." Luka walked up behind him, tapping his head. "Death is not an evil, because it frees us from all evils. You lucky bastard, we're freeing you."

"What philosopher is that?" I cut a look to my cousin.

The contented smile curving his lips and the fiendish glint in his eye were my only answers.

Luka was batshit crazy.

"Please," the fool whimpered. "It was years ago. And I was so very drunk."

We did it. It was the first step, penitence. We broke him.

"Boo!" Luka said in his ear with a pop.

Craig gasped. But the sharp intake became a strangled cry of pain. He clutched his heart.

"If I didn't have bigger problems than you, I would give you the antidote." I gave him a cold look. "I have it on the coffee table, in fact."

Craig scrambled forward.

But I clutched his shirt, dragged him to the bed, and sat on his legs. I forgot to breathe through my mouth. Lavender assaulted my sinuses. A sneeze prickled at the back of my nose. Pinching my nostrils, I held my breath so as not to spew DNA over the soon-to-be corpse.

"All that struggling and kicking is only going to kill you faster," Luka sang out.

"I can help you." Craig sat up, looking at me.

Bartering, the second step.

"How could *you* help me?" I drawled. "I eat little shits like you for breakfast."

"I have connections." The bastard's voice wavered. The words slurred.

The end was close.

"You touched my wife." I leaned in close. "You're going to die."

I rose. The moment the pressure on his legs was gone, he bounded off the bed. Stumbling like a deer in the thicket, he pushed past Luka.

Joining my cousin at the doorway, we watched the desperate man cling to life. He took the bottle of liquid, stabbed a needle into the top, and filled the syringe.

What he didn't notice was the open laptop facing him.

With a desperate gulp, he stabbed the needle into his vein and depressed the plunger.

Only then did he look up at where we stood watching.

"Suicide is a sin, right?" Luka laughed softly.

"To Church of Rome attendees like him, yeah," I drawled. "Of course, I doubt he repented of his other sins, so suicide is just the cherry on top."

"Suicide," he stammered.

"Read the note you wrote before you ended yourself." I jerked my chin to the laptop screen.

It talked about his raping and battering of women. Countless, countless women.

"We really were too easy on him," Luka huffed.

"Unfortunately." I crossed my arms.

Craig stumbled back. Lips blue, he slumped against the couch. "You said it was the antidote."

"Oops, did you trust the men who came to end your miserable existence to tell the truth?" Luka crowed. "Bra, you're stupider than you look. And you look like a bloody idiot."

"Goodbye, Craig Snell." I walked behind the computer monitor as the filth struggled for his next breath.

When it didn't come, and his body tensed, I moved toward the door, Luka hot on my heels.

Ellie and Johnny had the hotel cameras on a loop so we would go unnoticed. The email was already sent to Craig's family, and the computer microphone had been remotely disabled. It was a very clean kill.

Kazimir and Alex met us in the stairwell.

"Did you get the text from your father?" Kazimir greeted me.

I opened my phone. My chest constricted. *What now?* "Why does he want us in his office?"

"Vasil, me, and you all received it," Kazimir muttered dryly.

I turned to Luka.

"I didn't." He began to pout.

"Go find Laurel. Protect her at all costs," I snarled.

My youngest cousin snapped his gaze to me. "Dimi, I can help."

"You are. Protecting my wife is the most important task. Shit is going to get ugly tonight. I need to know that no matter what, she is safe. Can you do that for me, Luka?"

He gave me a short nod. "On my honor."

"On your life," I corrected, and then turned to jog down the stairs.

Chapter 61 – Laurel

It was worse than Luka could have said. Before he fell into a deep, bone-numbing slumber courtesy of the roofies I slipped him, he explained that some internal shit was going down. What he failed to mention was that Dimitri was in the viper's nest alone. While in all fairness he might not have known, I was pissed enough that I had no remorse for the dirty deed of knocking him out.

Pursing my lips, I watched Kazimir and Vasil long enough to make sure they weren't actually going to help Dimitri. They sat in a truck across the street, watching and waiting. Their lips moved animatedly. But they seemed resigned to stay put.

I shook my head and turned away.

In the time it took me to pull my drugs out of the secret pouch of my cosmetic kit and slip them into a cup of tea, not counting the time it took to steal a car and drive here, any number of fates could have befallen my mobster.

Why they let Dimi go into the lair of the cruel pakhan alone....

He's probably being heroic.

Well, screw heroism.

It was time for this villain to raise hell.

I couldn't manage navigating the abandoned building to the tunnel's secret entrance without the flashlight. But I pulled my hoodie over the lamp end to mute the brightness. The floor grate was closer to the door than last time, exactly as it should be. Well, this time, I wasn't a bundle of nerves. My purpose was clear, and my steps direct.

The latch was stuck fast. Shutting the light off, I pocketed it. My fingers screamed in protest as I cranked the nob. When the hinge groaned, I sighed. It took another five minutes, but I tugged the thing open.

This time, I ignored the damp, claustrophobic feeling of being underground. I *ran.*

Luka had helped me before, but tonight he needed to stay safely away. The pakhan would die. Nothing would stop me. But if Luka was involved? The bratva would turn on him.

Just like they would turn on Dimitri.

No, I would take full responsibility for this death—and its disastrous outcome. As an outsider, the wrath of the soldiers for the murder of their pakhan needed a scapegoat. I had nothing more at stake than my heart. And that little old organ could survive what came next.

Don't think about that now. Kill first, flee second.

I might not have a valiant, ruthless bratva soldier at my side to storm the fortress of horror, but I wasn't going in completely alone. There was one friend I could count on! I took the first tunnel to the left and scrambled up the metal rungs. Emerging from the exit to the kennel, I winced when the dogs began to bark frantically. I didn't have treats for them. Not that those would work. They were basically savage, and it would take a great deal of time to earn their trust. Rushing to Marena's cage, I slipped the bolt off the latch.

"What are you doing?" someone snapped behind me.

Mistake, buddy. Shoot first, ask questions later. Which was exactly what I did.

The stolen gun from Luka kicked high in my hand. It took everything I had not to let it go flying behind me!

The guard dropped with a groan. In the split second I saw his face, I realized it was one of the goons who'd helped beat Dimitri.

That knowledge helped settle the butterflies in my stomach that threatened to turn into worms.

Not only had this man come to step in the way of me reaching Dimitri, but he had hurt the mobster I loved.

Every instinct told me to escape. The shot was sure to bring other guards. The baying, savage animals gave me an idea. They could be just the thing I needed. The shot could be mistaken for the guard firing his own weapon—so long as he had something plausible to shoot at. Standing behind the doors, Marena at my side, I unleashed the guard dogs. They scented blood and rushed to the dying guard.

Any guards who came to help would think the dogs got free, and this one shot at the mutts.

Plus, they would be too busy rounding the loose animals to realize their dead comrade had a bullet hole in his chest.

The door beyond was open, but I didn't stick around to see if the dogs rushed to the exit after wrapping their muzzles around the lump of flesh. Marena and I dropped back into the tunnels, taking care to seal the door tight behind us.

Chapter 62 – Laurel

Standing outside the office door, I held my breath. It was cracked! Yet another thing going my way. I uttered a quick prayer and gave thanks, not to the universe, but to something...more.

The pakhan's voice was hard. "Get rid of her. I've lined up a suitable bride. They're sending her from Belarus capital."

"I'm not divorcing Laurel," Dimitri snapped.

He's alive!

"She's no one!" Matvei roared.

"She's mine, and I defy you to take her from me."

I winced. His declaration should have made me warm and soar. Instead, a cold sweat broke over my body. He broke form in front of the pakhan. He used a disrespectful tone. He talked back.

To defend me.

At my side, Marena shifted. Those great big brown eyes turned up to me.

"I know, baby girl, I know." I choked a breath out. "I hate it too." So freaking much.

We couldn't storm in there and shoot. If I took out the pakhan, the bratva would hate me. They would possibly try to kill me. But ultimately, they wouldn't respect the new boss if I wasn't punished.

Dimitri would choose me—he would always choose me.

I would have to end the pakhan when it was obvious Dimitri wasn't involved. As soon as Dimitri left, as soon as the pakhan was alone, I would kill him.

"You will get rid of her, and I don't mean divorce," Matvei snarled.

This time, I froze.

My stomach knotted. The fight or flight urge spiked, and my muscles begged to run.

"No!" Dimitri growled. "Laurel is *mine.*"

"Pathetic," Matvei spat. "Just like your whore of a mother. Soft. Weak!"

There was rummaging around.

"What are you doing?" Dimitri challenged.

"Taking care of the problem that should never have happened," Matvei yelled. "Since you're too fucking stupid to do it."

"I won't let you touch her," Dimitri said, voice deadly quiet. "You are my pakhan and my father, but I won't let you touch my wife."

"My greatest failure." Those words were followed by a soft click, Dimitri's cry of pain, and a deafening thud.

I banged the door open to find the horror playing out in front of me. Matvei, leaning heavily on his cane, held a gun.

Dimitri lay still on the floor.

"Look what you've done. You corrupted my son," Matvei sneered, looking at me like I was something on the bottom of his shoe.

Time slowed as he lifted the gun toward me.

There wasn't time to duck away. I couldn't charge fast enough. But Marena could.

Two bounds, and she latched her teeth around Matvei's frail wrist. The bullet shot wide. Marena took the pakhan to the floor, snarling and shaking the old man.

I lunged for the gun and wrenched it easily from my father-in-law's fingers. I held it over the pakhan and called Marena off.

She backed away, still snarling, and sat at my side.

I pointed the gun at Matvei, only it felt wrong. I risked a glance at the weapon. It was a strange, wide-barreled thing. The bullets were pointed.

"What did you do?" I cut my glaze to Dimitri, seeing a feathery tubular thing sticking from his neck. My beloved's chest rose and fell. It was possible these were just tranquilizers.

"You bitch," Matvei panted, clutching his hand to his chest. "I'll burn you alive in front of the whole Bratva! That's what we did with your sort in the olden days. You've bewitched him! You've turned my son against me."

I ran my tongue over my lip. "No, you did. You're done, old man."

Darkness swirled through my veins. My eyes closed, and I drew in a cleansing breath. "All the evil you've done," I spoke over his inane and unfocused raging as I moved to close the door. "Vengeance is coming for you."

Matvei stilled. His gaze flicked to the gun in my hand. "You wouldn't."

"No, I won't. But I won't save you."

Matvei hollered for help. The plaintive tone filled his voice.

"Where's your henchman?" I laughed and began to walk around him. The pakhan bellowed, struggling to his feet, but I kicked his cane away. "Ever since I've come, you've had nothing nice to say to me," I said in flawless Russian, enjoying the surprise flashing over his face. "You called me fat, bovine, and weak."

"I'm his father." The fight returned to the old man's face.

"And you should have *nurtured* him." Anger boiled through me. The sooner this scum was gone, the better. I crouched, running my fingers over Marena's head. "Dimitri is the strongest man I've met. And you do nothing but make him doubt that."

"He'll hate you for this," Matvei seethed, spittle flying from his mouth.

I shrugged. "Maybe. But I am not weak."

Each word came out as a poignant jab.

"I love your son. And I am never letting you hurt him again," I laughed. Switching to the sci-fi language, I whispered to Marena, "Throat. Kill."

Matvei must have sensed it. Because he brought his hands up in a feeble last defense.

Marena charged. Her fangs sank into the old man's throat, tearing the delicate flesh as though it was butter.

Meanwhile, I grabbed Dimi. Hefting him under the arm, I began to drag him toward the utility closet and secret passage.

A sob threatened to choke my throat. The heavy weight of my actions settled on my chest, making each breath an effort. The next step was going to be the hardest. To distract myself from the inevitable parting, I began to ramble under my breath.

"That's it! On Monday, I start weight training," I hissed. The words I managed to utter came out strained and hoarse, betraying the turmoil that churned inside me. "Although, thanks to the self-defense lessons, I already have far more muscle than ever. I need to be strong physically if I am going to survive in this world. I can trade some of my soft pounds for hard muscley ones, so long as I keep my curves. They look good on me—and drive my husband feral."

My husband who I wouldn't see again. This time, the sob pulsed painfully in my chest. A knot of raw emotion was lodged there.

Once in the utility room, I whistled for Marena. The hound came back, licking her chops.

"Gross, babe," I murmured.

Shutting the utility door tight, I opened the latch. The stairs helped with his weight. Dragging him down the tunnel, I realized I wouldn't be able to heft him up the ladder at the far end. He was too heavy.

These precious minutes in the stale, closed tunnel were my last with this wonderful, impossibly valiant mobster. There was no stopping the tears. But in the dark, no one could see. The great sobs threatened to crack me.

To distract myself, I focused on my anger.

I hate that fortress.

When we reached the end of the tunnel, my body shook from the exertion. But I knew my next course of action. Reaching into Dimitri's pocket, I pulled out his Zippo. I stopped by the boiler and furnace to shut off the gas line. After that, it was just a simple matter of going upstairs to douse the house with incendiary liquid.

One by one, the fires were lit.

Witch? If that was what the old man thought of me as, I would claim the title. But I preferred conqueror.

Coughing violently, I retreated to the safety of the tunnel. The secret door to the fortress closed tight. At the end, I squatted beside Marena.

"Keep him safe, girl," I sniffed.

Reaching out, I brushed my fingers over his head. By the light of the single flame, I saw things clearly.

There was only one way to ensure Dimitri wasn't blamed for his father's death. They needed someone to pin the death on. There needed to be a focal point for the bratva's pain and mistrust.

I squared my shoulders. One kiss on his forehead, that was all I allowed myself.

As I climbed into the secret, exterior entrance, I debated the best course of action. I stopped only to send a message to Kazimir. I dropped my phone under the tire before driving away.

Chapter 63 – Dimitri

"Where is my wife?" I bellowed through the dining room of Vasil's home. The pulsing headache was due in part to the tranquilizer, part to the tension radiating through every fiber of my being. But it was the raw, inconsolable ache in my chest that threatened to kill me. The pain was profound, deep in my bones. It was a dull, persistent throb, a reminder of the void that would be left in my life.

"There's simply not a trace," Kazimir insisted through the speakerphone set on the dining room table.

There had to be! I ought to have gone to his technology company instead of calling him. A few well-placed bullets in the squealing nerds, and there would have been results. My voice hardened. "This is the twenty-first century, people don't vanish."

Ilya stood against the far wall, arms crossed and aggression bristling off his body. "They can, and they do."

I narrowed my eyes. We were coming back to that statement. But not until I burned this whole saints forsaken city to the ground until I found my wife.

I was about to yell at Kazimir, but Vasil raised his hand. He pressed his phone to his ear, let out a clipped assent, and explained as he ended the call, "There's a middle-aged woman at the gate who has a letter from Laurel."

The words weren't even out of my uncle's mouth, and I was running through the door. The sharp prickle at the corner of my eyes made the world blur. I clenched my jaw, blinking rapidly. I had been a small boy the last time I gave into that physical reaction.

It was the bartender, the one with pink—now lime green—braids. "Where is she?" I snapped, not letting her get a word in edgewise.

A rougher voice that could have been from smoking or something else barked a laugh. "I don't know, Mister Vlasov. But Dolly P. gave me this and said you'd give me three grand cash."

She waved an envelope in my face.

My fingers itched, and I took a step forward, moving into the woman's space. "Where is my *wife*?"

"She ran."

The growl that exploded from my throat was the promise of a swift death. The woman flipped her hair and gave me a sassy look.

"Read this," she snapped.

A plain envelope slapped against my chest. I ripped it away, popped the seal, and began to read.

To the current pakhan of the Vlasov Bratva,

I did it. I killed the former pakhan, Matvei Vlasov. The responsibility is mine.

Take your crown, mobster. Wear it with pride; wear it well.

Let your bratva hunt me. I've migrated to warmer parts. It will be hard for them to trace me, because I'm changing my name—and my hair.

P.S. Julisa lent me three grand. I'm calling in my life debt from when we reconnected weeks ago. Up to half your kingdom, right? Pay her back and don't shoot her.

"Redbird," I breathed. Air refused to fill my lungs. *No! It can't be!* Clammy hands crumpled the paper.

This was goodbye. The undeniable crack that split my chest in two confirmed that. She was gone—gone!

My thighs trembled. The landscape swayed. The bright and warm sunlight of late March promised beautiful things. But it might as well have stayed winter.

You didn't have to go. The pakhan died in a fire from leaving a cigarette near the flammable substances used for preserving and torture that he kept in his office. That was what the Vlasov Bratva were told, and if they were smart, that was the story they would stick to.

Blindly, I stumbled backward. I didn't know where I went, but when my old friend's arms grasped me, I looked up through the suddenly blurry vision.

"Hire that woman as a bartender at Club MØ, give her a six grand cash signing bonus," I croaked. How those details clicked, I couldn't say.

Because...Laurel would want it. My heart bled. I absently touched my chest, trying to find the leak so that I could tear it open.

Ilya shook me. "We'll find her, brother."

I shook my head. "She's gone."

Ilya squirreled me indoors and into an empty room. He thrust a bottle into my hands, but when they shook too badly to drink, he uncorked it and forced it between my lips. "You need to pull yourself together, you fucking got that?"

My shoulder lifted and fell. "What's the point?"

His open palm cracked across my face. The sharp bite of pain cut through the suffocation. "You keep fighting. You keep looking. Until we put you six feet under, you don't fucking stop. Got that?"

Something within me snapped. It was a trail of song, both memory and a promise. My place was by her side, and my snowy beauty had forgotten that. *I'll stand by you.* I put the bottle between my lips and chugged. Fueled by the burn, I focused on the tendrils of fire.

My jaw set, the resolve hardening in my eyes as I stared down the challenge before me. The fear that had clouded my mind receded. There was a sharp focus that honed my thoughts and actions toward the goal. This was my moment, I realized, a pivotal point that demanded everything I had. And I was ready to give just that, every fiber of my being alight with an unyielding determination to overcome, to succeed, to prove that I could rise above and conquer.

The fear of losing her was banished.

"You're right," I gasped. An idea formed in the wake of the delicious trickle of the vodka.

Ilya plucked the bottle, downed a healthy gulp, and then slammed it on the side table. "Of course I am."

My phone was in my hand the next moment. I dialed a number. To hunt a ghost, it would take a ghost. The phone rang three times. Silence answered.

"I need you to find my wife," I breathed. "There's been a terrible mistake, and I can't fix it until I have her back."

"Da, pakhan." The line clicked silent.

Chapter 64 – Laurel

A Month Later

Yawning, I let myself into the rental house. It was small but it was cozy, and the locks were good. Minneapolis wasn't as bustling as Chicago, but the streets felt more unsafe if that was even possible. A favorite game amongst pre-teens was carjacking. Other crimes ran rampant, but so far my neighborhood was safe enough.

The coffee shop did not pay as much as bartending. But one, it didn't require an ID to work. Two, I was done with nightlife. Quiet and simple. That had been my motto. I pulled out my yoga mat and began my nightly routine. This last month had been all about rebranding myself.

That meant no singing.

Dimitri had resources. Even a video of a candlelit song could be traced back to me.

My wings were clipped, and I felt the loss in my soul.

Yoga, shower, and bed, only to leave me staring at the ceiling. I forbade thoughts of the past. It was gone.

A pang shot through my chest. I let out a shuddering exhale.

There was a noise. Thumping bass and several shouts. A car door slammed. The neighbors must be home. I rolled over, exchanging the ceiling for the wall.

My eyes fluttered closed only to flare open when wood creaked.

Sitting up, I flipped the lamp on. Or tried to.

Darkness continued to pool around me.

Heart jumping to my throat, I realized the power was out. Not a single light, including the stove on the other side of the studio, glowed.

Maybe he found me....

I scrambled out of bed only to be wrapped in strong arms.

Wrong arms.

There were no puckered scars. Something smelled different. *Not him.*

I screamed, but a sweaty palm covered my mouth. I tried to bite, but the man wrenched it back.

"Will you stop?" he hissed in Russian.

I stilled. The voice was familiar. "Dimi?"

"No. His cousin."

I jerked, but only to move around. "Luka's brother—Kolya? How did you find me? What are you doing here?"

"Yes. Not easily. Taking you."

Well, he was a talkative one. *Lovely.*

"I can't go back," I whispered.

"That's not my problem," the man growled. He clamped his hand around my wrist and dragged me to the wall.

No! I couldn't go back. I had to be the scapegoat. If I went back, Dimitri would have to shoot me. He wouldn't be able to shoot me. Desperation pulsed through every fiber of my being.

Fight! FIGHT!

My pulse roared in my ears. Muscle memory sent my leg sweeping out. His shin was hard against my bare foot.

I yelped.

He cursed—violently.

Okay, so maybe not completely a man of few words.

He wrenched open the door and the emergency floodlight poured on him. "Look here, lady. My cousin has torn Chicago apart. He's beside himself, but he won't rest until you're back at his side. You're coming with me. I need to finish this job, because there's another waiting. I don't do drama. Take up your issues with the pakhan." He narrowed his eyes. "What? Why are you staring at me like that?"

I reached out to brush my fingers against his cheek.

Kolya shied away.

Oh, shit! How freaking insensitive of me. "Not your scar," I rushed to say. The puffy red gash looked painful. I winced. "I just...has anyone ever told you how much you and Dimitri look alike?"

"All the time."

I reached out again. This time he closed his eyes. Hard breaths came through his nose. I kept my voice as gentle as possible as I murmured, "I know you're cousins, but...damn. You look so like him."

A shudder rippled through that big body.

I snatched my hand away. "I can't go back. I killed the pakhan."

His voice turned hard. "No one cares."

"I highly doubt that." I crossed my arms over my chest. "I'm not going with you."

The man flicked out his phone. He tapped the screen. There was a beat of silence.

Horror descended on me. I knew exactly what he was doing.

"Give me that," I screeched, scrambling up his big body.

"I found her," Kolya clipped in Russian.

A sob bubbled in my throat. The sound of Dimitri's voice whispered through the speaker. Water clogged my eyes.

"Hang it up. Please," I begged. "He'll hate me. I can't have him hate me."

"This delay is costing my hunt," Kolya growled. "She won't come with me."

"Put her on the phone."

Kolya held the device out.

I looked at it as if it were a snake. "I can't."

"Laurel. LAUREL. *LAUREL!* Take the saints damned phone this instant."

My hands shook, and I dropped the device.

Cursing, Kolya grabbed it and tapped the speaker button. "Speaker's on. Talk."

"Laurel, are you there? Is it you?" Dimitri's voice lacked proper breath.

Kolya let out a growl of disgust. "I said I found her. Therefore, I found her."

"Redbird, please—"

"I'm here," I croaked. The pain in his voice was too much. I couldn't be the cause of that. "I'm here, mobster. I'm here."

"Where are you?" he growled.

I flinched. "Minnesota."

"South Minneapolis," Kolya corrected. "In a dump."

Something clattered to the floor on the other end of the line. I flinched.

"Get her out of there, Kolya."

"She won't go. Do I have permission to bind her?" Kolya pinned me with a look.

"No, no!" Panic clawed at my throat. I backpedaled. My feet hit the bed in the middle of the room, and I fell.

"Call John Henry. Jet takes 90 minutes. She's your problem, not mine," Kolya clipped out.

There was a beat of silence. "Keep her safe."

"Always." He hung up.

"You don't understand," I pleaded. "I can't go back."

"Dimitri loves you." Kolya cut his hand through the air. "Don't hurt him."

But I already have.

Chapter 65 – Dimitri

The billionaire always had a jet fueled and ready at a moment's notice. He and his brother had habits of taking off across the country whenever the need to attend to business overtook them.

Not having cops in my back pocket, I drove just over the speed limit. It was hard to say whose territory we were in, but from the looks of the rundown buildings, the mayor of Minneapolis was doing as fine a job as the mayor of Chicago with the ghettos.

It was a shame children had to grow up in these places and call them home.

I tried to think of my cousin, tried to picture him growing up in these slums. But thoughts of Kazimir were replaced by the thunderous knowledge that I was nearly there.

One fucking month. That was nearly thirty days without the clever, merciless, enchanting songbird by my side.

Laurel had been my princess, but now it was time to make her my queen. I had a solid grasp on the bratva. Igor revealed it was Emil who'd put the hit on me. Boris confirmed that he'd been approached to help take me down. Neither had spoken up because they thought it was a trap orchestrated by my late father to weed out anyone loyal to his son.

I beheaded Emil in front of the entire body of our men, along with six others he'd recruited to his cause.

A new reign was in order.

They feared me, but they also loved me. Just as Laurel prophesied they would.

My grip on the steering wheel tightened. I blew through a red light, careened around a corner, and pulled up short in front of a terrible looking two-story house. It needed to be condemned. Bulldozed. Rebuilt, but kept affordable for working class families.

Jogging up the exterior stairs, I shouldered through the partially open door.

The breath left my lungs in a whoosh. "Redbird...."

That hair. Flaming locks of rich auburn, tinted with gold and brighter red, fell down her back.

Laurel seemed to realize what I meant, because she self-consciously lifted her hands to her head. "Oh! It's not real. I dyed it back, but it will grow out something like this and—"

I was on her the next minute. My mouth hungered for her taste.

Kolya coughed. "I'll give you two a minute. But we shouldn't linger, Dimi."

Her tongue darted out to swipe against my lips. Mine dove into her mouth. A groan ripped from deep inside. All available blood, boiling and fierce, raced to my dick.

My hands ran frenziedly over her body as if my touch could convince my broken heart she was really here at last—at long last!

I gripped her wrists. Laurel sucked in a harsh breath, but her body relaxed a moment later. She leaned into my body, and I think we would have fallen into bed.

If a gunshot hadn't broken the moment.

I raced outside, only to bump into Kolya as he dove back into the building, clutching his arm.

"Damned druggies," he hissed.

Scrambling into action, I peered out the door. A second bullet fired. The shooter was bad, because it hit the roofline far above my head. I slammed the door.

"He wanted Dance Fever," Kolya snarled. "He was convinced I was the dealer."

I was about to answer, when a groan and creak sounded behind me.

"Hey, asshole!" Laurel shouted. "No one touches my husband."

A shotgun exploded.

Laurel stumbled back with a soft yelp.

I was on her a second later, ripping the twelve gauge from her hands. "What the hell do you think you're doing?" I roared.

She shrugged. "That's my home defense system in case the locks failed."

Laughter, rich and righteous, broke out. I glared at Kolya, never having heard him do more than huff. Deep belly notes boomed from his mouth. He hooted and wiped his eyes.

"Felicitations, cousin. She's perfect for you," he finally gasped. "Taking out your enemies with a damn trap gun."

Laurel frowned. "Trap gun? It's the biggest shotgun they have."

"It's for target practice, not even hunting," Kolya hooted.

"So? It knocked the guy over," Laurel sassed back.

The temperature in the room instantly dropped.

"We've got to move," I snapped, and Kolya nodded.

Half lifting, half hustling, I forced Laurel from the space. I swept the chilly evening grass with my gun, but when there was no movement, I hurried her down.

Except my stubborn little wife stuck her heels in the wood. "No, no, no!" she cried out.

"Laurel." I shook her. "It's time to go."

"Not without—" She tore back into the dump.

Kolya snorted as he walked by. "Good luck with that one."

I stormed back inside to see Laurel scrambling with papers in a purple plastic basket by her bed. She shifted through them.

"These important to you?" I barked.

She shot me a glare. "Yes."

"Anything else?" I snatched them from her delicate fingers.

My heart skipped a beat when I saw the flash of her wedding ring.

"Um...not really, but I'm not dressed and—"

"No time." Once again, I tossed her onto my shoulder. The weight was the same as it had been weeks and weeks ago in the luxury hotel. But the feel of her was different.

Her fists pummeled my back, but I jogged from the building.

"She missed. But he fell and must have hit his head. He's breathing," Kolya updated me as I approached the still running vehicle.

It was dumb to leave a truck running here.

I dumped my bride in the passenger seat. "Stay," I barked.

Laurel bared her teeth and growled.

"Do that again, I dare you," I hissed, leaning in.

Her eyes heated and nostrils flared.

Slowly, she curled her upper lip.

I surged forward, caught it in my mouth, and sucked hard.

"Enough sexcapades." Kolya slammed his back door closed.

"This isn't finished," I promised. We had ninety minutes to kill on the plane ride.

I rounded the truck, and we were barreling through the chilly spring night in minutes.

Once in the airplane, Kolya went to the bathroom to stitch up his arm. The bullet had only grazed the skin and flesh. I offered to help, but as usual, he declined.

Laurel sat, clutching her purple basket.

"What are those?" I walked over, slinging back the chilled vodka the attendant gave me upon boarding.

Laurel narrowed her eyes. "My projects."

I cocked my head, hoping and praying she would tell me.

With a sigh, she handed the cheap plastic basket to me. "I've been song-writing. I'm not bad at it, but without a laptop to create beats, it's not easy. And I spent all my extra money on my hairdo, so I've been living off dollar store crap until I saved up enough for a small keyboard."

"But you have a shotgun."

"Oh, that." Laurel pawed the air. "I won it off a neighbor during a poker match."

I closed my eyes and drew in a deep breath. This woman. This tenacious, gorgeous woman. I didn't want to know how much danger she'd put herself in with this stunt. Clearly, she'd been busy.

I set the basket down and dropped to both knees. Tentatively, Laurel slid her hands into mine.

"Why didn't you want to come back, Laurel?" I asked the question as gently as I could.

She bit her lip, eyes darting behind me.

Kolya came out, took one look at us, and then put in headphones before taking a seat.

"Why didn't you want to come home, redbird?" I repeated.

A heavy tension filled the air. "I killed your father. Your bratva needed someone to pin the murder on, so you wouldn't take the fall."

I had to clench my jaw—hard. The muscles locked, and the force threatened to break my teeth.

"Dimi," she whispered, shifting in her seat. "They'll make you kill me."

"Instead of asking me," I ground out, "you made that decision. For both of us."

"If I left, your bratva could hate *me*. Don't you get it?! They wouldn't come after you for the death of your father and—"

"They were glad! They wanted him dead and wanted me on the throne. They rejoiced when his smoking habit *accidentally* lit his home on fire."

My words sank into Laurel. The great strategist blinked at me, the wheels of her mind turning.

"You were too focused on what was in front of you, Laurel. You didn't see that option. But we could have figured it out. If you had talked to me, if you hadn't fled!" I dug my fingers into her thick, tight thighs.

"But you would hate me," she whispered. "He was your father."

Her eyes flicked to my cousin, however. They narrowed.

"I should have done it years ago. Other bosses kill their fathers. As saints damned twisted as our world is, that's the reality we live in, redbird." I brought her hands up and lathed a kiss on the inside of her wrists. "You were the bravest of us, finally someone strong enough to stand up to him."

She shook her head vehemently. "You did it first. You stood up to him—for me. You said it was over your dead body I would be gotten rid of."

She'd been there.

Of course, she'd been there! Film reels of that terrible night flashed through my mind. While my father was preparing to harm me, Laurel had been lurking outside. I shuddered, suddenly feeling sick. She'd been so close to harm.

But instead of fleeing, she'd come to my rescue.

"Always, redbird, you're mine. I let being a son make me hesitate in my duties as a husband."

"You should get a DNA test, I doubt you were actually Matvei's," she snorted.

I frowned. "What makes you say—" I shook my head. "That's off topic."

I lifted her into my arms. She let me.

My mouth found hers, finally about to satiate the gnawing edge of desperation. But only the edge. There was no way I would ever have enough of her.

Carrying her to the small bedroom, I kicked the door closed. Her fingers scrambled for the button and zipper of my pants while I pulled the flannel pajama bottoms off her.

I groaned as I felt the slick heat of her pussy.

"Mobster," she rasped, pulling me down with her legs.

And there were days I thought I would never hear those words again.

There were more muscles, but those beautiful curves were still there. I placed my cock at her drenched entrance while my other hand gripped her hip hard.

The joining was cataclysmic.

Laurel arched off the bed, moaning my name.

I clenched my jaw again as each inch slid into her. There would be no holding back. Not after how long she'd made me wait.

I warned her, and she only laughed. "Come home, Dimitri. Come home."

Growling low and wild, I yanked her hips back, impaling her on my cock.

Our double cries rattled through the room. Desire burned in my veins. I took my wife with brutal savagery. Laurel dug her nails into my back, scoring the flesh the moment she tore the shirt from me.

"You can't get away from me again," I growled. "You're mine, Laurel."

"And you're mine," she choked out, teeth scoring my neck. "We killed for one another; we've bled for one another."

"We've fucking *wept* for one another," I hissed.

Laurel let out a strangled huff. "I'm yours, Dimi. I'm yours."

"And you're mine," I rasped.

Her tight little pussy felt like it was tearing with each brutal thrust. But she only burned hotter for me.

"You were made for me," I growled. "Now...come on your cock."

Laurel whimpered, but the muscles deep inside clenched viciously tight. I thrust harder and groaned as I emptied myself into her. Pleasure, harsh and bright, nearly blinded me. The convulsions were a chain reaction, rippling with savagery as they took every drop of me.

When the moment finally ebbed, we lay there, not ready to break apart.

Those delicate fingers traced up and down my spine. "Ya lyublyu tyebya, mobster." *I love you.*

"Ya tozhe tyebya lyublyu, redbird."

And we did.

Epilogue – Vivian

Dried tears glued my eyelids shut. It took far too much energy to tear them open. The new sun, cresting the horizon stabbed the pupils with sharp beams of light.

With a groan, I closed them quickly.

Dry. Everything was so dry!

My tongue was cotton, sticking to the roof of my mouth. I rubbed it. A trickle of saliva came to my rescue, but I desperately needed water or a sports drink—

Gatorade.

I sat bolt upright. Fear created a blinding panic as memories slammed into me. Sitting in the backseat of a car, still wearing the work uniform and salt stained sports bra and panties underneath, the evidence pointed that it wasn't a dream. This was a living nightmare.

The bastard drugged me!

But where is he? I peered out of the car.

While my body screamed in protest, I was able to ignore it because of the heavy adrenaline coursing through my veins. I had to sneak out of here! And then, run. Run, because my life depended on it. There was no knowing what my kidnapper meant to do with me.

Stupid, stupid!

How could I accept a drink from a stranger?

I emerged from the running vehicle and into the muggy late summer heat of the South. Bugs droned in the distance. Good, let their symphony play loud. It would cover my clumsy tracks. I stumbled away from the car and into the deep green woods. The ground was densely covered with smaller foliage. But I grit myself against the fear of poison ivy. What was a little itch, so long as I escaped?

The forest seemed to close in around me as I fled, every step a desperate struggle against the suffocating dehydration, the oppressive heat, and the quickly thickening underbrush. My throat burned with each ragged breath, the need for liquid made my mouth feel like sandpaper. And yet, sweat began to trickle down my face, stinging my eyes and making my skin slippery.

The rays of sunlight pierced the canopy. My eyes were constantly forced to adjust. The bile in my gut churned, threatening to make an appearance. While my legs felt like lead as I pushed forward, every muscle screaming in protest, I refused to give up.

A noise made me stop short.

He was back.

My clammy palm slapped over my lips to hide the whimper. He couldn't find me! He was too strong, and I didn't have a weapon. I looked up, but quickly banished the idea of climbing a tree. Putting distance between me and the monster, and then hiding was my only option.

I hurried away, trying to make careful, precise steps. The underbrush snagged at my clothes, roots and fallen branches threatening to trip me with every hurried step. Something slithered away, startled by my sudden appearance.

The sound of his muttering in a foreign language bounced off the trees. He was tracking me!

Was he a damned woodsman?

Or was I just sloppier in my panicked, dried out state?

The desire to survive surged through me, an electric current that kept me moving even as my body threatened to give out. The rustling leaves and snapping twigs seemed amplified, echoing in my ears and driving my heart rate even higher. I could hear the sound of my pursuer crashing through the foliage behind me, their footsteps growing louder, more insistent.

The forest was a blur of green and brown, the dappled sunlight flickering like a strobe light through the leaves. I stumbled over a hidden root, catching myself just before I hit the ground, but the jolt sent a sharp pain up my already aching legs. I couldn't afford to fall, couldn't afford to stop.

Move. Move!

The air was thick with the earthy scent of damp soil and decaying leaves, a stark freshness that contrasted with the foul stench of fear wafting off me. My vision tunneled, the edges growing dark as exhaustion threatened to take over. I needed to find somewhere to hide, to catch my breath and figure out a plan, but the relentless pursuit left no room for error.

My ears strained for any sign of help, a voice, a distant sound of civilization, but there was nothing but the forest and the monster stalking his prey. Desperation clawed at my chest, mixing with the physical strain of my exertion.

The trees ahead suddenly thinned. I crashed through a dense tangle of plants, nearly falling flat on my face, and emerged into a small clearing. My legs wobbled, but there was no time to rest, though. I scanned the area frantically, searching for any place to hide, any cover that might offer a few precious moments of respite.

Water. There was water ahead!

And if my kidnapper was in fact the man I suspected him to be, he couldn't swim well.

Decision made, I leaped over the muddy bank and into the swampy mess. This was not my beautiful lakes of the north, nor the ever warm water of the Gulf Sea.

The sound of my pursuer's approach was closer now, almost on top of me. My heartbeat thundered in my ears, drowning out rational thought. I kept moving; I had to survive. The thought of being caught sent a fresh surge of adrenaline through my veins, propelling me forward despite the exhaustion that threatened to pull me under the brown surface.

"Vivian," he called.

A sob choked my throat. No. *No!* I wasn't going to let him win.

"That water's pretty gross, sweetheart," he smirked. "Why don't you come out here and we can chat."

I shook my head back and forth. Further, deeper! My feet no longer touched, so I kicked out. If I made it to the opposite bank, there was no way he would find me quickly. I could disappear, hide, and –

"Vivian!"

Something in his tone had me turning around. That glacial blue stare locked with mine, panic dancing through the light blue depths.

"Come back to shore, Vivy," he said with forced calm. "You're in danger out there."

"No, Luka, if that is in fact your name," I hissed, hands fisted as my legs kicked the water. "I'd rather die."

"Well, that gator over there might just grant your wish." With that, my kidnapper kicked off his shoes and advanced, knife drawn.

Thank you for reading *Merciless Princess*!

Can you HELP me out? Would you please take just a second to hop over to Amazon and leave me a quick review? This is the most important thing you can do to help others know what a great story this was!

Bonus Scene for Merciless Princess

Merciless Princess has bonus content!

Do you want to see what happened eight-plus years ago?

Want to see how the dark prince crossed paths with the runaway princess?

Read Dimitri and Laurel's meet cute!

Sign up for my newsletter to read the exclusive epilogue *A Broken Wing*!

Grab a copy here: https://BookHip.com/MAVGVAA

And enjoy!

Sweetest
SCARS
ALEXA MICHAELS

Sweetest Scars

Luka

It was supposed to be a simple job.

Our bratva was hired to collect something, and in return, we would receive a favor from a powerful entity.

I should have known that something this good would come at a steep price. Still, when the new boss commanded me to complete the mission, I obeyed.

But once I meet her, once I taste her fire, I'm not sure any favor is worth losing her.

This might just be the first order I disobey.

I hope my boss is merciful, or else I'll make my confession and receive the last rites because nothing else can take me away from her!

Stalk Alexa & Become One of Her Villainous Darlings

Step into my spooky, seashore villa.

Welcome to Alexa's manor. There are many rooms here, plenty of space for another soul. The only light come from the glow of a candle or the whisp of moonlight through the vaulted windows. These looming, stone walls hold many secrets. Find the hidden passages that lead to the treasure vaults.

Join the virtual fun...if you dare.

Newsletter – This is the formal reception hall. Once a week, unless something comes up, Alexa sends a note straight to your inbox. The emails tell you important things going on, any giveaways you might want to join, and even recs for other authors. And! There's that exclusive bonus scene, *A Broken Wing* for subscribing.

Newsletter on Book Funnel: https://BookHip.com/MAVGVAA

Reader Group – a place where Alexa lets down her golden tresses, kicks back with her favorite sweet treat & glass of wine. You're encouraged to post, share pictures of how you picture your favorite characters, your reaction to her stories, or even what you're sweet treat of the week under the weekly thread. This is a casual, low key space. Somewhat like the poolside of the seashore villa.

Facebook Group: Alexa Michaels's Villainous Darlings: https://www.facebook.com/groups/1225286398132690

The Library – Floor to ceiling shelves, a sliding ladder, and a roaring fireplace. In this space, you'll find all of Alexa's published stories. Can you read them all?

Amazon Author Page: https://www.amazon.com/stores/Alexa-Michaels/author/B089NFZD4D

The Secret Chamber – Somewhere in the formal library, there's a secret passage. Find the rare book, pull the latch, and a door opens up to reveal a pitch black hall. Don't forget your candle as you traverse to the most secret of places. Once you arrive, you'll find a space with such treasures, you won't believe your eyes! Large WIP snippets, digital swag, early access, and even bonus content and access to my writing cave. All are welcomed with a letter and exclusive sticker. Alexa's Patreon is filled with possibilities. Only those who want it all dare to take up one of these treasures.

Patreon: https://www.patreon.com/alexamichaelsauthor

The Gardens – , , and – Three places you can follow and like! I attempt to post daily, but with so many villains to wrangle as they attempt to find their other halves, posting on the socials can be an added craziness. So forgive me if I'm not always tending the flowers. Besides, sometimes it's better to a let a garden grow a little wild so that there's something to bask in when you return.

Instagram: https://www.instagram.com/author.a.h.michaels/

Facebook Page: https://www.facebook.com/profile.php?id=1000869679023 13

Tiktok: https://www.tiktok.com/@alexa.h.michaels

A note from Alexa:

Thank you for indulging me as I painted a metaphor, comparing my digital presence to a haunted seaside villa. I've written the back matter in books for years, and this time, I would rather be clever and compare each place to a room instead of simply saying "Hey! I'm over here, oh, and I'm also over here." This expression of creativity soothes my soul and my hope is that it entices you to come over and stay a spell. So let's have a glass of iced tea on the front porch and get to know one another better!

Xoxo, Alexa

About The Author

Writing Day Dreams!
When Alexa isn't writing, she can be found with a book in her lap and a mug of coffee or glass of red wine within reach.
A native of the North Woods, Alexa is an avid lake-jumper, beach lounger, and sunshine lover. Alexa is living a happily ever after with her own steamy hero.
Summer 2023, Alexa and her husband moved to the South Coast, changing from the court of winter and ice and pledging their allegiance to the court of sun and sea.
Alexa loves any type of love story. So you can find her writing both contemporary romance and fantasy novels. Instead of making a separate pen name, Alexa just adds her middle initial to her fantasy genre books!
Alexa H. Michaels
"Monsters deserve love, too."

Made in the USA
Columbia, SC
11 January 2025

51604362R00270